Harlequin Cowboy Christmas Collection

Family and friends gathered around the tree, exchanging gifts and good food, sharing the warmth of the season…there's no place like home for the holidays. Especially after spending their days tending the ranch and riding the range, the rugged men in this special 2-in-1 collection value the place they hang their hats.

And this Christmas, these cowboys could be coming home to a few surprises in their stockings! They may not be looking to find that special woman, but romance has a way of catching solitary men under the mistletoe.

So join us as we celebrate these cowboys and the women who lasso their hearts!

If you enjoy these two classic stories, be sure to check out more books featuring cowboy heroes in Harlequin American Romance.

For the past eighteen years, *New York Times* bestselling author **Cathy McDavid** has been juggling a family, a job and writing and doing pretty well at it except for the housecleaning part. "Mostly" retired from the corporate business world, she writes full-time from her home in Scottsdale, Arizona, near the breathtaking McDowell Mountains. Her twins have "mostly" left home, returning every now and then to raid her refrigerators. On weekends, she heads to her cabin in the mountains, always taking her laptop with her on the chance inspiration strikes. You can visit her website at cathymcdavid.com.

Be sure to look for more books by Cathy McDavid in Harlequin American Romance— the ultimate destination for romance the all-American way. There are four new Harlequin American Romance titles available every month. Check one out today!

New York Times Bestselling Author

Cathy McDavid
and
Laura Marie Altom

RODEO MAN
UNDER THE TREE

H₸**ᴍ HARLEQUIN® COWBOY CHRISTMAS**

Recycling programs
for this product may
not exist in your area.

ISBN-13: 978-0-373-60988-8

Rodeo Man Under the Tree

Copyright © 2014 by Harlequin Books S.A.

The publisher acknowledges the copyright holders
of the individual works as follows:

Her Cowboy's Christmas Wish
Copyright © 2011 by Cathy McDavid

The Bull Rider's Christmas Baby
Copyright © 2010 by Laura Marie Altom

Printed in U.S.A.

www.Harlequin.com

CONTENTS

HER COWBOY'S CHRISTMAS WISH

Cathy McDavid

To my own darling Caitlin.

You were truly the most beautiful baby ever born. I'm not exactly sure when you grew up into this incredible, lovely and supersmart young woman, but it happened. And I couldn't be any prouder.

Love you forever, Mom.

Chapter One

The big buckskin reared—at least he tried to rear. His thick, rangy body was too confined by the narrow chute, so he achieved little height. Frustrated, he pawed the ground, then backed up and banged into the panel with such force the reverberation carried down the metal railing like an electrical current.

"He's an ornery one," the cowboy sitting astride the fence said. "And smarter than he looks."

Ethan Powell considered the man's assessment of the horse he was about to ride, and decided he agreed. The buckskin was ornery and smart, and would enjoy nothing better than stomping Ethan into the ground.

Exactly the kind of saddle bronc he preferred. The kind he'd hoped to draw when he'd competed professionally. Nowadays his rodeo riding was restricted to this small, local arena and for "personal enjoyment" only. No sanctioned rodeo, or unsanctioned rodeo for that matter, would allow him to enter.

He understood. He just didn't like it, and was determined to change the Duvall Rodeo Arena's policies, if not the entire Professional Rodeo Cowboys Association. Before he could do that, however, he had to prove he still had what it took to go up against men who were, for the most part, younger than him and, without exception, physically whole.

"You gonna stand there all night, Powell?" the cowboy asked.

In the chute beside Ethan, the buckskin lifted his head and stared straight ahead, every muscle in his body bunched tight with anticipation.

Just like Ethan.

"Yeah, I'm ready."

Shielding his eyes from the bright floodlights that lit the arena, he climbed the fence and straddled it alongside the wrangler. Then he took another few seconds to study the bronc up close.

"Good luck," the cowboy said.

Ethan would need more than luck if he expected to ride this bad boy for eight seconds.

He'd been on plenty of unbroken and green broke horses in the last year. There was, however, a world of difference between those animals and one bred and trained to give a man the ride of his life.

Drawing a deep breath, he braced a hand on either side of the chute and lowered himself onto the buckskin's back inch by inch. Twice he paused, waiting for the big horse to settle. Once in the saddle, he took hold of the reins and slipped his feet into the stirrups, careful to keep his toes pointed forward.

The buckskin, eager to give his rider a preview of what was to come, twisted sideways. Ethan's left ankle was momentarily pinned between the horse's broad body and the chute. It might have hurt if he had any feeling in his lower leg.

He didn't and probably never would, unless medical science developed a prosthetic device with artificial nerve endings that could transmit sensation to the wearer.

When his ankle was freed and the buckskin was once again in position, Ethan slid the reins back and forth through his gloved hands until the grip felt right.

The moment the horse committed, he nodded to the wrangler manning the gate and said, "Go," hoping like heck he wasn't making a huge mistake.

With a loud metallic whoosh the gate slid open. Ethan tried to straighten his legs and set his spurs. He didn't quite make it. The prosthesis he wore failed to respond as quickly as his real leg did.

The buckskin lunged out of the chute and into the arena. Only his front feet touched the ground. His hind ones were raised high above his head as he tried to kick the moon out of the sky.

Ethan didn't have time to mark his horse, much less find his rhythm. With his weight unevenly distributed, the buckskin easily unseated him and sent him sailing through the air. Ethan barely glimpsed the ground as it came rushing up to meet him.

His shoulder absorbed the brunt of the impact, which he supposed was better than his face or prosthetic leg. That was until he moved. Pain, razor sharp and searing hot, ripped through him. He decided it was better to just lie there for a second or two longer.

Shouting, which seemed to come from far away, told him the buckskin had been safely rounded up and was probably gloating.

"Need help?"

Ethan glanced up, then away. What he'd dreaded the most had just happened.

"Nope, I'm fine," he told the pickup man looming above him. At least the guy hadn't gotten off his horse before offering his assistance. That would have been even more humiliating.

Ethan pushed up on one elbow, the one not throbbing, then climbed to his knees. Getting his good leg under him was a little tricky, especially given the way the world was spinning. He could feel the eyes of the crowd on him, with everyone likely wondering if he was going to rise under his own power and take on another bronc.

The answer was *damn straight*.

In a minute, after he could move his shoulder and arm without having flashes of color pulsate before his eyes.

"The first time's the hardest," the pickup man commented.

"So they say."

Except this wasn't Ethan's first time bronc riding. It was his first time since losing his leg fifteen months ago, while serving in the Middle East. He'd loved the marines almost as much as he loved rodeoing. Now both were lost to him.

Maybe not rodeoing, he corrected himself.

Standing upright, he brushed off his jeans and readjusted his hat, which had miraculously stayed on during the fall. Then he walked to the gate, doing his best not to limp. It wasn't easy. Another cowboy held the gate open for him and clapped him on the back as he passed. The resulting pain almost drove Ethan to his knees, but he didn't so much as blink.

Outside the arena, he paused to catch his breath. This wasn't going exactly as planned.

"Hey, Ethan!"

He lifted his head to see his childhood friend Clay Duvall approaching, his gait brisk as usual. Ethan and

Clay had been close up until their early twenties, when Ethan's mother had died from complications following a heart transplant, and Clay's father had sold Ethan's family's land out from under them. Ethan had joined the marines and for almost eight years neither saw nor spoke to his former friend. His anger at the Duvalls had been too great.

It was Clay, however, who gave him the opportunity to realize his ambition of bronc riding again, along with a job breaking and training his rodeo stock. After a chance meeting with Clay three months ago, Ethan had realized he couldn't hold a twenty-one-year-old kid responsible for his father's actions, and the two had reconciled.

It had taken Ethan's brother, Gavin, longer to get over his animosity toward Clay. But now the two were partners in a mustang stud and breeding business, with Clay owning the wild mustang stallion and Gavin the mares.

Sometimes, when the three men were together, it felt as if all those years they'd been at odds with each other had never happened.

Ethan pushed off the railing, doing his best not to wince as invisible knife blades sliced through his shoulder. "How you doing?"

"I was going to ask you the same question." Clay grinned good-naturedly. "That was quite a fall you took."

"I'll survive." Ethan rolled his shoulders. Big mistake. He sucked in air through his teeth and waited for the spasm to pass.

"What say we have the new nurse check you out?"

"Nurse?"

Clay hitched his chin in the direction of the empty

announcer's stand. "She's here setting up the first-aid station for the jackpot."

"I thought you were bringing in an EMT and an ambulance."

"Too expensive. Found out I could hire a nurse for a lot less money and still meet the insurance company's requirement for providing on-site emergency care."

Ethan resisted. "I'm fine." He didn't want to be checked out. And he sure didn't want the other cowboys seeing him head for the first-aid station.

"Come on." Clay took a step in that direction. "We have a deal."

They did. Clay had agreed to let Ethan practice bronc riding as long as several conditions were met, one being that he have any injury examined by a medical professional. Ethan knew what a liability he was, that his chances of hurting himself were far greater than the next cowboy's. Clay was taking a sizable risk despite the waiver Ethan had signed.

If he didn't comply with his friend's conditions, there was no way on earth he'd be allowed to compete in the upcoming jackpot, much less practice for it.

Grumbling, he fell into step beside Clay, and the two of them headed toward the announcer's stand.

"You going to be ready in time?"

"Count on it." Ethan had until the Saturday after Thanksgiving, less than two weeks away, to last a full eight seconds on one of Clay's broncs. That was another of the conditions Ethan had to meet in order to enter the jackpot. "I'll be here every evening if I have to."

The door to the small room beneath the announcer's stand stood ajar. A minivan was backed up to it, the rear hatch open. As they neared, Ethan glimpsed plastic containers and cardboard boxes stacked inside the van and a handicap placard dangling from the rearview mirror.

Clay stopped suddenly and scratched the back of his neck, the movement tipping his cowboy hat forward over his furrowed brow.

"Something the matter?" Ethan asked.

"I was going to surprise you. Now I'm thinking that's not such a good idea."

"Surprise me with what?"

"My new nurse. You know her." He smiled ruefully. "That is, you used to know her. Pretty well, in fact."

Ethan had only a second to prepare before a young woman appeared in the doorway. She paused at the sight of him, recognition lighting her features.

Caitlin Carmichael.

She looked the same. Okay, maybe not the same, he decided on second thought. Nine years was a long time, after all. But she was as pretty as ever.

Her former long blond hair had darkened to a honey-brown and was cut in one of those no-nonsense short styles. Her clothing was equally functional—loose-fitting sweats beneath a down-filled vest. It was her green eyes, he noticed, that had changed the most. Once alive with mischief and merriment, they were now somber and guarded.

Something had happened to her during the years since they'd dated.

Was she thinking the same thing about him?

He waited for her glance to travel to his left leg. It didn't. Either she was very good at hiding her reactions or she hadn't heard about his injury.

"Hello, Ethan," she said, her voice slightly unsteady. "It's good to see you." She came forward, her hand extended. "Clay told me you were back in Mustang Valley and training horses for him."

"For a while now." He took her hand in his, remembering when their greetings and farewells had included a hug and a kiss. Often a long kiss.

An awkward silence followed, and he finally released her hand. "So, you're a nurse?"

She smiled. "I suppose that's hard to believe."

"A little." The mere sight of blood used to make her queasy. "I guess people change."

"They do." Her gaze went to his leg, answering Ethan's earlier question. She quickly looked away.

"I work mornings at the middle school and afternoons at the new urgent-care clinic in Mustang Village," she continued. "Have since the school year started."

"And now for Clay, too."

Her cheeks colored.

Why? Ethan wondered. It was on the tip of his tongue to ask how her husband or boyfriend felt about her busy schedule. Then it occurred to him maybe she and Clay were seeing each other. That would explain the embarrassment.

Ethan couldn't blame his friend. And it wasn't as if he had any kind of claim on Caitlin himself. Not after leaving her high and dry when he'd enlisted, following his mother's death.

"Speaking of which," Clay interjected, "Ethan's your first patient."

Her eyebrows rose. "You are?"

"It's nothing," Ethan insisted, sending his friend— soon to be *ex*-friend once again if he kept this up—a warning look.

He'd hardly gotten over the shock of seeing Caitlin. No way was he ready to be examined by her.

Any choice he had in the matter was taken from him when Clay all but shoved him through the door and into the dimly lit room.

The next instant, his friend was gone, leaving Ethan alone with the woman whose heart he'd broken, and who still owned a very large piece of his.

CAITLIN PULLED A flimsy metal folding chair into the center of the space and indicated Ethan should sit.

Gripping the back of the chair, he tested its strength. The legs wobbled. "You sure?"

She shrugged apologetically. "I'm still setting up." When he hesitated, she added, "There's always the cot."

He promptly sat, his long legs stretched out in front of him, his big frame dwarfing the chair. Ethan had always been tall, some had said too tall for a bronc or bull rider. What he'd done since they last saw each other was fill out. No longer lean and lanky, he'd grown into a wall of solid muscle. She supposed his two—or was it three?—overseas tours were responsible.

The extra weight looked good on him.

Who was she kidding? He just plain looked good.

Dark eyes, jet-black hair and a five o'clock shadow that should have looked scruffy but somehow managed to be sexy. And that smile of his. It had dazzled her at age seventeen, and never stopped during the four years they'd dated.

Wait. On second thought, he hadn't smiled yet.

He'd been pleasant and polite, but that devil-may-care charm was noticeably absent.

"I'm guessing you injured yourself?"

"My left shoulder," he said.

"Strained it?"

"Or something."

She stood in front of him and gently placed her hand on the afflicted area. He jerked at her touch.

"Does that hurt?"

"Some."

She suspected her proximity was responsible for his reaction more than anything else. There was a lot of history between them, after all, much of it unresolved.

"What happened?" She gently probed his shoulder.

"A horse decided he didn't much like me riding him."

It was on the tip of her tongue to ask how he managed that with a prosthetic leg, but she refrained. Clay had warned her that Ethan didn't appreciate reminders of his handicap, and refused to let it hold him back. Well, he'd always been competitive. First high school sports, then professional rodeo after graduation.

"Did you at least land on soft ground?"

"The arena."

"Thank goodness." She lifted his arm. "Tell me when it starts to hurt."

He said nothing, even when she raised it clear over his head. The clenching of his jaw told another story. She lowered his arm, then raised it again, this time to the side.

He squeezed his eyes shut, but remained stubbornly silent.

Bending his arm at the elbow, she pressed his hand into the small of his back. "What about now?"

"Okay." He released a long breath and shook off her grasp. "You win. It hurts."

So he wasn't invincible.

"You should see your doctor as soon as possible and get an X-ray," she told him, lightly massaging his shoulder. "You might have torn a ligament or your rotator cuff."

"I'll be better by morning."

He was back to being the tough guy.

"No, you're going to be worse. Trust me."

"I'll take some ibuprofen."

"Three a day, extra strength. Up to six if your stomach can tolerate it. Ice the shoulder for at least an hour tonight before you go to bed, and again in the morning. When you can't stand the pain anymore and decide I'm right, see your doctor."

He chuckled, and the smile she'd been missing earlier appeared, if only a shadow of the one she remembered.

"You have nothing to prove, Ethan." She laid her palm on his good shoulder. "See a doctor."

"You're wrong." He rose from the chair, either her touch or her words galvanizing him. "I do have something to prove."

One step on his part and they were standing toe to toe.

Unable to help herself, Caitlin looked up into his face. As his gaze raked over her, lingered on her mouth, the atmosphere surrounding them went from calm to highly charged.

So much for believing the attraction had died.

She retreated on unsteady legs. All these years apart, and he still had the ability to unsettle her.

"How's your family?" she asked. Breathing came easier with some distance between them. "Clay mentioned your brother's getting married."

"This spring. I suppose Clay also mentioned the two of them are partners in a stud and breeding business."

"No." By unspoken agreement, she and Ethan made their way to the door. "We really haven't talked much other than about setting up the first-aid station."

"Huh. I thought maybe you and he…"

"He and I what?"

"Had kept in touch." Ethan stepped aside, allowing her to precede him outside.

"We did up until he got married and moved away. I had no idea he was divorced and back in town."

"Then how did you wind up working for him?"

"He showed up at the school last Wednesday and asked me to run the first-aid station."

"Have you been at the school long?" They stopped beside her minivan.

"You really don't know?"

"Should I?"

"I thought maybe someone told you."

Mustang Village was a horse-friendly residential community, built in and named after Mustang Valley, the land Ethan's family had once owned, and where they had raised cattle for four generations. Their ranch, what was left of it, lay nestled in the foothills of the McDowell Mountains, and looked down on the village. Caitlin didn't think much happened that the Powells didn't know about.

She'd certainly heard about Ethan's injury, medical discharge and return home.

"I've worked at the school since August," she told him.

"That long?" he said, more to himself than her.

"Clay told me you're breaking horses for him."

"Trying to." Another half smile appeared. "Some of them aren't embracing the process."

"If anyone can change their minds, you can." Again she wondered how he managed such a physically demanding job. "Is your sister still living in San Francisco?"

"For five years now."

"But she visits, right?"

"Used to. Not much the last couple years."

"That's too bad."

"Sierra being gone so much is hard on Dad. He misses her. Misses Mom, too. Though he's doing a lot better lately since Cassie came to live with us. He's crazy about her."

Caitlin had met Ethan's twelve-year-old niece at the school. "I don't imagine recovering from the death of a loved one is ever easy."

"It's not."

The mention of his late mother put a damper on their conversation. It was right after Louise Powell died that Ethan had abruptly enlisted, leaving Caitlin to suffer the loss of not only a dear friend, but the love of her life.

A painful pressure built inside her chest.

Heartache.

It had been a long time since the memory of those unhappy days had caused such a profound physical re-action.

"How's your brother?" Ethan asked. "Gavin told me about the accident."

More pressure.

Discussing Justin was always hard for Caitlin. No matter how many obstacles he overcame and how many challenges he conquered, she could never forget that she was responsible for him being a paraplegic and having to spend the rest of his life in a wheelchair.

"He's graduating from Arizona State in December," she said, focusing on the positive. "With a master's in education."

"Good for him."

"We're all very proud. Now if he can just land a job."

"It's a tough economy."

"That, too."

Great strides had been made in the last few decades when it came to equal rights for handicapped employees, but Caitlin still worried about her brother's chances at finding decent employment.

Ethan distracted her by reaching into the back of her minivan and removing a carton of supplies.

"Hey, what are you doing?" She tried to take the box from him.

He swung it out of her reach. "Helping you unload."

"Ethan!" She sighed with exasperation. "You're hurt."

"My shoulder. Not my hands." He squeezed past her and carried his load inside.

She hurried after him.

"Where do you want this?"

Because she knew arguing with him was useless, she pointed to the folding table along the wall. "There. And don't even think about carrying anything else in."

He not only thought about it, he did it. She gave up and pitched in. Together, they quickly emptied the van.

"You're going to regret this tomorrow," she told him when they were done.

"You were never such a worrier before."

"It comes from being a nurse. So does being bossy." She leveled a finger at him. "Now get yourself home and take care of that shoulder."

"Yes, ma'am." One corner of his mouth lifted in an amused and very compelling grin.

Caitlin's heart fluttered. No doubt about it, the attraction hadn't died.

With the van unloaded, there was no reason for him to remain.

"Will I see you later?" she asked.

"Tomorrow, if you're here."

The thought shouldn't have appealed to her as much as it did. Ethan had hurt her. Terribly. She'd be wise to take care where he was concerned.

Even so, a sweet rush of anticipation cascaded through her.

"I'm sure Clay can do without you training his horses for a couple of days."

"Probably." Ethan buttoned his denim jacket. "I'm the one who can't do without the practicing."

"Practicing for what?"

"The jackpot."

She stared at him blankly. "You're not competing."

"I am. Or I will be if I can last a full eight seconds at least once before then. Clay won't let me enter otherwise."

"Is that how you fell tonight? Bull riding?"

"No, saddle bronc."

"Are you crazy?"

"A little, I suppose," he said jokingly.

"More than a little." She started to remind him that he had only one good leg, then stopped herself. "Bronc riding is dangerous. I really wish you'd reconsider."

"Not a chance." He turned to go, then paused. "I'm glad you're home, Caitlin."

A few minutes ago, such a statement would have elicited a breathy sigh from her, foolish though it may have been.

Not now.

He was saddle bronc riding again. With a prosthetic leg! Why didn't he just jump off a three-story building? The results would be the same.

Caitlin had cheered Ethan on from the sidelines all those years ago. She'd also encouraged him the same way she'd encouraged her brother. Winning competitions required a certain amount of risk, after all.

She'd learned too late that taking risks came with a steep price. In her case, her brother, Justin, was the one to pay.

It would be no different for Ethan, and she refused to be there when he injured himself.

Except, as the on-site emergency medical personnel for the Duvall Rodeo Arena, she most likely would be the one to treat him.

Chapter Two

Ethan hated to admit it, but Caitlin was right. His shoulder hurt like a son of a bitch. It had all night, affecting his sleep, his ability to dress himself and his mood.

What if he really had torn something? Then he wouldn't be able to enter the jackpot, that was for sure.

The idea of going to the doctor and getting an X-ray wasn't quite as distasteful to him as it had been the night before. Maybe he could go to the urgent-care clinic. If he was lucky, he might run into Caitlin again.

He no sooner had the thought than he dismissed it. More likely than not she was married or in a committed relationship. Of course, finding out wouldn't be all that hard.

And if she was single, then what?

He doubted she'd go out with him, not after the way he'd dumped her with hardly a word. Then there was the matter of his leg—or lack of it. Beautiful, desirable women like Caitlin Carmichael didn't date men with missing limbs.

Gritting his teeth, he shoved his arms through the sleeves of his undershirt and tried to pull it over his head. He didn't get far. The pain immobilized him.

The next instant a knock sounded.

"What?" he hollered, his breathing labored.

The front door opened and his brother came in. "Good morning to you, too." He stopped midstep and eyed Ethan curiously. "Having a problem?"

Ethan muttered to himself, not pleased at having an audience.

"What did you say?"

"I hurt my shoulder last night."

"Breaking one of Clay's horses?"

"A bronc trying to break me."

"Ah." Gavin wandered toward the newly remodeled kitchen. "Any coffee?"

"There's instant in the cupboard."

"Instant?" He grimaced.

"Beggars can't be choosers."

Ethan didn't particularly like instant, either. But he'd discovered since living alone the last few weeks that brewing a pot of coffee was a waste when he drank only one cup.

He and Gavin and their dad had resided comfortably in the main house for over a year. When Gavin's daughter, Cassie, moved in with them this past summer, they'd continued to get along. Soon, however, Gavin's fiancée, Sage, and her young daughter, Isa, would be joining the family permanently, and that was a little too much closeness for Ethan.

The old bunkhouse had seemed a good solution. Converting it into an apartment was taking time, though, and living amid the chaos of construction did get tedious. But Ethan didn't mind.

After a lifetime of cohabitating with others, including a barracks full of marines, he quite liked his solitude. No snoring, music or loud TV disturbing his sleep. No having to wait for someone to finish in the bathroom. No arguing about whose turn it was to wash the dishes or vacuum.

No one watching him put on his prosthetic leg, then turning away when he caught him staring.

"Want some?" Undeterred by the prospect of instant coffee, Gavin removed a mug from the cupboard.

"Naw. I already had my quota today." Readying himself, Ethan raised his arms, only to hesitate.

What was wrong with him? He'd endured far worse discomfort than this. The months following his accident—a nice, gentle euphemism for losing the bottom half of his leg in an explosion—had been a daily practice in pushing the boundaries of his endurance.

It hadn't stopped there. The first thing Ethan had done when he returned home was reveal his intentions to start training horses again, his job before enlisting. His family had tried to dissuade him, but eventually came to understand his reasons and the need that drove him.

Since no respectable cowboy wore athletic shoes when he rode, Ethan had used some of the money he'd saved during his enlistment to purchase two pairs of custom-made boots that fit his prosthesis. Within a few weeks, he was riding, and suffering a whole new kind of torturous pain. With determination, practice and continual exercise, he found the pain eventually lessened, though he still had his days.

He didn't start breaking horses until a chance meeting with Clay Duvall. Over beers at the local bar, his old friend had listened while Ethan outlined his ambitions. Then he'd offered him a job. In addition to the arena, Clay owned and operated a rodeo stock business that specialized in bucking horses.

The idea of competing again hadn't occurred to

Ethan until he'd watched the cowboys practicing at Clay's arena. What started as a vague longing quickly grew into a burning desire. Ethan was tired of people looking at him differently. Tired of their sympathetic smiles.

Once he started competing again, all that would change.

Ignoring the pain, he pulled on his undershirt, then walked through the partially framed living room to the freshly painted bathroom, where he removed a bottle of ibuprofen from the medicine cabinet.

"You need a day off to rest up?" Gavin hollered from the kitchen.

"Hell, no."

Both Ethan and his father worked alongside Gavin. With only thirty of the family's original six hundred acres remaining in their possession, they'd turned their ranch into a public riding stable. Many Mustang Village residents boarded their horses, took riding lessons or went on guided trail rides at Powell Ranch.

In addition, they'd started the stud and breeding business last month, after capturing Prince, a wild mustang roaming the McDowell Mountains.

"Maybe you should take it easy today," Gavin suggested, when Ethan returned to the kitchen.

"Don't worry about me." He glowered at his brother. "What are you doing here, anyway?"

"Prince is off his feed. I'd like you to take a look at him before I call the vet."

"I will. Later."

"I was hoping you could do it first thing."

Ethan thought his brother babied the wild mustang too much. Then again, the future of their family business relied heavily on Prince and his ability to breed.

While he'd successfully mated with several mares since his capture last month, it was still far too early to determine if any pregnancies had taken, much less what kind of foals he would produce.

Gavin studied him as Ethan downed the painkiller with a glass of water. "Have you considered seeing a doctor?"

"Caitlin told me the same thing."

That got his brother's attention. Instead of leaving, which was Ethan's hope, Gavin pulled out a chair at the dining table, removed his hat and made himself at home.

Great.

"You saw her?" he asked.

"Last night. She's working for Clay, running his first-aid station."

"Interesting."

Gavin's expression reminded Ethan of their father and, he supposed, himself. The Powell men all looked enough alike that most people immediately recognized them as family.

"That's what I thought, too," Ethan said, recalling the shock he'd felt when he first saw Caitlin. "She also works mornings at the middle school and afternoons at the urgent-care clinic."

"Uh-huh."

His brother was sure taking the news in stride. Then it hit him. "You knew she was back, didn't you?"

"We met when Cassie sprained her ankle in gym class, and the school called me to come pick her up."

"That was weeks ago. And you're only now telling me?"

"Figured it wasn't my place."

Another thought occurred to Ethan. "Caitlin ask you not to tell me?"

"No. Nothing like that."

"Did my name even come up?"

"We really didn't have time to talk. She was busy, and Cassie was complaining about her ankle."

Ethan started pacing the kitchen. Caitlin had known he'd returned to Mustang Valley and hadn't bothered to look him up.

Did he really expect her to, after the way he'd treated her?

Probably not. Change that to hell, no.

"Look," Gavin continued, "it just slipped my mind. I had a lot going on at the time. Capturing Prince. Starting the stud and breeding business. Sage and I getting engaged."

"Right," Ethan answered testily. He'd bet the entire contents of his wallet that running into Caitlin hadn't slipped his brother's mind. "I'm a big boy, bro. You don't have to watch out for me."

"Sorry. Old habits are hard to break."

Not exactly an admission, but close.

"Answer me this," Gavin said. "What would you have done if I told you she was back in town?"

"Apologize, for one." Which, now that he thought about it, wasn't something he'd done last night. "And make amends…if possible." He owed her that much.

"You going to ask her out?"

"Are you kidding?"

"Why not?"

"Even if I did, she'd turn me down flat. Besides, she's probably married by now."

"She isn't."

Ethan stopped pacing. "How do you know?"

"The subject came up."

"I thought you said you didn't have much time to talk to her."

"Doesn't take long to say, 'Hey, you ever get married?'"

Ethan groaned.

"What are you so mad about, anyway?"

Before he could reply, another knock sounded at the door.

"What now?" He stormed over and yanked the door open.

Clay stood on the other side. "You're in a fine mood." Without waiting for an invitation, he stepped inside. "I just came from Prince's paddock. He hasn't touched his food."

"We're heading there now," Ethan grumbled, snatching his jacket off the back of the couch where he'd left it.

"Any more of that coffee left?"

"It's instant," Gavin complained from his seat at the table.

Clay drew back in surprise. "Don't you have a coffeemaker?"

Ethan glared at him. "Don't you?"

Clay glared back. "What's bugging you?"

"He's mad that I didn't tell him Caitlin was working at the school." Gavin rose from the table.

"Can we not discuss this?" Ethan headed for the door.

"You going to invite her out?"

He ignored Clay's question.

"I already asked him that." Gavin went to the sink and deposited his mug. "He says no."

Annoyed, Ethan shoved an arm into the sleeve of his jacket, then swore loudly when his entire left side seized with fresh pain.

"How's the shoulder?" Clay asked.

"Fine." Ethan opened the door and stepped out onto the porch.

Clay came up behind him. "You don't act like it's fine."

"I'll be all right."

"What did Caitlin say last night?"

"Ice the shoulder and take ibuprofen. I've done both."

"Did she tell you to see a doctor?"

"I don't need to see a doctor."

"Don't believe him." Gavin joined them on the porch, shutting the door behind him. "He's hurting."

Ethan anchored his hat to his head as a strong gust of wind swept past them on its way down the mountain to the valley.

"See a doctor," Clay ordered. "Until you do, and until you're cleared, no bronc riding."

Ethan swung around. "Dammit, Clay!"

"Sorry. That's the rule. Same for you as everyone else."

"The jackpot is a week and a half away. I need to practice."

"Then I guess you'd better haul your butt to the doctor today."

AT THE BOTTOM of the long driveway leading from Powell Ranch to the main road, Ethan turned left. Three minutes later he reached the entrance to Mustang Village, with its large monument sign flanked by a life-size bronze statue of a rearing horse.

As he drove at a reduced speed through the equine-friendly community, he tried to remember what it had been like when there were no houses or buildings or people, only wide-open spaces and Powell cattle roaming them. He'd missed out on the construction of the community, having been in the service at the time. How hard it must have been for his father and brother to watch their family's hundred-year-old history disappear acre by acre, replaced with roads, houses, condos and commercial buildings.

He generally avoided Mustang Village. The reminder of all they had lost was too hard on his heart.

If not for his mother's failing health, they wouldn't have borrowed the money from Clay's father and used their land as collateral. If Clay's dad had honored the agreement and not sold the land out from under them, Mustang Village would never have been built. If not for the residents of Mustang Village, Ethan's family would be raising cattle rather than operating a riding stable.

A lot of ifs, and that wasn't even counting the most recent one—if he hadn't been standing where he was at the exact moment the car bomb exploded, he wouldn't have lost his leg.

Ethan turned his thoughts away from the past when Mustang Village's one and only retail strip center came into view.

It always struck him as odd to see hitching rails and bridle paths in a residential community. On any given weekend, there were almost as many equestrians riding about as there were pedestrians walking. Not so much during the week. Mustang Village resembled most other communities then, with school buses making runs, mothers pushing strollers, cyclists zipping along and dog lovers walking their pets.

Today, a work crew was busy stringing Christmas lights along the storefronts and hanging wreaths on lampposts. Already? Thanksgiving was still more than a week away.

A buzzer announced Ethan's arrival at the urgent-care clinic. This was his first visit. He always drove to the VA hospital in Phoenix for his few medical needs.

Inside the crowded clinic, a receptionist greeted him with a friendly "May I help you?" and handed him a clipboard. When he was done filling out the forms, she processed his co-pay and said, "Have a seat."

Ethan considered inquiring if Caitlin was working. But then the phone rang, followed immediately by a second line ringing. He left the receptionist to answer her calls, and sat in a chair next to a mother and her sniffling child.

He couldn't help thinking that if the bronc hadn't thrown him last night, he wouldn't be here now, anxiously waiting to see his former girlfriend again. Yet another if in a long, long list of them.

Except Ethan really wouldn't describe Caitlin as a girlfriend. She'd been much more than that to him, and he to her. Had his mother not died and he not enlisted, chances were good they'd have gotten married.

He really had to stop thinking about what might have been, or else he'd drive himself crazy.

"Ethan?"

His head snapped up when Caitlin called his name. "Yeah."

"Right this way."

He followed her down the corridor. Once he was weighed and his height taken, she escorted him to an examination room, where he sat on the table and she at the computer terminal.

"Why are you here today?"

Seriously? She knew darn well why. "I fell from a horse last night and hurt my shoulder," he answered, playing along.

"What part of your shoulder?"

"You examined me."

She gave him a very professional smile. "It's procedure."

He cupped his shoulder with his palm.

More questions followed, and she typed the answers into the computer. During the entire process, Caitlin treated him like any other patient, concerned, interested and like they hardly knew each other.

What did he expect? She was at work.

What did he want?

The answer was easy. To see that light in her eyes.

"The doctor will be right in to see you." Before closing the door, she smiled and said, "I'm glad you came in today."

He was tempted to jump to the wrong conclusion and reminded himself that her remark was medically motivated. Hadn't she urged him last night to have his shoulder looked at?

After a brief consultation with the doctor, Ethan waited again, this time for the X-ray technician. Returning from the imaging room, he waited a third time.

The doctor's news was good. Nothing was torn, only soft-tissue damage.

"Can I start riding again right away?" he asked.

"I recommend you take a few days off." The man studied him over a pair of reading glasses. "A week would be better."

"But there's no reason I can't ride."

"You could sustain further injury."

"Okay." Ethan nodded. He had every intention of getting on a bronc tonight, and he was pretty sure the doctor knew it.

"I'm going to prescribe an anti-inflammatory and a

muscle relaxant. If you aren't better in two weeks, call for a follow-up exam or see your regular doctor."

"Thanks."

"You know—" the man removed his reading glasses "—if you're really that determined to ride, you might consider physical therapy to speed your recovery."

"Appreciate the advice, Doc."

"The nurse will be in shortly with your prescriptions."

Another wait, this one not long. Caitlin returned with three slips of paper in her hand. Ethan had to admit the sight of her in pale green scrubs was as surreal as seeing her in sweats. In college, she'd majored in journalism, with ambitions of being a TV reporter, and always dressed fashionably.

Admittedly, the scrubs looked cute on her, the loose material not quite hiding her very nice curves.

"Here you go." She handed him the prescriptions. "The doctor wrote one for physical therapy as well, in case you need something for the VA."

"I'll probably skip PT."

"Why? It will help."

He stood, folded the prescriptions and placed them in his wallet. "The nearby facilities don't take VA insurance. And I can't afford the time off work to drive into Phoenix."

"What if...what if I provided your physical therapy?"

"You?"

"I have some basic training. I'm not licensed, but I've taken several classes. For Justin. During his rehab, he'd strain his upper body muscles. And now that he's involved in wheelchair athletics, he's always overdoing it."

"I can relate."

"You two are alike when it comes to that." Her expression softened, and suddenly she was the seventeen-year-old transfer student who'd been assigned to sit next to him in calculus class.

Ethan was caught off guard and needed a moment to collect himself. "I don't think the VA will pay for a private physical therapist."

"I won't charge you."

He shook his head. "I can't ask you to do it for free."

"Who said anything about free?" She smiled then, *really* smiled, and he caught another glimpse of the confident, carefree girl he'd fallen in love with. "I was hoping we could negotiate a trade."

She had his attention now. "I'm listening."

She motioned him into the hall.

"I'm on the Holly Days Festival committee," she said.

The residents of Mustang Village had put on a big community-wide event the previous Christmas. None of the Powells had attended, but they'd heard about it. From everyone.

"The committee, huh?"

"You know me."

He did. She'd been an involved student in both high school and college. Cocaptain of the cheerleading squad, student council, National Honor Society.

"I thought the festival was strictly for residents."

"I'm a resident," she said brightly as they entered the reception area.

"Really?"

"I'm renting a condo. In the complex right across the street." She nodded toward the window. "I get to walk to work every day. Well, not to the middle school. But here."

Working *and* living in Mustang Village. Was that

another bit of interesting information Gavin had conveniently forgotten to tell Ethan?

"The committee is hoping to try something different this year," Caitlin went on. "The parade was fun, but more people participated than watched."

"You saw it?"

"I did. I almost drove to the ranch, too."

Just how often *had* they narrowly missed crossing paths since his return home?

"Anyway, I remembered that old farm wagon of yours and was wondering if we could decorate it and have you drive people around the park."

"No one's used that wagon in years."

Her hopeful smile fell. "Well, it was just an idea."

Ethan had no desire to participate in the Holly Days Festival. Nothing involving Mustang Village appealed to him—with the exception of Caitlin. And she appealed to him far too much for his own good.

But hadn't he just told Gavin this morning that he wished he could make amends with Caitlin? Wagon rides at the festival wouldn't exactly clean the slate. But it was a start, and obviously important to her.

"We could pull the wagon out of storage," he said. "See what kind of shape it's in."

"Great!" Her green eyes lit up.

This was the moment Ethan had been waiting for, only her excitement was over an old wagon. Not him.

"Why don't you come out to the ranch?"

"When?"

Ethan massaged his left shoulder. "As soon as possible. I still haven't qualified for the jackpot next weekend."

"What about tomorrow, say around noon? I have a two-hour break between the school and the clinic. If the wagon is usable, we'll set up a schedule for your PT sessions."

"Sounds good."

"Hey, Caitlin." The receptionist held up a manila folder.

"I have to go," she said hurriedly. "Thank you, Ethan."

She collected the folder and called the next person's name.

Once again, Ethan was just another patient—and it didn't set well with him.

Chapter Three

In days gone by, Caitlin would have driven directly to the main house at Powell Ranch and parked there. Instead, she followed the signs and went around behind the cattle barn to the designated parking area.

"It's weird," her brother said from beside her in the passenger seat. "The place is totally different, but not different."

"Yeah, weird." She opened her door and stepped out.

Memories that had hovered the last few days promptly assailed her. Most were good, gently stroking emotional chords. One wasn't so good, and it quickly overpowered the rest.

"When was the last time you were here?" Justin asked, already maneuvering his legs into position.

"Oh, about nine years ago."

Nine years, four months and…she mentally calculated…eighteen days. Not that she was keeping track.

She'd arrived that last evening intending to join the Powells for dinner, something she often did in the past. Even before the meal was served, Ethan took her out to the front courtyard and sprang the news on her. He'd enlisted. Signed up a week after his mother's funeral. A rather important decision he hadn't even bothered discussing with Caitlin.

A fresh wave of hurt and anger unbalanced her now, and she paused, holding on to the van door for support.

Guess she hadn't moved past her and Ethan's bitter breakup, after all.

It must be seeing the ranch again. Or seeing *him* again—for the third day in a row.

Enough is enough, she told herself. She could manage working with Ethan, seeing him at the clinic, administering his physical therapy. He was nothing more than her patient.

With actions honed from much practice, she removed her brother's wheelchair from the rear of the minivan and carried it to the passenger side, where he waited.

She'd have set the wheelchair up for him, except he insisted on performing the task himself. Rather than argue, she gave in. Being independent was important to Justin, and she respected his wishes even though her instinct was to do everything for him.

After hoisting himself into the wheelchair, he and Caitlin made their way to the stables. She figured the office was as good a place as any to start looking for Ethan.

"Sure are a lot of people here," Justin commented, rolling his wheelchair along beside her.

A half-dozen riders were gathered in the open area near the stables. Several more were in the arena, riding alone or in pairs. One enthusiastic mother clapped while her preschooler trotted a shaggy pony in circles.

"I hear it's even busier when school lets out for the day." Caitlin remembered when the only people on the ranch were the Powells and the cowboys who worked for them.

"I'll wait here," Justin said when they reached the small porch outside the office.

He could easily maneuver the three steps leading onto it, but he probably wanted to give Caitlin and Ethan some privacy.

Easing open the door, she stepped tentatively inside the office. The sight of Ethan sitting with his back to her at an old metal desk gave her a start.

Not again, she chided herself. No more going weak in the knees every time she saw him.

Clearing her throat, she said, "Hello," then "Oh!" when the ancient chair swiveled around with a squeak.

The man wasn't Ethan.

"Hey." Gavin greeted her with a wide grin. "What brings you here?"

Caitlin vacillated between enormous relief and equally enormous disappointment. "I'm meeting Ethan."

"You are?"

Obviously he hadn't informed his family of her visit. She didn't know what to make of that.

"If he's not around—"

"He's here. Shoeing one of the horses."

"Is it all right if I interrupt him?"

"I'm thinking he won't mind."

Caitlin wavered, then blurted, "Can I ask a favor of you?"

"Sure."

"My brother's outside. Would you check on him for me? Without making it look like you're checking on him?"

"How's he doing?"

"Good. And he's perfectly capable of handling himself in new situations."

"But you worry."

"Constantly."

"Not a problem." Gavin's cell phone rang. "Let me take this call first."

"Thanks." Caitlin hurried across the office and out the door leading to the stables.

It was like stepping back in time.

The rich, familiar scents of horses and alfalfa filled her nostrils the moment she crossed the threshold. Daylight, pouring in from the large doorways on both ends of the long aisle, illuminated the interior better than any electric-powered lights could. Soft earth gave beneath her feet with each step she took. A barn cat dashed behind a barrel, then stuck its head out to peer warily at her.

Caitlin glanced around, her breath catching at the sight of Ethan not thirty feet away. He was bent over at the waist, the horse's rear hoof braced between his knees as he used a file to trim it.

How did he do that with a prosthetic leg?

How did he do that with a bad shoulder?

Fine, he was resilient. She appreciated that quality in an individual. Admired it. But shoeing a horse while injured was just plain stupid. So was bronc riding.

She started to say something, only to close her mouth when Ethan released the horse's hoof and straightened.

He stood tall, his blue work shirt rolled up at the sleeves and stretched taut across his muscled back. The leather chaps he wore sat low on his hips, emphasizing his athletic frame. She couldn't remember him ever looking better. Or sexier.

When they were in high school, Caitlin had liked him best in his football uniform. Next best in the tux he'd worn to their senior prom. She'd been the envy of every girl on the cheerleading squad, and had relished the attention.

What an idiot she'd been. Shallow and silly—placing too much importance on things that didn't matter.

Ethan turned, and she wished suddenly she was wearing nice clothes. Not an oversize hooded sweatshirt and scrubs.

"You made it."

"I did."

He set the file he'd been using down on a box of tools. Next, he removed his chaps and draped them over the box. "Ready to take a look at the wagon?"

"Is that Chico?" Caitlin advanced a step, then two. "Can I pet him?"

"Of course."

"I remember him. I can't believe he's still around." She stroked the old horse's soft nose, and he snorted contentedly.

"That's right. You and Chico are already acquainted."

Caitlin was never much of a horse enthusiast, though she'd tried her best to share that interest with Ethan. When they did go on a ride, Chico was her mount of choice.

"He's Isa's horse now."

"Isa?"

"Sage's daughter. Gavin's soon-to-be stepdaughter. She's six and in love with this old guy."

"I'm glad." Glad the horse Caitlin remembered with such fondness was adored by a little girl and that some things around Powell Ranch hadn't changed.

"Do you still ride?"

"No, not since Chico." She didn't want to admit to Ethan how much riding—or any physical activity that held risk—scared her. She hadn't been like that before Justin's accident. Quite the opposite.

"I'll take you sometime." Ethan moved closer.

Caitlin's guard instantly went up. She continued stroking Chico's nose in an attempt to disguise her nervousness—at Ethan's proximity and the prospect of getting on a horse again. "We should probably take a look at the wagon. I have to get to the clinic soon."

They left the stables. Chico, Ethan assured Caitlin, would be just fine tied to the hitching rail, and was probably already napping.

As they rounded the corner of the cattle barn, she noticed lumber stacked nearby, along with a table saw, ladder and toolboxes.

"What are you building?"

"We're converting the old barn into a mare motel for the stud and breeding business. Clay and his men are helping us."

Ethan took her elbow and guided her around more piles of construction material. She started to object and insist she was fine, then changed her mind. Like the other night when he'd insisted on unloading her medical supplies, it would be like arguing with a brick wall.

He led her to a corner of the barn where, behind a tower of wooden crates and beneath a canvas tarp, the wagon stood.

"Not sure we can get much closer," he said, stepping over a roll of rusted chicken wire.

Caitlin squeezed in behind him, acutely aware of his tall, broad frame mere inches from her.

He leaned over and lifted the tarp, revealing a wagon wheel. Without thinking, she reached out and touched the worn wood.

A memory of Ethan driving her around the ranch in the wagon suddenly surfaced, of her bouncing in the seat beside him and both of them laughing. How carefree they'd been back then.

She suddenly missed those days with a longing she hadn't felt in years.

Stop it!

Dwelling on that period of her life would do more damage than good. She and Ethan might have renewed their acquaintance, but that was all it was, an acquaintance. All it could be. Even if she finally got past the hurt he'd caused her, he rode saddle broncs for pleasure and broke green horses for a living. Caitlin wasn't capable of caring for someone who courted danger on a daily basis. Not after what had happened to her brother. She couldn't live with the constant worry and fear.

"Going to need a few repairs." Ethan wiggled a loose spoke.

Caitlin was relieved to get back on track. "And lots of cleaning."

"Hope you have enough volunteers."

She studied the wagon with a critical eye. "I might need more."

"I've been thinking. Would it be all right if we asked for a small donation? Completely voluntary, of course. Sage, my future sister-in-law, is starting a wild-mustang sanctuary here on the ranch, and she's having trouble obtaining funding."

"What a good idea. I can't imagine the festival committee having any objections."

"That'll make her happy."

Caitlin brushed dirt off the wheel. "When can we get started?"

"Saturday soon enough?"

"We'll have to be here early. I'm due at Clay's arena after lunch."

"Me, too."

"You're not riding!"

"Planning on it."

"Your shoulder!"

"I can't afford to miss any practices."

"Isn't it dangerous to ride with an injury? I'd think your reaction time would be slowed."

"I'll wrap it."

As if that would fix everything. His attitude was exactly the reason they would never date again, no matter how attractive she found him. Riding broncs was bad enough. Riding broncs with an injury was idiotic.

"I'll have a couple of the guys help me pull the wagon out," he said.

"I recommend you *supervise* a couple of the guys." She leveled a finger at him. "If you're going to ride on Saturday, you need to rest that shoulder and let it heal."

"Right."

He was impossible.

"I need to get going." She stepped over the roll of rusted chicken wire. "I don't want to leave Justin alone too long."

"You brought him with you?"

"He doesn't have class on Fridays and sometimes comes by for a visit."

"Justin drives?"

"A Honda Civic. Modified, of course."

"And he lives with your parents?"

"No, he has an apartment near campus with a roommate."

"Not that it's any of my business," Ethan said, "but if the kid lives on his own and drives, don't you think he'll be okay alone for a few minutes?"

She sighed with exasperation...at herself. "I can't help worrying about him. Call it big-sister-itis."

"His accident wasn't your fault."

Caitlin went still, swallowed a gasp. No one other than Justin and her parents knew of her guilt and the reason for it.

How in the world had Ethan guessed?

Stupid question. He'd always been able to read her better than anyone.

She averted her face, hiding the sudden storm of emotions churning inside her. Him, this place, the memories of happier times—it was all too much.

Ethan took her elbow again, helping her navigate the narrow path through the construction material. His fingers were warm and strong and far too familiar. Any hope Caitlin had for control flew out the window.

"You weren't at the river that day," he said, his voice gentle with understanding. "You couldn't possibly have been involved."

His compassion and sympathy were her undoing.

"I encouraged him to go," she admitted, her throat burning. "If he had stayed home, he wouldn't have landed on that rock and damaged his spinal cord."

"Come on. Name one senior at our school who didn't tube down the river and jump from the cliffs the week after graduation. It was a rite of passage."

"Justin didn't normally disobey our parents." As she had, she thought. "I told him he was eighteen and it was time he stopped acting like such a geek. I drove him to his friend's house, then lied to our folks about where he was going."

"Teenagers disobey their parents. It's what they do."

"Being popular was so important to me in high school. Justin was such a nerd back then. Shy and scrawny and brainy. He was practically invisible. I thought if he went tubing, he'd break out of his shell. Because of me, his life is ruined."

They came to a stop at the entrance to the barn. Ethan released her elbow, only to drape an arm around her shoulders.

"Trust me, you weren't the only one pressuring him to go tubing. His buddies were, too."

It would have been nice to lay her head on Ethan's chest as she'd done so often in the past, and let him comfort her.

She might have, if she wasn't convinced she'd be sending him the wrong message.

Wiping her eyes, she tried to ease away from his embrace.

He'd have none of it.

"When someone's seriously injured, like Justin, it's pretty common for family members and friends to blame themselves. My dad and brother were the same way. Kept thinking if they'd been there for me when Mom was sick, and after she died, I wouldn't have enlisted and been caught in that explosion. Eventually, they came to accept it was my decision to join the marines, and rotten luck I was standing where I was that day. Same with Justin."

Caitlin looked up at Ethan. "You don't think I was there for you when your mom died?"

At the time, she'd been so embroiled in her own misery over his abrupt departure, she hadn't considered the reason he left was because of her. How incredibly selfish.

"What? Of course not. I was the one unable to cope with my grief, so was pushing people away." He inhaled deeply. "I'm sorry, Caitlin. For abandoning you like that."

"I appreciate the apology."

"I know it's not enough to make up for what I did to you."

"No, it isn't."

He drew back at her brutal, but honest, admission.

"You're not the only one who had to deal with traumatic events," she said. "I did, too. And believe me, there were plenty of times after Justin's accident when I wanted to run away and leave everything behind. But I didn't. I stayed and dealt with my responsibilities regardless of how difficult it was. I just wish you had loved me enough to do the same."

CAITLIN'S REMARK HIT Ethan like a blow. How could she think he hadn't loved her enough? The whole reason he'd left was because he had loved her *too* much. She deserved more than a man who was emotionally devastated, out of work and whose family was financially ruined, thanks to one man's insatiable greed.

Before he could explain, Justin came wheeling toward them. Ethan was pleased to see the young man, even if his timing stank.

"Hey, there you are." He pushed his wheelchair forward, meeting up with Ethan and Caitlin outside the cattle barn. "How are you doing?"

"I'm good." Ethan shook his hand, which was sheathed in a worn leather glove with cutouts for his fingers.

"I was just talking to Gavin. He filled me in on all the changes round here."

"Lots of them. Some good, some bad."

"You miss the old days?"

No one had ever asked Ethan that. He took a moment to consider before answering. "I do sometimes. I miss the people, especially. My mom and sister." He glanced briefly at Caitlin. If she was aware of his unspoken inclusion of her, she didn't show it. "But all things considered, I can't complain."

"Me, either," Justin said, without the slightest trace of bitterness.

Ethan's respect for him grew by leaps and bounds. If Justin felt self-pity at losing the use of his legs, he certainly didn't wallow in it.

"You in a hurry to leave?" Justin maneuvered his wheelchair so that he faced Caitlin. "I was hoping Ethan could show us the mustang."

"I can't be late for work."

Justin checked his watch. "I thought you didn't have to be at the clinic until two."

"I like to arrive a little early."

She sounded eager to go.

Ethan wanted the chance to explain his real reason for enlisting and leaving her, and was determined to find the opportunity. "It won't take long. Prince's stall is just behind the barn."

Justin started wheeling in that direction. Ethan followed, as did Caitlin, her gait stiff and her steps slow.

If she so obviously didn't want to be with him, why had she come along?

"I have to warn you," he told Justin, "the way there's bumpy."

"Can't be any worse than hiking Squaw Peak."

"You've done that?"

"Five times. Four of them in my chair." Justin beamed, his geeky smile reminding Ethan of the undersize, asthmatic kid he'd known when he and Caitlin were dating.

The smile, however, was the only thing about him

that was the same. Justin had acquired some serious muscle on his upper body.

"Why do you keep him so far from the other horses?" he asked, guiding his wheelchair down the rocky slope to Prince's pen like a pro.

"He's too wild and unpredictable." Ethan kept his eyes trained on the ground, watching out for potholes and rocks. What would cause another person to merely stumble could send him sprawling. "And being near the mares tends to…excite him, shall we say. Better he's off by himself."

Where to house Prince had been an issue when they'd captured him last month. Clay solved the problem by erecting a temporary covered pen near the back pasture.

"I've been wanting to see Prince ever since I watched your brother on the news."

Ethan chuckled. "You caught that, huh?"

"Are you kidding? He was all over the TV."

The media had gotten wind of Prince's capture; a horse living wild in a ninety-thousand-acre urban preserve was big news. Several local stations had dispatched reporters to interview Gavin. The attention had resulted in a slew of new customers, giving the Powells' dire finances a much-needed boost.

"Watch yourself," Ethan cautioned as they drew near. "Prince is wary of strangers. He still doesn't like me and Gavin that much."

Justin showed no fear and wheeled close. Caitlin reached for his wheelchair as if she wanted to pull him back. After a second, she let her hand drop, though it remained clenched in a fist.

Was it only Justin's fall that had made her overprotective?

As they watched Prince, the stallion raised his head

and stared at them. Then, tossing his jet-black mane, he trotted from one end of the pen to the other, commanding their attention.

And he got it. Ethan couldn't wait to see the colts this magnificent horse produced.

"He's bigger than he looked on TV."

Ethan kept a careful eye on Justin, ready to run interference if he ventured too close to the pen. Caitlin, on the other hand, seemed content to observe from a safe distance.

"Have you ridden him yet?" It was the first she'd spoken since Justin joined them outside the barn.

"No. He's only halter broke, and barely that."

"But you are going to break him?" Justin asked.

"Oh, yeah. My goal is by Christmas."

"That doesn't give you much time."

"You're right. He and I are going to have to come to a new agreement soon about who's boss."

Prince pawed the ground impatiently, as if daring Ethan to try.

Justin grinned sheepishly. "Don't suppose there's a horse in that stable of yours I could ride."

"Anytime you want, buddy." Ethan immediately thought of old Chico. If he was trustworthy enough for a six-year-old, he'd do fine for Justin. "Give me a call. I'll take you on a trail ride."

Beside him, Caitlin visibly stiffened. "Justin, are you sure about that? You've never had an interest in riding horses before."

"I never played sports before, either." He slapped the arm of his wheelchair. "Turns out I'm pretty good."

"What do you like?" Ethan asked.

"Basketball. Baseball. Swimming. I'm considering taking up track and field."

"I'm impressed."

"Well, I couldn't do any of it without Caitlin's help. She's amazing."

Did Caitlin pay for her brother's athletic expenses? Ethan wondered. That would explain the three jobs and why she worked fifty to sixty hours a week.

"You'll do fine at riding, then," he assured him.

Caitlin removed her cell phone from her sweatshirt pocket and checked the display. "It's getting late."

After a last look at Prince, the three of them returned to the stables, Justin chatting enthusiastically about riding and Caitlin stubbornly silent.

When they reached her minivan, Justin hoisted himself into the front passenger seat.

"I'll get that," Ethan offered, and carried the wheelchair to the rear of the minivan, where Caitlin had the hatch open.

She closed it the second he'd stowed the chair. "See you Saturday."

"What about physical therapy?" If he was keeping his end of the bargain, she needed to keep hers. "I'd like to start right away."

"I don't get off at the clinic until seven-thirty most nights."

"Eight's fine," he said, ignoring her attempts to postpone. "If it's not too late for you." He rose at the crack of dawn and assumed she did, too, what with her schedule.

"No, eight's okay." She peered nervously at her brother, who was busy with his MP3 player. "We can start tonight."

"Anything special I should have on hand?"

"I'll bring my portable table. We can set up just about anywhere."

"Okay. Drive straight to the bunkhouse and park there."

"The bunkhouse?"

"I live there now. Moved out of the main house so Sage and Isa can move in."

"O…kay."

"If you don't want to be alone with me—"

"It makes no difference," she answered tersely.

Somehow, Ethan thought it did. He just wasn't sure why.

Chapter Four

"Easy, boy." Ethan held on to Prince's lead rope, gripping it securely beneath the halter. "That's right, there you go." He ran his other hand down the horse's neck, over his withers and across his back, applying just the slightest amount of pressure. Prince stood, though not quietly. He bobbed his head and swished his tail nervously.

On the ground beside Ethan lay a saddle blanket, which he hoped Prince would allow to be placed on his back. The step was a small but important one toward breaking the horse. If Caitlin arrived on time, she'd be able to watch him.

He resisted pulling out his cell phone and viewing the display. It was 8:18. He knew this because he'd checked the time four minutes ago when it was 8:14, and every few minutes before that for the last half hour. He doubted she was going to keep their physical-therapy appointment, not after the disagreement they'd had this afternoon.

"Uncle Ethan!" Cassie yelled. "What are you doing?" She and Isa came bounding toward the round pen.

The horse's reaction to the girls' approach was immediate. Prancing sideways, Prince tried to jerk free of Ethan's hold…and almost succeeded.

"Relax, buddy," Ethan soothed, his grip on the lead rope like iron. Luckily, he was using his right hand. Thanks to the way his shoulder felt tonight, his left arm was pretty much useless.

The mustang, eyes wide, stared at Cassie and Isa, who peered at him and Ethan from between the rails of the pen.

"You girls stay back, you hear me? And keep ahold of that pup. I don't want him getting kicked."

They complied, sort of, by retreating maybe six inches. Cassie did scoop up her puppy, Blue, a five-month-old cattle dog mix that was out of her sight only when she was at school or a friend's house.

"Gonna ride him, Uncle Ethan?" Isa asked.

Though not officially a member of the family yet, Sage's daughter had already started calling Ethan "uncle." Probably because Cassie did. Isa copied the older girl's every move.

Ethan didn't mind. In fact, he rather enjoyed the moniker—and his role of the younger bachelor uncle who constantly set a bad example for his nieces by swearing in front of them and periodically losing his temper.

Months of counseling after the car-bomb explosion had taught Ethan how to deal with his sometimes volatile and erratic emotions. Normally, he did a good job. On occasion, like earlier today, he wondered if maybe he'd quit attending counseling too soon, and should call the VA hospital for a referral. His buttons lay close to the surface and were easily pushed.

"Not tonight," he said, answering Isa's question. "Prince isn't ready."

"When *will* you ride him?" Cassie asked.

"Soon."

"That's what you said yesterday."

"Don't you girls have any homework?"

"We did it already," Isa volunteered.

"A TV show you want to watch?"

"We're still grounded until tomorrow," Cassie answered glumly.

"You're lucky that's all the punishment you got. If I'd pulled a stunt like you two did when I was a kid, Grandpa Wayne would have had me cleaning stalls every day before school and mucking out the calf pens."

Come to think of it, those had always been his chores. Both he and Gavin had helped their father and grandfather with the cattle business from the time they were Isa's age.

"Yeah, but if not for us, you wouldn't have captured Prince."

Cassie was right, even if her assessment of the situation was a mite skewed.

Last month, in an act of rebellion, she and Isa had taken off on horseback into the mountains without telling anyone where they were going. After a frantic two-hour search, they were found in the box canyon, along with Sage's missing mare and Prince.

The wild mustang had proved difficult to capture, requiring all of Ethan's and Gavin's skills as cowboys. It had also been one of the most exciting moments of their lives.

"Maybe not that night, but we'd have captured him eventually." Ethan continued stroking Prince, running his hand over the horse's back and along his rump. The movement aggravated the pain in his shoulder, but he ignored it.

"Did you ride a bronc earlier at Mr. Duvall's?" Cassie asked.

"I did." Ethan had gotten back to the ranch at seven and taken a quick shower just in case Caitlin showed up. He'd decided to work with Prince, because he didn't want to appear as if he was waiting for her—which he was.

"Did you make it a whole eight seconds?"

"Not quite. Almost four." Which was double his last time.

"Did you get hurt again?"

Why did everyone assume he couldn't fall without injuring himself?

"No, I didn't." He had, however, eaten a whole bucketful of arena dirt when he'd hit the ground. He should have taken another turn on a different bronc, but he figured one wreck a night was about all his body could handle.

He slowly bent and reached for the saddle blanket near his feet.

"What are you doing now?" Cassie asked.

"Hopefully, getting Prince used to this."

His plan didn't work. Prince reacted to the blanket as if a swarm of hornets might fly out from behind it at any second.

Wherever Prince had come from, and it was still a mystery, he'd never known human touch. Gavin claimed the horse was a descendant of the wild mustangs that had roamed the valley till the 1940s. Ethan thought that was impossible, but had yet to come up with a better explanation.

"Why don't you try a carrot or an apple?" Isa suggested. "That's what Mama used to train her horse."

"Good idea. What say you girls run in the house and see what you can find in the refrigerator."

Isa lit up. "Okay!"

"Uncle Ethan." Cassie turned and craned her neck. "Someone's here."

He saw the headlights of an approaching vehicle seconds before he heard the sound of tires crunching on gravel.

Had Caitlin finally arrived?

Excitement coursed through him when he recognized the familiar outline of her minivan.

Taking his eyes off Prince proved to be a mistake. The horse—possibly out of affection, probably out of dislike—butted Ethan in the shoulder. His injured shoulder.

"Shit!"

"Uncle Ethan!" Isa slapped her hands over her mouth. "You're not supposed to swear in front of us."

Cassie, a little older and a little wiser than her soon-to-be stepsister, appeared unfazed by the use of a four-letter word. "They parked in front of the bunkhouse," she informed Ethan, her eyes glued to the vehicle.

He unclipped the lead rope from Prince. "It's okay. You girls can go inside now."

Cassie and Isa didn't budge. Not until the minivan door opened and Caitlin stepped out.

"It's Nurse Carmichael from school," Cassie said with a very adult interest. "What's she doing here?"

Ethan slipped through the round-pen gate, leaving Prince inside. "If you must know, she's helping me with my shoulder." He set the saddle blanket on an overturned bucket by the gate, well out of Prince's reach.

"How?"

"Giving me physical therapy."

"Now?" Cassie furrowed her brow in an impressive imitation of parental concern. "Isn't it kind of late?"

"Seriously, you two," Ethan chided. "Get inside."

Unfortunately, Caitlin spotted them across the open area and started in their direction.

"Come on." Cassie grabbed Isa's hand. "Let's go say hi to her."

Ethan had no choice but to let them run ahead. He did well riding horses and walking from place to place, but he hadn't quite mastered the fifty-yard dash in under ten seconds.

Just as well. The extra time allowed him to study Caitlin. She didn't look as upset as she had earlier today. That, or she was hiding behind her nurse facade.

A tactic, he began to suspect, she frequently employed to keep people—him specifically—at a distance.

No more, now that he was onto her.

CAITLIN WAS SUDDENLY surrounded on all sides. "Well, hello, there."

"Nurse Carmichael." Cassie smiled exuberantly, her arm slung around the younger girl. "This is my stepsister, Isa. Well, she's not my stepsister yet, but she will be soon. Her mom's marrying my dad."

"Hi." The little girl stuck out her hand, her enormous grin adorable despite two missing teeth.

"Nice to meet you, Isa." Caitlin shook Isa's hand while gently disengaging her pant leg from the puppy's fiercely clenched teeth. "I heard you've been riding my old horse."

"Chico?"

"Uh-huh. He and I were good pals a lot of years ago."

"My dad never told us that." Cassie appeared suitably impressed.

"He may not have remembered."

"I don't know. He's got a pretty good memory. He's

always boring us with stories about when he was our age."

"Yeah," Isa agreed, imitating Cassie's tone. "Boring us."

"He's not the one who took me riding." Caitlin glanced up as Ethan joined them, a familiar fluttering in her middle. "Your uncle Ethan did."

"Oh," Cassie said, as if she suddenly understood everything. "I see."

"Isn't it time for you two to hit the sack?" Ethan came up behind the girls and patted them on the head.

"Do we have to?" Cassie complained.

"Do we have to?" Isa echoed, only whinier.

"Get yourselves inside. Whether or not you go to bed is up to your parents."

"Just when it was getting good," Cassie mumbled under her breath.

"What about Prince?" Isa asked.

"He's fine in the round pen. I'll put him away later."

"Uncle Ethan's breaking Prince," Cassie announced with pride.

"He told me." Caitlin sent him a silent reprimand. "Except he's not supposed to do anything that might hurt his shoulder."

"Like bronc riding? 'Cause he went to Mr. Duvall's earlier."

"Exactly like bronc riding."

Would he ever learn? Ever change?

And what if he did?

"Scoot," Ethan admonished the girls, his voice warm with affection. "You've gotten me in enough trouble for one night."

"I'm not sure you need any help," Caitlin admonished.

"Never did."

So true. And for much of that trouble, she'd been his cohort. How many times had they sneaked out together when they were supposed to be home in bed? Or skipped class to head to the river? Or risked being caught making love when her college roommate was due back any minute?

No sooner were the girls out of earshot, the puppy chasing gleefully after them, than Ethan said, "About this afternoon—"

"It's okay. Really." Caitlin didn't want to talk about it. Not tonight. Maybe not ever. "Water under the bridge."

"I did love you. More than anything."

Why did he have to say that? "If you don't mind, Ethan, I've had a long day."

That did the trick, and he shut up.

They walked the short distance to his bunkhouse. Caitlin wasn't sure what to expect, having never been inside before. It had always been occupied by two or three ranch hands when she and Ethan dated.

They stopped at her van for her duffel bag and the portable table, which Ethan insisted on carrying despite her protests.

"This is nice," she commented upon entering the modest stucco structure.

"There's still a lot of work to do."

She noticed the partially framed walls dividing the single large room into a living room, bedroom and hall, and the smell of fresh paint lingering in the air. "It's bigger than I thought it would be."

He leaned the portable table against the kitchen counter. "To be honest, I didn't think you'd come."

"Like you said before, we have an agreement. And

I don't back out on agreements just because the other person says something I don't like or don't agree with."

"Me, either."

"Good." Caitlin lightened her tone. "Because the committee is really excited about the Holly Days wagon rides." She removed her jacket and reached into the duffel bag, more than ready to get down to business. "I usually start with some heat therapy."

"Shirt on or off?"

"A T-shirt's fine."

Without any hesitation, he stripped off his denim jacket and work shirt and tossed them onto the couch.

Oh, boy. Clearly, she should have better prepared herself on the drive over. Whoever thought plain white T-shirts could be so sexy?

Tearing her gaze away required effort. She looked at his feet. "You might want to change out of those boots." Then she remembered his prosthesis. "But it isn't necessary."

"Be right back."

He stepped through the partially framed wall into the bedroom. Sitting with his back to her on the corner of the bed, he removed his boots. She thought she heard the sound of a zipper.

Rather than stare, she busied herself setting up the portable table and warming a hot pack in the microwave.

Ethan returned a few minutes later wearing a pair of athletic shoes.

"Have a seat." She indicated the kitchen chair she'd pulled out. "I brought these for tonight." She touched the pair of two-pound hand weights she'd set on the table. "Do you by chance have any of your own?"

"Not here. There might be some in the storeroom. It's been a while since I've worked out."

Caitlin remembered when Ethan had played football and basketball. While he'd lifted weights in the garage, she'd kept him company, talking and flirting and doing her best to distract him. Most of the time, it hadn't worked. But there were times it had....

Removing the hot pack from the microwave, she tested the temperature before laying it on his shoulder. Next, she busied herself readying the portable table. In truth, there wasn't much to do. She wiped it down twice with disinfectant spray just to avoid standing around. Ethan, she was sure, would attempt to fill the lull with conversation of a personal nature, and she was determined to keep their session completely professional.

"Is Justin the reason you became a nurse?"

Caitlin had been fluffing a small travel pillow. At Ethan's question, she set it down. Usually when people asked, she answered that she'd always wanted to be a nurse. Ethan, however, knew better.

"Yes." She smoothed the last remaining wrinkles from the pillowcase. "After the accident, I took an active role in his care. Found out I could actually stand the sight of blood. I'm a pretty good nurse. Who'd have guessed?"

"Me."

"Right." She gave a small laugh. "The last thing I was interested in when we were going together was taking care of other people."

"You're a softie. The first to jump in when someone needs assistance. Of any kind. I always figured you'd work in a people-oriented field."

What had Ethan seen in her all those years ago that she hadn't seen herself?

"Let's start on those exercises," she said briskly.

She spent the next twenty minutes showing him several simple exercises designed to loosen his muscles, build strength, decrease pain and restore mobility. Some of the exercises were done with weights, others without. Some standing, some sitting. When they were finished, Caitlin instructed him to lie on the table.

"Face up or down?" he asked.

"Up."

She thought she'd prepared herself for this part of the session. Once again, she was wrong.

Bending over Ethan, she wrapped her arms around his upper body, leaning in so that their faces were inches apart. Their positions, and the ones that followed, sorely tested her ability to remain detached. His dark eyes locked with hers. His chest rose and fell with each breath he took. His masculine scent filled her nostrils and triggered an onslaught of sensual memories.

The cheerfulness he'd exhibited earlier slowly vanished, and his features went from animated to stoic to strained. He, too, was being affected by their close proximity.

Levering a hand beneath his shoulder, she lifted his arm over his head, stretching it as far as his constricted muscles would allow. Unable to stop herself, she looked down at his face, bracing herself for the jolt of awareness that would race through her.

It didn't happen quite like she imagined.

Ethan tensed, his upper body involuntarily lifting several inches off the table. "Son of a bitch! That hurts."

"Sorry." Caitlin immediately relaxed her grip. "I didn't realize.... Justin usually lets me know right away when I'm pushing him too hard."

"That'll teach me to tough it out." Perspiration beaded his brow.

"Yes, it will." She kneaded his shoulder, noting when the tension ebbed away. "I really didn't mean to hurt you."

"You sure? I was thinking it was your way of getting back at me for all the misery I caused you."

"You *are* joking, right?" When he didn't reply, she said, "Ethan!"

"Yes. I'm joking."

His words didn't reassure her.

"Caitlin." He reached for her hand and clasped it in his.

She made a token effort to pull away, then gave up. Seeing him on the table, knowing he was in pain, tugged on that soft spot in her heart he'd talked about earlier.

All at once, he sat up and swung his legs over the side of the table.

"Wait," she protested. "We're not done."

"No, we're not."

It took her a second to realize he wasn't referring to their physical-therapy session.

"You misunderstood me." She tried to back away.

He gripped her hand, holding her firmly in place. "I want to see you again. And not just for more PT or when you and your crew are here working on the wagon."

"Ethan, we can't. I can't."

"Give us a chance."

"It's impossible."

"I know you haven't forgiven me yet."

"I'm working on it."

"Is it my leg?"

"God, no! That doesn't matter to me in the slightest." Despite her vehement objection, she could see by his expression he didn't believe her. "It's your bronc riding. And breaking horses for Clay. And the mustang. And telling Justin he can come here and ride anytime he wants."

"Why can't he?"

"It's too dangerous."

"Probably no more dangerous than basketball or baseball. Especially on old Chico."

"He could fall."

"He could have tipped his wheelchair on the way to see Prince."

"That's different, and you know it."

"I wouldn't put him on any horse that wasn't dead broke. And we have safety equipment if he wants. Helmets. A harness."

"It's not that. Justin gets enthusiastic. Tries to do more than he can."

"Don't you think he's the best judge of his limitations?"

She frowned. "I should have figured you wouldn't understand."

"You're wrong. I understand your brother very well. A whole lot better than you do, I'm guessing."

"That's not what I mean."

"A guy being disabled doesn't give other people the right to run someone's life or make decisions for him. Not even family. No matter how good their intentions are or how guilty they feel."

She flinched as if struck.

"Caitlin." Ethan released her and pushed off the table, landing on his feet. "I'm sorry. I get defensive sometimes. Shoot off my mouth."

"You take chances, Ethan." She squared her shoulders. "Big chances. Without the slightest fear. Justin does, too."

"There was a time you liked that about me."

Oh, she had. Very much. "But not anymore."

"Justin's accident wasn't your fault!"

"That's not true. He got hurt pulling a stupid stunt I convinced him to do." Reaching for the hot pack, she began packing her duffel bag. "When I first became a nurse, I trained in a trauma center. I thought it would help me better understand Justin's needs. You can't imagine the injuries I saw."

"Actually, I can. I spent two months in a military rehab center."

"Then you have to understand where I'm coming from." She shoved item after item into the bag. "I lost count of how many people I treated who were victims of sport or recreational-related accidents. Skydiving, drag racing, skiing and, yes, horseback riding."

Ethan came up behind her. "People get hurt just walking across the street."

Damn. He was close. Too close. If he touched her, she'd give in or break down or otherwise embarrass herself.

No, not happening. She was strong and could resist him and these feelings whirling out of control inside her.

"Fewer people get hurt walking across a street than they do jumping off a cliff into the river or riding a wild bronc." She paused, steeling her resolve. "I can't handle someone I care about being hurt. Or worse. Not again." Her voice warbled on the last two words.

"Does that mean you care about me?"

Not the response she was expecting. She zipped the duffel bag closed. "Of course I do."

"Would you go out with me if I wasn't riding broncs or breaking horses?"

"I don't know. Maybe."

"Okay." He grabbed his shirt and put it on, not bothering to button it.

Okay?

"Are you saying you'd quit bronc riding and breaking horses for me?"

He replied without missing a beat. "No. I don't believe people have the right to demand someone to give up their passion as a condition of the relationship. That's unfair. I wouldn't ask you to give up nursing, just like I wouldn't ask my brother to give up what's left of this ranch."

This time he gave her the response she'd expected to hear.

It also confirmed what she knew to be true. There was no chance for her and Ethan. Not as long as he cared more about what he wanted than he did about her.

Chapter Five

Ethan didn't think he'd ever seen Clay's rodeo arena so busy. At least forty men had shown up to practice for the jackpot next weekend. The majority of them were bull riders, the rest bronc riders. Family members or girlfriends tagged along, bringing ice chests and folding chairs and lap blankets to ward off the chill. Those who didn't gather around the lowered tailgates of their trucks sat in the bleachers observing the practice rounds with interest. Even more stood by or straddled the fences, chatting up the cowboys.

"What's with folks in these parts?" Conner asked, settling into a vacant spot on the fence alongside Ethan. "Don't they have anything better to do on a Friday night?"

"I was just thinking the same thing."

Like Clay, Conner had been Ethan's friend since grade school. Conner sometimes helped the Powells, leading trail rides and giving roping lessons. He'd also been with them on that night in the mountains when they'd captured Prince. Conner's regular job was systems analyst for a large manufacturing plant in Scottsdale, though no one would guess by his well-worn jeans, scuffed boots and weathered cowboy hat that he held two degrees, one in computer science and the other in business management.

"Your brother invited me for Thanksgiving dinner."

"You coming?"

"Can't, pal. Going to be at the folks'."

"Come over later for dessert if you want."

This Thanksgiving would mark the first holiday the Powells had celebrated since Ethan's mother died. Of course, Ethan hadn't been home for most of those Easters, Thanksgivings and Christmases. He was really looking forward to the dinner this year, brightened considerably by the addition of Cassie, Sage and Isa.

"Are you riding tonight?" Ethan asked as he watched the young man preparing to go next, studying his techniques and comparing them to his own. The kid was inexperienced but showed real potential. He might do well at the jackpot.

"Hell, no." Conner snorted. "I'm not about to risk scrambling my brain."

According to Caitlin, that was exactly what Ethan did on a regular basis.

"You used to like bronc riding. Bull riding, too."

"Yeah, before I grew up."

What did that say about Ethan?

His attention wandered to the makeshift first-aid station beneath the announcer's stand. Caitlin had arrived a half hour earlier, unloaded several boxes and grocery sacks, then disappeared inside. She had yet to emerge. He hoped she was simply busy and not avoiding him after their...what? Second disagreement?

He didn't much like the habit they'd fallen into of late.

"Something bothering you?" Conner asked.

"Just got a lot on my mind."

"Like qualifying for the jackpot?"

"Oh, I'm going to qualify. If not tonight, then tomorrow."

Ethan had put his name in about ten minutes before Conner arrived. He figured he had a little time before heading over to the chutes.

"Clay letting you practice with that bum shoulder?"

"It's better." And it was better. Marginally. He hadn't included that qualifier when he'd talked to Clay, however. "I have to go in for a follow-up exam before the jackpot."

Another chance to see Caitlin.

"Then what's with the scowl?" Conner asked.

Ethan decided he didn't care for old friends who knew him too well. "I did something stupid last night."

"What else is new?"

He drew back in mock offense. "That's a fine thing to say."

"And true." When Ethan remained silent, Conner burst into deep, rich laughter. "Come on. Fess up, buddy."

"I sort of asked Caitlin out."

"Sort of?" Conner's brows shot up.

"I might have suggested that she and I test the relationship waters."

"Relationship waters! Just how much Dr. Phil do you watch?"

"You're not helping."

"All right." He laughed again. "What did she say?"

"In a nutshell, no. Not so long as I'm riding broncs and breaking green horses."

"You going to quit?"

At that moment, Caitlin emerged from the first-aid station. Shielding her eyes from the bright floodlights, she scanned the arena and nearby stands. Ethan guessed she was searching for Clay. Her gaze lit on him momentarily. No sooner did his pulse skyrocket than she nonchalantly looked elsewhere.

"No, I'm not going to quit," he told Conner.

"Why not?"

"Hell, I've barely started again."

"Why continue? We all know you can do it."

There it was again, the reference to him having something to prove.

"Except I *haven't* done it. Not for eight seconds."

"Is bronc riding really that important?"

"It's not the bronc riding."

"What then?"

"I just want to be Ethan Powell again. Not Ethan Powell who lost his leg while serving in the Middle East."

"That isn't how people think of you."

"Not you, maybe. But everybody else does."

"When did you become a mind reader?"

Ethan ignored Conner. People who were physically whole didn't understand. Didn't notice the stares. Ethan noticed. There were at least a dozen individuals casting discreet glances in his direction this very moment. And if he possessed superhearing, he was sure he'd catch his name being mentioned in every conversation at some point during the night.

Conner rested his forearms on the fence and shifted his weight from one foot to the other. "What makes you sure everyone walks around thinking there goes Ethan Powell, the peg-legged cowboy?"

Conner was lucky they were such good friends. If not, Ethan wouldn't let him get away with that last remark, teasing or not.

"I don't know," Conner mused out loud. "If it were me, and a gal as pretty as Caitlin Carmichael asked me to give up something for her, I'd be inclined to oblige."

Ethan's attention zeroed in on Caitlin. She stood beside the announcer's booth, pushing a breeze-blown lock of hair back from her face. He liked the shorter cut, once he'd gotten past the initial shock. The strands curled attractively around her face in a way they hadn't before. She wore jeans tonight and, unlike all the other loose garments he'd seen her in, they fit her to perfection.

Conner nudged Ethan in the ribs. "Why don't you go over and talk to her."

"We didn't exactly part on good terms last night."

After his declaration, she'd hurriedly packed her things. Refusing his help, she'd carted the portable table out to the van and hightailed it off the ranch without so much as a backward glance.

Ethan had spent another restless night, this one less from shoulder pain and more from mentally kicking himself for being such a fool.

"Ethan Powell!" The young woman Clay had recruited to help out checked off Ethan's name on the clipboard she was holding. "On deck."

He pushed away from the fence. "Guess I'm up."

"You sure about this?" All trace of joking was gone from Conner's voice.

Ethan shot Caitlin another glance. No question this time, she was staring straight at him. Even at this distance, he could discern the worry on her face. Or was that pleading?

If he wanted to, he could turn around, walk away from the chutes and toward her. Show her he was willing to compromise in order to test those relationship waters he'd mentioned earlier.

But when he took that first step, it was in the direction of the chutes. He sensed her tracking him the entire way. He also sensed her disappointment.

It wasn't enough to make him change his mind. Not with the dozens of spectators also tracking him and waiting for him to fail, thinking maybe he'd lost a part of his mind in that explosion along with his leg.

As the big brute he was about to ride greeted him with bared teeth and flattened ears, Ethan began wondering the same thing.

CAITLIN WATCHED ETHAN amble over to the chutes, her agitation mounting with each step he took. She so wished he'd give up this stupid—make that insane—idea of riding broncs. What was the matter with him? With all men? They had some kind of ridiculous ambition to risk life and limb just to prove they were tough.

Without consciously planning it, she moved trancelike toward the arena fence. Ethan had disappeared behind the chutes, preparing for his turn. Just as she reached the railing, he reappeared. Scaling the fence, he straddled the top and waited, conversing with the cowboy beside him.

Caitlin's initial thought was how lucky that the first-aid station was fully stocked and operational. Her second one—she hoped to heck he didn't need it.

"Think he'll go a full eight seconds this time?"

"Don't know. I still can't believe he's trying. If anything goes wrong…jeez, he's already lost one leg."

The people next to Caitlin were discussing Ethan. She had to agree with the second man's opinion.

Ethan slowly lowered himself onto the bronc's back.

Caitlin's stomach constricted into a tight fist of worry. He'd survived two other rides that she knew of, but not unscathed. It could be worse tonight.

Standing on tiptoe, she craned her neck to see over the high wall of the chute. The only thing visible was the crown of Ethan's tan Stetson.

All at once the gate next to Ethan's chute opened and a figure on horseback burst through it. The ride lasted a few harrowing seconds and ended with the cowboy sprawled on his back in the dirt, his chest visibly heaving. So was Caitlin's. The horse, kicking his hind legs, loped in a victory circle until the pickup men were able to safely herd him to the far side of the arena and through the exit gate.

Caitlin, hands on the railing, ready to bolt into the arena if necessary, expelled a sigh of relief when the cowboy rolled over and clambered to his feet. The crowd rewarded him with a round of applause as he walked, then jogged to the gate in order that the next participant—Ethan?—could go. Thankfully, the cowboy didn't appear in need of any medical attention. But another man had earlier in the evening. He'd suffered a nasty gash on his chin when his face collided with his saddle horn.

Caitlin had advised him to take the rest of the week off from bronc riding. He hadn't heeded her advice, but instead had gone right out and put his name in again. Crazy.

Like Ethan.

How did these wives and girlfriends here tonight stand watching the men they loved without constantly breaking down? Caitlin couldn't do it.

The wrangler manning the gates pulled the center one open, scrambling out of the way as he did. All at once a large, dark-colored horse hurtled into the arena, all four feet off the ground and Ethan astride his back.

Caitlin understood very little about bronc riding, despite having watched Ethan a hundred times in years past. There was more, she knew, to a successful ride than just remaining in the saddle for eight seconds. Something to do with how high the horse bucked and how expertly the cowboy rode him.

Both seemed to be happening as she watched Ethan. The horse achieved tremendous height, humping his back into a tight arc while Ethan hung on and rode the tar out of him.

Eight seconds had never lasted so long. Caitlin vaguely registered the sound of a buzzer going off. As the pickup men flanked the horse, one of them grabbed the bucking strap and jerked it loose. The horse immediately stopped kicking and began trotting. The other pickup man extended his arm to Ethan, who reached for it.

Caitlin relaxed, let her shoulders sag. The worst was over.

Suddenly, the horse gave a last mighty buck and unseated Ethan, launching him into the air. Caitlin stifled a cry and clung to the fence railing with such force the coiled wire cable cut into her palms.

By some miracle, Ethan righted himself and landed on his feet…only to pitch face-first onto the ground. The crowd let out a collective gasp.

Caitlin found herself hurrying along the arena fence, stopping when she was directly across from the spot where he had fallen. The first pickup man rode his horse over to check on Ethan, blocking her view. She was just about to move when Ethan began to rise. The crowd applauded as he stood and hobbled awkwardly away.

Hobbled! Had he hurt his good leg? What would he do? How would he get around? He must be in terrible pain.

She followed him from the other side of the fence, zigzagging between people in an effort to keep up. She lost sight of him when he exited through the gate and had to make a detour around the cattle pens. By now, she was practically running.

Where had he gone?

Finally, thankfully, she located him standing behind the chutes, talking to a group of men. Hands braced on his hips, he leaned forward at the waist. It was a posture Caitlin often observed in people who were injured.

Enough was enough. She'd drag him, kicking and screaming if necessary, to the first-aid station and examine him. Keep him still long enough to listen to her advice to take it easy.

She set out, resolute. At the same moment, one of the men clapped Ethan on the back and laughed loudly. Caitlin was shocked. Did the cowboy have no consideration for someone in pain?

"Ethan," she called.

He turned then. And rather than a grimace, his face wore a wide, exuberant grin.

Sweet heaven, he was handsome. She came to an abrupt halt, her mind emptying of everyone and everything save him and what they'd once had together. What they could have together now if he would just come to his senses.

He limped toward her. "Did you see?"

"Yes. Are you all right?"

"I couldn't be better."

Realization dawned. Slowly, but it dawned. The men surrounding Ethan were congratulating him. Because he… She recalled hearing the buzzer. He had gone a full eight seconds. He'd said something about that the other night. If he lasted eight seconds, Clay would allow him to compete in the upcoming jackpot.

Dammit!

Fury bubbled up inside her. More at herself than Ethan. What a fool she'd been to think even for a few seconds that they could rekindle their former relationship.

"I just wanted to make sure you were okay."

She expected him to return to his friends. After all, her tone had been anything but inviting.

Only he didn't. He kept coming straight toward her. Before she could object, he hauled her into his arms and swung her in a wide circle.

"Put me down before you hurt yourself again."

"I did it!"

"Ethan, please. Your shoulder."

He released her. The moment her feet touched the ground, he lowered his mouth to hers, stopping a fraction of an inch shy of kissing her.

"I've been wanting to do this for the last three days."

Three days? Was that all?

She'd been waiting the past eight years, eleven months and twenty-one days to kiss him.

Just like that, their years apart melted away. Ethan's lips moved expertly over hers, applying just the right amount of pressure to coax a melting response from her. He'd always been an amazing kisser. That, or they were just amazing together. Their bodies fit perfectly. Her soft curves nestled against his hard planes as his arm circled her waist and drew her against him.

Caitlin was tempted to lose herself in his kiss. Set aside her worries and concerns and embrace the moment. And she did…until sanity returned, giving her a big, solid kick. The hoots and hollers of Ethan's cowboy friends might have had something to do with it, too.

Just how many people were watching them?

Caitlin broke off the kiss and pressed a hand to her flaming cheek. Ethan didn't appear the least bit embarrassed. Of course not.

"That shouldn't have happened," she stammered, and backed away.

Ethan started after her. "But it did happen," he said in a low voice. "And for a minute there, you were liking it every bit as much as I did."

Had they really kissed for more than a minute?

Wilting beneath stares from dozens of eyes, she executed a hasty retreat.

"Caitlin." Ethan appeared beside her.

"I don't want to talk." She couldn't. Her thoughts were in a jumble. She'd wind up saying something she'd regret. "Not now." She brushed past him.

"I need— Wait up, Caitlin!"

Through the haze of fog surrounding her, she heard the note of urgency in Ethan's voice. Still fuming, she almost didn't stop.

Almost.

She spun around just in time to see him crumple, a look of pure agony on his face.

"Ethan! Are you all right?" Instinct took over, and she ran to him. Dropping to her knees, she touched his head and back with gentle fingers. "What happened?"

He pushed himself to a sitting position. "I thought you were mad at me." Labored breathing punctuated each word.

"I am mad at you."

His grimace turned into a lopsided smile. "Then how come you didn't keep walking?"

"I'm a nurse."

"That's not why."

She made a sound of frustration. "Are you hurt or not?"

"It's my leg."

"Did you sprain it?"

"No." He groaned and shifted his weight.

Between their heated kiss and Ethan's fall, they'd drawn a sizable audience. Some of Ethan's friends expressed their concern and offered assistance.

"I'll be all right," he insisted. "My leg came loose in the fall."

His prosthesis. Thank goodness that was all.

Two of his buddies hauled Ethan upright. Still grinning, he slung an arm around their shoulders.

"Where to?" the taller of the pair asked.

"The first-aid station."

Caitlin hurried ahead of them to open the door and flip on the light. The men brought Ethan inside and deposited him in the same metal folding chair he'd sat in that first night.

"You need anything?" one friend asked.

"Naw, I'm fine." He nodded at them both. "Appreciate the lift."

The taller man tipped his hat at Caitlin and followed his buddy outside.

"What can I do?" she asked.

"I've got it." Ethan didn't exactly push her away, but he made it more than clear with his gesture and tone that he didn't want her hovering. Bracing his hands on the chair seat, he managed to stand, though unsteadily. His loose prosthesis hung at an odd angle in front of him.

She rushed forward, stopping short when he snapped, "I've got it!"

"Okay."

Patients often refused help. She had learned to navigate the fine line between respecting their wishes and providing the care they needed. She watched him intently from beside the table, ready to jump in if necessary.

With his free hand, he reached for his belt buckle and unfastened it with a flick of his wrist.

Her breath caught. "What are you doing?"

"Putting my leg back on."

Naturally. How silly of her.

In order to get at his prosthesis, he had to remove his pants. There was no other way.

What had she been thinking?

Once he had his jeans unzipped, he slid them down his hips and sat back in the chair. His shirttails covered him. Only the lower part of his blue—blue?—boxer shorts was visible. Caitlin averted her gaze, concentrating on his feet.

The prosthesis, caught in the pant leg, didn't cooperate. Without thinking, she knelt in front of him and grabbed it by the boot.

"You don't have to." Ethan's hands grappled with hers.

"Let me," she said softly. "Please."

She lifted her face to his. She could read in his eyes how difficult this was for him. He didn't want people seeing him at his most vulnerable.

Gripping the hem, she pushed the prosthesis back up his pant leg.

Ethan didn't move at first. Then, taking hold of the prosthesis around the cup, he fitted it to his stump.

There was a quiet whoosh as air escaped. When he was done, he secured the elastic cuff, which had slipped off during his fall.

She said nothing, knowing the more professional she acted, the easier it would be for Ethan. Easier for her, too.

As soon as he was done, they both stood. She placed a hand on his lower back to steady him while he pulled up his jeans and tucked in his shirt.

"Thank you," he said, buckling his belt.

"That's why I'm here, and what Clay pays me for."

"Is that the only reason?" He pinned her in place with those dark brown eyes of his.

If only she could lie. Say that helping him was just her job. Nothing more.

But her mouth refused to listen to her brain's instructions. What they'd just shared had in some ways been more intimate than their earlier kiss. To lie would be dishonoring that moment and the undeniable, yet impossible, connection they shared.

"No, Ethan. It's not the only reason." She straightened, set her mouth in a resolute line. "But we both know it should be."

Chapter Six

Ethan stood outside the round pen. He'd been up since five this morning, working with Prince. His deadline for breaking the mustang, as he'd told Justin the other day, was fast approaching, and he was determined to make some real progress. After two patience-testing hours, ones that aggravated his shoulder considerably, Ethan had the saddle blanket on Prince's back, along with a lightweight pack saddle.

Prince didn't like either, and alternately trotted and loped in circles as if he could outrun them. Each time he stopped, he glared menacingly at Ethan.

"Not yet, pal. A little while longer."

Prince stomped his left foot, then started trotting again.

Gavin came up beside Ethan. "I'm impressed."

"Don't be. The pack saddle may be on his back, but he's far from accepting it."

Prince came to an abrupt halt across from them. Reaching his head around, he took hold of the blanket with his teeth and gave an angry yank. Ethan imagined Prince trying that same move with his pant leg when he finally managed to mount the horse.

"You ready to help me with that wagon before Caitlin gets here?" he asked.

Gavin hitched his chin at Prince. "What are the chances that blanket will be in shreds and the pack saddle in pieces when we get back?"

Prince was now sniffing the cinch holding the saddle in place, and making irritated snuffling sounds.

"I bet he'll quiet down the second we're gone," Ethan said.

"Hmm."

"He always has to put on a show. Let everyone know how tough he is."

"He's not the only one."

"Are you referring to me?" They set out in the direction of the old cattle barn.

"I heard about your fall last night."

"Did you also hear I qualified for the jackpot?"

"I did. And congratulations. So, how badly were you hurt?"

"My leg came loose is all."

"Is that why Caitlin kissed you?"

Now it was Ethan's turn to grin. "It was more the other way around. I kissed her."

"Clay said she didn't act like she objected."

"He was there?" Ethan scratched his head. "Really?" What else had he missed when all his attention was riveted on Caitlin?

"Am I to assume the two of you are back together?"

"No. She's made it pretty clear there's no chance of that."

"Then why the kiss?"

"I'd just finished my ride. And she looked really pretty. I couldn't help myself."

"Be careful you don't hurt her again."

Ethan had been having similar thoughts. But then he'd recall Caitlin's lips, soft and pliant and molding to his. She might be resisting him at every turn, but there was no denying her response.

She still cared, and the knowledge pleased Ethan enormously.

As far as what he'd felt when she'd helped him with his prosthesis, he still wasn't sure. Not since his last visit to the VA hospital had he allowed anyone to view his prosthesis up close, much less touch it. He could argue Caitlin was a nurse, but that wasn't the reason he'd accepted her help.

He trusted her. Simple as that. Unfortunately, she didn't trust him in return.

It was a situation he intended to rectify.

He and his brother spent ten minutes unburying the wagon, and another ten rearranging the surrounding junk, as Gavin called it. They were just rolling the wagon into the open area near the horse-bathing rack when Caitlin's minivan pulled up, an older model sedan following in its wake. Ethan was surprised to see Justin in the passenger seat of her van, considering she didn't want him anywhere near horses.

"Hi." She greeted Ethan and Gavin with a bright smile that revealed nothing other than her delight at finding the wagon ready for her crew of volunteers to clean, repair and decorate.

Introductions were made. Four helpers beside Justin had accompanied Caitlin—an older man, a middle-aged woman and a couple in their early twenties who were obviously boyfriend and girlfriend. That relationship didn't prevent Justin's gaze from constantly traveling to the young woman.

Poor guy. He looked on the verge of falling head over heels for a woman who was completely unavailable.

Ethan was no different.

"I'm going to check on Prince," Gavin said after a bit. "Nice to meet you all."

Ethan probably didn't need to hang around the volunteers, either, but he couldn't make himself leave.

The older man proved to be quite handy with a hammer, wrench and electric drill. Together, he and Ethan repaired the broken wheel, cracked seat and loose running board. They also replaced a half-dozen missing bolts. The rest of the volunteers cleaned—and cleaned. Ten years of neglect had resulted in a mountain of dust, dirt and grime.

"Would it be all right if we gave the wagon a fresh coat of paint?" Caitlin asked. "We'd buy the paint, of course."

"Sure. As long as you use John Deere green."

She laughed. "I think we can manage that. It'll go perfectly with the wreaths and Christmas lights."

The volunteers were taking a well-deserved break, refueling with doughnuts the older gentleman had brought.

"Justin seems taken with Tamiko," Ethan said. He and Caitlin sat on a pair of old crates, away from the rest of the volunteers.

"I noticed that, too." She cast a worried glance at her brother, who maneuvered his wheelchair in order to be closer to the young woman. "I hope she doesn't break his heart."

"Looks to me like she's more interested in him than she is in her boyfriend."

Justin was holding the hose and filling a bucket with water while Tamiko poured in a capful of liquid soap. There was no mistaking the exchange of smiles and frequent eye contact.

"Tamiko's a sweet, funny girl," Caitlin said. "But to be honest, I don't think Justin stands a chance with her."

"Because she already has a boyfriend?"

"That—" Caitlin turned back to Ethan "—and because he's in a wheelchair."

"Don't underestimate him. Or her."

She said nothing, perhaps because this conversation had started to sound too much like the one they'd had in his bunkhouse earlier in the week.

They finished their doughnuts and spent the next several minutes watching an advanced riding class in the arena. Their break would soon be over, and Ethan didn't think he'd have another chance to speak to Caitlin alone.

"About last night…"

She immediately straightened. "We both agreed kissing was a mistake."

"I didn't agree."

"Ethan." She looked over at her crew of volunteers before continuing. "Can we discuss this later?"

"When later?"

"I brought my table and duffel bag. We can have another PT session today if you're available."

"After what you said, I assumed we weren't continuing."

"I told you, a deal's a deal." She gathered up their trash. "Besides, you need physical therapy if that shoulder's going to heal properly."

He did need it, what with the jackpot only a week away.

And the prospect of Caitlin's hands on him, even if they frequently caused him excruciating pain, was too appealing to resist.

CAITLIN WAVED GOODBYE to her brother and friends. Had she been wrong, making arrangements for Justin to return home without her? He sat in the backseat next to Tamiko. Her boyfriend, for some reason, occupied the front passenger seat. Given his angry glare, he wasn't too happy about the arrangement.

Tamiko was only being nice, Caitlin told herself. She wouldn't intentionally lead Justin on. But he was following nonetheless.

Work on the wagon had gone well, better than Caitlin had expected. Her emotional state, however, was in turmoil…a continuation from the previous night and this afternoon.

She should avoid Ethan, her common sense urged. The problem was they had an agreement, one that would bring them together often in the coming weeks.

The prospect unsettled her. Made her a little nervous.

It also thrilled her.

Telling herself over and over that she was here for one reason only, she returned to her minivan and drove it to the bunkhouse. Ethan wasn't there. He'd left after bidding Caitlin's friends and brother goodbye. She could see him in the round pen across the way, unsaddling Prince under Gavin's watchful eye. Unless she was mistaken, the horse wasn't making much of a fuss.

A step in the right direction.

Hopefully, Prince would be as gentle when the day came for Ethan to ride him.

He'd been lucky last night at the rodeo arena. Very lucky. His next fall could end differently.

She carried her portable table from the van to the bunkhouse, determined to complete the task before Ethan showed up and did it for her. Again. When he arrived a few minutes later, Caitlin, the table and her duffel bag were all waiting on the porch.

"Sorry I'm late," he said, nudging the door open with his good shoulder.

He kept his left arm tucked close to his chest, as he had all morning. What was wrong with her? She should have insisted he leave all the wagon repairs to her crew. But then she wouldn't have enjoyed his company for over two hours.

It reminded her a little of their senior year in high school, when she'd coerced him into helping her with decorations for the winter formal. He'd hated it, and his football teammates had ridiculed him. Still, he'd done everything she'd asked, and though she hadn't appreciated him as much as she should have, she'd never forgotten.

"Have you been icing your shoulder twice a day and taking ibuprofen?"

"Yes, Nurse Carmichael," he teased.

"How much did it hurt last night?"

"Before or after my ride?"

"Both."

"It hurt before. A lot more after."

"Didn't appear to affect your ride much. You lasted eight seconds."

"The horse was having a slow night." Ethan unbuttoned his long-sleeved work shirt, wincing slightly as he peeled it off. "I won't be nearly so fortunate next time."

After only one PT session, he pretty much knew the drill and completed the exercises with minimal instruction from her. She was glad to see he'd found the old set of weights and was using them. His range of motion, she observed, had improved minimally.

When he finished with the exercises, she patted the table. "Ready?"

He hopped on, then lay on his back. "You going to your parents' house for Thanksgiving?" he asked once she began rotating his arm.

She remembered from their first session that Ethan liked to talk during therapy. Justin did, too. It probably helped them tolerate the pain better. Except she wasn't fooled. The strain in their voices along with clenched jaws and muscle tremors gave them away.

"Actually, they're going to my aunt and uncle's in Green Valley."

"Don't your relatives usually come up here?"

"Not this year. Uncle Lee just had back surgery and can't handle a long drive. They invited me and Justin. He hasn't decided for sure, but I'm not going."

"Why not?"

"I'm scheduled to work at the clinic Wednesday evening and will be here Friday morning to work on the wagon. Driving to Green Valley and back in one day is too much for me. I'll be wiped out."

"If you want," Ethan said through gritted teeth as she applied more pressure, "come to the house for dinner."

"I couldn't impose."

"Trust me, you won't be. Dad and Sage are doing all the cooking. Can't guarantee you won't get stuck with cleanup duty."

How many times had she done exactly that after dinner with the Powells? Too many to count. "I don't know...."

"This will be our first Thanksgiving dinner in nine years."

She didn't think he was trying to make her feel guilty as much as expressing his pleasure that the family had finally moved on enough after his mother's death to celebrate the holidays.

"Thank you." She lifted his arm high over his head. "But I'd better not."

"Is it because I kissed you last night?"

"Yes." That was only partially true. The bigger reason was that she'd kissed him back. Enthusiastically. "It wouldn't be right encouraging you when there's no hope of us ever…picking up where we left off." She couldn't bring herself to say *falling in love again.*

"My bronc riding," he said flatly.

"I explained already. And now that you've qualified for the jackpot, I'm assuming there's no chance you'll give it up."

"None."

"Turn on your right side," she instructed, hoping the change in position would put an end to their conversation.

It didn't.

"I care about you, Caitlin. And I think you still care about me."

"Of course I do. Just not like I used to."

"Then why are you always putting up your guard whenever we're together?"

"I'm a nurse." Lifting his shoulder off the table with one hand, she pushed down on his elbow with the other. "You're my patient."

"It's also easier to deny your feelings when you distance yourself."

"You're wrong."

"I don't think so."

The wound she'd believed long healed suddenly tore open, catching her unawares and leaving her feeling vulnerable. "I was devastated when you left."

That got a reaction from him—he winced.

Then again, her fingers were digging with excessive force into the soft tissue surrounding his shoulder.

"I don't regret enlisting, only how I handled telling you." His voice seemed to hold genuine regret.

"What about losing your leg?"

"Don't get me wrong, I'd rather that hadn't happened. But I was luckier than a lot of soldiers. At least I came home."

"I'd have gone with you."

"It doesn't work that way."

"Even if we were married?"

"I wanted to ask you."

"Then why didn't you?" Emotion thickened her voice.

"I was afraid something would happen to me. That I'd be killed and you'd be all alone. Like my father was after my mother died."

"Isn't that what you did? Left me alone? Only, instead of dying, you took off."

Neither of them spoke for a moment, and Caitlin relaxed her grip, the tension seeping out of both of them as she massaged his shoulder, upper arm and back.

Lying on his side, his eyes closed, the dim light softening his features, he looked seventeen again. Caitlin's anger faded, and she felt vulnerable all over, but for different reasons.

"I was an idiot," he said, breaking the silence. "I ran away from the very person I needed the most, because I couldn't handle my grief. You have no idea how much I wish I hadn't."

"Thank you for being honest. But it changes nothing." She stepped away from the table.

He sat up so abruptly the table shook. "That's what you're doing, too, Caitlin. You're running away."

"I wouldn't be here right now if that was true."

"Then come to Thanksgiving dinner."

"I told you, I can't."

"Trust me, I have no expectations where we're concerned—despite the kiss last night." He held up his hand when she would have protested. "We were swept up in the moment is all. No big deal."

Maybe not for him. It had been a very big deal for her.

"Come on." He grinned imploringly. "No one should be alone on Thanksgiving. And Dad would love to see you again."

"Justin may be—"

"Bring him, too. He's more than welcome."

Caitlin couldn't imagine making a bigger mistake, considering her knee-buckling reaction to Ethan's kiss. If only she didn't dread spending Thanksgiving alone in her little condo. And Justin would probably love coming to the ranch....

"All right," she said, relenting. "I accept your invitation. As long as we're clear—*friends only.*"

"Yes, ma'am," he answered, his solemn tone in direct contrast to the twinkle lighting his eyes.

Caitlin sighed tiredly.

Had he heard even one thing she said?

Chapter Seven

Ethan's father stood in front of the open oven door, fussing over the roasting turkey as if he was competing in a professional cook-off and about to be judged.

"It's not browning right."

"Looks okay to me." Ethan peered around his dad's head. "I'm sure it'll taste fine."

"Humph."

Evidently not the right thing to say to someone who took food preparation seriously.

Wayne Powell shut the oven door with more force than was necessary. Grumbling to himself, he went to the counter and checked on the girls. They'd been assigned the task of peeling potatoes, an entire five-pound sack.

He wasn't annoyed with Ethan, at least not as much as he pretended. He liked being in charge of the kitchen, liked making a fuss. Up until Sage and Isa had entered their lives, cooking was the only chore he regularly performed on the ranch, choosing instead to remain a semirecluse. Even Cassie, his one and only grandchild, coming to live with them hadn't rescued him from the deep depression he'd succumbed to after his wife died. All that had changed when the girls went missing.

Finding them in the box canyon had not only resulted

in Prince's capture, it restored Wayne Powell to his former self and his family.

This was truly a day to be thankful.

The reason foremost in Ethan's mind was Caitlin coming to dinner. He hadn't spoken to her about Thanksgiving since inviting her last Saturday, though he'd seen her twice for physical-therapy sessions. He worried that bringing up the topic of dinner might cause her to change her mind. Better to keep cool. Lie low. Feign disinterest.

Yeah, tell that to his gut, which had been churning all morning from nervous tension.

"How's the pico de gallo coming?" Ethan's father asked.

Sage stood at the counter beside the girls, chopping tomatoes, cilantro, green chillies, garlic and onions. "Almost done, and then I'll be out of your way."

Normally Ethan's father would have resisted serving pico de gallo and tortilla chips as an appetizer at Thanksgiving. But he loved Sage and Isa and welcomed their contribution, even if it wasn't a traditional dish.

"Nice day." Gavin appeared at Ethan's side and gave his brother a hand with putting the extra leaf in the dining table. "We haven't had this much commotion in a long time."

"Yeah, real nice." They'd always been a close family. It was just that for the last decade, they'd been a broken one. Like his brother, Ethan was glad to see their family on the mend.

"Too bad Sierra isn't here." Gavin slipped the extra leaf into place, then helped Ethan push the expanded table together.

"I don't know what's wrong with her. She hasn't called yet, and Dad's starting to worry."

"It's still early, and that job of hers keeps her busy."

"On Thanksgiving?"

"It's possible."

Ethan had his doubts. Something was wrong with his sister and had been since her last visit a year and a half ago. Everything had gone well, as far as he knew. Really well. But shortly after she returned to San Francisco, she'd stopped answering her phone, stopped emailing regularly and was always busy when someone did finally get ahold of her.

"Let's wait till dinner's over," Gavin said. "Then we'll call her."

He was always the more reasonable of the two brothers, and Ethan would be wise to listen. Still, he couldn't ignore his instincts, and they warned him to be on the watch where Sierra was concerned.

"I'm going to bring in more wood for the fireplace," he said.

"What about your shoulder?"

"I'm fine." Ethan wasn't exactly fine, though he was considerably improved, thanks to a constant regime of ibuprofen, ice packs and physical therapy. In fact, he was enough better that his confidence was growing. Despite not making eight seconds again since his ride last week, he'd changed his goal from just competing in Saturday's jackpot to placing in the top five positions.

If you want to be a winner, you have to think like one.

His high school coach's advice still rang in Ethan's ears, and he heeded it.

Escaping the bustle of the busy kitchen, he went outside to the woodpile behind the house. On his third trip carrying an armful of cut pine logs, he spied Clay's truck pulling through the main gate. His renewed friendship with his childhood buddy was yet another reason to be thankful today.

"Need a hand?" Clay asked, meeting him on the back porch.

"I think I've got enough for now." Ethan did let Clay open the door for him. "See your dad today?"

"Nope."

"Talk to him?"

No answer.

"Isn't it about time you two buried the hatchet?"

"We will. One day. Just not yet."

Clay and his father had suffered a terrible falling-out when Bud Duvall had refused to honor his agreement with Ethan's dad and had sold the Powell land out from under them. There was likely more to the story, but Clay chose not to elaborate, and Ethan respected his friend's privacy.

Taking his share of money from the family's cattle operation, Clay had struck out on his own, purchasing a large parcel of land a few miles down the road. He'd used the remaining funds to construct the rodeo arena and bankroll his rodeo stock business. Somewhere in between, he'd married and, after six short months, divorced. But that subject was also off-limits.

While Clay shook hands and dispensed hugs to the other Powell family members, Ethan carried the last load of firewood into the living room, placing it in the log bin along with the rest. He was just glancing at the mantel clock and wondering if Caitlin had changed her mind, after all, when a small commotion rose from the kitchen.

"Nurse Carmichael's here!" Cassie's high-pitched voice echoed throughout the house.

Ethan headed for the kitchen, presenting a welcoming smile that he hoped hid the turmoil in his heart. Caitlin wanted to be friends, and he'd rather have her in his life as a friend than not at all.

It wasn't, however, what *he* wanted.

"Happy Thanksgiving."

He envied the girls, who clung to her with the tenacity of baby possums riding their mother's back.

"Same to you." She smiled brightly. "Sorry we're late."

To his delight, she extracted herself from the girls' clutches and gave him a casual but decidedly warm hug. He resisted the urge to fold her in his arms and bury his face in the soft, fragrant skin of her neck.

Justin appeared in the doorway, having taken a bit longer to cross the porch. He rolled his wheelchair over the threshold and into the kitchen, which was now crowded with nine people.

"Hi, everybody."

Reintroductions were made along with new ones. When it came to Isa, the little girl hovered behind her mother. She wasn't normally shy, and Ethan suspected Justin's wheelchair had something to do with the change in her behavior.

"Hello, I'm Justin." He tilted his head so he could see her better and winked. "What's your name?"

"Isa," she answered timidly.

"Well, Isa, I was hoping for a tour of the house. Maybe you can show me around."

She crouched even farther behind Sage.

"That's too bad. Because I brought this box of chocolates, and I need someone to help me eat them." He produced a wrapped package from the backpack on his lap. "Possibly two someones."

That was enough encouragement for Cassie. She rushed forward. "Can I touch your chair?"

"Sure." Justin shifted sideways, and Cassie stroked the armrest.

"Wow!" She bent and examined the wheels. "Cool."

Isa slowly emerged from behind her mother to stand next to Cassie. At Justin's smile of encouragement, she also stroked the wheelchair's armrest.

"Come on, you two. Let's get out of here before the grown-ups put us to work."

"Yeah," Cassie agreed. "I hate peeling potatoes."

Including himself with the "kids," even though he was considerably older than them, sealed the deal. Justin and his young tour guides left the kitchen to explore the rest of the house.

Caitlin's smile followed them.

"He's very good with children," Sage observed.

"He's going be a teacher when he graduates."

"A good one, it looks like."

"What can I do to help?" Caitlin held up a container. "I brought a pumpkin pie."

She was instantly recruited to slice the freshly baked bread.

Ethan offered Clay a beer. Gavin joined them, and the three men retreated to the calm of the living room. Taking a seat on the couch, Ethan stared at the fire with its leaping flames and crackling logs. The woodsy scent filled the room, giving it that special holiday feeling.

"Sounds like the girls have coaxed Justin into a game of Uno," Gavin said, craning his neck to see through the archway and into the family room.

"He's a good sport," Ethan answered.

"A real nice guy," Clay concurred, and took a long swallow of his beer. "Shame about the accident."

"Doesn't seem to have slowed him down any."

"You're right about that." He turned to Ethan. "How's the physical therapy going with Caitlin?"

"Great. I have an appointment at the clinic tomorrow. I'm sure the doctor won't find anything."

"I wasn't talking about your shoulder." Clay shot Gavin a conspiratorial look.

Ethan's brother shrugged.

"Caitlin and I are friends," Ethan insisted. "That's all."

Maybe if he said it seven hundred more times, he'd start believing it.

"You weren't acting like friends the other night when you were kissing." Clay looked at Gavin again and received another shrug.

Ethan sipped his beer. He and Caitlin hadn't acted like friends when they were kissing because it hadn't felt that way.

"What are you going to do?" Clay asked.

"Nothing. She says there's no chance for us as long as I'm riding broncs and breaking horses."

"Then give it up."

"Are you nuts?"

"Isn't she worth it?"

Conner had made a similar comment the other night at the rodeo arena.

"It's not like I wouldn't—won't—give up bronc riding eventually." When he'd erased all doubt from his and everyone else's minds that he was no different than before the car bomb explosion. "Breaking horses, that's another thing. It's my job."

"She's the love of your life."

"*Former* love of my life," he corrected. "And that was years ago."

"She could be again." Clay sent Gavin another look. This one was met with a confident nod.

Ethan was less sure about his feelings for Caitlin and hers for him. Could he ever give up his cowboy ways for her? He'd almost rather lose his other leg.

It was a quandary he continued to ponder all through dinner as he sat across the large table from her. He did his best to keep up with the lively conversations, but was completely distracted by her green eyes and the memory of them drifting shut as his mouth claimed hers.

"I HAD A WONDERFUL TIME. Thank you so much for inviting us." Caitlin wrapped her arms around Wayne Powell's generous waist and squeezed.

He returned the hug with great enthusiasm. "It's wonderful to have you back. Just like old times."

She agreed. The only difference was the absence of his late wife, who'd been mentioned often during dinner.

"Give your parents my regards." Wayne released Caitlin. "And don't be a stranger, you hear?" He tapped the tip of her nose with his finger.

"I won't."

If only Caitlin was certain she could return for a social visit. No matter how often she told herself she wasn't interested in Ethan romantically, there was no denying the rush of awareness that stole over her whenever she caught his dark eyes observing her.

"Goodbye, Justin." Isa hung on to his wheelchair, which earlier in the day had intimidated her. "If you come back, I'll let you ride my horse, Chico."

"Deal, kiddo." He bumped fists with her before wheeling himself through the back door.

Caitlin's steps momentarily faltered. Was Isa's invitation spur-of-the-moment or had Justin and the girls been talking about riding? Considering his last visit to the ranch, Caitlin should have seen this coming.

"I'm right behind you," she called to her brother, who beat her out the door.

She'd said her farewells to everyone except Ethan, who'd disappeared at the last second. She tried not to let the obvious slight bother her. They'd see each other again tomorrow when she and her volunteers came by to work on the wagon.

Sound reasoning did nothing to alleviate her disappointment.

"Take your time," Justin called to her.

She scarcely noticed the hint of amusement in his tone, she was so distracted. Once outside, she almost ran over Ethan.

"I'll walk you to your car."

That would probably be a mistake. It would be much less nerve-racking to say goodbye here, with his family watching from the doorway. Only she didn't, and he fell into step beside her.

Lately, it seemed, the harder she tried to keep him at a distance, the closer he got.

Or was it the closer she allowed him to get?

"Thanks again for coming," he said.

She hoped he wouldn't take her hand, as he had in the bunkhouse. Touching him would break down the last of her defenses.

"I really enjoyed myself. Justin did, too."

"Dad insists I ask you back."

"That was nice of him."

No commitments. Better for both of them in the long run.

"What time will you be here tomorrow? I'll make sure everything's ready."

"Really," she insisted, "I don't want to put you through any more trouble than I already have. It's enough that you're letting us use your wagon during the festival—and will be driving it."

"I like your friends. And I like you."

Here was where she was supposed to say, "I like you, too," but that would be asking for trouble.

"Let's schedule one last physical-therapy session before the jackpot," she said instead. "How about tomorrow after we're done working on the wagon?"

"Yeah, sure. I appreciate all you've done. My shoulder's doing great."

Justin had already hoisted himself into the front passenger seat and collapsed his wheelchair, leaning it against the open door. Ethan went over to him, and, after saying goodbye, grabbed the chair.

Caitlin knew better than to insist he let her get it. Whenever Ethan was around, he carried things. Maybe to show everyone he wasn't an invalid. More likely, that was the way Wayne Powell had raised his sons.

When Ethan had finished loading the chair, he came around to join her at the driver's-side door. For an awkward second or two, Caitlin debated what to do.

"See you tomorrow," he said.

"Ten sharp."

Another second passed. Two. Three.

Oh, what the hell, she thought. Throwing caution to the wind, she looped her arms around his neck for what was supposed to be a brief, casual hug....

Only she was the one to hold on, not Ethan.

The day had been filled with memories. Of the ranch house. Thanksgiving dinner. The Powell family. In truth, the past two weeks had been a constant trip down memory lane. She'd responded to Ethan's kiss the other night out of habit, her body instinctively nestling against his as it had so often in the past.

As it did now.

Emotions, tender and bittersweet, weakened her resolve. She leaned into him and rested her head in the crook of his neck. He stroked her hair, then combed his fingers through it. Another familiar gesture that stirred yet more memories.

She removed her arms, now strangely limp, from around his neck. "I have to go."

"Take care."

Thankfully, Ethan didn't acknowledge the hug.

It would serve her right if he did, after she'd been so adamant that there could never be anything between them again.

Before she quite knew what was happening, she was standing on her tiptoes and pressing her lips to his cheek, her hands resting gently on his chest.

He smelled amazing. Fresh and clean like the outdoors, where he spent most of his time. His flannel shirt was smooth beneath her palms, and the bristles of his five o'clock shadow tickled her lips. She shivered ever so slightly.

I wish you hadn't left.

The thought came from nowhere. No, not nowhere. It came from a tiny corner of her heart where it had remained lodged for nine long years.

Mystified and annoyed at what had come over her, she backed away from Ethan, ready to apologize for her lack of control.

One look at his nonchalant expression and she promptly shut her mouth.

Seriously! Was she the only one whose world was just rocked?

Evidently so.

Muttering something unintelligible, Caitlin dived into the minivan, dreading having to explain her actions to Justin.

How could she expect Ethan to believe all her talk about them being just friends when she'd rushed head-long over the line she'd vehemently insisted he not cross?

Chapter Eight

Caitlin stood over a box of Christmas decorations, painstakingly unraveling a knotted mess that promised to be a string of lights. Over in the round pen, Ethan was working with Prince. He hadn't stopped by to help her and her crew, hadn't even waved at them. Considering the way they'd parted yesterday, he was undoubtedly avoiding her. With good reason. One minute she was insisting they couldn't see each other, and the next she was, well, all over him.

The sound of happy laughter distracted her, and she looked over at her brother and Tamiko. They were attempting to twine a string of lights through the spokes of a wagon wheel, and it didn't seem to matter that their efforts weren't producing the desired results. They were having fun.

There was a lesson in there somewhere for Caitlin. She worked too hard. Not just at her various jobs, but at making her and Justin's lives safe. Predictable. Structured. Comfortable.

Thinking back, she hadn't been playing it safe when she'd responded to Ethan's potent kiss at the rodeo arena, or when she'd lost her head yesterday during their hug.

Her glance fell again on Justin and Tamiko. Too bad

Tamiko already had a boyfriend. She and Justin were cute together. As she bent close to talk to him, her long black hair fell like a silky curtain, momentarily shielding them from view.

Attraction at its earliest and most innocent.

Perhaps not so innocent, given the yearning in her brother's eyes when Tamiko straightened.

Caitlin's heart broke a little. Her brother was obviously smitten and understandably so. Tamiko was gorgeous, bright and chock-full of personality. But she was also taken. Compared to the strong and towering young man painting the wagon's sidewall, Caitlin doubted her brother stood a snowball's chance. Tamiko was simply being kind to him, not realizing how hard and fast he was falling for her.

Caitlin chuckled mirthlessly to herself. She and her brother were quite the pair. Here he was chasing a girl who wasn't available, while she was trying her hardest to stop Ethan from chasing her.

"You finished with that string of lights?" Howard asked.

"Almost." Caitlin smiled. The older man had turned out to be a big help.

She and her crew of volunteers weren't the only people at the ranch this Friday morning after Thanksgiving. At least a dozen riders were exercising their horses in the main arena. Another group was readying for a trail ride. In a small arena adjacent to the main one, a lone woman riding with an English saddle took her horse over a series of jumps. Clay and four or five of his men were hard at it, hammering, sawing and raising a ruckus as they labored to convert the old cattle barn into a mare motel. Once in a while, one or two of the men wandered over to Ethan's bunkhouse, carrying a toolbox or a ladder or sheets of drywall.

Gavin waved to her as he left the barn and headed to the round pen.

Caitlin did a double take. Ethan had finally gotten a saddle and bridle on the mustang. She stopped working on the lights to watch.

The moment Gavin reached the pen, he and Ethan entered into a heated discussion. Ethan waved off his brother, who in turn demanded to be heard. When Ethan didn't respond, Gavin climbed through the rails and into the pen. The argument continued.

Prince behaved relatively well, all things considered. He was calmer, at least, than when Caitlin and Justin had visited him in his stall. Then again, these were the two people who spent the most time with him, and he was used to them.

The brothers' loud voices eventually drew a crowd of ranch hands. Clay emerged from the barn and, after quickly assessing the situation, hurried over.

Gavin cautioned everyone to stay back. He stood at Prince's head, gripping the lead rope attached to the halter Prince wore beneath his bridle. Ethan positioned himself at the horse's right side, the reins bunched in one hand. With his other, he stroked Prince's neck over and over.

Suddenly, he lifted his good leg and placed his foot in the stirrup.

He was going to ride Prince!

Caitlin dropped the lights and ran toward the round pen to join the others.

"Hey, come back," Howard called after her.

She ignored him.

"Sis!"

She slowed for Justin, who quickly caught up with her.

"Where are you going?"

"Ethan's riding Prince."

"Cool."

That wasn't how she would describe it.

She wormed her way between two ranch hands. As much as watching Ethan terrified her, she had to be there in case something went wrong.

Through the railings, she saw Ethan swing up into the saddle. Prince stood still, a perplexed expression on his face. He slowly craned his head around and sniffed Ethan's leg, his ears twitching. Snorting once, he turned away.

Caitlin expelled a giant sigh of relief. Everything was going to be okay. All that worrying, and Prince was a lamb at heart. Once again she'd overreacted.

"Good boy," Ethan murmured to the horse.

Suddenly, Prince emitted an ear-piercing squeal, his entire body quivering. With no warning whatsoever, he started bucking in place again and again. Ethan was shaken so violently, his hat flew off. Just as quickly, he was flung backward when Prince reared.

By some miracle, he hung on.

The ranch hand beside Caitlin gave a loud whoop and jostled his neighbor's arm. "Did ya see that? Ride 'em, Ethan!"

Caitlin stared, transfixed. She hadn't been this afraid since the day of Justin's accident.

THE TECHNIQUES USED for breaking a green horse weren't the same as for riding a bucking bronc.

Ethan transferred all his weight to the lower half of his body. Sitting squarely in the saddle, he pointed his heels toward the ground and squeezed Prince's flanks with his calves. His goal was to hang on until the horse tired, which he hoped would be soon.

He heard his name being called above the whoops and hollers of the people watching him, and thought he caught a glimpse of Caitlin from the corner of his eye. Prince twisted sideways, and from then on, all of Ethan's attention was focused on outlasting the horse on their wild roller-coaster ride. With both hands gripping the reins, he pulled back, keeping Prince's head tucked close to his body, and preventing him from rearing. Gavin stood in the pen, dashing out of harm's way when necessary, but otherwise keeping a close watch on horse and rider.

Clumps of dirt exploded from beneath Prince's hooves as he bucked and bucked, showering nearby spectators. Ethan barely noticed. This was a contest of wills, and he had every intention of winning.

As suddenly as it started, the rocking motion ceased. Prince transitioned into a choppy lope, lungs heaving and nostrils flaring. Ethan took a chance and gave the horse a little more rein. Prince extended his forelegs, and the ride became considerably smoother.

Cheers and applause erupted. Gavin wore a grin the size of a dinner plate. Ethan's chest swelled with satisfaction and accomplishment. This was hardly the first horse he'd broken, but it was definitely the best.

Prince, always eager to be the center of attention, shifted into a high-stepping trot. Head raised, tail arched, he showed off in front of his admirers, understanding on some level that he was equally interesting to them with a human on his back as he was without one.

Ethan let the horse have his fun. Hell, he was having fun, too. The time of his life. One of his first questions to the doctors when he'd woke after losing his leg was whether he would ever ride again.

They'd uttered all the platitudes, that anything was possible with hard work and determination. But Ethan had glimpsed the uncertainty in their earnest expressions.

Too bad those doctors weren't here now. Not only could he ride, he could break green horses and compete in saddle bronc events. He might even win at the jackpot tomorrow. It was less of a long shot today than it had been yesterday.

After a few more circuits of the pen, Ethan brought Prince to a halt and dismounted with Gavin's help. He held out the reins to his brother.

"Your turn."

Gavin took them. "Thanks." He clapped Ethan on the shoulder—his *good* shoulder. "For everything."

Ethan heard what his brother didn't say. There had been a time, after the explosion and during rehab, when Ethan wasn't sure if he wanted to come home and help his family with the failing remains of their once thriving cattle operation. Coping with that loss on a daily basis was more than Ethan could handle. But he had come home, and together he, his brother and father built a new business with the potential to be just as profitable as the old one. Adapt or perish. Wasn't that the saying?

The Powells had adapted and, despite the odds, were succeeding.

Ethan held Prince's lead rope while Gavin swung up into the saddle. The horse's eyes went wide at this sudden change, and he initially balked. Once Gavin was situated, however, he settled down, obediently trotting in a circle.

Ethan moved to the center of the pen, watching

Prince and making mental notes for future training sessions.

"See if you can get him to lope," he instructed Gavin.

Prince did, after significant urging. Even then, he refused to lead with his left leg. Training him would take patience and a strong hand. Ethan couldn't wait. And once Prince was fully broke, his intelligence and reliable disposition proved, his value as a stud would increase.

Gavin finished his ride. Ethan once again held Prince's head so his brother could dismount without incident. The horse was doing well for a first day, but he was unpredictable at best, and it was wise to err on the side of caution.

If anything, the crowd had grown in size. Caitlin, Ethan noticed, had yet to move from her spot at the fence.

He went first out the gate, keeping the admirers at a safe distance while Gavin led the horse away. Ethan watched them go, his elation giving way to disappointment.

They had agreed that Ethan would break the horse. In some ways, and on most days, he worked more closely with Prince than his brother did. But there was no doubt Gavin and the horse shared a special bond. It had been Gavin who'd tracked the horse for months and insisted on capturing him. Gavin who'd juggled the family's finances so they could purchase Prince at auction, only to lose him to Clay. Gavin who'd set his differences aside in order to form a partnership with Clay that would benefit them both.

Prince knew who was responsible for his cushy new lifestyle. From the moment they'd brought him to the ranch, he'd tolerated Gavin best, allowing him into his stall when no one else could get within ten feet of him. It had been Gavin's jacket pockets he nuzzled, searching for treats.

Ethan wasn't one to waste time envying others, but his brother did have it all. A beautiful, wonderful fiancée who came with a great kid. A terrific daughter. A job he loved. Loyal employees. Friends. Respect in the community. An incredible horse.

Ethan wouldn't mind having a few of those things for himself.

A voice behind him roused him from his reverie.

"Hell of a ride, pal!" A beaming Clay handed Ethan his hat.

"We still have a long way to—"

"I swear," one of the wranglers interrupted Ethan, "I've never seen anything like that."

Someone else shook his hand. Then another person. His father was there, too. Ethan didn't remember seeing him at the round pen. The next thing he knew, he was pulled into a mighty bear hug.

"I'm proud of you, son."

Ethan swallowed, his throat tightening. "Thanks, Dad."

He recalled a similar celebration when he'd just returned home from rehab. His father had expressed his pride then, too. But there had been an underlying sadness to the gathering of friends and family that dampened the mood.

Ethan had been a wounded man.

Now he was a warrior once again.

And the person he wanted most to share this incredible moment with was Caitlin.

Where had she gone?

He searched for her, spotting her with Justin on the

fringes of the now dispersing crowd. He made his way over to her, mindless of the people calling his name and tugging on his jacket sleeves.

Justin's boyish face lit with pleasure at the sight of Ethan. "Dude, that was awesome! I took pictures with my phone. Here, I'll show you." He started fiddling with the device. "Darn it," he grumbled when the photos didn't immediately fill the screen. "Hold on a second."

Ethan gave Caitlin a crooked smile. "Did you see?"

"Yes."

He'd been so caught up with his ride and how great it had gone, he hadn't really looked at her. She wasn't smiling, and her brows were drawn together in a pronounced V.

"Is something wrong?" he asked.

"Not at all."

"She was worried you were going to fall," Justin answered.

"But I didn't fall."

"You could have." Again Justin replied for his sister. She glared at him.

"Hey, don't get mad at me. It's true."

"I break three or four horses a month," Ethan said. "If not one of Clay's rodeo stock, then a client's horse. I'm good at my job."

"She gets scared easily."

"All right!" Caitlin snapped. "I do get scared easily. Who wouldn't? The horse was going crazy."

Ethan liked that she worried about him. It was another sign she cared. What he didn't like was her disapproval, which was tarnishing an otherwise memorable day for him and his family.

"You're upset with me," she said.

"Of course not." Only he was.

"Here we go," Justin announced enthusiastically, and passed Ethan his phone.

There were five photos, two fuzzy and out of focus. In one, Ethan's head and Prince's legs were cut off. The remaining two were quite good for having been taken with a cell phone.

He tried to see his ride through Caitlin's eyes. Prince, his nose to the ground, his back legs straight up in the air, could appear dangerous to a novice. But not once had Ethan lost control or so much as slipped in the saddle. Surely she'd seen that. Everyone else had, and was thrilled and excited for him.

"Thanks, bud." He returned the phone to Justin.

"I can email these to you if you want."

"That'd be great. I'll have Gavin post them on the ranch's website."

"Hey, Caitlin!" Howard hollered though cupped hands. "We have a problem."

"I need to go." She started out at a brisk walk.

"Wait!" Ethan went after her, cursing himself.

She stopped and pivoted slowly.

"Why can't you be happy for me?" he asked.

"I am."

"You have a strange way of showing it. I rode Prince. I'm fine. Not a single scratch."

"You're right."

"I get that you're scared."

"I don't think you do." Her voice shook. "I don't think you have the slightest inkling of how truly terrified I was, watching you ride."

"Caitlin—"

"I admit it, I'm a neurotic mess."

"You're not neurotic. A little obsessive, maybe."

"This isn't a matter of whether my worrying is obsessive or reasonable." She placed a hand over her heart. "It's how I feel, and it won't change or go away because you or I want it to."

"I'm sorry."

"Me, too." She walked away from him then.

Ethan stared after her. Until that instant, he hadn't believed their differences were insurmountable.

No more.

"Go easy on her."

It took Ethan a few seconds to realize Justin had wheeled up beside him. "Yeah?"

"She's crazy about you."

It went both ways. "Could've fooled me."

Ethan wasn't sure where he should go—after Caitlin, back to the stables or to the office. "You want a beer?"

Justin glanced at his watch, shrugged, then grinned. "Sure. I'm not driving. Nothing motorized, anyway."

"Let's go."

Neither said a word on the short walk to Ethan's bunkhouse until they reached the porch.

"Can you—"

"No problem."

Justin reversed his wheelchair and backed it up to the bottom step. Leaning forward, he cranked the wheels and climbed the two short steps inch by grueling inch, the muscles in his arms straining.

"You're pretty good at that."

"I've had a lot of practice." Justin maneuvered the chair through the bunkhouse door, which was just wide enough to accommodate him. "This is nice," he said, and parked himself adjacent to the couch.

Why his sister constantly fretted about him, Ethan

didn't understand. Justin was obviously capable of handling himself.

Ethan recalled his own months of rehab, learning how to stand, walk off a curb, climb a ladder, manage stairs. More than once he'd landed face-first on the floor.

"Thanks," Justin said, when he passed him a cold beer from the refrigerator.

Ethan sank onto the couch and propped his feet on the old footlocker that served as a coffee table. The beer tasted good, and for several moments they savored it in silence.

"It's not Caitlin's fault she's the way she is," Justin said finally.

"It's not your fault, either."

"Hell, no, it's not." He took a swig of beer. "She changed after the accident. We all did."

"I can relate." Ethan lifted his bottle in a toast, which Justin returned.

"Don't take this wrong, okay? But when you lost your leg, your family wasn't there. They didn't see you at the hospital afterward."

That was true. Gavin had wanted to fly out to Germany, where Ethan had been transferred for surgery immediately after being stabilized. Unfortunately, the ranch was barely sustaining itself in those days, and they didn't have the money to finance a trip to Tucson, much less halfway around the world.

"Caitlin and my parents spent some pretty harrowing weeks while I was in a medically induced coma. They didn't know if I'd survive, much less walk again."

"I can imagine."

"Caitlin blamed herself, which was ridiculous. I chose to jump off that cliff. She had nothing to do with it. I was bound and determined to show everyone I wasn't the loser they called me behind my back and to my face."

Justin's need to prove himself in front of others was a lot like Ethan's—except his attempt had ended in tragedy. Ethan had a decidedly different outcome in mind for himself.

"Have you told her you don't hold her responsible?"

"Dude, I've practically had it engraved in stone. She doesn't listen."

Ethan pondered Justin's remark while finishing the last of his beer. "Want another one?"

"Sure. Why not? I doubt Caitlin's missing me."

"Caitlin or that girl? What's her name?"

"Tamiko."

"She's cute."

"And has a boyfriend."

"You haven't let anything stop you from doing what you want before now." Ethan retrieved two fresh beers from the refrigerator.

"Her boyfriend, Eric, may be dumber than a bag of hammers, but I think he can take me."

"It's not his decision who she dates. It's hers."

"You're right." Justin copied Ethan and raised his beer in a toast. "And the same could be said for you, my friend."

"About Caitlin?"

"You want her. Don't let anything stop you."

"I'm up against a lot more than a boyfriend. You saw her today. A five-ton steamroller couldn't break through those walls she's erected."

"Chicken."

"Me?" Ethan snorted. "Have you looked in the mirror lately?"

Justin laughed. "Tell you what, let's make a deal. I'll go after Tamiko and you go after my sister. Who knows? Maybe we'll both get lucky."

Ethan stood and hitched up his jeans. "You're on."

Justin's challenge might have been issued in jest, but Ethan took it seriously. If any two people deserved a second chance, he and Caitlin did—and he was determined to see they got it.

Chapter Nine

"Is it gonna hurt?" The little girl's eyes brimmed with unshed tears.

"No, I promise, sweetie." Caitlin dabbed antibiotic ointment onto the girl's cut with a cotton swab. "There, see?"

"Ow!" She jerked her knee away, although the ointment couldn't possibly have stung.

The cut wasn't serious. Caitlin had seen far worse this past week alone.

"I don't know how she fell." The mother anxiously smoothed her daughter's disheveled hair. "I swear she wasn't out of my sight more than a minute."

"We were running, and Becky Lynn pushed me."

The girl sat in a folding chair, the same one Ethan had occupied when Caitlin had examined his shoulder, and again when she'd helped him put his prosthesis back on. She hoped to see him today—safe and sound after his ride, not in the first-aid station for a third time.

"You and Becky Lynn have to be careful." The mother hovered, watching every move as Caitlin placed a bandage over the cut and pressed down on the adhesive tabs. "There are a lot of people here today. You shouldn't be running around and not paying attention."

There *were* a lot of people. Caitlin hadn't known how

many to expect, considering this was Clay's first jackpot. Someone mentioned fifty-six entrants had registered and by Caitlin's estimation at least two hundred people packed the bleachers.

The little girl was Caitlin's second patient this afternoon, and the event hadn't officially started yet. She'd also treated one of Clay's wranglers after a bull stomped on his foot while they were transferring livestock from the paddocks to the holding pens behind the chutes. Though the cowboy's foot was only bruised and not broken, she'd advised him to take it easy for the rest of the day.

FYI, he hadn't. She'd seen him twice so far, limping as he went about his tasks.

He reminded her of Ethan.

"Can I go now?"

"Sure thing." Caitlin rolled down the little girl's pant leg, covering the bandage.

She hopped off the chair and flexed her knee as if testing the bandage's sticking power.

"What do I owe you?" her mother asked.

"Not a thing. It's part of the service."

"You sure? I really appreciate the help."

"If you'd like, you can make a donation to the Powells' Wild Mustang Sanctuary. There's a collection jar at the chuck wagon."

"I will." The woman's tentative smile bloomed.

Her daughter tugged on her hand. "Hurry, Mommy. We don't want to miss Daddy's ride."

"Oh, honey, don't worry. The bull riders go last, after the bronc riders."

Caitlin thought of Ethan breaking Prince yesterday.

"Isn't it hard watching your husband ride bulls?"

she asked the woman, surprised at the boldness of her question. "Aren't you afraid for him?"

"'Course I'm afraid. I start shaking the second that chute opens, and don't stop till he waves at me from the other side of the arena fence."

"Why put yourself through that?"

Why let him do it? was what she really wanted to know.

"My Micky's no champion bull rider and not likely to ever be one. These jackpots, they're his moment to shine, you know? For eight seconds, he's king of the world. I wouldn't dare miss it, and I wouldn't dare take it away from him, either."

"Mommy!" The little girl tugged harder on her hand. "Let's go."

"You be careful," Caitlin told the girl. "I don't want to see you back here."

"And I'll be sure to put a donation in that collection jar," the mother promised as they left.

Caitlin spent the next several minutes cleaning up after her patient and thinking about the woman's remarks. Her support of her husband was admirable. But what if he fell and hurt himself? His loving wife and beautiful daughter depended on him. He put not only himself at risk when he went into the arena, but his family, too.

"Hey." Clay's large frame filled the doorway. "I see you've had a couple visitors already today."

"Your wrangler T.J. was one of them. He should be resting somewhere, elevating and icing that foot," she admonished.

"I told him to take the day off."

"FYI, he didn't listen to you."

"He needs the money, Caitlin. It's a tough economy, and he has bills to pay."

"Right."

"You annoyed at me specifically or the world in general?"

"Sorry." Caitlin was immediately contrite. "That was uncalled for."

"Does your mood have anything to do with Ethan competing?"

"Not at all."

"You sure?" Clay stepped fully into the room. "Because he mentioned you being mad at him. Something to do with breaking Prince yesterday."

Caitlin hadn't been particularly close to Clay when they were younger, even though he was Ethan's best friend. They were always in competition for Ethan's time and attention. Caitlin had wanted him to herself, while Clay was constantly luring Ethan away for football or rodeo or fishing or a night out with the boys.

Working for Clay, however, had changed their relationship. He really was a decent guy, and Caitlin felt bad that his brief marriage had ended disastrously.

"A couple of weeks ago he injured his shoulder," she told Clay. "Then his prosthesis came off. Next time could be a lot worse."

"He knows what he's doing."

"He's at a disadvantage. I heard him telling Justin at Thanksgiving dinner he sometimes has trouble keeping weight on his left leg, and it throws him off balance."

"He's learned to compensate."

"How would you feel if something happened to him?"

"Like shit," Clay answered honestly. "But I wouldn't blame myself, if that's what you're asking."

"Not even a little? You did give him permission to enter the jackpot."

"He's a grown man. He makes his own decisions."

Ethan had tried to tell her the same thing about Justin. That he was the one who chose to jump off the cliff.

But there was a difference. While Clay allowed Ethan to ride broncs and enter the jackpot, he hadn't encouraged him. Goaded him. If anything, he'd discouraged Ethan.

"You care, and that's sweet." Clay watched her as she meticulously organized the tray of supplies. "Did you ever think your constant worrying makes him feel like an invalid and not like the normal guy he wants to be?"

Her hand slipped, knocking a box of gauze pads to the floor. She stooped to pick it up. "Did he tell you that?"

"Not in so many words."

"I don't think of him as an invalid."

"You just said he's at a disadvantage because of his artificial leg. That sounds like you're calling him an invalid."

"I'm not," she argued hotly. "Not on purpose."

"Then go watch him compete. Saddle bronc riding is the first event."

"Leave the first-aid station? What if someone gets injured?"

"This place isn't that big." Clay grinned affably. "We'll find you."

"I…can't."

"Why not?"

"Watching him would be like giving my stamp of approval, and I don't approve. It has nothing to do with his prosthesis. Anyone who climbs on a bull or bronc is an idiot in my opinion."

Clay's response was a loud laugh.

"This isn't funny."

"You're right." He promptly sobered, studying her intently.

"What?"

"I was just thinking how lucky Ethan is to have you."

"He doesn't *have* me."

Clay laughed again. Her steely glare had no effect on silencing him.

The overhead speakers did the trick when they came to life and a man's crackling voice announced the start of the jackpot.

"I'd better get going." Clay hesitated at the door. "Hope you change your mind about watching Ethan."

"I won't."

"This is a big moment for him. He wants you there."

Caitlin was still thinking about what Clay had said five minutes later as she listened to the announcer call the names of the first three contestants.

How many men were competing in bronc riding today and how soon until Ethan's turn?

What did it matter? She wasn't going to watch him. She managed to stick to her guns until the announcer, during color commentary between participants, mentioned the Powells, their mustang sanctuary and Ethan's military service.

Caitlin dashed out the door and raced toward the area behind the bucking chutes where the cowboys typically gathered to debate the various merits of the bucking stock. He was there, engrossed in conversation with two men.

He noticed her only when one of his companions elbowed him in the ribs and nodded in her direction. If he was surprised to see her, he hid it well.

She slowed, her courage evaporating as quickly as it had come.

He broke away from his friends and met her halfway, ignoring the good-humored jeers they hurled after him.

"Hey."

"I...uh..." She tipped her head back in order to see his face, and promptly lost her train of thought. His dark eyes had a way of doing that to her.

"If you're here to tell me I shouldn't ride, you've wasted a trip."

"I'm not."

His brows rose. "Good."

"I didn't want you getting on that horse thinking I was mad at you. I'm not, and I apologize for my behavior yesterday. I really am happy you broke Prince and proud that you're competing today."

"Thanks." His mouth lifted in a sexy, knee-weakening grin. "Don't suppose I could have a kiss. For luck."

She should have seen that coming. "How 'bout a hug?"

"I'll take what I can get."

Determined not to lose control as she had during their last hug, she looped her arms around his neck, her spine ramrod straight, her cheek averted. She lasted two full seconds before her entire body melted with a gentle sigh and she relaxed into his embrace.

When they parted, he caught her chin between his thumb and forefinger. "I'm going the full eight seconds."

"I just want you to be safe." Her voice quavered.

"I can do both."

She carried that promise with her to the stands, where she perched on the front row of the bleachers, her foot tapping nervously.

Ethan watched Caitlin walk away, her hands stuffed in the pockets of her hoodie, her slim shoulders hunched. It wasn't cold. In fact, the sun shone brightly in a perfect, cloudless sky. But Caitlin looked cold.

Or was she sad?

"Hey, Powell!"

Hearing his name, he sauntered back to his buddies. He couldn't afford to be distracted, by Caitlin or anyone. His upcoming ride was too important. He'd made it this far, paying the price in pain and sweat, and refused to screw up.

"You drew a mean one."

Micky's comment prompted Ethan to reevaluate Batteries Included, the bronc he was about to take for a spin. He'd helped train the big, rangy black, one of Clay's first purchases when he'd started his rodeo stock business, and knew to expect the unexpected. Batteries Included possessed enough bucking power to give a cowboy a championship ride, if he could stay in the saddle. Most who rode the horse ended up in a pile on the arena floor.

Ethan didn't plan on joining their ranks.

"You ready?" Micky asked.

There was a lot that could be read into the question. Was he ready to make a fool of himself in front of a huge crowd? Or was he ready to show everyone he still had what it took to compete professionally, even if he couldn't enter Professional Rodeo Cowboys Association–sanctioned rodeos?

Micky could also be wondering something as simple as whether or not Ethan had his nerves under control.

The answer to that last question was no. He hadn't been this jittery since he was fourteen and competing in his first junior rodeo. He'd fared poorly, getting bucked off in every event. He'd also learned many valuable lessons that stayed with him even today.

"I'm ready," he said, nodding confidently. "Ready to beat the two of you and look damn good doing it."

The three men chuckled.

Letting loose took a little of the edge off his tension and, oddly enough, helped him concentrate.

They moved from the stock pens to the chutes, where they discussed in detail the competitors going before them. Micky straddled the top railing, worming his way between a pair of cousins from Tucson, while Ethan stood beside T.J., his left leg braced on the bottom railing. He could climb the fence, and would have, were he not competing shortly. No point putting unnecessary strain on his prosthesis.

A dozen men were ahead of him, allowing him time to wait. To think. To stress. To envision the worst... and the best.

All day long he'd glimpsed people staring at him, wearing he-must-be-crazy expressions. Who entered rodeo jackpots with a missing leg?

Half a leg, Ethan corrected.

What was the difference? Half or whole, he was still handicapped.

God, he hated that word, and refused to let it define him.

He searched the audience until he found his family. Gavin, their dad, his niece Cassie, Sage and her daughter, Isa. He didn't want to disappoint them. His brother and father especially. He owed them an eight-second ride if for nothing other than the unconditional support they'd given him since his accident.

Not far from his family, Caitlin sat in the front row. So she was going to watch him compete. He hadn't been sure despite the hug. Gladness filled him, and he felt his mouth break in a wide smile. If she was able to conquer her fears enough to sit through his ride, then maybe they stood a chance. Their gazes connected across the distance and held, convincing Ethan she shared his optimism for their future.

Thirty minutes later, another ten contestants had gone. Ethan liked being one of the last, as it gave him the opportunity to analyze the competition and determine what he needed to do in order to beat their scores. Contestants in jackpots were often weekend enthusiasts and not at the same experience level as those competing professionally.

On the other hand, there was always one or two serious contenders. Ethan studied them the closest.

"Powell, on deck!"

Ethan moved into place beside the chute where Batteries Included waited. As he climbed the fence, the horse twisted and snorted, the whites of his inky-black eyes showing. Ethan swung his good leg over the top rung. The horse kicked out with his front hoof. The clang of iron shoe against metal railing rang out like a challenge, one Ethan accepted.

Muscles clenched, nerves strung tight, he lowered himself onto the bronc's back. Placing his feet in the stirrups, he pointed his toes. Next, he checked the reins and tugged the brim of his hat low over his eyes. When he was satisfied, he whispered a silent prayer to his mother.

One last shift in the saddle, and he uttered the word that could possibly give him back the life he'd lost.

"Go!"

The gate opened. Batteries Included charged into the

arena, his powerful body rocking forward and backward with enough strength to jar Ethan's teeth loose.

Acting on pure instinct, he marked the horse. Hand raised over his head, he leaned back in the saddle and found his rhythm.

Time slowed. He heard the roar of air rushing into his expanding lungs, the creak of leather stretching and bending, his bones grinding together, someone hollering his name. He slipped once, righted himself and dug his heels into the horse above the shoulders, urging him to buck higher and harder.

From nowhere, the buzzer sounded.

Ethan's heart exploded. He'd done it!

The pickup men materialized beside him. With a strong arm, the nearest one hauled Ethan out of the saddle and deposited him on the ground. The crowd applauded. Ethan readjusted his hat, dusted off his jeans and began striding across the arena to the gate, his glance repeatedly darting to the scoreboard. Finally, the numbers changed and the announcer's voice blared from the speakers.

"That'll be an 83 for Ethan Powell."

Applause followed. Not wild applause. Ethan had done well enough, though he wouldn't place in the top three. Possibly the top six if he was very, very lucky. Still, it was a decent score for a man with a prosthesis.

Stop thinking like that!

"Good ride." Micky sidled up beside him.

"Not bad."

"You've done worse."

He had. In professional rodeos before he'd enlisted. He'd also done better. A lot better.

"You going to try bull riding again?"

"Probably not." Ethan knew his limits.

"Bareback?"

He'd considered it. Without stirrups he might have even more trouble maintaining his balance. Then again, he might have less. "Soon, I'm thinking."

"Glad to hear it." Micky left to join the other bull riders.

Ethan's buddies congratulated him as he made his way to the pens. Like Micky, they didn't go overboard with their praise. He'd finished, and that was worth acknowledging. Not, he'd finished, and that was an unbelievable accomplishment.

He liked being treated the same as anyone else.

His enjoyment was cut short when the audience gasped loudly. A young man lay prone on the ground. While the pickup men went after the loose horse, wranglers streamed into the arena, surrounding the fallen rider.

The next instant, Caitlin was running pell-mell across the arena, her shoes sinking into the soft dirt. She pushed her way through the wranglers and dropped to the ground, examining the man with expert hands. Not long after, she assisted him to a sitting position, then to his feet. Cheers rose as he limped toward the gate, Caitlin holding his elbow on one side and a wrangler on the other. The announcer wished him well and promised the audience an update on his condition before the jackpot was over.

Returning to work after that was hard for Ethan. He kept thinking about the young man as he supervised the transfer of stock from pens to chutes. News soon spread that the rider had sprained his back. Ethan could easily imagine Caitlin recommending the young man see his regular doctor, and him insisting he was all right. Just as Ethan had done.

He was glad the rider had sprained rather than broken his back. Not only because the injury was less severe. If he'd been driven to the hospital in an ambulance, there would be no convincing Caitlin bronc riding was only moderately dangerous.

Yeah, moderately.

Why was he trying so hard to sway her when she'd insisted there was no chance in hell they'd resume their relationship?

But there had been that hug before he'd competed, and the one at Thanksgiving.

No matter how much she denied it, she liked him. Possibly even loved him, deep down.

He couldn't give up on them.

Two hours later, the Duvall Rodeo Arena's first jackpot came to a close. A brief ceremony followed, and the top three contestants for each event received their belt buckles and winnings. Ethan applauded along with everyone else. He'd rather have been part of the ceremony with Micky and the others.

Soon, he assured himself.

He hung around as long as possible, supervising the wranglers as they returned the remaining livestock to the paddocks and pastures. Every now and then his gaze wandered to the first-aid station. When he saw Caitlin loading up her minivan, he made an excuse to the men and hurried over.

"Need help carrying anything?"

She spun around, nearly dropping the tower of plastic bins in her arms. "Thanks. I've got it."

Not the warm welcome he'd been anticipating after their hug.

"Did you see my ride?" Stupid question. She'd been watching from the bleachers.

"I did." She loaded the plastic bins into her van. "Congratulations. You must be pleased."

"I am."

"Are you celebrating tonight?"

"Hadn't thought of it." He immediately warmed to the idea. "You free? We could have dinner."

She exhaled wearily. "It's been a long day, and I'm exhausted. I'm sure you are, too."

Not really. If anything, he was energized. Had been since his ride.

"Sure. No problem." He hesitated, searching for a reason to stay. "When are you coming out to the ranch next?"

"I'm glad you asked." She brightened, noticeably relieved at the change of topic. "Next Saturday, if that's okay with you."

"Great."

"Any chance we can take the wagon to the park for a test drive? I'd like to experiment with a couple different routes. See which one works best."

"Call me."

No dinner. And a full week before he saw her again. No physical-therapy sessions, either.

So far, this plan he had with Justin to go after his sister was a complete and total bust.

"Good night, Ethan. Congratulations again." She got in her van and left.

As he walked back to the holding pens for a final inspection, he decided he didn't much like being treated the same as every other guy out there.

He much preferred to be special, after all, at least where Caitlin Carmichael was concerned.

Chapter Ten

Caitlin waited at the entrance to the park, shielding her eyes from the brilliant morning sun. She could just make out the wagon with its team of two horses plodding along Mustang Valley's main road at a gentle pace. Vehicles going in both directions slowed at the unusual procession, their drivers used to yielding the right-of-way to horses.

The wagon carried two passengers besides Ethan. Cassie and Isa sat with him on the bench seat, their excited chatter reaching Caitlin's ears from a half block away. Musical tones blended with the girls' voices, and it took Caitlin a moment to recognize the source.

Jingle bells hanging from the harnesses! Ethan must have added them after Caitlin and her crew had finished decorating.

How nice of him.

Guilt needled her with pointy barbs. For the past week, ever since the rodeo jackpot, she'd purposefully avoided Ethan, speaking to him only once midweek to firm up their plans to drive the wagon route before the Holly Days Festival. Evidently he'd gotten her message loud and clear, because he hadn't attempted to contact her, either.

Caitlin should be relieved. Happy, even. Instead, she

jumped every time her cell phone rang or the clinic buzzer heralded the arrival of a patient.

This morning was no exception. Her insides fluttered annoyingly at the sight of Ethan's broad shoulders and tall physique, and her palms leaked perspiration.

She wiped them on her jeans, then waved. Only the girls returned her greeting. Was Ethan angry with her for turning down his dinner invitation? As the wagon drew nearer, she noticed Gavin sitting in the bed on a bale of hay and holding on to the sidewall.

Good. More passengers. She'd been a wreck for days, uncertain how she would handle being alone with Ethan. As it turned out, her obsessing had been a complete waste of time.

The horses' clip-clopping hooves on the pavement, the girls' lively chatter and the ringing of jingle bells combined to create a merry cacophony. Caitlin stepped out from her spot beneath an ironwood tree as Ethan expertly turned the horses into the park entrance.

"Whoa, there!" He pulled back on the long reins, and the wagon came to a creaky stop.

Caitlin walked over and gasped softly. "The lights are on!" She hadn't noticed their multicolored flickering in the bright sunlight.

"We're testing the electrical system." Gavin climbed out of the wagon bed, using the rear wheel spokes like a ladder to reach the ground.

Vehicles continued to pass them in a slow procession, the drivers honking or waving. A pickup truck didn't drive past but parked behind the wagon. Caitlin recognized the woman at the wheel. Sage must have followed to prevent potential tailgaters from creeping too close.

The truck door opened and she emerged. "Morning, Caitlin!"

"How are you?"

The two women met up near the wagon. Caitlin liked Gavin's fiancée and their daughters. Another time and place, she and Sage might have become good friends.

Why not now? a voice inside her asked. *Surely not because of Ethan.*

Avoiding Ethan's family on the off chance he might show up did seem ridiculous. What was the worst that could happen?

Plenty. One smoky glance from him, one caress of his lips on her skin, and she'd be all over him.

Not going to happen, and four co-passengers were the perfect deterrent.

"Come on, girls," Gavin said, climbing out of the wagon. "Let's get a move on."

"You're leaving?"

Caitlin wasn't the only one protesting.

"Aw, Dad, please. Can't we stay with Uncle Ethan?"

Yes, can't they stay?

"We have an appointment," Sage reminded them in a motherly voice. She pulled Caitlin to her for a quick hug. "Maybe after the holidays we can meet for coffee or lunch."

"That would be nice," she mumbled, releasing Sage reluctantly.

The girls continued to whine.

"Tomorrow afternoon I'll take the two of you for another ride," Ethan said. "How's that?"

"Really?" Isa clapped her hands.

"Will you teach me to drive?" Cassie asked.

"Yes and yes."

He helped the girls down off the wagon seat into Gavin's outstretched arms, Isa first, then Cassie. They both kissed Ethan's cheek before being lowered, their slim, girlish arms circling his neck.

"Thanks, Uncle Ethan."

"I love you, Uncle Ethan."

"Love you, too, kiddos."

Watching them, Caitlin felt her racing heart slow, then turn to mush. He was incredibly good with the girls, and they seemed to adore him. It had never occurred to her what a terrific father he'd make.

"All aboard!" Gavin beckoned her to the front of the wagon.

"Me?"

"You are riding with Ethan, aren't you?"

She pasted a brave smile on her face. "I am."

"Well, let's do it. Unless you can climb into this wagon by yourself."

Caitlin might be taller than the girls, but she wasn't nearly as nimble. She needed help. Mentally measuring the distance from the ground to the wagon seat, she decided she might need wings.

The footrest was on the same level as her chest. No way could she lift her leg that high.

"Are you kidding me?" She gaped at Gavin.

"Right foot here." He patted one of the wheel spokes. "Left foot here." He tapped the footrest. "Then swing yourself up into the seat."

He made it sound so easy.

The horses chose that moment to shift restlessly, causing the wagon to rock.

Caitlin instinctively drew back. "I can't."

"You'll be fine," Ethan said. "The brake's on."

She wavered, angry at herself. She'd done this before. Granted, that was years ago, when she'd have walked through fire to be with Ethan.

"Okay, okay." She lifted her foot as instructed and placed it on the wheel spoke. Then nothing. Gravity had a hold on her and wouldn't let go.

"Here."

She glanced at Ethan. He'd placed the reins in his left hand and was holding his right one out to her. It was large and strong and appeared more than capable of hauling her safely up into the seat.

"Hang on." Gavin gave her a boost.

She rose up, her left foot automatically seeking purchase. Before she quite knew what was happening, Ethan caught her by the forearm and yanked. Her world tilted crazily. Then she was seated beside him, and everything returned to its proper place.

It had been like that before, when they were young. He had only to touch her, hold her, and all was right once more.

"It's high up here." Higher than she remembered. Her fingers gripped the thin and unreassuring metal armrest. "No seat belts, huh?" She laughed nervously.

"I don't remember you being so afraid of horses."

She hadn't been, only since Justin's accident. She hadn't been afraid of fast cars, roller coasters, bungee jumping or heights before then, either.

"I haven't ridden for years."

"We should go one day. Get you used to horses again."

"Get me used to the wagon first. Then we'll see about horses."

"One step at a time." Before she could wonder if he was really talking about them, he said, "Molly and Dolly are the two calmest horses on the ranch next to Chico. I wouldn't take you or anyone for a drive if I thought for one second we'd have a runaway."

Runaway! Why had he mentioned that? "How reliable is that brake?"

She immediately imagined the horses galloping hellbent for election through the park like in those old black-and-white Westerns she used to watch as a kid.

As it turned out, she'd panicked for nothing. The horses, under Ethan's careful guidance, traveled along at a sedate walk. After several minutes, Caitlin started breathing again. Before long, she relaxed enough to appreciate the advantages her elevated position offered. She had a clear view of the workers erecting the miniature Santa's workshop and the obedience trials under way in the dog park across the expansive green. In the far distance, Pinnacle Peak, with its distinctive silhouette, reached skyward as if to capture the sun.

"How beautiful."

Ethan smiled, and they drove for a while in companionable silence.

Eventually, Caitlin pulled a map of the park from her pocket. "I figured we'd have the wagon pickup and drop-off station near the picnic area, next to the Santa's workshop."

He grunted approvingly.

"We could set up a table here—" she tapped the map "—and take donations for the mustang sanctuary. Pass out literature if you have any."

He grunted again.

"Do you think Cassie would be willing to dress in an elf costume and be one of Santa's helpers?"

"Probably."

When he said no more, Caitlin continued examining the map and the routes she'd sketched out. "What do you think about this one?" She angled the map for him to see.

He grumbled instead of grunting.

Fine. He was keeping conversation to a minimum. That suited her, as well. Folding the map, she returned it to her pocket, sat back and kept quiet.

For two full minutes.

"Did I do something to upset you?"

"Not at all."

"I'm sorry about refusing your dinner invitation last Saturday. I figured it was better if we—"

"You're not going to give me the let's-be-friends speech, are you?"

Her cheeks burned. That was exactly what she'd been planning. "No. Don't be ridiculous."

"Because I won't be friends with you."

That stung.

"I want more."

"More?" Her voice sounded small.

"Much more."

Oh, dear.

"Look at me, Caitlin."

She did, tensing as his smoldering gaze raked over her.

"Don't expect me to make small talk with you when what I really want is to make love."

"I'm sorry." Caitlin sucked in air, then released it in a shuddering breath.

"Don't be. I'm not propositioning you, simply stating a fact."

She and Ethan were no strangers to intimacy. They had been each other's firsts, consummating their love shortly after high school graduation. The night had been one of the scariest of her life, and the most memorable. Scary for Ethan, too. Revealing his true feelings had endeared him to her and broken down the last of her defenses. When she gave herself to him, it was without reservation and without regrets.

Magic had happened that night and for many nights afterward. Making love with Ethan had been extraordinary. Fulfilling, satisfying and fun. But physical pleasure—and there had been a lot of it—was never more important than their emotional connection, which only grew stronger the longer they were together.

Yet another reason why his abrupt enlistment in the marines had devastated her. How could he have loved her so completely and so thoroughly and then abandoned her like that?

The horses plodded along the side street circling the park, the sleigh bells chiming in rhythm to the cadence of their hooves.

Seconds ticked by, then minutes.

"Was there anybody after me?" Caitlin was shocked at her own audacity.

Ethan answered without pause. "I dated some in the marines."

"No one special?"

"No one I fell in love with." He clucked to Molly and Dolly, who had stopped at the sight of an elderly couple walking a shaggy terrier.

"What about since your discharge?"

"Haven't had the time."

Was that true? Or did the loss of his leg have something to do with it?

Justin had been painfully shy around girls as a teenager, frequently becoming tongue-tied. After his accident, he'd refused to even be alone in the same room with someone of the opposite sex.

Not anymore, Caitlin mused, remembering him and Tamiko together.

When had Justin changed? And what had prompted it?

"How about you?" Ethan's sidelong glance gave nothing away. "Date much?"

"Not hardly at all until after college. Caring for Justin took up most of my free time. And then there was homework and work-study programs. I met someone a few years ago."

"Tell me about him."

He wasn't you. The thought came from nowhere and traveled straight to her chest, where it curled around her heart.

Caitlin averted her head to hide the tears that sprang unbidden to her eyes.

"We went out for about two years," she said when she'd composed herself. "Then it just kind of fizzled. No big fight. No drama. We parted friends."

"Too bad."

What she didn't tell Ethan was that her boyfriend had wanted to marry her, and had repeatedly proposed. Caitlin couldn't bring herself to take the next step—because of Ethan or Justin or both, she really wasn't sure. Eventually, her boyfriend grew tired of waiting. There'd been no one since, not even a casual date. Which also meant that Ethan's kiss at the rodeo arena was her first one in years.

"I thought maybe we'd have the wagon rides on Friday and Saturday nights only," she said. "From six to nine." The small talk sounded trite after such a personal conversation. "Is that too long? I don't want to tire the horses."

"I'll have two teams. One for each night."

"Will you take the other team out for a test run, too?"

"Tomorrow. With the girls. Want to come along?" He studied her face intently.

Were there tearstains on her cheeks? She instinctively touched them. Dry, thank goodness.

"I, um, promised Mom I'd go Christmas shopping with her."

If she didn't already have a legitimate excuse, she would have manufactured one. Her resistance to him was at an all-time low. It would be so easy to say she didn't care about his bronc riding, scoot closer and rest her head on his shoulder.

"You having Christmas Day at your place?" he asked.

"Oh, gosh, no!"

"Condo too small?"

"That, and too empty."

"Still moving in?"

"I've been waiting to see if I'm…" *staying in Mustang Valley* "…keeping the condo. I don't have one Christmas decoration up or one card displayed. Mom and Dad are having dinner at their house. My aunt and uncle and cousin are driving up from Green Valley. Some friends from Dad's work will also be there."

"You'll have fun."

"Is Sierra coming home?"

"She hasn't committed one way or the other." Ethan absently clucked to the horses. "I don't know what's with her lately. She's cut herself off from the family almost completely. Dad's pretty upset."

"Is it a man?"

"I hadn't thought of that."

"Getting involved in a relationship is one reason people ignore their families and friends."

"Why wouldn't she tell us?"

"Maybe she's afraid you won't approve of him."

Ethan stared at the road, his jaw working.

"I'm not saying it's a man. Could be anything."

"It makes sense, though."

Caitlin left Ethan to his thoughts, concentrating instead on her own. When they rounded the last bend on the route, the towering Christmas tree the Holly Days committee had erected in the center of the park came into view. Caitlin felt a sentimental tug on her heartstrings. This was her favorite season.

"If you could have just one wish for Christmas," she asked, "what would it be?"

Ethan didn't immediately answer. She assumed he was thinking of Sierra and his bronc riding. Of his desire to compete professionally. His job training horses. Her, and his desire for them to get back together.

"That was a silly question," she blurted when the silence stretched. "You don't have to answer it."

"What I'd want most of all is for things to go back the way they were. Before my mother got sick and we were still raising cattle."

Ten years ago she and Ethan had been planning a wedding in the not-too-distant future. Ten years ago, he had yet to enlist.

"But that isn't possible." He shook the reins. If the horses were supposed to walk faster, they didn't pay attention. "So, I guess I'd wish for the riding stables to do well and Gavin's stud and breeding business to take off. He's trying hard to preserve what little we have left in order to pass it down to his children."

A noble, selfless wish. "What about you, Ethan? What do *you* want?"

He turned his head, the ghost of a smile lighting his lips. "For us, you and me, to be happy. And I don't mean together, necessarily," he added, as if anticipating her objection.

No?

Neither of them had been happy apart.

"I'd like that, too," she said softly, realizing it was her Christmas wish, as well.

ETHAN WALKED THE PERIMETER of the last stall in the nearly completed mare motel. "Looking good."

"I agree." Gavin nodded approvingly.

The crew had finished hanging the twenty-four stall doors an hour earlier, shortly after Ethan returned home from his ride with Caitlin. While there was a long punch list needing completion, and minor modifications here and there, the mare motel was operational and ready for "guests."

"If I hadn't seen it myself," Clay said, his deep voice resonating with awe and admiration, "I wouldn't have believed this was once a cattle barn."

Indeed, the transformation was nothing short of amazing. Ethan could hardly remember what the barn had looked like in "the old days," as his niece was fond of saying—the remark accompanied by an eye roll.

A wave of nostalgia overcame him, bringing with it memory after memory. He, Gavin and Conner had spent considerable time in this cattle barn while growing up. Working, not playing. Wayne Powell had been a taskmaster, requiring his sons to give one-hundred-and-ten percent. They hadn't really appreciated his strict work ethic until they were adults.

Clay had worked alongside them on occasion, when he wasn't busy with his father's cattle operation. Back then, the future had seemed both certain and endless. Gavin would take over the family business. Ethan would run it with him, after winning a world championship at the National Rodeo Finals. And Sierra would marry a local boy—Conner, possibly—and move to a house just down the road. The three siblings would produce a passel of rascally children to try their parents and entertain their grandparents.

It hadn't turned out that way. All things considered, their lives weren't so bad.

"Mom would be proud," Ethan mused out loud as he, Gavin and Clay strode down the bright and airy aisle.

"She would," Gavin agreed.

Clay smiled fondly. "When is Camelot Farms arriving with their mares?"

The farm's half-Arabian, half-quarter-horse animals would be the first to reside in the mare motel.

"In the morning," Gavin answered.

"How many are they bringing?"

"Just two."

Gavin hoped to keep all twenty-four stalls filled. Unfortunately, a stud and breeding business took months, if not years, to establish. Prince had proved himself capable of impregnating mares, as a recent veterinarian exam had confirmed. But it wasn't enough. His foals had to be born healthy, inherit their sire's best qualities, then grow into fine horses. Only then would customers beat down the Powells' door.

Patience was required, and Gavin's was in short supply.

Even now, as he stared at the cooling fans suspended from the barn ceiling, he seemed distracted. More than once Ethan or Clay had to repeat themselves because Gavin wasn't listening.

"Anything in the bunkhouse the men need to finish before I send them home?" Clay asked.

"Nope." Like the cattle barn, Ethan's bunkhouse barely resembled its former incarnation. During the past two weeks, the workers had pushed hard. "They finished constructing the built-in bookcases yesterday."

"You buy an automatic coffeemaker yet?"

"Very funny." He had bought one, but he wasn't about to tell Clay. The bunkhouse, now an apartment, suited him fine without making accommodations for anyone.

Except for Caitlin.

He'd be willing to change his bachelor ways, and pad, for her. Make concessions. Alter his habits. Compromise.

He wasn't willing to give up bronc riding and breaking green horses.

Until then, there was no point even imagining sharing living quarters with her.

"Gavin," Clay said. "Gavin!"

Ethan jerked. His brother wasn't the only one who was distracted.

"Yeah." Gavin blinked as if orienting himself. "What?"

"I asked where the backup generator is located."

"Nowhere for now. We need to decide, and hook it up."

"You okay?"

"Fine." Gavin grinned stupidly.

"You're not acting fine."

"I'm preoccupied." His stupid grin grew even wider.

Ethan couldn't recall seeing his brother act like that, other than the day he'd proposed to Sage. "Is there something you're not telling us?"

"No." Gavin shook his head, then laughed. "Yes."

"Which is it?"

"I'm not supposed to say anything."

"Sage is bred," Clay uttered bluntly.

Leave it to a cattleman to use animal vernacular when describing a pregnancy.

"Is she?" Ethan felt his own mouth stretch into a smile.

"She took the home pregnancy test this morning. We'd planned on waiting before having a baby. A year at least."

"Congratulations." Ethan pumped his brother's hand, then captured him in a headlock. "Dad's going to be thrilled."

"Don't say anything," Gavin warned, after enduring a suffocating hug from Clay. "I promised Sage. She wants to wait until she sees the doctor."

"Let's celebrate," Clay suggested. "Lunch at the Rusty Nail. My treat."

The local saloon and grill had been one of their favorite hangouts in years past.

"I'm in."

"Call Conner. Maybe he can cut loose from work and join us."

An hour later, the four friends were seated at a table, having beer with their hamburgers and reminiscing about their high school years and all the trouble they'd managed to get into.

Gavin didn't stop smiling, except when he talked about Sage or Cassie. Then his expression grew soft and his voice low. Ethan was truly happy for his brother. He was also jealous and wouldn't mind having a little happiness for himself.

With Caitlin.

Ethan couldn't see himself loving and living with any

other woman but her, which explained why he'd dated only occasionally since they'd broken up.

Caitlin wasn't his better half, she was his *other* half. The piece of him that had been missing for years.

Maybe he should consider quitting busting broncs. After the jackpot last week, everyone knew he could still ride with the big boys.

He toyed with the idea of giving up his lifelong dream, and to his shock and alarm, it no longer frightened the hell out of him.

Chapter Eleven

Caitlin stood in line behind a dad and his pair of pre-schoolers. The girl, the older of the two, wriggled excitedly and chattered incessantly. The boy wore a solemn expression and chewed nervously on the tip of his mitten.

"Look at the horses!" The girl grasped her brother by the shoulders and shook him. "Real horses."

Caitlin decided the family must not be from Mustang Valley. Most of the residents owned horses, had neighbors with horses or rented them at the Powells' stables. They wouldn't get that excited over the prospect of seeing "real" ones. As she glanced around, it occurred to her there were quite a number of unfamiliar faces at the Holly Days Festival. Articles in the local newspapers and advertisements on radio stations must have attracted people from all over the Phoenix metropolitan area.

A moment later, the man finished his transaction with Sage. "Come on, kids," he said.

The girl skipped alongside him as they headed to the decorated wagon. The boy lagged behind. Caitlin was convinced he would be as enthused as his sister by the time they returned from their ride. She didn't see how much money the dad had given Sage as a donation, but her cheery, "Thank you so much and Merry Christmas," led Caitlin to believe the amount was generous.

"How's business?" she asked, stepping up to the folding table that was serving as a ticket counter. Tamiko had painted a large poster advertising the wagon rides and the mustang sanctuary, and had taped it to the front of the table.

"Couldn't be better!" Sage gushed. "Most people are giving more than what we're asking for the tickets."

"I'm so glad."

"This was a fantastic idea you had. I can't thank you enough for getting the committee to agree."

"We couldn't have done it without Ethan and his family." Caitlin glanced over at him. Ethan sat in the wagon with his back to her, but they'd exchanged looks often during the evening, each one giving her a small tingle. "The festival is everything we had hoped it would be, and they're a big reason why."

During the past week, the stately pine tree in the center of the park had been decorated with silver and gold ornaments and candy canes. The white lights strung through its boughs flickered merrily. Santa's workshop, complete with artificial snow, a replica North Pole and a life-size Rudolph the Red-nosed Reindeer, had been erected across from the tree. Santa sat on a makeshift throne, his pudgy belly hanging over his belt, his white beard covering his chest. The line of children waiting to have their pictures taken with him extended clear to the back of the workshop.

Cassie and Isa, dressed in elf costumes, complete with fake pointed ears, assisted Mrs. Claus with crowd control.

"I still can't believe how many people are here." Caitlin stepped aside to let another customer purchase tickets from Sage.

"There'll be a lot more tomorrow night, I bet."

The festival was scheduled for a full three days, as long as the weather held, which the forecasts predicted it would. Friday night, all day Saturday, and Sunday till four.

Caitlin couldn't be more pleased with the attendance and the positive feedback she'd been receiving. The hard work of the various committee members and crews of energetic volunteers was paying off.

"Excuse me." A woman leaned around Caitlin. "Four tickets, please."

"This wagon is full," Sage apologized with a bright smile. "You'll have to wait for the next ride, in about half an hour."

"How's Ethan holding up?" Caitlin asked Sage when the woman left, tickets for the next ride clutched in her gloved fist.

"You haven't talked to him tonight?"

"Not yet."

Caitlin didn't admit she'd seen him only once since the previous weekend, when he'd taken her for a drive in the wagon, and that was for a PT session. Nor did she admit how much he'd been on her mind. It seemed for a while there they'd been seeing each other every few days. Lately, hardly at all.

She missed him.

A small part of her wondered if she'd acted too hastily when she'd told him there was no chance for a reconciliation.

"He's fine," Sage said. "Though I bet he'll be exhausted by tomorrow night. Driving a wagon is more tiring than you might think, and it takes hours and hours to get ready. He's been at it since noon. Grooming the horses. Cleaning the harnesses. He even washed and ironed his shirt." She winked at Caitlin. "I like a man who does his own laundry."

"Is his shoulder holding up?"

"He hasn't complained."

"He wouldn't."

"You're right about that. He's still doing his exercises, or so he says."

"That's good."

"Where'd all the customers go?" Sage glanced around. "Oh, well." She used the lull to transfer money from the cash box to a press-and-seal plastic bag. "If I give you my keys, would you mind running this to my truck for me? It's in the parking lot. I don't like sitting here with all this cash."

"Glad to," Caitlin said. The stack of bills Sage stuffed in the bag, mostly small denominations, was three inches thick. "Wow, that is a lot of money."

"I'm hoping by the end of the weekend we'll have enough collected to bring two mustangs down from the Bureau of Land Management facility in Show Low. Our first foster horses for the sanctuary."

"Are they injured?" Caitlin tucked the bag of money inside her jacket and out of sight.

"Only superficial wounds sustained during the roundup."

Caitlin really didn't have a reason to stick around talking to Sage, other than she enjoyed the company. She just couldn't bring herself to leave while the wagon was still parked at the corner.

While Ethan was nearby.

As she watched, he clucked to Molly and Dolly and

set out amid whoops and cheers from his passengers, the sleigh bells jingling and the lights blinking.

Caitlin attempted a smile, but her mouth wouldn't cooperate.

What was wrong with her?

Sage paid no attention and continued prattling on about the foster mustangs.

"These two horses are what the BLM considers unadoptable. Even with a reduced price of twenty-five dollars each, no one would purchase them."

"Why? Are they mean?"

"No, just wild and not adapting to confinement. But they're so beautiful and spirited. I'm convinced, with the right training, they can make really nice horses for someone. Ethan's skills will be tested for sure."

"He'll train them?"

Of course he would, Caitlin thought, answering her own question. He broke rodeo stock for Clay and green horses for the Powells' clients.

"He did a fantastic job with Prince," Sage declared. "You won't believe how well that horse is doing. You should come out to the ranch and see him."

"Prince wasn't unadoptable."

"He was wild," Sage explained. "Living in the mountains. You can't get much more unadoptable than that."

"If these mustangs aren't adapting, are you sure it's safe for Ethan to try and train them?"

"As if I could keep him away."

As if anyone could. Certainly not Caitlin.

...when what I really want to do is make love to you.

How often had she heard him say that in her head this past week?

What would it be like making love with him now?

she wondered. Different from when they were younger, certainly. They weren't the same people anymore.

Discovering the changes would be interesting. Exciting. Thrilling.

Enough was enough. She wasn't getting back together with Ethan, and she definitely wasn't going to have sex with him.

She patted the bank bag inside her jacket. "I'll put this in your truck and be right back."

"No hurry."

While Caitlin was crossing the parking lot, she glimpsed the wagon with its multicolored lights and excited passengers. It was a charming sight, one straight off the front of a Christmas card.

Ethan really was working his tail off for the committee.

For *her*.

She should do something for him, she decided. A token of appreciation.

Nothing personal. It wasn't as if she was trying to bridge the distance that had developed between them.

When she returned to the table, Clay was there. Caitlin arrived just as he was pulling Sage out of her chair and into his arms.

"Congratulations," he boomed.

She laughed and pushed him away. "Who told you?"

"Who do you think?"

"What's going on?" Caitlin asked, her interest piqued.

"Nothing." Sage took the keys from Caitlin's outstretched hand, her cheeks flushed a deep crimson and her eyes sparkling.

"Come on. Something's up. Tell me."

"Tell her," Clay coaxed. "You know you want to."

Sage sighed. "I was going to make an appointment

at the clinic next week, so I suppose you'd have found out eventually."

"You're pregnant!" Caitlin guessed.

"Not so loud." Sage placed a finger to her lips. "I haven't told Isa yet."

"I'm so happy for you!" Caitlin reached across the table and clasped Sage's hands in hers.

"We were going to wait. It was an accident."

"The best kind of accident."

They didn't have much time to talk because a large group of Red Hat ladies descended upon them. Clay convinced the women to add another ten dollars to their donation.

When they left, Sage asked him, "How's that cowboy who got hurt?"

"Better."

Caitlin stilled. "Who got hurt?"

"Micky Lannon," Clay said.

"Micky?" The father of the little girl with the cut knee. "What happened?" she demanded.

"He got bucked off last night."

"From a horse?"

"A bull." Clay and Caitlin continued their conversation while Sage passed out flyers. "Broke his leg in three places. They had to operate this morning, insert some pins. I just came from the hospital. He's going to be released tomorrow."

"Poor guy." Caitlin pressed her hands to her cheeks. "How's his wife holding up?"

"All right, I think."

"What about his job?"

"He's taking a medical leave of absence. Six to eight weeks."

Caitlin wished she had been there to help. Unfortunately, Clay had hired her only for jackpots and rodeo events, not regular practices. There probably wasn't much she could have done anyway. Not with a break that severe.

"What about health insurance?"

"He has it."

Even with coverage, there would be costs. Hefty costs. And he'd be out of work almost two months, which would put a strain on his family and finances. He should have thought of that before climbing on a bull.

"The men are taking up a collection for him. Didn't Ethan tell you?"

Why did everyone think she and Ethan spoke on a regular basis?

"No. I haven't seen him recently." Even if she had, she doubted he'd have mentioned Micky's fall, knowing how upset she'd get.

"Can I interest you two lovely ladies in a hot chocolate?" Clay asked.

"Mmm." Sage rubbed her palms together. "Yes, please. It's getting chilly."

Caitlin was so engrossed in her thoughts she barely noticed Clay leaving.

Her mind raced. It could have easily been Ethan in the hospital, recovering from a serious surgery. Her chest constricted at the image of him lying with his leg—his one good leg—elevated in a fiberglass cast.

She couldn't bear it if he was hurt like that.

A moan of distress involuntarily escaped her lips.

"Caitlin? You okay?"

She looked over to discover Sage staring at her, a curious expression on her face.

"YOU'RE HERE!" CAITLIN hurried over to Justin and her parents. She'd spotted them in the parking lot while making yet another money run to Sage's truck. "I wasn't sure you'd make it."

"Sorry, I got stuck at the office." Her dad slung his arms around Caitlin and her mother. "How soon till the festival closes?"

"Nine."

He whistled. "Doesn't give us much time."

The lateness of the hour and the dropping temperature had no effect on the crowd. People were still arriving in droves.

"Is Tamiko here?" Justin asked, wheeling along beside Caitlin.

That didn't take long.

"Yes. But so is what's-his-name."

What *was* his name? Eric, right?

The presence of Tamiko's boyfriend didn't appear to deter Justin. "Hook up with you later," he said, and was gone.

"Who is this Tamiko?" Caitlin's mother asked in a concerned tone. "He hasn't mentioned her before."

"One of my volunteers. They met at the ranch when we were decorating the wagon."

Typical father, her dad asked, "Is she pretty?"

Typical mother, her mom asked, "Is she nice?"

"Both." Caitlin laughed. "And she likes Justin."

There was just the matter of that pesky boyfriend.

The three of them strolled to the festival grounds. Caitlin often marveled at how easily her parents had adjusted to her brother's loss of mobility and independent lifestyle. Sure, they had worried when he was first injured. And periodically in the years since, especially when he moved away from home and into his own apartment. But never for long, it seemed.

Caitlin was the one who fretted. The one who couldn't cut the apron strings.

Then again, she was the one consumed with guilt over Justin's paralysis. How could her parents, knowing the part she'd played, love her as they did, forgive her as they had?

Justin, too.

Her mother stopped to take everything in. "Are the wagon rides still going on?"

"There's one more at least, maybe two."

"We'd better hurry and buy our tickets." She was off, leaving Caitlin and her father in the dust.

When they reached the table, Caitlin's dad purchased the last two tickets and gave a very large donation that had Sage practically in tears. "Thank you, Mr. Carmichael. Mrs. Carmichael. Can I add you to our list of newsletter subscribers?"

Caitlin could tell one more foster mustang would be arriving from Show Low.

"Too bad Justin's going to miss out," Caitlin's mother mused. "He'd enjoy the wagon ride."

"He's going," Sage said brightly. "He bought a ticket right before you."

"Wonderful."

No, it wasn't.

Apparently Caitlin was the only one who wondered how he'd get up into the wagon without a lift, and how embarrassing it might be for him with all these strangers watching.

"Doug, let's check out the craft tables while we're waiting." Her mother latched on to her husband's arm.

"Send a search party if we're not back in three days," he called to Caitlin.

"Any chance I can recruit you to help me tomorrow night?" Sage asked as they walked away.

"Sure. I was planning on being here, anyway."

Ten minutes later, the wagon returned from its run, the passengers singing Christmas carols. By the time Ethan reined the horses to a stop at the drop-off point, dozens more people milling nearby had joined in with the carolers.

Cheer spread from person to person, carried by a smile.

Caitlin felt her own mouth curve up at the corners. She had spent considerable effort and energy working on the festival. This was, however, the first moment she'd felt truly touched by the Christmas spirit.

She sought out Ethan. He must have sensed her gaze on him because he turned and looked at her...and kept looking. The warmth within her that had started with the caroling continued to build.

Ethan was responsible for this wondrous night. She'd asked for his help and, as always, he'd given it. Unconditionally. Even during the past couple weeks when she'd been avoiding him as much as possible.

She wanted to give him a gift of appreciation—and affection. And suddenly she knew just what it would be.

"We'd better hurry." Caitlin's mother carried three plastic sacks, last-minute Christmas purchases from the craft tables. "Where on earth is Justin?"

The passengers had stopped singing and were climbing down from the wagon one by one, their faces radiant. They exchanged greetings with people lining up for the next ride.

"Here he comes," Caitlin's dad said.

She saw her brother wheeling toward them. Tamiko walked beside him. They made a striking couple, Justin with his fair complexion, Tamiko with her long black hair and exotic beauty.

Not a couple, Caitlin reminded herself.

Where was her boyfriend, Eric?

"Who's this?" her mother asked when Justin and Tamiko joined them in line, even though Caitlin had already told her.

Tamiko put out her hand. "Hi. I'm Justin's friend Tamiko."

Justin's friend? Not, Caitlin thought, one of the festival volunteers.

"Nice to meet you." Caitlin's mother's eyes were bright with curiosity. "Do you attend ASU, too?"

Justin stared at Tamiko with such raw longing, Caitlin couldn't bring herself to watch them. He'd get hurt if he wasn't careful, and there was nothing she or anyone could do to prevent it.

"You coming, honey?" her father asked.

"I didn't buy a ticket."

"They won't charge you. Not with all the work you've put in."

She could always give Sage a donation tomorrow night.

And the wagon ride would be fun. "Sure, why not?"

Caitlin and her family fell into line. The wagon, with its hay bale seats, could easily accommodate ten people and two or three small children sitting on laps. Another person, usually an older child or teenager, rode shotgun next to Ethan.

While the passengers boarded, he stood, stretched and rolled his bad shoulder. It must have been an arduous day for him.

Justin wheeled to the rear of the wagon and waited

for a woman with incredibly inappropriate stilettos to be hoisted up by her husband.

Caitlin had to intervene. "Dad, are you going to help Justin?"

"If he asks me."

"Aren't you concerned how he'll get in the wagon?"

"Not as much as you are."

She grumbled to herself. They could possibly fit the wheelchair into the bed if a bale of hay was removed. That would require a pair of strong arms.

"You first," Justin told Tamiko.

"Hey, what gives?" Her boyfriend abruptly stepped in front of them. Had he been there all along? "He's not riding with us."

"Yes, he is," Tamiko answered coolly.

"I bought a ticket, dude." Justin held up an orange stub.

"Yeah? Well, news flash, *dude*. No room for your wheels."

"I'm not hooked to this chair by wires," Justin said with a chuckle.

Caitlin willed herself not to say anything. She'd interfered before, only to incur her brother's anger. He insisted on fighting his own battles.

Her parents didn't appear to be concerned. They watched their son closely but made no move in his direction.

"Come on, Tamiko." Her boyfriend snatched her hand.

"What about Justin?"

"You heard him. He's not hooked to that chair."

The other passengers had all boarded and were watching the scene unfolding before them with rabid interest.

"This is better than reality TV," one woman said.

The hell with making Justin mad. Caitlin had reached her limit. "Okay, guys—"

"Stay out of it," her father ordered.

"Dad!"

"I mean it, honey."

"I'm not leaving Justin," Tamiko said stubbornly.

"You'd pick him over me?" Eric demanded.

"We're friends. Why can't you be nice?"

"This is stupid." Caitlin took a step forward.

A large, strong hand on her arm pulled her back. She pivoted, intending to tell her father they should—

It wasn't her dad restraining her. It was Ethan.

"Let me handle this," he said, and brushed past her.

Caitlin started to follow.

"Young lady!" Her father's stern voice stopped her in her tracks. "What did I tell you? Butt out."

"Dammit," she grumbled. Why did she have to butt out and not Ethan?

He walked over to Justin. "You ready?"

"If you are."

A look of understanding passed between them.

Ethan bent down and placed one arm beneath Justin's legs and the other behind his back. He lifted her brother out of the chair and carried him the short distance to the wagon. Another man sitting on a hay bale jumped up. Without being asked, he took Justin from Ethan and gently deposited him on the nearest empty seat. The three of them worked together so smoothly, they might have done this before.

And just like that, it was over.

Caitlin's father helped her mother and then Tamiko into the wagon. Her boyfriend clambered up after her, scowling as he squeezed by Justin.

"You coming, honey?"

"Yeah, Dad."

Ethan appeared next to her. "You can sit with me if you want."

She turned to her father, but he was already halfway in the wagon. "I guess I will."

Conner sat in the seat, holding the reins, while T.J. gripped Dolly's bridle. The two cowboys had been helping Ethan with the horses all night.

Ethan climbed up first. Once he had hold of the reins, Conner jumped down. Molly and Dolly, tired after their long night, didn't so much as twitch an ear.

Ethan held out a hand to Caitlin.

She tried to remember where to place her feet. Wheel spoke left? Footrest right?

"Need help?" Conner didn't wait for an answer, and gave her a boost.

By some miracle, she made it into the seat, clumsily plopping down beside Ethan. Before she was quite settled he clucked to the horses and they were off.

She glanced over her shoulder at her brother. He appeared fine. Not the least bit self-conscious. He seemed to be enjoying himself, talking with the man who'd helped him. Smiling at Tamiko.

Such a change from the shy, geeky kid he'd been.

If Caitlin hadn't encouraged him to go to the river that day, it might have been him sitting next to Tamiko. Taking her to a dance. Walking with her down a church aisle one day.

"He's all right," Ethan said.

"I was checking on my parents."

"Liar."

She sighed. "Am I that transparent?"

"Only to those of us who know you well."

He did know her well, and she him. Which made this game they were playing—drawing toward each other, then stepping back—all the more frustrating.

"Thanks for helping Justin out."

"He's a good kid."

"Yeah, he is. And I'm sure he appreciates what you did for him." She bit her lower lip, worrying it between her teeth. "So do I," she finally admitted.

His reply was a simple, "You're welcome."

"I apologize for the mixed messages I've been sending you."

"Maybe they weren't so mixed."

Maybe they weren't.

A tiny sliver of awareness arrowed through her.

"I'm here for you, Caitlin, and I'm willing to wait. For however long it takes."

That wasn't what he'd said before. He'd left on a whim, broken her heart.

Could she trust him again?

Perhaps the more important question was, did she want to live the rest of her life without him?

Chapter Twelve

"Isa, come back here!" Sage muttered an expletive in Spanish under her breath. Jumping down from the wagon, she chased her daughter across the green to the Santa's workshop.

"Just think," Ethan ribbed Gavin, who sat on the seat beside him. "Soon you and Sage will have another kid to wear you down and teach you a second language."

"Yeah." His brother grinned, something he'd been doing a lot lately. "I can't wait."

None of the Powells could. Sage's resolve had weakened yet again, and this morning she'd broken the news of her pregnancy to the rest of the family. The girls had squealed with excitement. Ethan's father had cried.

"By the way, you're going to have to buy a new suit," Gavin said. "We're moving up the wedding date from May to February. Sage doesn't want to be fat as a cow in her wedding dress. Her words," he added emphatically, "not mine."

"Can you pull everything together by then?"

"I think so. If we keep it casual and simple."

"Let me know what you need help with."

"Consider yourself on notice." Gavin swung out of the seat, landing easily on the ground.

"Clay can be in charge of the bachelor party."

Gavin moaned. "Whatever you do, don't tell Sage." He headed to the horses to check on them.

Ethan chuckled. He was glad for his brother.

Six months ago, the Powells were barely making ends meet, and their future looked bleak. Gavin had believed it was entirely up to him to put their riding stables in the black. He'd done it, with a little help from the rest of the family and good friends, including Clay. He'd also gained a fiancée and stepdaughter in the process.

Quite an accomplishment for a man who, until recently, considered himself unmarriageable and a poor excuse for a father.

Ethan held a similar opinion of himself. Though lately, with the help of Cassie and Isa, he was learning how to be a good uncle. That was a start.

"Isa forgot her hat." Cassie, in full elf costume, held up a striped stocking cap with an enormous tassel on the end.

She, Isa and Sage had ridden in the bed of the wagon from the ranch, while Ethan's father followed in the truck. He and Gavin had been tapped to help Ethan tonight with the horses.

"Come on, Dad." Cassie scrambled out of the wagon. "I'll show you and Grandpa Santa's workshop."

"You okay alone for a bit?" Gavin asked Ethan.

"Go on. Have fun."

The pair met up with Ethan's dad on his walk over from the parking lot.

All the Powells were together for an outing. Ethan didn't have to search his memory for the last time that had happened. He remembered it clearly—Fourth of July fireworks, right before his mother's body rejected the donor heart, and she succumbed to infection.

He'd taken Caitlin to the fireworks display, naturally,

and they'd kissed under the brilliantly lit sky, pledging their love and devotion. No wonder she was still angry at him. If she had up and left him shortly after a night like that, he'd have trouble forgiving her.

She would be here tonight, helping Sage sell tickets and take donations. Ethan intended to get her alone at some point before the evening ended. A small wrapped package was burning a hole in his jacket pocket, and he was eager to give it to her. The gift wouldn't make up for all the grief and misery he'd caused her, but he hoped she would see the meaning behind it and think a little better of him.

One of the horses lowered his head and pawed the pavement, more ready than his buddy to get started.

Ethan had brought a different team tonight. They weren't as nicely matched as Dolly and Molly, but equally dependable. The geldings had been full of energy when they left the ranch. A two-mile walk down the long road had tired them out some, and by their third trip around the park, they'd be beat.

So would Ethan. He hadn't worked this hard since basic training, but he'd do it again in a heartbeat if Caitlin asked him.

Ethan noticed her then, taking the same route as his father from the parking lot across the green. She carried a large tote bag pressed close to her side, as if the contents were fragile or precious.

Caitlin went straight to the table, waving briefly to him, and seemed perplexed to find no one there. She looked around, set her tote bag down, then picked it up again.

He'd have gone over to talk to her if he could leave the horses. Instead, he imagined her coming to him.

In the next moment she did, wearing a radiant smile.

She aimed it at him, and he swore they were back at the fireworks display, sitting beneath the brilliantly lit sky.

Before she reached him, his father and Gavin met up with her. She gave his dad a hug and a kiss on the cheek. Ethan was jealous. Gavin received the same treatment, and Ethan was even more jealous. He was seriously considering leaping down from the wagon and collecting his kiss and hug when she came to stand by him, her hand resting on the wheel.

"Hey."

"Can I interest you in a ride, ma'am?"

"Maybe later." She laughed softly and transformed once more into the old Caitlin. They were young, flirting outrageously and unable to get enough of each other. "I promised I'd help Sage tonight."

"The supplies are in the truck," Wayne said. "If you're looking for them."

"I'll wait for Sage." She shrugged, causing her tote bag to slip. She hefted the straps back onto her shoulder, running her fingers tentatively down the side.

"She might be a while. I can fetch them for you."

"Do you mind? I'll go with you."

Ethan saw his opportunity and grabbed it. "I'll do it. Gavin, get over here and watch these horses for me."

"Did you want to leave your stuff here?" Ethan asked. "Dad will watch it."

"No." Caitlin hugged the tote closer. "That's all right."

They walked side by side, though not close and not touching. Small talk came easy.

"Are you ready for Christmas?"

Her question reminded Ethan they'd seen little of each other lately.

"Me? No. I'm a last-minute shopper." He thought of the gift in his pocket. "Usually. But Sage and the girls have transformed the house. There's a tree in the living room, a wreath on the front door and cookies baking in the oven every day. Dad's trying to set some kind of record."

"Sounds wonderful."

"It is." The preparations took him back to when he was a kid and his mother had gone all-out for Christmas with the same gusto as Sage and the rest of his family. "What about you?"

"I've finished my shopping."

"More than I can say."

"Still haven't done anything with the condo or even sent out one card. I'm so bad."

"You're busy."

"Not that busy."

"By the way, Clay's having another jackpot the Saturday after Christmas."

"I'll be there." She hesitated a beat before asking, "Will you?"

"Yes, but not riding. Working the stock."

"Not competing?"

He thought he detected a hint of optimism in her voice, and hated disappointing her. "This jackpot is for high school students. There's a statewide junior rodeo coming up in January. Clay wants to give the kids an opportunity to practice before then."

"High school students? They're so young."

"I was competing at that age."

"I know." Deep creases knitted her brow.

"We don't use the same rodeo stock for them. The

bulls and horses tend to be smaller. And Clay will require every participant to wear safety equipment or they don't compete."

He could see the topic distressed her. Too late, he remembered that Justin had been a senior in high school when he'd had his accident.

Fortunately, they reached Gavin's truck, and the discussion came to an end. Digging the keys from his pocket, he unlocked the door and retrieved the box of supplies.

"I'll carry it for you," he said when she held out her hands.

"Wait."

"Just this once, Caitlin, let me carry something for you without giving me a hard time."

"I don't care about the supplies." She hesitated, did that lower-lip biting thing that signaled she was nervous. "I'd planned on giving you this later tonight." She lowered the tote from her shoulder. "Now might be better, so you can put it in the truck."

His curiosity was piqued. "What is it?"

She removed a wrapped present from the tote bag and held it out to him. "Merry Christmas, Ethan."

He was floored. She'd gotten him a present, too.

Setting the supplies on the hood of the truck, he took the slim, rectangular package from her. "Thank you."

"It's nothing special… I hope you like it."

He tugged at the tape holding the colorful wrapping paper. "I'm sure I will."

The corner of a wooden picture frame peeked out. A moment later, he held a framed photograph in his hands, emotions rioting inside him.

"I noticed you don't have any pictures on the walls

in your apartment yet," Caitlin explained. "I thought maybe this could be your first one."

"This is great." He smiled at her and tilted the picture for a closer look in the fading daylight. "I really like it." He also liked the effort she'd gone to and the thoughtfulness behind the gift.

"I hoped you would."

The photo was of him breaking Prince. It was one Justin had taken with his phone, now enlarged to an eight-by-ten. The angle was perfect. Both Ethan and Prince wore determined expressions, Ethan's goal to stay seated and Prince's to throw his rider. At the moment the photo was snapped, no clear victor was evident.

He rewrapped the picture and placed it on the floor in front of the passenger seat.

"Don't take this wrong, but I'm kind of surprised."

"Why?"

"You don't much like me bronc riding and breaking horses."

"Yes." Caitlin tipped her head appealingly to one side. "But it's your life and what you choose to do. I respect that and admire it, too. You've always been true to yourself, Ethan."

That wasn't quite accurate. If he was really true to himself, he'd haul Caitlin into his arms and kiss the socks off her.

"Be careful. I might start thinking you're not as tough as you claim."

"Maybe I'm not."

He was tempted to jump to all sorts of conclusions, and warned himself not to read too much into what she said. Becoming more tolerant of his chosen profession wasn't an open invitation back into her life.

"I have something for you, too." He reached inside his jacket pocket and removed his gift for her.

"Oh." Her eyes lit up. She accepted the present and, unlike him, tore at the paper with careless abandon. "Haverson's?" she asked, reading the name stenciled in gold.

"You've heard of them?"

"Yes." She cradled the box in her hands. "Before I open this, I'm going to say you shouldn't have. Everything in that store costs a small fortune."

Ethan chuckled. "One of the owners is a client of mine. He gave me a discount."

Nestled inside the tissue paper was a handmade Christmas tree ornament. Caitlin lifted it by the silk string and held it up. The wagon, a miniature replica of the one Ethan drove, spun in a circle, the glow from the parking-lot lights glinting off its shiny green paint.

"Ethan," she breathed. "It's charming."

"I know you said you weren't decorating this year because you hadn't decided whether to stay in Mustang Valley or not. I thought you should have something. Blame Sage and the girls. They've corrupted me with their Christmas spirit and—"

Caitlin didn't let him finish. Clutching the front of his jacket, she pulled him to her for a kiss. "I love it," she said, and pressed her lips to his.

Ethan was very glad he'd stowed away the picture she'd given him. Having two free arms enabled him to slip his hands inside her unbuttoned coat and draw her fully against him.

In the span of an instant the kiss went from sweet to sensual to searing. The moment his tongue touched her lips they parted for him. He took full advantage, and she encouraged him, unlike the night they'd kissed at the rodeo arena and she'd held back.

She tasted exactly as he remembered. Her body, firm yet yielding, molded to his. She teased and tortured him by sifting her fingers through the hair at the base of his neck and rocking ever so slightly.

Her soft moan was answered by a low groan from him.

The need to touch her became overwhelming. Too many clothes hampered his efforts, causing him great frustration. He settled for taking hold of her hips and aligning them with his.

"Caitlin?" Sage's call carried from the park.

Ethan cursed his future sister-in-law's lousy timing.

He broke off the kiss, gulping air to fill his deprived lungs. He tried to talk. All that came out was Caitlin's name and a ragged breath.

She sighed contentedly, smiled coyly. Standing on tiptoes, she captured his lower lip between her teeth and tugged. It was something she used to do when they were younger, and it always drove him crazy.

Nothing had changed. His body jerked reflexively in response.

He kissed her again, hard, deeply, then pulled away while he still could. "I want to see you. Tonight. After the wagon rides."

"All right."

No objections? No arguments? No insisting he listen to reason?

"I'll get Gavin and Dad to take the wagon and horses home."

Caitlin leaned forward and rested her forehead on his chest. In a quiet voice she said, "We can go to my place."

"You sure?" Ethan lifted her face to his, not wanting there to be any misunderstanding between them.

"I'm sure." She retreated a step, and his hands fell away.

She'd made her decision about them and about tonight. Ethan didn't quite know what that decision was. He could only guess…and hope.

"Thank you, sir." Caitlin put the donation for the mustang sanctuary in the jar. "The last ride will be leaving in about twenty minutes. The line starts over there."

They'd been busier tonight than last night, for which she was glad. The constant stream of customers over the past three hours had enabled her to avoid thinking of Ethan and what might occur later.

She'd invited him to her condo! That hadn't been her original intention. After they'd kissed, her mind shut down and her heart had come up with the idea. She could rescind the invitation, concoct some excuse. Only she didn't want to.

The ornament—Ethan must have had it custom-made for her—wasn't the only reason for the sudden change. He cared for her and showed her as much with his kindness to her brother and his respect for her feelings even when he didn't agree with them.

Hearing jingle bells, she turned her head. From this distance, the wagon looked like a wind-up toy. No, like the ornament. The illusion faded as the wagon drew nearer. Ethan sat in the driver's seat, the collar of his sheepskin jacket pulled up to protect his neck from the cold wind that sailed through the valley, his hat settled low on his brow.

Soon they would be leaving for her place. Her insides tingled with anticipation.

It was then she noticed the teenager sitting next to him was holding the reins, not Ethan. She heard him instruct the boy, "When we get to that tree, pull back and tell 'em 'whoa!'"

The wagon rattled to a stop a minute later, and the passengers, all in high spirits, piled out. Those waiting in line for the last ride of the night eagerly took their places.

Karen Lawler, the chair of the festival committee, stepped into her line of vision.

"Caitlin, my dear, the wagon rides have been an incredible success. Did you see the picture in today's newspaper?"

"No, but I heard about it."

"You should get a copy." The reindeer antlers Karen wore on her head tipped back and forth as she gestured excitedly.

"I'll check my computer in the morning. See if the picture's in their online edition."

"Do you think the Powells will be willing to give wagon rides again next year?"

"I have no idea. You can always ask."

"I was counting on you to do that, seeing as you're so close to them." There was no mistaking Karen's implication. Like half of Mustang Valley, she'd concluded Caitlin and Ethan were romantically involved.

Caitlin waited for a flood of embarrassment to heat her cheeks and tie her tongue. It didn't happen.

Interesting.

"I'm also counting on you to volunteer again," Karen continued.

A few weeks ago, Caitlin might have hesitated or declined, unsure if she was remaining in Mustang Valley or not.

"Of course I'll volunteer."

"Lovely," Karen trilled, and clasped Caitlin to her. "Merry Christmas, my dear. I must run. I'm meeting up with my grandchildren."

All the passengers had loaded up, and the wagon was ready to depart on its last run of the festival. Caitlin started clearing the table.

"You don't have to do that," Sage admonished, hurrying toward her. "Let me. You were only supposed to relieve me, and you ran the table the entire evening."

"You and the girls were enjoying the festival."

"Go get yourself an ice cream or a cup of coffee before all the vendors close for the night," Sage suggested.

"Okay. If you're sure you don't need me."

Caitlin didn't get ten feet away before discovering she really wasn't interested in food. If no one claimed the seat beside Ethan, maybe she'd go on the last ride with him.

The thought was barely formed when Cassie plunked down beside him and Gavin went over to talk to him.

Well, it had been a good idea while it lasted.

A minute later, the wagon still hadn't pulled out, and the passengers were getting restless. While Caitlin watched, the brothers traded places, with Gavin taking over the reins. He settled next to Cassie, while Ethan climbed carefully down, landing stiffly on the ground.

His leg must be bothering him. Or he was sore. Probably both.

She walked over to him. "Is something the matter?"

He smiled, a not-at-all-tired smile. "Gavin's taking the last ride for me, and then he'll drive the wagon home."

"Did you tell him about our plans?"

"Not a word. He's just giving me a break. It's been a long two nights."

The wagon pulled out at last to a chorus of cheers from its passengers.

"Do you mind if we take your van?" Ethan asked. "Dad's going to follow Gavin home in the truck."

"Of course not."

It wasn't until they were leaving the parking lot that Caitlin realized Ethan had no way home from her condo unless she drove him.

Chapter Thirteen

"You haven't been here before?" Caitlin asked.

"Actually, no."

Ethan didn't intend to gawk at his surroundings, but he couldn't stop himself. They stood at her front door while she fitted the key in the lock. He was quite certain the dirt road that used to cut through the center of Mustang Valley, the one he, Gavin, their father and the ranch hands had driven on a weekly basis, had been right where he was standing.

A surreal feeling came over him, as if he'd walked into someone else's dream.

"Everything's changed. So much."

"Must be hard on you." She twisted the knob and pushed open the door.

"Not as much as when I first came home. I haven't spent much time in Mustang Village." Hardly any until meeting Caitlin again.

They stepped inside her condo, and he was suddenly struck with a case of cold feet.

He was here at her invitation, which told him she was ready for more. But how much more? He'd hate to jump to the wrong conclusion.

She flipped a switch, and an overhead lighting fixture illuminated the empty entryway. To their right was a staircase. Directly in front of them, a hallway. To their left, an open archway led to the living room.

"Public rooms downstairs. Bedrooms and bathroom upstairs." She laughed. "Though calling the second bedroom a 'room' is a stretch. I've seen bigger closets."

"This is nice."

Caitlin removed her jacket and held an arm out for Ethan's. He gave it to her. "It would be nicer with more furniture."

"Would you rather have a house?"

"Sure, eventually. For right now, this suits me. I don't have the time to take care of a yard or keep up on the maintenance a house would require."

She hung her jacket in the hall closet and draped Ethan's across the banister.

Was she planning on him making a fast exit?

"What about you?" she asked. "Ever think of living anywhere other than the ranch?"

"The bunkhouse is fine for now. Kind of cramped if I were…"

"Married with kids?" she finished for him.

"Something like that."

"You're really good with Cassie and Isa."

"Their parents might disagree. They've learned a few words from me that aren't, shall we say, appropriate for young ladies."

He followed Caitlin into the living room, which reminded him a little of his bunkhouse. The minimal necessities were there, a couch, a chair, a side table. What was missing were the decorative touches that turned a place into a comfortable home.

They were quite the pair, the two of them, moving through life, staying in different places but never putting down roots. What were they running away from?

What were they running to?

"I didn't even consider having kids for a long time." He sat on one end of the couch. "Not while I was in the marines."

"That's understandable."

Caitlin had brought the wagon ornament inside with her. She removed it from the box and placed it on the table beside an old lamp Ethan was sure had come from her parents' house. The ornament looked out of place sitting there all alone. Had he been wrong to get it for her? Maybe she wasn't ready to stay in one place.

Stay here with him.

"What about you? Want kids?"

"Two for sure. Maybe three," she added with a shy smile.

They'd never discussed having children, that Ethan could remember. In fact, they'd rarely discussed anything of a profoundly personal nature. Having fun had been their priority. Perhaps that was why when his mother died he hadn't turned to Caitlin and confided in her.

"Can I get you something?" she asked, a little too brightly. "Coffee? Beer? Eggnog?"

"Eggnog? I haven't had that for a long time. My mom used to make it."

"I'm afraid the kind I have comes in a carton from the grocery store. I can add a splash of brandy to it if you'd like." A mischievous glint sparked in her eyes.

He hadn't seen that glint since before he'd left for the marines. These days, she was always so serious.

"I'd like to, but you have to drive me home."

"That won't be for a while."

Oh, boy.

She went to the kitchen. Ethan waited on her couch, his heart chugging like a piston. It was just a cup of eggnog, he told himself. Nothing else.

But there had been that glint in her eyes....

She returned shortly and handed him a glass of frothy, creamy eggnog filled to the brim. Sitting on the other end of the couch, she kicked off her shoes, tucked her legs beneath her and sipped at her glass.

Her relaxed pose did nothing to slow the piston inside his chest.

He tasted his eggnog. "Not bad."

They talked after that, about nothing and everything. Gavin and Sage's wedding plans, old friends—who'd moved where and done what—and some of the more memorable shenanigans they'd pulled as teenagers.

More than once Caitlin's eyes misted with sentimental tears. They'd shared so much when they were younger. Ethan couldn't believe he'd walked away from it. From her.

After a particularly good laugh, she stretched out her legs on the couch. Her feet, in colorful Christmas socks, were inches from him.

What would she do if he pulled her feet into his lap?

"Another one?" Caitlin held up her empty glass.

"No, thanks." The eggnog hadn't been particularly strong, but it was probably better that they refrain from having more. "I should be getting home."

The talking had been enjoyable. A good beginning to wherever it was they were heading. Given the choice, he'd move a whole lot faster, but Caitlin was setting the pace, and he was very willing to let her.

"So soon?" She arched a foot toward him.

It was a very small movement, one that could easily

be misread. He did nothing at first, then she arched it again. This time her toes brushed his thigh, light as a butterfly's wing.

What the hell.

He rested his hand on her ankle. When she didn't jerk it away, he began kneading her foot, something he'd been aching to do since she'd shed her shoes.

She tipped her head back and closed her eyes. "Mmm…that feels good."

He couldn't take his eyes off her. The smooth expanse of her bare neck cried out for his kisses. Her slightly mussed hair curled sexily around her pink-tinged cheeks.

His hand moved from her foot to her calf. She made a contented sound as he continued massaging her with firm strokes.

In another minute, he wouldn't be responsible for his actions.

"I really need to go. Or not." He'd leave the choice to her.

Caitlin opened her eyes and sat up. Slowly pulling her legs away from him, she set her feet on the floor.

Disappointment cut through him.

Perhaps next time there would be a different ending to the evening.

He braced his hand on the armrest and started to stand.

She slid across the middle cushion separating them. "Or not," she stated.

Ethan sat back down and studied her face, searching for any sign of indecision or distrust. There was none. "Do you know what you're saying?" Honor dictated he give her one last opportunity to change her mind.

She linked her arms around his neck, snuggled against him and whispered, "Stay."

One word, and a whole world of possibilities opened up.

CAITLIN MIGHT HAVE questioned her actions right up until the moment she and Ethan kissed. They weren't just going to hit rough patches along the way, they were starting out in the middle of a big one.

But being intimate with him felt right and always had. She loved hearing her name on his lips, repeated over and over between heated kisses.

His hand, large and strong and warm, slid down her back and under the hem of her shirt to caress bare skin. Her breasts flattened against his broad chest as she wriggled closer...closer...closer. His low exhalation of breath deepened into a groan as he tore his mouth away, to trail more kisses along the column of her neck.

She'd all but forgotten.

How could she?

Her fingers sought the buttons of his shirt, toyed with them, finally succeeded in unfastening the top three. A T-shirt impeded her quest for skin-to-skin contact, and she swore impatiently.

Ethan shifted beneath her, almost upending her. In one swift, deliberate move he stripped off his shirt and T-shirt, tugging them over his head and tossing them aside.

"Yes." She skimmed her palms along his hard muscles, felt them constrict as he sucked in air though his teeth. When she would have explored further, seen what other reactions she could arouse in him, he clasped both her hands between his and held them over his heart.

"This is no one-night stand. If it is for you, we stop now."

"No one-night stand." She sealed the promise with a kiss that instantly turned explosive.

The hair-trigger passion they ignited in each other was the same as when they were younger. It was also different. There was a hardness in Ethan she hadn't seen before, an intensity that was almost unbearable at times.

She imagined he noticed changes in her, too. The adventurous teenager had all but disappeared, replaced by an overly cautious woman afraid to take risks.

Except when it came to sex.

Then, and now, Caitlin had no qualms letting Ethan know what she wanted, with actions and quietly murmured demands.

Suddenly, he broke off the kiss and set her away from him.

"What?"

"Not here." He caressed her cheek with his fingertips. "Upstairs."

She rose from the couch, her body weightless like a bird taking flight, and extended her hand. Ethan took it. She turned, but before she could slip away, he wrapped his arms around her waist and pulled her to him, fitting her back to his front. His erection pressed into her as his lips nibbled the sensitive flesh where her neck joined her shoulder.

"So long," she murmured. "We waited so long."

He groaned in agreement.

She craved more but was loath to leave the warmth of his arms. Her burning need won out, and she led him to the stairs. As they climbed single file, she sensed his gaze on her and purposefully didn't hurry, even when they reached her bedroom. Inside the door sat a dresser with a small lamp. She turned it on. Light bathed the room in a warm yellow glow.

Ethan went to the bed and sat on the edge of the mattress. When she went to sit beside him, he tugged her between his open legs. Resting his hands on her waist, he laid his head on her chest.

"There's been no one for a long time." She couldn't explain her need to reveal such personal information.

"For me, either."

She brushed a fallen lock of black hair from his face. Leaning down, she kissed him again, holding his face in her palms she ran her lips over his. He sat very still, hardly breathing.

"Touch me," she whispered.

He covered her breasts with his hands, squeezing them through the sweater she wore.

Waves of pleasure cascaded over her, and she tugged frantically at her clothes.

"Let me," he insisted, his voice a husky growl.

Who was she to object? She lifted her arms so he could remove her sweater. Her bra came next.

Filling his hands with her breasts, he ran his thumbs over her nipples until they hardened to tight peaks. It wasn't enough. At her urging, he leaned forward and drew one nipple into his mouth, then the other.

Her eyes drifted shut; her knees buckled slightly.

"Sweet. So sweet," Ethan murmured.

His mouth didn't stop there. It moved to other erogenous zones. The ridge of her collarbone. The valley between her breasts. Her navel.

She was wearing way too many clothes, Caitlin thought, and reached for the clasp on her jeans.

"I have protection," he said.

"Good."

He sat forward, removed his wallet from his pants pocket. "I'm only carrying this because—"

"I don't care why." She stroked his jaw. "I'm just glad you have it."

"Me, too."

She shimmied out of her jeans and panties, liking that he watched her every move with hungry eyes. Naked at last, she stood in front of him.

"You're incredibly beautiful." His gaze traveled from her toes to her face.

"Your turn."

Pushing himself off the bed, he attacked his belt buckle. When the clasp and zipper on his jeans defeated him, she came to his aid. Hooking his thumbs in the waistband, he slid his pants down. This time there were no shirttails to cover him, and Caitlin very much liked what she saw.

He sat back down, extending his left leg.

She knelt in front of him and removed his right boot. Then she grabbed his prosthesis by the ankle.

"Caitlin, sweetheart."

"Let me. I don't want there to be any barriers between us."

After a long moment, he swallowed and nodded. Once he'd loosened the cuff, she pulled gently. The prosthesis came off, sliding out of his pant leg. Giving it only the briefest of glances, she set it on the floor near the dresser.

Ethan removed his jeans, and she rested her hands on his thighs. Tenderly, she ran her fingers over his stump which began a few inches below his knee. He flinched once before relaxing as her gentle caresses continued over skin that was rough and riddled with scars in some places, and surprisingly smooth in others.

Caitlin's throat closed, and she swallowed a sob. In her mind, she could see him lying in some Middle Eastern street, buried in a pile of rubble, broken and bleeding. "This must have hurt."

"It still does some days."

"I'm sorry."

He tucked a finger under her chin and raised her face to his. "Don't be. I'm one of the lucky ones."

She straightened and went into his arms. "You have no idea how glad I am for that."

Ethan pulled her onto the bed and laid her on her back. She didn't stop to think about what he could or couldn't manage when it came to lovemaking. She had every confidence he'd show her.

They spent long minutes reacquainting themselves with each other's bodies. Ethan was still ticklish on his neck. She still broke out in goose bumps when he sucked on her earlobe. She delighted in the reactions her tongue and touch evoked in him. He grinned whenever she sighed softly or shivered with unrestrained pleasure.

She was past ready when Ethan nudged her legs apart and began stroking her intimate places. Her breathing went ragged, then stilled as his mouth moved down her torso to the inside of her thighs.

"I've dreamed of this," he said, placing his mouth on her.

So had she. Often.

Within minutes, seconds maybe, she was arching off the bed and hovering on the brink of climax.

"I want you inside me."

He crawled up her body, his mouth following the same trail up as it had down.

"Hurry!" she urged.

One quick tear and he had the condom open. Levering himself over her, he said, "Look at me."

She did, and he thrust inside her.

A shattering climax seized her almost immediately. She became a piece of driftwood riding a wild, storm-churned sea. He followed soon after, clinging to her as if she alone was responsible for anchoring him to the bed.

Eventually, he loosened his grip. When he started to roll off her, she held him and pleaded, "Not yet."

"For as long as you want, baby doll."

Baby doll. That was the name he'd called her in high school.

Caitlin felt her throat close again. She wasn't usually this weepy, but it had been a long time since she'd let down her guard. A long time since she'd felt so cherished.

"What if I want you with me a really long time?"

"I can do that." He rubbed his cheek along hers.

"I'm serious, Ethan."

He lifted his head to peer at her, his expression filled with—did she dare think it?—love.

"Me, too."

They would talk, needed to talk. Eventually. But not tonight.

"What would your family say if you didn't come home till morning?"

He did roll off her then and lay beside her, his good leg draped over her. "Probably that I finally came to my senses. And that you lost yours."

She punched him lightly in the arm. "Not possible."

"I won't hurt you again, baby doll. I swear."

Caitlin believed he would try his best to keep that vow. She also wasn't naive. Things changed without warning. Shit hit the fan. Worlds fell apart. It had happened to her before and could again.

They needed to proceed cautiously. Lift the lid of this box that was their new relationship one corner at a time.

As Ethan's hands roamed her body once more, inducing tiny tremors in her, she forgot all about erring on the side of caution.

Pushing him onto his back, she straddled his middle, determined to drive every thought from his mind.

GETTING TO THE RANCH early wasn't a problem. Ethan and Caitlin hardly slept all night. When they did doze, it was wrapped in each other's arms. He could still feel her tucked against him, warm and giving. Could taste her lips and skin, smell the light, flowery fragrance of her hair.

He'd brought only one condom with him. That hadn't stopped them from enjoying each other. They'd been careful and innovative, and next time—there would be many, many more next times—Ethan would be better prepared.

"When do you have to be at the festival today?" he asked.

Stifling a yawn, she turned her van into the driveway leading to the ranch.

"Not till ten. I can probably show up at eleven and no one will notice. I just need to be there when we close at four."

"Go home and take a nap," he told her, squeezing her hand.

"I think I will. What about you?"

"We're usually busy on Sundays, but with the festival, I doubt we will be today. If the girls don't pester me to take them on a ride, I might squeeze in a little shut-eye, too."

Any hopes they had of not being caught were dashed the moment Caitlin pulled into the open area in front of the stables. Gavin and Sage, up for an early morning outing, were helping the girls onto their horses.

Sage, Isa and Cassie waved, with big, welcoming smiles on their shining faces. Gavin simply nodded.

"Looks like you caught a break," Caitlin said airily. "No trail ride duty today." She didn't appear the least bit embarrassed at being spotted sneaking Ethan home.

He decided he shouldn't be, either. What he and Caitlin did in the privacy of her condo wasn't anybody's business, though there would be questions, he was sure, 'om Sage. His future sister-in-law didn't ascribe to the same to-each-your-own philosophy his father and brother did.

Caitlin continued to the bunkhouse, driving slowly, and parked out front. Their goodbye kiss went on and on.

"Any plans tonight, for after the festival?" he asked, thinking he could never get enough of her lush, ripe mouth.

"Nothing definite. I was considering buying a tree."

He liked the idea. It rang of permanence.

"Why don't I pick you up at four-thirty? We can go for an early dinner and then head to the tree lot."

"A date?"

"Yeah, a date."

"Mexican?"

"Wherever. You pick the place."

She paused for so long he thought she was going to say no. "Mexican it is."

"Good." *Very* good.

"We can talk."

"Ah." He'd been expecting that. "I suppose we have to."

"Yes, we do."

"I wish I could tell you I'll stop riding broncs."

"I wish I could tell you I have no problem with that." She lifted his hand and pressed the knuckles to her cheek. "Be patient with me. I swear I'll try my hardest to cope."

"I don't want you to always be worrying about me."

"It comes with the territory. Because of who I am, my profession, my brother and because of how I feel about you."

He was tempted to ask her exactly how she felt about him but decided to wait until dinner tonight.

"One day at a time, okay?" she said.

"Sounds good to me."

"See you at four-thirty."

"If not sooner."

Her eyebrows rose.

"I was so busy with the wagon rides, I never got a chance to check out the festival. Is it possible to get a tour?"

"I'll see what I can arrange." Her mouth curved up in a smile that proved irresistible.

They were going to be all right, Ethan thought during another lingering goodbye kiss. This time, their relationship would last. It wouldn't be easy, but unlike when they were young, they knew full well the obstacles facing them, and that would make all the difference.

Chapter Fourteen

Caitlin could hardly believe it was Christmas Day already. The ten days following the Holly Days Festival had flown by in a blur. A happy, exciting, cloud nine kind of blur where she and Ethan were together every possible minute. They didn't run out of things to talk about or places to go. Neither did they tire of making love. Most nights they ended up at her place—no prying eyes and nosy family members, particularly those age twelve and under.

Missing the lower half of his left leg affected Ethan very little. He was an incredible lover. Attentive, considerate and generous. He also brought an emotional intensity to their lovemaking that hadn't been there years ago. She found that aspect more exciting than anything else.

She had wanted to spend today at the ranch with the Powells, but that wasn't possible because of her family obligations. No way on earth would her mother have tolerated her missing Christmas dinner.

By late afternoon, Caitlin couldn't wait a moment longer to see him, and after calling Ethan, left for the ranch with a promise to return to her parents' by seven. Or seven-thirty. Maybe even eight.

"You made it." He hurried across the back patio to meet her.

"Finally!" Eight o'clock for sure.

Caitlin had attended Christmas Eve service with the Powells, their first time stepping inside a church together since Ethan's mother's funeral. It had been a sentimental and moving experience, for Caitlin, as well.

Afterward, they'd returned to the ranch for coffee and dessert. Isa had hot chocolate. Cassie insisted on drinking coffee like the grown-ups. Her face as she forced down each sip had had everyone in stitches.

"I've missed you." Ethan lifted Caitlin off her feet and held her tight.

"Me, too." She liked being eye level with him, and showed him how much by giving him a smacking kiss on the lips.

He set her down then, but was slow to release her. "Hungry?"

"Are you kidding? Mom made enough food to feed five families."

"Same here. We'll be eating leftovers for a month."

"Everyone inside?"

"Mostly outside. Gavin wants to try riding Prince again today."

"Is he still giving Gavin a hard time?"

"It's funny. Gavin and Prince have always had this special connection. But for some reason, Prince doesn't like him riding him. He hasn't been able to get on the mustang since the day we broke him."

They strolled in the direction of the stables. Caitlin could see Gavin in the round pen with Prince.

"It's Christmas," she said. "Don't you guys ever take a day off work?"

"Riding Prince isn't work."

"Spoken like a true cowboy."

The setting sun gave everyone and everything it fell on long, skinny shadows, and a strong breeze from the east tousled hair and jackets. After the hectic family celebration, Caitlin welcomed the quiet change of pace the ranch afforded.

And she'd missed Ethan.

They hadn't resolved any of their issues. He was still riding broncs at Clay's arena. They didn't talk about it, and Caitlin chose not to think about it. Avoidance, yes. Denial, absolutely. And the day would come when they'd have to deal with both his lifestyle choices and her fears.

Next week, maybe, after New Year's and the high school jackpot. She wasn't about to put a damper on the holidays. Till then, she could almost pretend Ethan didn't court danger on a regular basis. It was easy as long as he didn't show up in her clinic injured, and she didn't have to watch him ride broncs at the rodeo arena.

"Merry Christmas," Caitlin said to Gavin when they reached the pen.

"Same to you," he answered distractedly, without taking his eyes off Prince.

At the sight of Ethan, the horse nickered and bobbed his head.

"He likes me better," he whispered to Caitlin.

"Who could blame him?" she whispered back.

He leaned over and gave her a peck on the cheek, which turned into a brief kiss, then a deep one.

"Ew!"

The comment came from Isa, who rode up on old Chico, the horse's dull clip-clop an excuse for a trot.

Cassie was noticeably absent. She'd gone to visit her mother back in Connecticut during the school break between Christmas and New Year's.

"No comments from the peanut gallery," Ethan admonished the little girl, though his voice was hardly stern.

"Caitlin, see my new boots?" Isa stuck out her foot to show off a brand-new pink boot with black trim.

"Very pretty." It had taken some coaxing to get both girls to call her Caitlin away from school and the clinic. "How's Cassie doing?"

"She's coming home next week!" Isa squirmed excitedly. "I can't wait. Mama's going to take us to buy dresses for the wedding."

"Really?" Caitlin looked at Ethan for confirmation. "She's coming home?"

Gavin's custody arrangement with his daughter had been only temporary. There was a chance when he'd put her on the plane to Connecticut that she might not come back until the following summer, if then.

"Cassie called this morning to tell Gavin the news," Ethan said. "She asked to live with him permanently, and her mother agreed."

Caitlin's heart soared. What a truly wonderful Christmas present for the Powells. "I'm so glad for both of them."

"Gavin's happy. Or he was," Ethan corrected, "until today." He stooped and climbed through the rungs into the pen.

Caitlin watched, leaning her forearms on the second rung. Isa also watched, from her vantage point atop Chico.

Prince was in a mood, for sure. He alternately pawed

the ground impatiently and swung his head from side to side. Twice he bared his teeth at Gavin.

Ethan approached the horse with less caution than Caitlin deemed prudent. She bit her tongue to stop from crying out.

"Easy, boy," he crooned.

To her surprise, Prince settled almost immediately. Even pushed his nose into Ethan's hand.

"Try getting on now," he suggested to his brother.

Gavin collected the reins, took hold of the saddle horn and raised his foot to put it in the stirrup.

Huffing loudly and humping his back, Prince danced sideways. He got only as far as Gavin's hold on him allowed.

"Stand!" Gavin commanded.

Prince stared at him, challenge burning in his eyes.

"What's with him?" Caitlin muttered.

"There's some new mares in the motel," Isa answered. "He always acts stupid around mares."

Caitlin didn't want to think about how knowledgeable Isa was on horse breeding.

Ethan reached out to stroke Prince's neck. The stallion permitted it, though he stood stiff and tense.

"That's it…" Ethan murmured.

Caitlin studied the two brothers, alike and yet so different. Both were intense. Ethan, however, was outgoing and gregarious, whereas Gavin tended to be reserved and private. Both loved passionately and both had suffered immeasurably when they'd lost a loved one. While Gavin withdrew, Ethan ran.

What would happen if Ethan was confronted with another devastating loss? Caitlin couldn't bear it if he left again.

"Go on, you ride him." Gavin nodded at Ethan. "One of us ought to."

"I'll warm him up for you."

With the ease of an experienced horse trainer, Ethan swung up into the saddle. Prince's legs trembled violently. But when Gavin released his hold on the bridle, the mustang circled the pen, responding perfectly to Ethan's cues. Walk, trot, lope and walk once more.

Man and horse were so beautiful. Ethan, tall and rugged in the saddle. Prince, strong and athletic, his long black mane and tail flowing in the wind like silky banners.

Caitlin wasn't the only one captivated. She glanced at Gavin and Isa and noted the two of them couldn't stop staring, either.

Ethan nudged Prince into a fast lope, then reined him to a sudden stop that ended with a shower of dirt exploding from beneath his hooves.

Caitlin let out a small gasp.

"Back, boy, back."

Prince lowered his hind quarters and dug his hooves into the ground, each backward step given reluctantly— a hard-won victory for Ethan. Such strength and power in the horse, yet Ethan controlled it with ease. Thrived on it. Reveled in it.

It must be like that when he rode broncs.

Who was Caitlin to take that from him for purely selfish reasons?

After a half-dozen more turns around the pen at a comfortable trot, Ethan brought Prince to a halt beside his brother, an elated grin on his face.

"Your turn."

"What do you think?" Gavin asked the horse.

Prince rubbed his head on Gavin's jacket sleeve and exhaled lustily.

"All right, partner, if you say so." He patted the horse and took hold of the bridle so Ethan could dismount. "Let's give it a go."

Ethan grabbed the saddle horn and removed his left foot from the stirrup. Prince stood quietly, and Caitlin dared to relax. She could do this, she thought—watch Ethan ride and not suffer a panic attack.

One second the air was still, the next a cold gust of wind whipped past them. An empty plastic bag tumbled through the rails and into the round pen.

Prince balked and snorted, disliking the object and the crackling noises it made. That might have been the end of it if the plastic sack hadn't brushed against his underside. The horse went into a frenzy, kicking out with his back legs.

"What's wrong?" Isa asked in a small, scared voice.

Before Caitlin or anyone could answer her, Prince bolted, galloping around the pen. Ethan held on, his prosthesis flapping uselessly.

"Whoa, whoa!" he hollered, sawing on the reins.

Prince came to a stop, only to rear, his front legs slashing the air. Gavin dodged out of the way, escaping one sharp hoof that came perilously close to his face.

Ethan leaned forward in the saddle, struggling to maintain his balance.

Caitlin pressed her hands to her mouth, willing him to stay seated. He'd ridden a crazed Prince once before, on the day he broke him. He could do it again.

At last Prince came down. Nostrils flaring and flanks heaving, he stood quietly, even hanging his head.

"Is it over?" Isa squeaked.

Caitlin dared to breathe. "I think so."

"Easy there," Ethan murmured, and visibly relaxed.

Without warning, Prince tensed, then bucked again. High.

Ethan flew out of the saddle. Sailing head over heels, he landed in the dirt with a gut-wrenching thud, then lay immobile.

"Uncle Ethan!" Isa screamed.

Blood-chilling fear galvanized Caitlin, and she ran to the gate.

"Stay back!" Gavin shouted.

At the sound of his voice, Prince spun and charged, flinging Gavin against the railing.

Rearing yet again, the horse came down on Ethan's still form, his front hooves striking him repeatedly in the center of his back.

Free at last of both humans and the terrifying plastic sack, Prince loped in circles, stirrups bouncing and reins dangling.

"Are you all right?" Caitlin hollered to both men.

Neither one answered.

Disregarding her own safety, she flung the gate open. "Look out!"

At Gavin's warning, Caitlin dived to her left, narrowly avoiding being trampled by Prince as he lunged through the opening and thundered toward the stables.

Caitlin raced into the round pen. "Ethan, can you hear me? Ethan!" She dropped down beside him, frantically taking in every detail. The closed eyes. The irregular breathing. The cuts and contusions. "Ethan, sweetie, can you hear me?"

His eyelids fluttered once, then went still.

Gavin stumbled toward them.

She looked up at him. "Do you have a cell phone on you? Call 911."

"Give him a minute. He'll come around."

"A minute? Are you insane?"

She was normally levelheaded in a crisis, one of the qualities that made her a good nurse. With Ethan hurt, being levelheaded flew out the window.

"Call 911 and do it now!"

Removing his phone from his pocket, Gavin placed the call.

Caitlin touched Ethan's bare head, his arm and back with just the tips of her fingers. She didn't dare disturb him, having no idea the seriousness of his injuries. A concussion, no doubt. Fractured bones. Internal injuries. A broken neck. Oh, dear God, he'd landed so hard, and his left arm lay at an unnatural angle. His hat sat upside down on the other side of the pen.

"Ethan, please." Tears blurred her vision, and her voice splintered. "Talk to me."

"He's going to be okay."

She was only dimly aware of Gavin's voice as it penetrated her escalating terror.

"You don't know that."

Her composure crumpled. She was once again in the hospital, pacing the halls, waiting for the doctors to deliver news of Justin's condition. And when it finally came, it had devastated her and her parents.

Sobbing, she barely felt Gavin's hand giving her shoulder a comforting squeeze.

"Go fetch your mother," he told Isa, who scampered off.

"Stay with me, sweetie..." Caitlin would give anything to hold Ethan in her arms, lay his head in her lap and stroke his hair. All she could do was watch helplessly as his chest rose and fell with each shallow breath he drew.

Where was the closest fire station? She couldn't remember.

Ethan groaned softly.

"I'm here. I'm here." She tentatively stroked his cheek with her index finger.

"See, I told you," Gavin said. "He'll be fine."

Only, Gavin was wrong. Ethan didn't rouse, and his face lost even more color.

"Gavin!" Sage came out of nowhere. "What can I do?"

"Keep everyone away. Direct the emergency vehicles here. And tell Javier to find Prince."

How could he care about that damn stupid horse after it had nearly killed his brother?

Finally, mercifully, she heard the distant wail of a siren.

"Help's on the way, sweetie," she told Ethan. "It won't be long now."

Long until what? The doctors came to the hospital waiting area and delivered a hopeless prognosis?

Ethan had been through so much already. He'd lost his mother and his leg. Plus the cattle operation that had been in his family for a hundred years. It wasn't fair. He didn't deserve tragedy heaped upon tragedy.

The paramedic unit pulled up alongside the round pen. Two uniformed men rushed through the gate, lugging equipment. A fire truck came next. As Gavin guided Caitlin out of the way so the paramedics could examine Ethan, more uniformed men arrived. Seven altogether.

They asked questions Caitlin couldn't answer. When

she pressed them for details on Ethan's condition, they gave noncommittal responses.

"I'm a nurse."

"Then you know to let us do our jobs," one of the men said, not unkindly.

Within minutes, they had Ethan hooked up to a heart monitor and an IV. They'd checked his respiration, taken his pulse and his blood pressure, and assessed his injuries. He came to, but only fleetingly, and wasn't coherent.

Understanding every move the paramedics made, every medical term they used, just made the situation worse for Caitlin. His vitals weren't good, and his failure to respond was of concern.

The ambulance arrived with its EMTs. Ethan's head and neck were immobilized, and he was carefully lifted onto a stretcher, then transported to the vehicle.

"Can I go with him?" Caitlin beseeched, her gaze going from Gavin to the EMTs.

"It would be better if you met us at the hospital."

The female EMT slammed the ambulance door shut, the sound echoing through the empty corridors of Caitlin's heart.

ANOTHER HOSPITAL, ANOTHER waiting room. Caitlin hadn't bitten her nails since she was in middle school, but her right thumbnail was now gnawed to the quick. She was starting on her left one when Justin wheeled into the waiting room.

She jumped up from her chair. Although she was glad to see him, his presence evoked memories of the terrible night she and her parents had spent after his fall from the cliffs.

"Any word?" he asked, throwing his arms wide.

She bent and held him for many seconds. "He regained consciousness in the ambulance. Was able to answer questions, like what's his name and what day it is."

"That's good."

"Yes, but he doesn't remember the accident."

"He may not."

True. Hadn't Ethan told her he still didn't remember the car bomb explosion?

"He's in surgery now."

"What for?"

"Six broken ribs, one close to his lungs. They also want to make sure there are no internal injuries."

The Powells sat huddled together on the couches where they had waited along with Caitlin for the last hour and a half—Gavin, his father, Sage and Isa. Their worried expressions told a silent story. Wayne Powell was a wreck. When he wasn't pacing he was staring out the window. Was he thinking of his late wife, just as Caitlin was thinking of her brother?

"You okay?" Justin asked.

"Fine."

"You sure? Your hands are shaking."

Were they? Caitlin glanced down, startled to see that her brother was right.

"It's nothing." She rubbed her palms on her pants.

"Mom and Dad said to call if you need anything."

Justin took her back to the Powells. They greeted him like one of the family, then everyone fell silent again.

Just when Caitlin was about to crawl out of her skin, the surgeon made an appearance and was instantly mobbed.

"How is he?" Ethan's father asked before anyone else could.

The doctor's eyes were somber, and she didn't mince

words. "He's in stable condition, but make no mistake, his injuries are serious. Had the horse landed differently, your son might not be here. He's a very lucky man."

Ethan had said almost the same thing about the explosion when he'd lost his leg. How often could a person escape death?

"What are his injuries?" Gavin asked.

"He sustained a concussion in the fall, and right and left rib fractures when the horse stepped on him—eight in total. One of the fractured ribs missed puncturing his lung by only a few millimeters. His spleen is bruised. Thankfully, it didn't rupture. We need to watch that closely over the next few weeks. And two herniated disks."

The surgeon went on to explain Ethan's treatment, expected hospital stay and rehabilitation.

"When can we see him?" Wayne Powell asked.

"As soon as he's been moved to a regular room. About a half hour to an hour. When you do see him, tell him I said to be more careful next time."

Once the surgeon left, everyone started talking, their relief needing an outlet. Sage broke into racking sobs.

Caitlin wanted to cry, too, but something prevented her. She kept remembering the surgeon's warning.

Had the horse landed differently, your son might not be here.... Tell him I said to be more careful next time....

Next time.

She should never have told him she would try to cope with his bronc riding and breaking horses. Never given him that photo.

Would he have stopped for her?

Maybe, maybe not. She'd basically given him her blanket approval.

This was her fault.

All right, maybe not all her fault. But partially her fault.

Like Justin's injury.

"You okay, sis?"

Caitlin blinked, shook her head to clear it. "Yeah. If you want to leave now, go ahead."

"I'll stay until after you've seen him."

"Thanks." She swallowed.

"Ethan's going to be fine."

"Until the next time."

Gavin turned to stare at her.

She hadn't meant to say that out loud.

Justin didn't seem to notice. "He's tough."

But was she? Caitlin had her doubts.

"You heading back to Mom and Dad's or going home?" she asked.

"Neither. Tamiko's family is having an open house tonight and they invited me. I thought I might drop by for an hour after I leave here."

"What about her boyfriend?"

"He'll be there, too. Unfortunately."

"Oh, Justin."

"Quit worrying about me, sis."

"I can't. I won't. You're my brother." She'd almost said *baby* brother. He wouldn't have liked that.

"Tamiko can do better than him. When she finally wises up, I want to be there, waiting in the wings."

"What if she doesn't wise up? I hate to see you get hurt."

"Life comes with risks."

"We can minimize them."

"We can also live in a bubble." He smiled at her. "What fun is that?"

Not long after, a nurse came by to inform the family that Ethan could receive visitors.

"Don't overwhelm him," she advised. "He's still pretty groggy and needs his rest."

"Isa and I will wait for you," Sage said.

"But I want to see Uncle Ethan," Isa pouted.

"We will, *mija*, tomorrow. You can draw him a picture."

Isa was only slightly mollified.

"I can come back tomorrow, too," Caitlin said. Now that the moment to see Ethan had arrived, she was having reservations.

"No," Gavin said. "He'll be furious with us if we let you leave."

They took the elevator to the fourth floor. Outside Ethan's door, Caitlin hesitated. His brother and father went ahead of her. She watched from the doorway, her feet frozen to the floor.

She was a nurse and knew what every beep and read-out on the monitors meant. He was stable; she could see that at a glance. His complexion was pasty, he barely moved and his responses were slow. But his injuries weren't life-threatening, and according to the surgeon, he'd make a full recovery.

Except, at this moment, she wasn't a nurse who thought logically and dispassionately. She was scared and worried and guilty as hell. Seeing Ethan's prosthesis leaned up against the chest of drawers intensified her emotions.

He's a very lucky man.

She gave his brother and father time alone with Ethan. He was considerably more alert than she'd expected. Like Justin had said, Ethan was tough.

He asked about the fall, had Gavin repeat the story

twice. He also wanted to know the details of his injuries and what procedure had been performed during the surgery. As they continued talking, he became more and more groggy. Between his injuries and the pain medication, it was to be expected.

"Did the doctor mention how soon until I can ride again?" he asked.

Ride again! How could he even be thinking of that?

"Six weeks at least," Gavin answered. "Depends on how fast you recover. Knowing you, it won't be long."

Gavin was encouraging him. What kind of brother was he? Had he not heard the doctor's warning?

"Maybe you should give it a while," Wayne Powell said, the only sane person in the room as far as Caitlin was concerned.

"Come on, Dad." Ethan smiled crookedly. "Didn't you teach us when we fall to get right back in the saddle?"

And that was exactly what Ethan had done when he'd lost his leg. Why would she think a concussion, a half-dozen broken ribs and a multitude of minor injuries would stop him?

She didn't stand a chance.

"Where's Caitlin?" he asked, slurring her name.

"She's here." Gavin turned and motioned her into the room.

One step was all she could manage before walking into an invisible wall.

"Hey," Ethan said, lifting his head. He peered at her with unfocused eyes, then fell back on the pillow. "Sorry, I'm a little dizzy."

Caitlin, too. Her own head swam and her stomach roiled.

"I'll come back later." She grabbed the doorjamb, desperately needing support. "When you feel better."

"No, don't leave," Ethan croaked.

The invisible wall wouldn't let her through.

"Come on, Dad." Gavin patted him on the back. "Let's give them a minute alone."

They squeezed past her into the hallway, leaving Caitlin alone with Ethan.

She mustered all her courage. For such a small room, it was a very long walk to the bed. She attempted to draw on her nursing experience, use it as a shield.

It didn't work. She wasn't in love with her patients.

"How are you?"

It should have been her asking him the question.

"Me? You're the one who got bucked off a horse." And nearly killed. She leaned down and kissed his forehead, a lump rising in her throat.

"I'm sorry," he said.

"For what?"

"Ruining your Christmas."

"You didn't," she said, because that was what he needed to hear. Inside, she was dismayed and distraught. The day had gone from one of the most joyous she'd spent to one of the worst. "I'm just glad you're going to be okay."

"What about us? Will we be okay?"

The lump in her throat burned.

She wanted to reassure him. Tell him that nothing had changed. They were as good as they'd always been. But the past two and a half hours had taken a terrible toll on her, and she had yet to assess the damage.

"Let's talk tomorrow."

"That sounds like a brush-off." He was fighting to stay awake.

She would not have this conversation in the hospital with him lying there in pain and doped up on medication.

"You need to rest," she said.

"That's Nurse Carmichael talking."

"Yes, and she knows best right now." Rest for him, space for her.

"It was an accident."

She hated that word. People used it when they didn't want to claim any responsibility for a bad decision they'd made.

"I'll see you in the morning."

"You're running away." The medications he was on didn't disguise the reproving tone of his voice.

Why was it okay for him to leave and not her?

His eyes drifted closed and the frown he'd been wearing vanished. Seconds later, he was sound asleep.

She had no trouble crying now. Tears streamed from her eyes as she staggered past the nurse's station to the elevator.

She was in the parking lot before it dawned on her she had no vehicle, having ridden over with the Powells. Were they still in the hospital? She didn't remember seeing them in her hasty exit. Or Justin. Maybe he could drop her off at the ranch to fetch her van, on the way to…where was it he was going? Tamiko's parents' open house.

Thinking was hard, more than Caitlin could deal with at the moment.

Tears continued to fall. Someone asked her if she was all right. Fortunately, sobbing people weren't uncommon at hospitals.

Caitlin found her way to a bench outside the entrance, sat and waited for her composure to return. It did, though her hold on it was fragile and, she feared, temporary.

With quaking hands, she located her cell phone and dialed Justin's number.

"What's wrong?" he asked upon hearing her voice.

He knew what she'd been through after his fall, and would understand her better than anyone else.

"I can't keep doing this," she blurted. "I just can't."

Chapter Fifteen

Ethan hobbled to the pasture behind the barn and the specially designed paddock. Prince greeted him with a friendly whinny and a head toss.

"Don't try and get on my good side. It's too late for that."

He stroked the horse's head and sleek neck. They'd come a long way since his capture, he and this once wild mustang. Had forged a lasting bond against all odds.

Ethan wished he could say the same for him and Caitlin.

While he and Prince still had considerable work ahead of them, they were well on their way. He understood the horse, accepted him for what he was, flaws and all. Tempered his high hopes with reasonable expectations. Prince, Ethan was convinced, felt the same about him.

He wished he had some idea—*any* idea—of how Caitlin felt about him.

She hadn't returned even one of his phone calls in the six days since she'd fled his hospital room. He still wasn't quite sure what had happened. Damn concussion and pain pills had messed with his memory.

What he did remember was that she'd left in tears. Based on what his brother had witnessed in the waiting room, and the previous disagreements Ethan had had with Caitlin, he guessed his cowboy ways were the cause.

How were they supposed to resolve their differences if she didn't take his phone calls?

Justin was no help. He was busy job hunting now that he'd finished college. Ethan had talked to him once, and his advice was to be patient. Caitlin would come around.

Ethan had contemplated jumping in his truck and driving to her condo, surprising her with an unannounced visit, but he'd barely made it to the paddock without stopping four times to rest and let an excruciating spasm recede. Coughing hurt. Yawning, too. Sneezing nearly knocked him to his knees.

Dammit!

Ethan removed his hat and drove his fingers through his hair. He despised this helplessness. He was a doer, a fixer, a problem solver. And he was convinced he could fix whatever had gone wrong with him and Caitlin if he could just talk to her.

"Happy New Year, buddy." Clay came up beside him, his arm raised.

Ethan glared at his best friend. "You clap me on the back, and I swear, I'll deck you."

Clay chuckled. "And I'd deserve it." He gave Prince a lengthy appraisal. "You two make up yet?"

"I was never mad at him to begin with. He's a wild animal. Former one, anyway. I let my guard down when I shouldn't have." Ethan noticed Clay's clothes for the first time. "You going somewhere special?"

"Conner's party. Want to come along?"

Ethan had forgotten all about it. He and Caitlin had planned on going, before he got hurt. Even if he was up to it, which he wasn't, he wouldn't attend without her.

"Maybe next year."

"I noticed the clinic was open tonight. Guess they're having extended hours on account of the holiday."

"And your point?"

"Caitlin's van was in the parking lot." Clay leaned against the stall. "She's on duty and can't leave the clinic. If you were to, say, show up, she'd have no choice but to listen to you."

Ethan grinned. He'd always liked the way Clay thought. "I'd need a ride. I can't drive yet."

"Let's go."

Ethan spent a few minutes cleaning up before leaving with Clay. Caitlin's van was indeed parked in the clinic lot, just as his friend had said, and a handwritten sign on the door advertised extended hours.

"I don't know how long I'll be," he told Clay.

"I don't care, I'm not sticking around."

"You're not?"

"You'll have to find your own way home. I'm counting on Caitlin."

Ethan was, too.

Thanks to his busted ribs, the door to the clinic weighed about three times as much as it had before. Clenching his teeth, he pushed it open and stumbled inside, setting off the buzzer.

"Hi, can I help you?" a pleasant young woman at the counter asked. There was no one else in the waiting room.

"I'm here to see Caitlin Carmichael."

"She's on duty. Is this an emergency?"

He didn't hesitate. "Yes."

"Can I have your name?"

This time, he did hesitate. "Ethan Powell."

The woman picked up the phone and pressed a button. After a moment, she said, "There's an Ethan Powell here to see you. He says it's an emergency."

Seconds ticked by. So many he started having serious doubts.

Finally, the woman hung up the phone. "She'll be out in a minute. Have a seat."

Ethan didn't. Getting up again would be too strenuous. He waited by the window, which gave him an unobstructed view of the door to the exam rooms. The minute the receptionist had promised stretched into five, then eight, then—son of a bitch, what was taking her so long?

A young couple came into the clinic, the man looking like death warmed over and complaining of flu symptoms. While they filled out the paperwork, Ethan debated asking the receptionist to page Caitlin again.

Before he could make his way to the counter, she came through the door.

"Sorry I'm late. I was with a patient." Lines of tension etched her face, and dark circles surrounded her eyes. She hadn't been sleeping well.

"I thought you might be avoiding me."

She didn't acknowledge his joke. "Is everything okay? Are your injuries bothering you?"

"I'm fine."

"You said it was an emergency." She eyed him suspiciously.

"It is. We need to talk."

"I'm at work," she replied in a low, terse voice.

"Take a break."

Her lips thinned.

"Ten minutes. That's all I ask. I wouldn't be here if you'd answered any of my fifteen or twenty phone calls."

"Fine. Let me get my coat and tell Dr. Lovitt."

She returned a few minutes later, slipping her arms into her coat sleeves as she walked to the door.

He beat her there and opened it for her, paying the price as a spear of agonizing pain sliced through him.

"Honestly, Ethan," she snapped. "You don't always have to do things for me, especially when you're hurt."

"My father raised me to be a gentleman."

She squeezed her eyes shut. "I didn't mean to insult you."

"You didn't."

He gestured toward the tables and chairs in front of the coffee shop next door. Caitlin pulled her own chair out when he would have done it for her. She sat gracefully, Ethan with considerable effort.

"How are you doing?" she asked.

"I'll live."

His answer had been intended as another joke, but it was obvious by her sudden stiffening that he'd struck a chord. He hadn't had long to mentally compose what he wanted to say to her tonight, but talking to her had consumed his thoughts for days. He should've done a better job of breaking the ice.

"It was an accident. Not your fault, not my fault. Not even Prince's fault. The best-trained horses spook sometimes at nothing."

"I know that. I don't blame myself or Prince."

"But you blame me?"

She remained stubbornly silent. When she spoke at last, her words were measured.

"You are who you've always been. You like taking risks. Tempting fate. Pushing your limits. It's what made you a good soldier, good at training horses and a competitive athlete."

"And you don't like taking risks."

"No." Her eyes were full of misery and regret. "And I don't think I can be with someone who does."

A suffocating pressure closed around his chest, worse than when he'd broken his ribs. On some level he'd been expecting this.

"I'll quit riding broncs. Breaking horses, too."

"I wouldn't ask that of you. You were right when you said it isn't fair for one person to force another to give up something that's important to them."

"No, I was wrong." God, he was losing her. He could feel her ebbing away like the ocean at low tide. "People have to make compromises for a relationship to work."

"Giving up your dream isn't a compromise, and I refuse to be the cause of your unhappiness."

A sense of déjà vu came over Ethan, crushing him. He remembered a similar conversation from nine years ago that had gone much like this one. Except he'd been the one saying, "I refuse to be the cause of your unhappiness."

"The day you were hurt was a nightmare for me," she continued, a tremor in her voice. "The sight of you in that hospital bed—I couldn't deal with it. I nearly broke down. I did later, outside the hospital."

"Why? You're a nurse."

"Not that night I wasn't." She sniffed. "I should have come over to see you after you were released. But telling you when you were laid up…"

"Telling me what?" Ethan braced himself, instinctively knowing that whatever came next was going to change his life irrevocably. Again.

She sat up, determination in her expression. "I'm sorry, I can't see you anymore."

"You're part of me. The missing piece."

"One you can live without." She stood, her chair squeaking as it scraped across the concrete. "You have before."

She left him there, alone in the cold.

Sometime later, a few minutes or an hour, Ethan couldn't be sure, Clay appeared. Had he waited all this time?

"Come on, buddy. I'll take you home."

Ethan went with him, needing help finding the truck. He thought he might be lost for the rest of his life.

CAITLIN SAT ON THE CLOSED toilet lid and stared at the double pink lines on the testing wand she held. Reality, which she'd successfully kept at bay since yesterday morning, hit her full force. The wand dropped to the floor as she caught her falling head in her hands. Home pregnancy tests weren't one-hundred percent accurate. Which was why she'd taken a second one this morning. The chance that both tests showed a false positive was astronomical.

She was pregnant.

How had that happened?

Of course she knew how it happened, but...*how*? They'd used protection. Condoms weren't infallible, as she'd heard doctors tell patients many times. And there was that first night she and Ethan had spent together after the Holly Days Festival, when they'd had only one.

She mentally counted backward. Three, no, four weeks along.

What was she going to do? She pressed her fingertips to her throbbing temples and rubbed.

If she told Ethan, he'd go all Ethan on her. Want to get married. Raise the baby together. On top of all the other problems they had, they'd be adding having an instant family to the mix. Not the best way to start out.

She could leave Mustang Valley, maybe even Arizona. Go stay with her college friend in Columbus and have the baby there.

Then what? She couldn't come home, not if she didn't want Ethan to find out. And he would, eventually. Someone would see her and the baby and mention it.

No, she either told him outright and dealt with the consequences, or left Mustang Valley for good.

Not the kind of decisions a new mother should have to make. This was supposed to be a joyous moment she would treasure the rest of her life.

And, suddenly, it was.

She was pregnant! Going to have a baby! Elation bubbled up inside her, then spilled out in a giddy laugh. Tomorrow or next week was soon enough to decide what and if to tell Ethan. She was barely a month along, after all. For now, she would keep her condition a secret, bask in her happiness alone until the right moment to share it.

She no sooner emerged from the bathroom than her cell phone rang. A glance at the caller ID informed her it was Justin. Guilt needled her. She hadn't spoken to her brother much these past two and half weeks. Or her parents. She'd taken the breakup with Ethan hard. Loss of appetite. Insomnia. Churlishness. Depression. You name it, she had it.

After one look her parents would instantly know something was wrong. Caitlin wasn't up to fielding their questions. Justin would be worse. He'd pester her until she spilled her guts.

Briefly, she considered not answering his call, but another prick of guilt compelled her to press the receive button.

"Hey."

"Why didn't you tell me you and Ethan called it quits?"

"We weren't actually going together." A few weeks didn't constitute a relationship.

They were, however, long enough to create a life.

"I knew you were upset with him, but I figured you'd resolved it."

"How did you find out?" Caitlin asked.

"Ethan told me. He's really bummed."

"You saw him?"

"I'm here now. At the ranch."

"You are?" She wanted to ask how Ethan was doing. Instead, she voiced the second question on her mind. "What are you doing there?"

"Tamiko and I signed up for riding lessons."

"Riding lessons!" This conversation couldn't get any weirder. "Since when?"

"I thought you'd be here, considering it's Sunday afternoon, and I'd surprise you."

Wait a minute. Rewind. "Riding lessons? I thought you agreed that wasn't a good idea."

"I never said any such thing. You lectured and I listened."

"Look what happened to Ethan." Fear gripped her and shook her like a rag doll.

"I'm not riding bucking horses."

"I don't care if you're riding a pony. It's too dangerous."

"No more dangerous than white-water rafting on the Colorado River."

She'd been a wreck when he'd taken that harebrained trip last summer. "At least you were wearing a life jacket."

"And this time I'll be wearing a helmet."

She had to stop him. "I'll be right there."

"Don't come if you're planning on making a scene."

"When have I ever made a scene?" She grimaced. "Okay, I take that back. I have made a scene or two, but only because I care."

"See you when you get here," he said, and disconnected.

Caitlin didn't waste any time. She grabbed her purse and keys and hit the door at a run.

Turning into the Powells' driveway, she reduced her speed to the legal limit and was immediately ashamed of herself. She didn't usually drive like a maniac.

Upon reaching the open area in front of the stables, she started searching for Justin.

And, yes, Ethan.

She'd missed him. And this place. His family, too. How had they become so important to her after only a few weeks?

Maybe because they always were.

She scoured the main arena, where a dozen riders were exercising their horses, none of them Justin.

At last she spotted him in the round pen. The same pen where Ethan had been injured when riding Prince. Justin sat astride a horse, Ethan standing beside him. Tamiko straddled the fence, the empty wheelchair not far from her.

Where was her boyfriend?

Caitlin drove her van right up to the pen, hit the brakes and slammed the vehicle into Park. Shoving the door open, she bailed out, tripping over her own feet in her haste.

"Justin!"

"That didn't take long." An exuberant grin split his face.

"Are you okay?" She was aware of Ethan watching her, studying her.

Her body, always attuned to him, hummed in response.

"Great! This is amazing." Justin shielded his eyes from the afternoon sun and regarded the horizon. "I can't believe how far I can see. Look at the mountains."

The motion unbalanced him and he teetered in the saddle.

Caitlin let out a yelp. "Ethan, help him!"

"Whoa!" Justin grabbed the saddle horn.

Ethan reached up and placed a steadying hand on Justin's leg. "Hang on."

He looked considerably better than the night he'd shown up at the clinic, but not strong enough to catch Justin if he fell. Someone else must have lifted her brother onto the horse. Someone else should be here now.

"No problem." Justin let go of the saddle horn.

Ethan started walking, leading the horse, which Caitlin now recognized as old Chico.

She was going to kill both Ethan and her brother.

"He's doing great, don't you think?" Tamiko said.

Caitlin looked around. "Where's...um..."

"Eric? I really don't know."

She didn't have time to process Tamiko's answer because Justin clucked to Chico, and the horse broke into a run.

All right, not a run. A very, very sedate trot.

Ethan walked beside the horse, letting the lead rope dangle. If Chico reared or bucked, there was no way he could restrain him. Justin would be hurt.

At least he was wearing a helmet and, she noticed upon closer inspection, a safety vest. If Ethan had been wearing a helmet and vest when he fell off Prince, he might not have broken his ribs or sustained a concussion.

Wait! Justin didn't have a harness. Ethan said at Thanksgiving that he had harnesses Justin could use. What if he slipped again?

"Be careful," Caitlin said, sounding like the broken record she was, her white-knuckled hands gripping the railing. Thank God there was no wind today. She scanned the immediate vicinity for stray plastic bags anyway.

"I can't wait for my turn." Tamiko glowed.

Caitlin, on the other hand, couldn't speak. Her heart had lodged in her throat.

Was she the only one terrified?

Yes, she was—the only one. Not Justin or their parents or Tamiko. Certainly not Ethan. And he should be more than anyone, after what had happened to him.

All right, she was a little overprotective. A lot overprotective. But she was hardly unreasonable.

Was she?

She looked at her brother, really looked at him. He was enjoying himself. Now that she thought about it, he always seemed to be enjoying himself. For the past several years, anyway. Ever since he took up wheelchair athletics.

He grinned confidently at Tamiko as he rode past her, a far cry from the insecure, self-conscious geek he'd been in high school.

Caitlin had to stop seeing him as disabled and start seeing him as what he was, a capable, competent young man with endless potential and no need of a hovering older sister.

"Yes, he's doing well," she said, sensing a shift inside her.

After a few more circuits, Ethan led Justin through the gate. They stopped in front of Caitlin and Tamiko.

"What do you think?" Justin preened. "Are we ready for the races?"

Tamiko's smile was radiant and for him alone. "You were awesome."

"I'm impressed," Caitlin admitted, her pride overflowing.

"You're not just saying that?"

"Definitely not."

"Any chance I can ride around the ranch?" he asked Ethan.

"Not by yourself. Not yet."

She sent Ethan a silent thank-you.

He nodded, and the yearning in his eyes reached into her, tugging at her heart and her belly, where she carried their child.

"Can Tamiko take me?"

"How about your sister? And just up and down in front of the stables."

"Me!" she squeaked. "What if Chico starts bucking? I can't hold on to him."

"He won't buck. He has the temperament of a kitten." Ethan thrust the lead rope into Caitlin's hands. "Go on. You can do it."

He was talking about more than her brother riding a horse, she was sure.

"It'll be okay, sis," Justin said, also talking about more than riding.

Yes, it would be okay.

The shift in her was suddenly complete and seamless.

Giving Ethan one last long glance, she took a step, then another. Chico followed like the good, dependable horse he was.

As she and Justin passed the office, he said to her, "Thanks. I know this isn't easy for you."

She didn't respond, afraid she might start crying. Must be hormones.

"You have to stop feeling bad about the accident," Justin said. "I don't. Haven't for a long time."

"But you lost the use of your legs."

"Pretty incidental in the larger scheme of things."

"No, it isn't!"

"It is. I'm better off now than I ever was. I've got my degree. Have two job offers I'm considering. I play sports. White-water raft. I'm learning to ride a horse." He patted Chico's neck. "Have a girlfriend."

"Tamiko? What about Eric?"

"She dumped him. For me. For *me*," he repeated, wearing the goofy grin of a besotted man.

Caitlin wasn't just proud of him, she was impressed. "I'm glad." As long as he didn't get hurt.

She had to stop thinking like that—*would* stop thinking like that.

"I'm happy, sis."

He was. She could see it in his face, hear it in his voice.

The weight she'd been carrying for the last six years didn't lift entirely, but it decreased. Eventually, soon, she'd be free of it.

"You should be happy, too. Ethan loves you."

"I messed up with him." She sniffed and Chico gave her arm a sympathetic nudge.

"Nothing you can't repair."

"I don't know how."

"Talk to him. I guarantee, he'll listen."

"I'm not sure there's a point to it. I can't handle his bronc riding. You saw how I was at the hospital."

"You'd be surprised what you can handle if you have to. Look at me. Look at Mom and Dad."

He made a good argument. And she already felt stronger. Amazing what release from guilt could do for a person.

Chico turned abruptly and started walking in the opposite direction.

"Hey, there!" Caitlin pulled on the lead rope, then gave the horse his head. Chico was going exactly where she wanted to—back to Ethan.

He must have noticed a change in her because his whole countenance lit up at her approach.

"Can we go somewhere to talk?" she said when they were close enough.

His shoulders straightened as if he, too, had had a weight lifted from them. "I'll find Conner and T.J. so we can get Justin down."

"I'm fine," Justin said. "Tamiko will lead me around for a while."

Tamiko jumped off the fence in eager anticipation. Caitlin passed her the lead rope, and the pair took off.

By unspoken agreement, Caitlin and Ethan headed in the direction of the office.

"Do you think they'll be all right?" she asked. Old habits were hard to break.

"They'll be fine."

Caitlin sat on the top porch step, keeping Justin in sight, but not fretting about him. Not like she had, anyway.

Ethan lowered himself down beside her, his movements still stiff.

"How are you doing?"

"Better. The doctor suggested physical therapy. Know a good therapist?"

"I might."

They both laughed and, just like that, the tension between them evaporated.

"You first," she said.

He took a moment before continuing. "Being laid up the last couple of weeks has given me a lot of time to think. About my job. About rodeoing. About us." He cleared his throat. "I've made a decision."

His tone was so serious. Had she misinterpreted his intentions? Good heavens. He was breaking up with her. Now, after she'd finally come to her senses.

"I love you," she blurted.

"Good." He sagged with obvious relief. "That makes what I'm going to tell you a whole lot easier." He fitted his palm to her cheek and rubbed his thumb along her jawline. "After my discharge, I wanted to…needed to ride broncs. To prove to myself and everyone else I was the same man I'd been before I lost my leg."

"I understand. And you don't have to give up rodeoing for me."

"I want to." His dark eyes searched hers. "It isn't important to me anymore. Having you, loving you, is. Nothing I do matters without you in my life. You make me the man I want to be. If Justin hadn't tricked you into coming here today, I would have gone after you myself and begged you to give us a second chance." He chuckled. "Guess that would be a third chance."

"Justin tricked me?" She tried to be mad at her brother, but couldn't. "Remind me to thank him."

Ethan cupped her other cheek and held her face between his hands. "If you'll have me, I'll also give up breaking horses."

"That's your job."

"I'll find another one."

"Not on your life, cowboy, you hear me? You're a Powell."

"Caitlin, baby doll—"

"No. Quitting bronc riding is enough." She remembered Justin's words. "I can handle breaking horses, though. I'll need help. Lots of support and understanding."

"You'll have it."

He kissed her then, and it was the sweetest kiss he'd ever given her.

"Life is full of risks," she said dreamily. "And they're not all bad."

She'd taken a huge one minutes ago when she'd asked to talk to him, and it was already paying off.

"Marry me, Caitlin. I love you, too."

Her eyes went wide. "What did you say?"

"I'd get down on one knee, except between my bum leg and broken ribs, I'm not sure I could get back up."

She drew in a ragged breath, her earlier indecision fleeing. "There's something you need to know first."

"If you're worried about honing in on Gavin and Sage's wedding next month, I can wait. Not long, mind you."

"It's not that."

"We'll buy a ring. Sorry I proposed without one."

"No, no, no. I don't care about a ring. Well, I do, but not this second."

"Then what?"

"Marriage is life changing." She wavered, scared and yet bursting with excitement. "Having a baby is, too."

He stared at her blankly.

She huffed impatiently. Did she have to spell it out? "I'm pregnant."

His dumbfounded expression transformed into one of unabashed delight.

Ethan struggled to his feet. He barely made it and doubled over, a low sound exploding from him.

"Ethan, are you all right?" She was instantly up and grabbed his arm.

"My ribs." He was laughing, and the sound grew louder as he straightened.

She laughed with him.

Gavin threw open the office door. Caitlin hadn't realized he was in there.

"What's going on?" His glance traveled from Ethan to Caitlin. "I take it you two are back together."

"More than back together." Ethan stopped laughing and pulled Caitlin to him. "You did accept, didn't you?"

"Yes, I'll marry you." She put her arms around him gently, drunk on happiness.

Gavin barreled down the steps and embraced them both, ignoring Ethan's protest to take it easy. "It's about damn time."

Justin and Tamiko came over, her brother still mounted. "What's going on?" he asked.

Ethan let go of Caitlin and shouted through cupped hands, loudly enough for the entire ranch to hear, "We're getting hitched and we're having a baby."

After that, everything was a blur. Caitlin was aware of hugs and kisses and lots of congratulations. Wayne Powell suddenly appeared. He must have come out of the house to investigate all the commotion. Sage and the girls were with him.

"Ethan's mother would be so happy." Wayne kissed Caitlin on the cheek. "Another grandchild."

Someone had helped Justin down from the horse, for

he was suddenly in his wheelchair. He held her fiercely when she leaned down to hug him.

"Thanks," she whispered. "For the advice and for tricking me into coming here. You're the best."

"Anytime, sis."

"Guess I'd better let Mom and Dad know."

Ethan put an arm around her. "We'll drive out there later. Tell them together."

She beamed at him. "Really?" That was exactly the right thing to do.

"You could have a double wedding," Tamiko suggested gleefully, then reddened when everyone stared at her.

Ethan found his voice first. "What do you think? I know it's kind of short notice."

Caitlin could tell by his eager grin that he liked the idea. He'd want to get married as soon as possible, what with the baby coming. "Gavin and Sage may not want—"

"Gavin and Sage *absolutely* want," Sage answered for them both. "All the arrangements are under way. It makes perfect sense."

"Okay." Caitlin shrugged, suddenly warming to the idea, as well. "Let's have a double wedding."

They took their celebrating inside to continue over supper.

Caitlin sat at the kitchen table next to Ethan, across from her brother, and with the family that had come to mean as much to her as her own.

When the meal was nearing an end, Wayne tapped his water glass with his fork. Everyone fell silent. "Here's to my second future daughter-in-law. Welcome to the Powell family." Wayne smiled at Caitlin affectionately. "I've been waiting nine years to say that."

She'd been waiting nine years to hear it.

The passage of time, the trials and tribulations she and Ethan had confronted and conquered, made the moment all the more meaningful.

Christmas wishes could and did come true.

Beneath the table, Ethan took her hand and linked their fingers. *"Stay with me tonight,"* he mouthed.

As if she would ever leave him or this place again.

* * * * *

Laura Marie Altom of Tulsa, Oklahoma, is a bestselling, award-winning author of over forty books. Her works have made several appearances on bestseller lists, and she has over a million books in print worldwide. This former teacher and mother of twins has spoken on numerous occasions at both regional and national conferences, and has been married to her college sweetheart for twenty-six years. Visit her online at lauramariealtom.com.

Be sure to look for more books by Laura Marie Altom in Harlequin American Romance—the ultimate destination for romance the all-American way. There are four new Harlequin American Romance titles available every month. Check one out today!

THE BULL RIDER'S
CHRISTMAS BABY

Laura Marie Altom

Belated congrats for my June graduates:

Terral Lynn Altom III, Hannah Marie Altom and Russell Shook.

I'm not only crazy-proud of all of you, but I can't wait to see what amazing grown-ups you become! That said, no matter how old you may be, you will always be my babies and as such are expected to forever believe in Santa, the Easter Bunny and the wondrous healing powers of a great big Mom hug! I love you!

Chapter One

Oklahoma rain drummed the rental car's roof, drowning out Hank Williams on the radio. For mid-September, the air was unbearably muggy. Feet swollen and the bagel she'd downed at Baltimore-Washington International threatening to make a break for it, Wren Barnes peered out her side window, praying she'd turned onto Cash Buckhorn's driveway and not merely another country road.

Thankfully, the drive stopped.

The downpour didn't.

Barely able to make out Cash's home through the rain, Wren prayed for the umpteenth time she'd made the right decision. Although regardless, there was no turning back now.

Since this would be a hasty mission, she'd leave her overnight bag on the passenger-side floorboard, but in case she needed tissues or antacid, she snatched her purse. Forcing a deep breath, she charged from her vehicle, running through the rain. Seconds later she stood on Cash's covered front porch, dripping.

Even in the midst of a storm, the home was lovely. A modern mix of stone walls and sheets of glass for windows. The place reeked of money, meaning as usual, she didn't fit in—would never fit in until she'd finished her training. But that was okay. She and her baby wouldn't be in Weed Gulch long. And then, back in Baltimore, the two of them would create the family she'd always craved.

Wren had just raised her hand to knock on a weathered copper-plated door when from around the corner stepped a cowboy and all that that implied. Through the steady downpour Wren couldn't get a complete image. Even squinting netted her the same sort of mouthwatering, wholly masculine, leather-chaps-wearing silhouette that had first gotten her into this mess. Mouth dry, pulse erratic, she managed to stammer, "C-Cash?"

"In the flesh, darlin'. What can I—" Having rounded the edge of an immaculate wildflower garden, he stepped onto the porch, not in the least concerned about the water dripping from his hat. "Oh. It's you."

The fact that her baby's father didn't even remember her name brought on a fresh wave of nausea. Bolting toward the rail, with as much grace as she could manage she upchucked the meal she'd tried so valiantly to keep down.

"Hey, whoa!" He stepped up behind her, taking firm hold of her heaving shoulders. "The gardener's gonna have my hide."

"S-sorry." Wren tried standing, but having had hardly any sleep for as long as she could remember, exhaustion clung like lead weights to her body.

"That's it," he soothed, tempting her to lean against the muscular chest forever seared into her memory. "Take it easy."

Never had she wished more that she was a delicate Southern belle prone to fainting. Alas, she'd been born in Philly to deadbeat parents. Forced from the tender age of two to survive in a church-run orphanage. The experience had delivered steady lessons in self-reliance. Because of which, she drew a deep breath, tugged her sweater over her nearly-six-month baby bump and refrained from any further leaning.

"You're Dr. Wren, right? We, ah, played your profession and then went on to dabble in mine?"

She cringed. Did he have to speak of such things in broad daylight? "Yes, um, unfortunately, that would be me."

"Well, hell, there wasn't anything unfortunate about that night. Unless you happened to catch a glance at our bar bill."

She'd forgotten his laugh. A slow, drawn-out chuckle of sorts during which he flashed strong white teeth and dimples in both of his whisker-stubbled cheeks. Cash wasn't merely handsome—with short, dirty-blond curls and eyes as green as daffodil stems, he was take-a-girl's-breath-away gorgeous. And he knew it. Confidence oozed from his every pore. Along with the knowledge that most every woman on the planet from age nine to ninety-two was helpless in the battle against his charm.

Except her. She'd already fallen once, and just as soon as she did the right thing in telling him he was going to be a father, she'd forever be on a *mostly* Cash-free diet.

"What's the matter?" he asked, removing his cowboy hat to whisk water droplets from leather chaps. Before seeing him ride bulls in that Vegas rodeo, she'd thought they'd been worn only in movies. "Missed me and thought you'd come round for more?"

"N-not exactly," she muttered. "I'm afraid it's more complicated. Would you mind going inside? I'm a little chilled."

"Sure." He opened the door and gestured for her to lead. He hadn't noticed her enormous belly, which, at the moment, suited her. The home was as spectacular on the inside as it was outside. With Native American motifs, buttery-soft leather sofas and lounge chairs placed around a soaring stone fireplace, she could only imagine how inviting it would be during a snow. Warm and cozy with a floor-to-ceiling view of rolling prairie and tumbling flakes. "Have a seat. Can I get you something to eat or drink?"

"No, thank you." Where to start? As wet as she was, she chose a wooden rocker.

He sat on the polished stone hearth. "Gotta say you're the last person I expected to see today."

"Yes, well, I—*we*—have had a problem arise." Not unlike her queasy stomach. "You might recall that when we, um, found pleasure on the balcony that the condom broke?"

"Oh, hell…" The tan slid from his face. "You're not tellin' me…"

"Cash, I'm pregnant with your baby." Before he got a grip on her last statement, she hit him with another. "But I'm not here to make demands—financial or otherwise." Curving her hands to her belly, she added, "If you'll recall, in Vegas I was celebrating my med-school graduation—the trip was a gift from a good friend— and was due to start residency in Baltimore mid-July. Well, as you can guess, this—"

"Ma'am, with all due respect, could you please stop yakking long enough to give a man time to think?"

"I'm chronically on the run. I don't have time to yak—more like hastily convey as-needed information."

Snorting, he said, "Hate to be the bearer of bad news,

but honey, we've got a lot more to worry about than se-
mantics."

"You think?" Standing, she paced, struggling to ignore the way the room had begun to spin.

"Being in your condition, shouldn't you sit? Better
yet, get in bed?"

"Exercise is healthy." That said, her current degree
of dizziness was not.

"Are you sure?" Though his expression seemed to
hold genuine concern, it also held a fair amount of panic.

She nodded.

"Damn, I didn't see this coming." He'd taken a red
bandanna from his back pocket and now wiped it across
his forehead. "Yes, indeed, this does present some problems."

"But it doesn't have to. That's the beauty of my plan."

"Your plan?" He chuckled. "From where I'm sitting,
looks like the bun in your oven is pulling our strings."

"Like I said, your life doesn't in any way need to
change. I'm here on a fall break from my residency. I
felt it best you hear this news in person. Now that you
have, I'll be on my way and our baby no longer needs
to be your concern."

He half laughed. "That's where you're wrong."

"Excuse me?"

"The baby growing inside you is a Buckhorn, and
lady, I don't know diddly-squat about your family, but
one thing you should know about mine is that our offspring don't go anywhere until they're old enough to
decide they want to."

Though she'd thankfully returned to her rocker, now
he was the one pacing. "Yes, sirree, this does present
a problem."

"Only if you let it." Her nausea and dizziness returned with a vengeance. Couldn't he be a gentleman and make this easy for her?

Slapping on his hat, he ambled with a slight limp toward the door.

"Where are you going?" she called, jumping to her feet. "We still have a lot to—"

Cash glanced back just in time to watch the very beautiful, very pregnant Wren Barnes crumple to the floor.

"You'll be fine," Doc Haven said to Wren thirty minutes later. She'd hardly budged since Cash had hefted her onto the sofa.

Cash thanked his lucky stars that the white-haired country doctor who'd been wearing the same wire-framed glasses since Cash was a little boy had been on a neighboring ranch when he'd called.

Checking her watch, Wren asked, "Does that mean I'm free to leave? It's a long drive back to Tulsa, and I've got a 5:00 a.m. flight."

"If that's the case," Doc said, rocking back on his heels, "we might have a situation."

"How so?" Wren wrinkled her pert nose. "I've got studying to do back home and am operating on a very narrow timeline."

"Sorry to hear that." After jotting a few notes in a black journal, Doc said, "Your fainting spell and sky-rocketing blood pressure tell me you need to be off your feet for no less than a week before I'm clearing you to travel as far as the local feed store, let alone halfway across the country."

"I *am* leaving," Wren assured him, "and I would *never* faint."

Cash snorted. "Mind explaining why I had to scoop you up from the floor?"

Not meeting his gaze, she said, "I was tired. It's been a long day."

"Um-hmm." Doc wrote on a scratch pad, then tore off the top sheet and handed it to Cash. "I'll run tests on the blood and urine samples, and you head down to the pharmacy and pick her up some iron tabs. Call if anything changes. In the meantime, you two kids behave."

With the doctor gone, Wren struggled for the right thing to say. Not only had she planned to be headed home already, but she was stuck staying with a man she hardly knew? No. Easing upright on the sofa she said, "Now that we're on our own, if you'd be so kind as to help me to the door, I'll…" Hand to her forehead, she used every ounce of her strength to hold her spinning nausea at bay.

"Can it," Cash said, sliding his hands under her before lifting her into his arms.

She squeaked, automatically circling her arms around his neck. "Put me down."

"Why? So you can get yourself all riled up only to faint again? Not happening on my watch. You gave me a hell of a scare. For the next week, you just plan on keeping that luscious booty of yours in bed."

Reddening at the memory of his hands on her bare *booty,* she said, "But I have to get…"

With a long stride, he'd already headed down a shadowy hall, grunting as he veered to his right to enter a sumptuous bedroom. Featuring another wall of windows, this one overlooked a free-form pool and hot tub surrounded by low rock walls and more wildflowers that looked as if they'd always been there. Wheat-colored carpet cushioned his footfalls. A rough-hewn log bed had been made in down linens.

Cash set her on the bed as carefully as if she were a porcelain doll. At the moment, as wretched as she felt, she appreciated his help. Though admitting any sort of weakness had never been her strong suit, this was one case in which she felt as if her own body was betraying her. "Bathroom's in here," he said, laying a throw blanket over her before ducking through another door to flip on lights to bathroom luxury fit for a five-star spa. "After you've rested for a while, help yourself to whatever you need. There should be towels and spare toiletries. Food's in the fridge. I..." He sharply exhaled. "Sorry, this has all caught me off guard. I need to get out of here for a while. I've gotta have time to think."

"Sure," she said, casting him a faint smile. "I understand. Take all the time you need."

IN THE BARN, surrounded by his favorite smells of oats, straw and horses, Cash dropped to sit hard on a hay bale, in the process jamming his screwed-up knee. He grimaced at the pain. If it hadn't been for a nasty spill he'd taken in Oklahoma City just three weeks prior and in the process tearing the medial collateral ligament, he wouldn't even be here. Pending further MRI readings, National Bull Rider tour docs had put him on a minimum six-week leave.

Taking out his phone, he hit speed dial for his big brother, Dallas. Though Cash was a respectable twenty-seven years old, on this particular afternoon he felt all of six, facing his father after having accidentally blown his math book to bits with a superstrength firecracker.

"What's up?" Dallas answered on the second ring. "Finish exercising the mares?"

"Yes, but—"

"And you got them in the barn before the storm?"

"Not yet, but—"

"Dammit, Cash, you're killing me. I know you've got a full plate, but we're trying to run a business here, and—"

Cash had never been what one might call an expert communicator, so before heartburn churned up his gut, he blurted out, "I'm pregnant."

"What?"

"Yeah. You know how Ruby dumped me right before that last ride I had in Vegas?"

"Uh-huh…" Even Dallas's grunts didn't sound happy.

"To celebrate, I hooked up with this uptight brunette from out East, only turns out she was actually pretty wild, and—"

"Holy hell," Dallas roared, "would you get to the damn point!"

"Condom broke. She's pregnant."

His big brother, the rock of their family since their father had died three years earlier, had apparently fallen speechless.

"You there?"

"Oh, I'm here, all right. When's the wedding? Mama didn't raise us to not do right by a woman. If she catches wind of this before you put a ring on that gal's finger, you'll never hear the end of it."

"I know, which is why I'm calling. I realize everyone will expect me to do the so-called right thing, but what if I can't?"

"So help me, if this is one of your practical jokes…"

"Honestly, would I joke about something like this? Vegas was hot, but God's honest truth, right now I'd swear off women forever. Had my eye on a smoking-hot redhead that night in OK City when I took my fall. Should've had my mind on business. Females are nothing but trouble, and—"

"Would you hush? Your voice is bringing on a migraine. In the meantime, you need to reassess your marriage views before Mom gets wind of this."

"Thanks, bro. You've been a lot of help." Especially considering Cash hadn't even gotten around to telling his brother he was now stuck with the woman living in his home for an indefinite length of time.

Dallas grunted. "And my whole damned life you've been a walking—or in this case, limping—pain in my ass."

Wren rested on her side, staring out the bedroom window, trying to regroup. She was drowning in fear. In hindsight, hopping a plane and showing up on Cash's doorstep hadn't been one of her brightest ideas. Should she have stayed in Baltimore? Told Cash he was going to be a father via internet or phone?

Eyes stinging, the ever-present knot in her throat hurting more than usual, she indulged in a brief crying jag before forcing a deep breath. Her entire life she'd been on her own. The orphanage had taught her to become an island. Self-sufficient and independent. Knowing she wanted more for her future family, she'd studied hard. Won scholarships. Fought her way to the top of her college and then med-school classes.

An unplanned pregnancy went against everything she'd fought so hard to become. That said, she hugged her womb, knowing that despite this momentary setback, she wouldn't trade her baby for the world.

When the front door slammed, Wren jumped.

"Hello?" Cash called.

"In here." With the backs of her hands she wiped still-damp cheeks.

Even barefoot, he towered over her. Despite the room's airy, open feel, the walls closed in around her. She'd never been the claustrophobic type, but his larger-than-life personality made it hard to breathe. Or maybe it was just those damned chaps!

A muscle ticking in his jaw, he turned his glare out the window. "I owe you an apology."

"Oh?"

"I should've handled this better. Truth is I'm kind of freaked out. This isn't the sort of thing that happens every day."

"Tell me about it." Even though Wren had had plenty of time to adjust, there were still days she couldn't get a grip on how far off course she'd strayed.

"When you get a chance," she said, "could you please get my rental agreement and overnight bag from my car? I'll call the agency for an extension."

"Will do. But let me give you a credit card to cover the extra days."

"Not necessary," she argued.

"How about you lie there making our baby and let me worry about everything else?"

"Seriously? You're able to say that with a straight face?" The sooner she got out of his home, the better. With that attitude, Cash Buckhorn sounded like a throwback to the days before Oklahoma had even been a state.

"What?" He blasted her with his smile. As usual, her traitorous body hummed under his spell. Just looking at him made her all hot and bothered. Luckily, there wouldn't be any additional touching between them. "You are making a baby, right?"

Having nothing more to say, she rolled over, blocking his powerful dimples from view.

"Not to change the subject," he said in a perfectly normal tone implying he still didn't *get* what he'd said to tick her off, "but I've got a big family. They're a bunch of busybodies. If you're going to be here a week, they're going to find out about it, and when they do, it's only fair I give you a heads-up."

"Regarding what?"

"The fact that you're carrying my child but don't have my ring on your finger."

"Isn't that archaic? The notion that a woman has to be married just to have a baby?"

He shrugged. "I couldn't agree more, but around here, folks see things differently."

"Is that what you want? To get married?"

"No offense, but no freaking way."

Though it was good news that his Old West chivalry ended at the very idea of a shotgun wedding, the vehemence behind his statement made her feel about as welcome as ants at a picnic. She'd always been so goal oriented that allowing a man into her life had never even been a priority. Sure, she'd let loose on a few weekends here and there, but for the most part, she stayed to herself, keeping her eyes on the prize of one day becoming a respected doctor. She dreamed of losing the stigma of having been a throwaway child. She wanted to feel needed and useful and above all, loved. "I appreciate your honesty. It's good we're both on the same page."

He actually sighed with relief. "So you don't think we should marry, either?"

"Of course not," she managed to say with a forced laugh. Although one day marriage was very much on her to-do list, for now it was out of the question.

Chapter Two

"You're pretty as the south pasture view." Georgina—Cash's mother and queen of the Buckhorn empire that included everything from cattle and quarter-horse breeding to oil—surveyed the mother of his child as if she were a filly up for auction. "A little on the scrawny side, but that's easily fixable with plenty of home cooking. Isn't that right, son?"

"Yes, ma'am," Cash muttered, wishing he hadn't told Dallas *everything* concerning Wren's visit. That way, he could've eased his mom into the matter. Kind of like you didn't want to jump into a cold pond on the first swim of summer, it wasn't a good idea letting your mom know you'd gotten a virtual stranger pregnant. If his mother found out, she'd have them to the courthouse within the hour. Which was why he was grateful to Wren for hiding her belly with an oversize purse. Cash had been all for keeping Wren's temporary presence on the ranch a secret, but she'd insisted on meeting his mother. Since in the twenty-four hours Wren had been in his home the color had returned to her cheeks, he'd agreed to a short outing before putting her back to bed.

"When Dallas told me his little brother had a woman staying with him, I didn't believe it. Now that I've seen it with my own eyes, I need to know everything. How you met. Where you're from. Who your parents are. Don't skip a single detail."

Wren opened her mouth to speak, but thankfully Stella, nanny to Dallas's twin daughters, rounded the corner from the hall leading into the vaulted living room. The Western-themed grandeur of the ranch's main home made his look like a playhouse. "Whew. Betsy and Bonnie are at their friend Megan's. They're eating there, too, which means I'm free until at least eight." Only just noticing the stranger in the room, she said, "I'm sorry. I didn't know we had company."

"Stella Ward, meet Cash's new girl, Wren Barnes, from—I'm sorry. I never did hear where you're from." His five-ten mom wore her white hair in a low ponytail, and had tucked her blue plaid Western shirt into the waistband of her jeans. Out of her back pocket a pair of red leather gloves hung like a turkey wattle.

"Baltimore," Wren said.

"You're a long way from home," Stella noted. "How did you two meet?"

"At the Venetian in Vegas," Wren said.

"Yeah, we, um, fought over the same slot machine." Cash forced a grin. "She won."

Alongside Wren, he slipped his arm around her waist, begging her with a squeeze to keep her mouth shut about the reality of their situation.

Her pinched smile told him the jury was still out on her decision. Thank the Lord for that humongous purse!

"Must've been a good machine," his mother noted, lowering herself onto the custom sectional his dad had had commissioned the year before he'd died. "I'm assuming this epic battle took place during your last rodeo out there?"

"Yes, ma'am." Cash further tightened his hold. "We've

talked every night since. But then I got to thinking it was high time I saved myself some money by just flying the girl out here."

"But Henry told me there's a strange car parked at your house. Your daddy and I didn't raise you to make a guest travel all that way unaccompanied." Count on Henry not to keep his big mouth shut. The old guy had been working the ranch since Cash had been in diapers.

"It wasn't a big deal, Mrs. Buckhorn." She shifted her weight from one foot to the other, and it occurred to Cash that considering her condition, Wren might need to sit.

Come to think of it, the way his knee throbbed, copping a squat wasn't a half-bad idea.

Stella snorted. "Would be to me. Wren, I wouldn't have put up with that if I were you. Plus, I imagine that must've set you back a pretty penny."

"I'll pay her back," Cash said. "In not only money, but kisses." He smooched her cheek.

At which point she shoved him away. "Enough's enough. Mrs. Buckhorn, Stella, I'm sorry to have participated in this sham for even five minutes, but the truth of the matter is that..." Down went her purse, taking Cash's sinking stomach along with it. "I'm pregnant, and—"

"Oh, dear," said Georgina. "The way you carry on, Cash, I worried about something like this."

"Carry on? Before meeting Wren I'd been faithful to Ruby for two long weeks."

"That's my point. Two weeks? You're incapable of holding a meaningful relationship." She paced. "Your good looks were bound to get you in trouble. Even though you and Ruby had been on and off for years, she was all the time worrying about one of those buckle bunnies throwing themselves at you and one day coming away with the prize."

"Stop right there," Wren interjected. "I'm certainly not a buckle bunny, whatever that is, and Cash is hardly a prize, but my worst nightmare. For as long as I can remember, I've wanted a baby, but not like this. As we speak, I'm supposed to be deep into my first year of medical residency. Not stuck in Oklahoma with a no-good cowboy who doesn't even have the sense to buy a condom that won't break."

Georgina and Stella began talking at once.

Cash slipped his fingers into his mouth to whistle them quiet.

"First—" he directed his words to Wren "—it took two to tango, and honey, I don't recall hearing any complaints from you. Second," he said to his mother, "before you start nagging, I'm a full-grown man and don't need a lecture. Third—" he glared at his nieces' busybody nanny "—you stay out of this. It's none of your concern."

"It is," Stella countered, "if I have a wedding to put together in only a few days."

"Stop the bus," Cash said, holding up his hands. "No one said anything about a wedding. Wren and I agree the whole idea is archaic. Besides which, as long as her blood pressure checks out, she'll be gone within a week."

"If you were raised in a barn, getting married is archaic," his mother interjected.

Hands up, Wren said, "Please, the last thing I intended was to start all of this bickering."

"Yeah, well, you failed miserably." Cash shot her a glare before walking out the front door. "Couldn't you have held up the purse a few minutes longer?"

On her own with a pack of female wolves, Wren was unsure what to do with her hands. "You, ah, certainly have a lovely home, Mrs. Buckhorn."

"Thank you," Cash's mother said with a cold formality Wren didn't like nearly as well as her earlier, friendly way.

Clearing her throat, Georgina said, "I've never been one to beat around the bush, so here goes... While I certainly can't force you and my son to marry, the fact that you're carrying his child means a great deal to me." Crossing to an oak rolltop desk, she withdrew a checkbook and proceeded to write. "How much will it cost me to keep this baby in the family, starting by having it born with the Buckhorn name?"

"Y-you can't be serious," Wren said. "This isn't about money. At all. I wouldn't even be here if a freak fainting spell hadn't forced me to temporarily stay."

Stella asked, "Are you and the baby okay?"

"Fine," Wren assured her, "but my blood pressure was unusually high. Dr. Haven felt it was best that I stay off my feet this week—just to be safe. After that, I have to complete my residency as planned and Cash can, well..." She fidgeted with her hands. "Do whatever it is Cash does."

Sitting hard on the desk chair, Georgina Buckhorn didn't try hiding the fact that she'd started to cry—in the process making Wren feel all the worse for standing by her conviction to not only finish her education, but remain single while doing it.

"Georgina, hon," Stella soothed, up from the sofa and rubbing the older woman's back. "Everything's going to be okay."

"How?" Cash's mother wailed. "Both of them are clearly not in their right minds. In my day, when a woman got pregnant, she got married. There was none of this career mumbo jumbo."

"But you helped Duke with the ranch," Stella pointed out.

"That was different. This land was our mutual love," she said with a sniffle. Looking to her friend, she said, "Stella, would you mind fetching me a cool glass of sweet tea?"

The nanny scampered off.

"If you don't mind my asking—" Georgina shifted in her chair "—what do your folks think about all of this?"

"Honestly, ma'am…" Wren raised her chin. "I don't have *folks*. I've been on my own for as long as I can remember, which is why keeping this baby is so important." Cupping her hands to her belly, to the tiny life inside, she added, "More than anything, I want a family. Unfortunately, in order to properly care for my baby, I first need to finish my training. By no means is this the perfect scenario I've always dreamed of, but I'm a firm believer in playing the cards I've been dealt."

"WHO'S RUBY?"

Early evening, Cash looked up from shoveling manure to find the source of his consternation. Wren had changed from her uptight suit into a pair of jeans and a Johns Hopkins Med School T-shirt. Impressive. With a school pedigree like that, he could see why she wouldn't want to waste her life in Weed Gulch. "Shouldn't you be in bed?"

"Probably, but I'm going stir-crazy cooped up in the house."

Scowling, he asked, "What's wrong with my house?"

"Nothing," she assured him. "It's lovely. I'm just not used to having so much downtime."

"Oh." To avoid seeing the strain her nice, full breasts put on her shirt, Cash went back to shoveling. It was just his luck to not only be stuck with a pregnant hottie in the house for the next week, but not even be able to touch her. Maybe if he ignored her, she'd go away.

"You never answered my question. Ruby?"

No such luck. "Ruby was my somewhat recent past."

"Please stop being evasive and answer the question."

Leaning on his pitchfork, he wasn't sure where to begin.

"I gather you've known her awhile."

He grunted. "Like Mom said, on-and-off high school sweethearts—mostly *off.*"

"If she meant so much, why haven't you married her?"

"Truth?" His facial features hardened. "Bull riding meant more. Which I guess gives us something in common, huh, Doc?"

Hefting herself onto a pile of hay bales, she made the universal sign of scales with her hands. "Riding bulls/ saving lives. I fail to see the correlation."

"You wouldn't." Turning his back on her, he returned to work. His daddy had always said nothing cleared a cloudy mind like weary muscles. His aching knee knew the adage to be true.

"Whatever." After a deep sigh, she said, "Back to Ruby. If you wouldn't stop riding bulls long enough to marry her, why would your mother expect you to marry me? Makes no sense."

"Nope." Wishing she'd hush, Cash quickened his pace, hoping the harder he ignored her, the more she'd get the hint he wanted to be left alone.

"I mean, beyond sharing this baby, you and I have

no connection. That means you're free to date, and one day marry, any woman you want."

"That simple, huh?" Judging by the furrow between her eyebrows, she wasn't quite as sold on the idea of him hooking up with another gal as she'd like him to believe. Good. If he was hurting from having to look at her gigantic pregnant boobs, he'd feel better knowing she wasn't happy, either.

Wren struggled for a coherent thought, eventually sputtering, "It could be—simple. If you'd let it." It wasn't fair that Cash had removed his shirt, turning her mind to mush. Having that bare chest pressed to hers had brought on the kind of heavy, sexual wanting she'd never dreamed possible. Which, in light of her current condition, was a fact she'd do well to remember. This time around, he was strictly hands-off. Especially since with his golden curls kissed by honeyed evening sun, it was easy to imagine how beautiful their son or daughter would be.

"I've got work to do," he snapped.

"I only made an innocent comment. Why are you defensive?"

"You really wanna know?" Stabbing his pitchfork in hay, he raked his fingers through his hair. "Because aside from one insanely hot night, I don't even know you. Because what happened in my life before we met is none of your business. Because I just want a few minutes to myself to process the fact that like it or not I'm going to be a father. I've got a million reasons. Need more?"

Mutely, she shook her head.

He was right—on all counts. So why did that fact hurt? Why did she even care? In a week she and her baby would be on their way, and aside from what would hopefully be civilized holiday visits she'd rarely see him again.

"Damn, if I don't feel married already." After smacking the stable wall, he marched toward the house.

Upon noticing his backside was equally impressive, Wren felt her mouth go dry. If only she didn't have those wild Vegas flashbacks to contend with. Maybe then she'd stand a fighting chance at keeping her mind on task. As for where her body was headed…

The baby she carried pretty much said it all!

THIRTY MINUTES LATER Cash pushed himself out of the pool and grabbed for a towel. A swim always cleared the fog from his brain. Too bad his knee still hurt like hell. The morning's rain was long gone and with sun beating on wet prairie, the day had been a scorcher. The scent of drying chlorine already rose from the pavement.

He reluctantly headed for the house. Wren carried his child. Shouldn't he at least feel warm and fuzzy toward her? Instead, the notion of not only seeing her again, but being stuck with her for a week was incomprehensible.

What would they talk about? Would his mother keep riding him about marrying? Couldn't she just accept the fact that he had reasons he wasn't ready to head down the aisle—damned good ones?

He found Wren in his guest room, lying crossways on the bed reading, damn near camouflaged by clothes. T-shirts, shorts and silky, lacy unmentionables, the mere sight of which had him shifting his fly to a more comfortable position. Their night in Vegas hadn't been merely hot, but more like an inferno. Where was *that* woman now? And how the hell had she squeezed so much into an overnight bag?

"You okay?" he asked.

"Sure." After raising her gaze from the pages of what looked to be a steamy, pirate-ravishing-a-maiden saga, she rolled onto her side. "Why?"

"You look like an old cat I used to have. She'd spend hours ripping up my room, then lounge among the wreckage, purring like a feline queen."

Wren laughed. "No purring for me. Just exhaustion. I got off to a great start unpacking, but I seem to have a tenth of my normal energy. It's a drag."

"Sorry." Not sure what to do with his hands, he settled on crossing his arms.

"What're you apologizing for?"

"Not to brag, but it was my superhuman seed that got you into this predicament." After capping off his outrageous statement with the slow grin that universally got him out of hot water with women of all ages, he yanked off his towel, using it to wipe down his still-water-beaded chest.

Wren rolled her eyes. "Never have I encountered an ego bigger than yours."

"Thanks." He rubbed his damp hair. "I think." He'd just started unfastening his swim trunk's button-fly when the good almost-doctor cleared her throat.

"Do you mind?" Slapping down her book, she raised her eyebrows a good inch.

"Mind what?"

"Not undressing in front of me."

"In case you've forgotten, we might be strangers when it comes to knowing each other's favorite colors and foods. But in the biblical sense, back in Vegas, we pretty much became experts on each other's anatomy. Think it's a little late for you to now turn shy."

It didn't take special psychological training to see that she struggled keeping her eyes off him.

"It's all right, you know." He gave his chest and abs a flourish. "You're allowed to look."

Not only did she grab for the nearest eye covering, but she said, "For the duration of my stay, it would be most appreciated if you'd disrobe in your own room."

On that, he had to laugh. Two could play this game. "Oh, honey, I'll keep my naked body behind closed doors as long as you quit waving those she-devil scraps you call panties in front of your face."

Yanking them down to see that she had indeed covered her eyes with lace, she growled.

He smiled and took his sweet time sauntering all the way into *his* shower.

Chapter Three

"Could you please speed it up?"

Standing in front of a pen filled with adorably chirping, fuzzy yellow chicks, Wren shot Cash a dirty look. They'd shared a house for all of two days and already the man drove her nuts. "Since I'm still dizzy, I told you I could ask your mother to drive me to town for shampoo. Then I wouldn't have had you nagging me over every little thing."

"And I told you, nobody carts around my pregnant woman but me. You're my responsibility. Besides, even if Mom had driven you, I was already headed to the feed store, so what was the point in wasting two tanks of gas?" In honor of their being out in civilization—if Weed Gulch and all ten of its downtown stores could even be considered civilized—Cash had at least worn clean boots and a long-sleeved baby-blue shirt that did wicked-good things to his green eyes. Not to be too formal, he'd left his shirttails loose. His straw cowboy hat looked as if it had been sat on one too many times and then run over by a tractor. Despite that fact, even at the feed store Cash drew women the way cupcakes drew kindergartners.

"Afternoon, Miss Lucy." He tipped his hat to a pigtailed five-year-old who was kicking the fool out of a gumball machine. "What seems to be the problem?"

"It took my money."

Kneeling, he plucked her fallen quarter from the concrete floor. "Wouldn't happen to be this money, would it?"

Arms around him for a hug, she said, "Thanks, Cash."

"You're most welcome."

Moving a few aisles farther, he asked Wren, "Want me to buy you some chicks?"

"What would I do with them?"

He shot her an indecipherable look before moving deeper into the store. His long-legged stride made it impossible for her to keep up, so she didn't even try, instead losing herself in the novelty of a place that sold not only live chickens but veterinary supplies, denim overalls and Crock-Pots. The rich scent of grain mingled with that of freshly popped popcorn—given away free with every purchased can of coconut popping oil.

Mouth watering, she grabbed a still-warm bag as well as everything needed to make the snack at home.

"Cash Buckhorn," said a big-haired blonde near a cardboard weed-killer display, "as I live and breathe. Been doing much dating since that knee has you stuck in town?"

"Nope." He took two pairs of leather gloves from a rack. One pair large. The other small. "Heard you stood up for Ruby at her wedding."

Eyes closed, the woman hugged herself, expression dreamy. "It was the most gorgeous ceremony ever. You know how Ruby's daddy prides himself on having the prettiest barn in three counties? Well, he had it decked out so fancy you'd be hard-pressed to even tell horses usually live there."

"That's nice." A muscle ticked in Cash's jaw.

"Ruby thought it might've been awkward had she sent you an invitation."

He shrugged. "She'd have been right."

Careful to remain in the shadows of rakes and hoes, Wren continued peeking around the wood handles, curious as to where this conversation was leading.

"You poor thing." Hands on her hips, the mystery woman cocked her head. "You're as heartsick as a kitten leaving its litter. Come to the Grange Hall dance with me Saturday night. It'll be just what you need."

"Love to," he said, "but besides my bum knee, I can't."

"Oh?"

"Yes, ma'am." He sidestepped the woman to snag a gaping Wren around her waist. "Please meet the mother of my child, Dr. Wren Barnes. Since she'll be bunking with me till week's end, even if my knee worked, it'd hardly be proper for me to go dancing with you."

Before Wren could answer, Cash planted on her lips a kiss so hot that she thought if he kept it up much longer, her popcorn-making supplies would burst without a stove!

"WHY'D YOU DO THAT?" Wren demanded once Cash had her back in his truck.

"You being a city gal," he said with a sideways glance while backing out of the lot, "and looking about twenty months pregnant, you wouldn't understand."

"Try me." As amazing as the kiss had been for a feverish few seconds, the aftermath had been a nightmare. She'd always been a private person, and it had never occurred to her that it was even possible to know every single person in a store. But Cash did. And now all those people were under the impression that she was Cash's *girl*. Only, she wasn't. Fortunately, she'd soon be gone, leaving him on his own to chase the tails of whatever lies he'd spun.

Since her companion obviously had no logical explanation for his unappreciated—although decidedly expert—advances, Wren focused on the scenery. Weed Gulch boasted one main road, which also happened to be a state highway. On that road there were two stoplights. One at the intersection in front of the town hall. The other at the entrance to the local school that housed kindergarten through grade twelve, all on the same campus. According to the Kiwanis Club sign, the Weed Gulch Wagoneers had been 1A state baseball champs in 1989.

Here and there were housing subdivisions mixed in with mobile homes and barns. Reasor's Grocery stood adjacent to a pasture filled with grazing cattle. A fieldstone library was squeezed between a mom-and-pop barbecue restaurant and the shell of an old convenience store that now served as a used-car lot.

"You may not understand that kiss," Cash said out of the blue, "but trust me, sometimes these things have to get done." Veering onto the county road leading to the dirt road that led to the ranch, Cash said, "Ruby used to be mine. Now, all because I didn't feel the timing was right for me to settle down, she's already gotten herself married to another guy. Tell me, does that sound right?"

Wren angled to face him. "In other words, in a perfect world she should have spent her whole life waiting for you to be ready?"

"I never said anything of the sort."

"Uh-huh." Frowning, she added, "Which leads us right back to my question of if you didn't want to marry her, why do you even care that some other guy did?"

"I don't. Not really." One hand on the wheel, with his other he fished a stick of Big Red from the pack he kept on the dash. Her mouth watered from the sweet cinnamon smell, but she refused to give him the pleasure of asking for a piece. "Truth is we'd long ago grown apart. The twentieth time around with her only told me what I already knew—together we had smokin' chemistry, but little else." Thoughtfully chewing, he added, "This is more of an ego thing. I'm easily the best-looking man in the county. Can't have people thinking I'm not worthy of marriage."

"Your head gets any bigger, you'll have to add a sunroof for you to fit in your own truck."

He winked, leading her to the conclusion that her dig hadn't bothered him in the least. What did was the notion of him being with this Ruby in an intimate manner. Why, she couldn't say, but with his baby growing inside her, she couldn't bear to think of his skilled hands being on any other woman's curves.

"What's wrong with your knee?" she asked, to clear her mind of irrational jealousy.

"Nothing."

She pressed, "Then why do you sometimes walk with a limp and you told the blonde back at the feed store that your knee's *bum*?"

"Long story," he said with a glance out his window. He didn't say another word, and his clenched jaw and tightened hold on the wheel told her to stay out of his business.

A GOOD FIFTEEN MILES down the road, Cash slowed upon finding Doc Haven's white cargo van pulled in front of Delores Hawke's place.

Slamming on the brakes to avoid hitting the town doctor who'd run into the middle of the road, Cash instinctively stretched out his arm to brace Wren. "Hold on…."

The white-haired doctor jogged to Cash's side of the truck.

Cash lowered his window. "Need help?"

"And then some," the older man said, struggling to catch his breath. "Delores took a tumble from her kitchen stool. Not only broke her hip, but put a nasty gash on her head. County ambulance is clear over in Marquette dealing with a cardiac arrest. Can you help me get her stabilized and in the back of my van?"

"Absolutely," Cash said, already pulling to the side of the road.

The elderly woman's home was stifling, reeking of Bengay and mothballs, and at least ten degrees warmer than the muggy eighty outside. Sidestepping stacked newspapers and yarn-filled baskets, they finally reached the moaning woman.

Kneeling alongside Delores, oblivious to the blood, Wren took the woman's hand, smoothing the top, assuring her everything would be okay.

Wren helped herself to alcohol swabs from the doctor's bag and cleaned Delores's forehead. Though the wound had bled a lot, it looked to be superficial. Cash had been hurt enough during his rodeo days that he knew the difference between a major blow and one that'd let you finish out your rides.

Wren distracted the older woman further by making

small talk and then holding firmly to her hand while Cash and Doc hefted her onto a gurney.

Within minutes, the pain meds Doc had loaded into Delores's IV conked her right out.

"Whew," Doc said once they'd gotten the patient settled in the back of the air-conditioned van. Removing his cowboy hat, he used his shirtsleeve to wipe sweat from his brow. "I sure am glad you two came along when you did."

"Why didn't you call the house?" Cash asked.

"I did. Only, no one picked up." Looking to Wren, the man said, "I appreciate the help, but why are you out of bed?"

Wren looked sheepish. "We just made a quick run to the store."

"Hmmph." Doc Haven frowned. "Well, try to take it easy from here on." He paused, then added, "You certainly have a way with patients and seem familiar with a head wound. Nurse?"

"She's nearly a doctor," Cash offered, unexpectedly proud of Wren's achievements. "Graduated from Johns Hopkins."

Doc whistled. "Dang, girl. With a fancy pedigree like that, you probably already know more than me."

"I would hardly say that." Wren reddened. Her flushed cheeks made her look younger. Less world-weary than her usual concentrated expression. Patting her belly, she said, "I'm supposed to be in my residency now, but life sort of got in the way."

Eyeing Cash and then her, he harrumphed. "In my day, folks got married before having babies."

Cash grinned. "Back in your day, you also didn't have microwave ovens or HDTV."

"Your point being?" The doctor put his bag on the truck's passenger side.

"Only that whether we're married or not doesn't make a hill-of-beans difference to this little guy or gal." He cinched his arm around Wren's waist. He couldn't pinpoint why, but it made him inordinately glad that she was as forward thinking in her anti-marriage views as he was.

"YOU'VE HARDLY SAID a word since we've been home." Cash finished unloading the feed from the truck to find Wren at the kitchen table, a cookie in one hand and her pirate book in the other.

"You're still not talking to me?" Easing onto a counter stool, he noted, "And seeing how much you like hearing your own voice, I must've done something pretty bad."

She treated him with a glare.

"At least you're looking at me. Somewhat of an improvement." He pitched a wadded napkin at her.

"Stop," she barked. "I'm at a good part and would appreciate not being disturbed."

"I'm sorry, okay? Whatever I did this time for you to be mad at me, I'm a miserable excuse of a human, lower than the manure lining the soles of my work boots." Off the stool, he was suddenly behind her, folding his arms around her, squeezing her tight.

Breaking free, she fairly flew to the side of the cramped room that he wasn't on. "Lay off the charm. I'm immune."

"You wish." He winked, and as if on cue, the butterflies in her traitorous tummy fluttered. "Come on," he coaxed, moving close to her. "You know you wanna tell me why I'm the most wretched beast to ever roam the earth."

Tired of fighting, Wren allowed herself a few minutes' surrender. Leaning against him, soaking in his strength was akin to removing twin bricks from her shoulders. "It's stupid."

"The reason you're upset?"

She nodded. He'd wrapped her in a backward bear hug and she circled his muscular forearms with her hands, resting her cheek on his shoulder. His T-shirt smelled clean and fresh, his skin like baked-in sun and soap and that unique something she inherently knew was him. Like it or not, a part of him grew inside her.

"Out with it," he urged.

"All day you've told anyone who would listen that I'm carrying your baby. When the doctor asked if we were tying the knot, you seemed to delight in telling him we aren't."

Tensing against her, he noted, "I don't *delight*— ever."

"Whatever you want to call it, I got the notion you were sticking it to everyone who's ever told you what to do. Using our baby to thumb your nose at their conventionalism."

He took a long time to answer. "That's not true. I'm just relieved you feel the same way about getting hitched. I'm not ready for that, and to be honest, I'm not sure I ever will be."

Fighting the knot in her throat, Wren said, "Fair enough. But if you're so relieved to be free of a binding relationship, then why did you kiss me? Why are you holding me?"

Slowly, softly he spun her to face him. "Beyond the

baby, the night you and I shared was hands down the hottest of my life."

Heat roared through her, flustering her mind to the point that it was impossible to think.

His touch was tender, radiating warmth as he brushed her throat with his thumbs. "Dare you to tell me you haven't replayed it a hundred times."

She wanted him so badly to kiss her that her lips actually hurt. "I—I'm also mad at you for not trusting me enough to tell me what's wrong with your knee."

"It's nothing to get worked up about. You and me, however..." He sharply exhaled. "Remember how we started out fast, but ended up slow? Which time do you think it was?"

Sliding his big hands along her silhouette, past the sides of her aching breasts, in at her waist, out at her hips, he knelt before her, lifting the hem of her T-shirt, pressing his open mouth against her womb.

Between her legs a low hum both dizzied and thrilled. Hands in his hair, steadying herself against his advances, she felt her breathing turn shallow. Her pulse became frenzied.

"You know, like how did we make our baby? On the lanai lounge chairs? Standing with your back pressed against the sliding glass door? In that big, soft bed with you riding me until—"

"Stop," she begged. Her voice was unrecognizable. Thick with ghost passion from a night she'd tried to forget. "It doesn't matter how our baby was made, only that he or she has become our future. Trouble is, I already have one—in Baltimore. I have to focus on that." *I can't afford to lose myself in you.*

"Once the baby is born, you don't want any contact with me?"

"In a perfect world, that'd be great." Ducking her head, she escaped to the fridge for a refill on her decaffeinated iced tea. "That said, it's not my intention to keep you from your child."

Jaw hard, he nodded and stood.

"It's entirely up to you how much contact you want." The tea was refreshing. Cash's cold stare? Not so much.

"But if I want that connection with my son or daughter, I'll have to go out East to get it?"

Chapter Four

"Sorry about not having the latest on-site ultrasound," Doc Haven said Friday during Wren's thirty-week pregnancy exam. Assuming everything went well, he'd clear her for travel. He bustled about the room that was decorated in a Sesame Street theme. "Tulsa has everything a body could ever need in regard to medical gadgets. If I run into something I can't handle I send folks to one of my associates over there. Speaking of which, remember our patient with the broken hip?"

"Cash's neighbor, Delores?"

"That's the one. Her surgery was a success and she's convalescing nicely at a short-term care center. Thanks again for your help."

"All I did was hold her hand."

"Sometimes that's what's most needed."

A freckle-faced redhead sporting a high ponytail and pink scrubs took Wren's blood pressure. "One forty-eight over ninety-two."

"Smidge higher than I'd like. Anyway, I'll give Cash Delores's address. If you happen to be that way, you might stop by. I'm sure she'd love the company." Taking a fetal Doppler monitor from a countertop charging station, he squeezed a dollop of ultrasound gel on her belly, and then applied gentle pressure until he found her baby's heartbeat. "He's a strong little fella."

"I think it's a girl," Wren said. Hearing her future child's galloping pulse never failed to thrill. She'd invited Cash to sit in on this portion of her exam, but he'd declined. Probably just as well. The more attached he grew to their child, the harder it would be for him to let him or her go.

"You don't want to find out for sure?"

Wren shook her head. "I've always liked surprises."

"Me, too," he admitted while checking her wrists, hands and ankles for fluid retention. "I miss that part of birthing babies. If God had meant us to know every little thing about these tykes, he would've installed a peephole."

Wren laughed.

Her ultimate dream—although, with the baby, it might now be out of reach—was to become a heart surgeon just like her idol and friend Dr. Abigail West, but she could see where being a country doctor would have its upside. On a good day Doc Haven covered every specialty from obstetrics to geriatrics. She supposed a country practice would be satisfying, but in a different way. Not the kind of rush stemming from a successful open-heart surgery, but more of a quiet satisfaction grounded in knowing his patients for a lifetime.

The baby's position was charted and then a lab technician popped in to tell the doctor that her urine sample checked normal for sugar, but high for protein.

"Thanks for working me in," Wren said once her examination was complete.

"My pleasure. I'm proud to say I delivered all three Buckhorn boys and the lone girl."

"Cash has a sister?"

Snapping off his gloves, the doctor nodded. "Took off a while back. No one's sure where. Georgina misses her something fierce. It's a mystery to me why she even left. Oklahoma has everything a soul could ever need."

Wren wasn't so sure. "What's your verdict? Am I free to make immediate flight plans?"

He shook his head. "Before your appointment I had a conference call with your big-city ob-gyn, Dr. Patten, and she agreed that if your blood pressure and urine protein were still up, we feel it's best you stay calm and relaxed. As much as you can, it also wouldn't hurt you to stay off your feet."

"But that's ridiculous. I have to get back to my residency. I owe my roommates rent money and have other obligations I can't just abandon."

Sighing, the older man crossed his arms. "Let me put it this way. Right now we're concerned. Plainly, your body was telling you that in your current condition, travel is a major stressor. You've been at rest for a week, and your levels are still not anywhere near normal. I'm not ready to diagnose preeclampsia yet, but you're close. Unless you want to be an ideal candidate for stroke, heart disease, kidney failure, delivering your baby premature or God forbid, even stillborn, you need to heed this as a warning. Slow down and let that man out in the waiting room take care of you."

Refusing to let the doctor's words take root, Wren asked, "What does that mean for my residency? I'll be back in another week or so?"

"Considering the fact that you had high blood pressure before you even got here, added to your now high protein levels and recent fainting spell, it is my and Dr. Patten's professional opinion that you remain on bed rest for the remainder of your pregnancy."

"That's ridiculous," Wren snapped. "I can't just—"

"Whoa. Cool that temper of yours right on down, little lady." Reaching for the blood pressure cuff attached to the wall, he took a reading. "One fifty-five over ninety-four."

"Are you sure?"

His stern expression told her that not only was he insulted by her second-guessing his reading, but fed up with her arguments.

Preeclampsia was nothing to fool around with. Bottom line, no matter how badly she wanted to get back to work, she wanted a healthy baby more.

Ten minutes later she returned to the waiting area to find Cash asleep in a chair, long legs sprawling in front of him, his straw hat covering his eyes. His light snoring didn't bother an elderly woman's knitting or a mother settling a fight between her two little kids.

"Cash?" Hand on his shoulder, she gave him a gentle shake.

He jolted awake. "Time for the baby?"

She squatted to pick up his hat from the floor. "Still ten to twelve weeks."

"Oh." Rubbing his eyes with the heels of his hands, he said, "I was just dreaming that I was at a rodeo when you went into labor."

"I suppose that could happen." After handing him his hat, resigned to the fact that she wasn't going anywhere soon, she made her way to the check-out clerk to schedule her next appointment. "Are you entered in one around then?"

"You ask too many questions. And wait a minute…" Just outside the office he stopped and eyed her. "Why'd you make an appointment with Doc Haven? Thought you were going home?"

"Surprise," she said with deadpan enthusiasm. "My blood pressure's still sky-high and I've been ordered to stay off my feet for the duration."

"Yeah, but what's that mean?" Even confused, he was much too handsome. How was she ever going to manage living with him until her baby's anticipated Christmas delivery?

"Basically that through no decision of our own, we've become roomies for the duration of my pregnancy—barring an unlikely blood pressure miracle."

"So you're still sick?"

She nodded and headed toward the truck. But he wasn't finished questioning and he snagged her wrist.

"But as long as you don't overdo it, you and the baby are going to be fine?"

"Yes," she said, hating the pleasant tingles he caused with his slightest touch. Her whole life, she'd been in control. Now not only didn't she decide where she lived or who she lived with, but her body betrayed her, too, whenever Cash was around.

"It won't be that bad."

"You're not upset?" Because she certainly was.

"About you staying on?" He grinned. "Might be fun. The doc didn't say anything about you restricting certain athletic bedroom activities, did he?"

She wrenched her arm free to give Cash a swat.

The day was clear and warm with the winds at peace. Why couldn't she shake the feeling that until she escaped Oklahoma, she might never feel that way? Should she take a chance with her and their baby's health? Betting that her blood pressure wouldn't become too great a problem if she flew home?

Still grinning, Cash used a remote to unlock his

black truck. The doors had Buckhorn Ranch arched across them, with battling rams beneath.

Upon opening her side, he offered his hand. "Yep, this could definitely work to my advantage. We could exchange sex for butler service. Kinky good fun, huh?" That white-toothed smile of his flipped her stomach. She would've liked to blame it on the baby, but considering the heat between them every time they touched, no one but Cash could be to blame.

"You're horrible! I would never have sex with you."

Clearing his throat, Cash reminded her with a laugh, "Hate to be the bearer of bad news, but judging by the size of my bun in your oven, you kind of already did."

Ignoring him, she rolled her eyes.

He circled to his side of the truck, climbed in and started the engine.

"Back to a more polite conversational topic, you never answered my rodeo question. Will you be around during the holidays?" Hoping to counteract the stifling heat, Wren turned on the AC.

"Officially, yes, I am supposed to be riding in a holiday rodeo, but because of my knee, I'm suspended from the pro tour. Happy?"

"No." She adjusted the vents to blow gale-force cooling wind on her face. "That's the last thing I want."

"Then why even bring it up?"

"I was curious. That's all. No hidden agenda."

Maneuvering Weed Gulch's main drag with its assortment of pickups, slow-moving blue-haired women in Caddies on their way to Alma's Kut & Kurl and too many harried moms in minivans, Cash hardened his jaw.

What was he thinking? During their time together, would she ever learn to decipher his multitude of expressions? Considering the fleeting nature of their relationship, would she even want to? The whole point of her staying was about maintaining or improving her current level of health while bringing an equally healthy baby into the world. Nothing about that plan involved becoming fast friends with her baby's father.

"Hungry?" Cash asked.

"Always. What'd you have in mind?"

"Queenie's twisty cones are always good on a warm day. Want one?"

"Will they dip it in that chocolate stuff that hardens into a shell?"

Glancing her way, he grinned. "You like your ice cream that way, too?"

Disregarding the pleasant tingle that was becoming a habit every time Cash smiled, she said, "Doesn't everyone?"

SHARING A PICNIC TABLE in the dappled shade of a pecan tree, Cash reckoned he got more pleasure from watching Wren devour her cone than he did eating his own.

She had this sexy-sweet habit of licking the base that was causing a tremendous amount of below-the-belt discomfort. Trying to get his mind out of the bedroom, he noted, "All kidding aside, hope you're not too upset about not getting to go home. Promise, I'll try making your stay as stress free as possible."

"Thanks." Lick, lick.

Cash shifted his fly.

"I never realized how much stress affects me. It's scary."

"I'm sure." Reaching for her free hand, he gave her a squeeze. "Now that we're a team, though, it's okay to chill. At least let me shoulder some of the emotional burden you've been carrying." It had to have been tough—not only finding out she was pregnant on her own, but then having difficulties. Just thinking about it got him all choked up. What if something bad happened to her or the baby? "Sorry."

"For what?" She'd finished her cone and now wiped her fingers with a napkin. His mind's eye saw her one day down the road, fastidiously helping their little boy or girl clean after a sticky treat.

"Going through the majority of your pregnancy alone. I should've been there."

"Stop. My purpose in being here isn't to ply you with guilt. I'm entirely to blame for not telling you sooner." Head bowed, she haltingly admitted, "For not admitting to myself that I needed help sooner. Guess now my body's making the call for me."

Leaning forward, elbows on the sun-warmed wooden table, he asked, "Why were you reluctant to come to me? Did you think I wouldn't care?"

Swallowing hard, she focused on the family foursome next in line for ice cream. "You have to understand that my whole life, I've been on my own. To even acknowledge I need help is a big step. Huge."

"What do you mean you've always been on your own?"

Meeting his gaze, she said, "My earliest memories are of a church-run orphanage. While I was more than adequately fed, clothed and educated, when it came to affection, there was precious little to go around— especially once I grew older." Shrugging, she wiped tears from her eyes when she thought he wasn't looking. "After a while I figured I was better off without any touchy-feely stuff. When it came to my studies, I compensated for a lack of outside attention by overachieving. Inside, I wasn't happy with anything less than the best. Up until now, that ideal has served me well."

"But to a certain extent—I mean, aside from your deciding to sleep with me—neither pregnancy nor your residency being interrupted was in any way under your control."

After a faint laugh, she wadded her napkin into a tight ball. "No kidding."

Save for the air conditioner's steady humming, the ride home was mostly silent. Cash's mind wandered to images of Wren as a small girl, sitting alone in the corner of some institutional playroom with few toys and even fewer friends. Though he knew it was the last thing she'd have wanted, his heart went out to the lonesome little girl. He had the craziest urge to shower her with pretty, girlie things and ensure she always had a surplus of hugs.

Growing up, he'd been blessed with an overabundance of not only material things, but parental attention. His dad was a local legend. Famed for being a shrewd oilman and cattleman. Always fair, yet firm. His dad had been as manly as they come, but not so much that he ever shied from giving his boys plenty of pats on their backs and all-around affection. Duke Buckhorn had been such a remarkable parent and husband that often Cash felt lost in his shadow.

When he rode and crowds cheered, he temporarily escaped. Now, with his messed-up knee, even that respite was at risk.

Truth be told, that was why he never wanted to marry or spend his life working this family ranch. How would he ever live up to his father's monumental ghost?

"DR. WEST?" ONCE HOME, after calling the rental car agency and arranging to drop it off, Wren stood in

Cash's den, hoping she stayed strong through the duration of this second call.

"Well," Wren's idol said in a friendly tone, "if it isn't my favorite resident. Are you back at the hospital?"

"N-not exactly." She explained her situation. "With all of that in mind, I'm temporarily stuck—but excited about getting back to work as soon as I'm physically able."

"Of course, I understand." The petite powerhouse, who wore a no-nonsense bob that always managed to look impeccable, sighed. Never a good sign. "That said, I can't help but find myself wishing this baby had never happened. I'm happy for you, but sad at the same time."

"I understand." Wren could feel Dr. West's disappointment in her.

"I've lost a lot of promising candidates due to so-called love, and I refuse to lose you, Wren Barnes. As long as we're on the same page about that, I'll move heaven and earth to get you back into the program."

"Thank you." Wren's whole body quivered with relief. Up until now, she hadn't realized just how afraid she'd been of potentially being booted from her chosen resident program, but with Dr. West on her side, she had nothing to fear.

THAT NIGHT, WATCHING the sunset from the back-porch swing, Cash sipped from a longneck beer. The scent of barbecued chicken on the grill made his stomach rumble. Damned if the day hadn't been so messed up he'd forgotten to eat. "Is it just me, or is this whole setup a little…"

"Awkward?" The soon-to-be mother of his child flashed a faint smile.

"I was going to say surreal, but your word works,

too." Since they shared the porch's only seat, necessity forced his thigh against hers. He wore jeans and a T-shirt. She'd changed into khaki shorts and a pink maternity tank that managed to all at once be sexy and demure. Their shoulders brushed as they shifted position. The sensation was electrifying—and all too reminiscent of the night that had brought them to their current predicament.

He cleared his throat and stood.

"Hard as I try," he said, "I can't wrap my head around what's happened. You showing up at my place. Pregnant." Worse yet, his body hadn't gotten the memo that he wasn't supposed to still be attracted to her. "Now sick and forced to stay."

"I know."

Ambling off the porch, trying to hide his limp, he took another drag from his beer before turning the chicken and brushing on more of his famous sweet sauce he usually reserved for special occasions.

Edging sideways, she raised her feet onto the swing, hugging her knees. "For what it's worth, I am sorry about you missing your holiday rodeo—and any others, too. If you have a miraculous recovery, please feel free to leave me in the housekeeper's care. That way, once I have the baby, I can head home and for you, it'll be like I've never been here."

"Way to make a man feel needed." He lowered the lid on the grill.

"Of course you are."

Shaking his head, he laughed. "You're some piece of work."

"What's that supposed to mean?"

The fact that she saw no potential problem with her plan to take their baby off to Baltimore and rarely see him again irked Cash to no end. Even better, it put his attraction for Wren into perspective. What he felt for her was physical—nothing more. "The chicken will be ready in about twenty minutes. I'm going to make a salad."

"Need help?"

"No, thanks."

"Cash…" She rose, hugging herself as if she were chilled. "When I decided to try finding you, I'd hoped we could be friends. This afternoon, over ice cream, I thought we'd made giant strides toward that end. Now I'm getting the sense that we're right back where we started."

Why, he couldn't say, but her statement struck him as asinine.

Turning his back on her, he went inside. He had developed a major soft spot for Wren, but then she'd reminded him that her real name was Miss Independence. She didn't need him, or anyone else for that matter. If it hadn't been for her high blood pressure, she'd have long since put her sweet behind on an eastbound plane.

Unfortunately, she followed. "Think about it. Like it or not, we'll now be sharing birthdays and holidays and milestones like first words and steps and graduations. Do you really want to spend all of those precious moments wearing a scowl?"

What he wanted was never to have been put in this situation, but that was a moot point. He couldn't put his finger on why, but he was suddenly mad as hell at the woman. Not about the baby. He'd been the one who'd purchased a faulty condom. But dammit, he'd lived twenty-seven years as a carefree bachelor and he wasn't even ready to have kids, let alone a ready-made, move-in wife.

Rummaging in the fridge for the prepackaged Caesar salad they'd picked up at the store, he found it, then conked his head on the top shelf as he straightened. "Damn!"

"You all right?" Her voice brimmed with soft concern. As if she genuinely cared about his well-being. At his side, she fished her fingers through his hair. "Let me have a look."

"I'm fine," he said, drawing away. It further irked him that she was being nice while he struggled for baseline civility. "Just hurts like a son of a—well, you know."

She closed the refrigerator door. "Since you don't need help with your head, want me to make the salad?"

"You're pregnant."

"And?" Leaning against the counter's edge, she folded her arms.

"You should be sitting." He took a glass bowl from the cabinet alongside the stove. "Doing a good job of growing my baby."

After a long pause and expression hot enough to start a barn fire, she got all up in his face. "Look here, Cash Buckhorn, I've had just about all I care to take of you blowing hot and then cold and your asinine, archaic pregnancy observations. Either you straighten up or I'm figuring out a way to safely hightail it back to Baltimore. It might be rough going, but nothing could be as bad as living with you like this."

Chapter Five

"Truce?" Wren glanced up from the book she was reading to see Cash at her bedroom door, waving a few sheets of toilet paper. He looked so ridiculous, she didn't have the heart to stay mad, especially since she'd skipped Cash's barbecued chicken and she was now starving. "We happen to be fresh out of white flags."

"Okay, truce," she said, resting her novel on her lap.

When he entered the room, all the oxygen left. The night was warm, with crickets singing outside open windows. Cash wore no shirt and his blond curls were a rummaged-through mess. His sleepy-sexy grin made it impossible for her to stay mad.

Perched on the foot of the bed, he said, "Sorry for earlier. Not sure what got into me."

"Probably the same initial rush of frustration and apprehension and excitement I've already been through." Smiling, she added, "You forget, I've already had a while to accept the inevitable."

"So? How did you work it out?" Looking away and then back, he admitted, "Straight up, I'm angry with you, but I don't know why."

"Do you resent me showing up on your doorstep, pretty much taking over your life?" Adjusting the pillows behind her, she leaned forward.

"Oddly enough, no. I don't think that's it."

"Then why?" With their new forced proximity, she needed to know what was broken between them in order to fix it. But then, seeing as how there was no "them" outside one wild night, maybe that was the problem.

"I'm miffed you waited six months to tell me I'm going to be a father. What? Was I so horrible to be with you couldn't bear to see me again?"

Tears stung her eyes. "I already told you, I prefer handling things on my own."

"Our baby isn't an item on your to-do list."

"I never said it was."

Shaking his head as though he was exasperated, he turned to leave.

Wren called out, "Please, stay."

He stopped, but didn't face her. "Why?"

"Because I'm sorry I didn't tell you sooner. I should have. But regardless, you deserved to be along for the *ride,* start to finish." She grinned.

"And I'm damned good-looking." He turned and sat next to her on the bed, every spellbinding, muscular ripple on his chest entirely too close for comfort.

"Wh-what?"

"Admit it."

"I will not." Even if it was true.

"You owe me that much."

"Why? Are we back to your bruised ego again? Because if you're worried about something ridiculous like I didn't find you attractive enough to be in my life, then you're certifiable."

"But in a hunky sort of way, right?"

His expression suddenly held such genuine concern, she couldn't help but laugh.

"This isn't funny."

"It is to me," she said with another giggle. "How are you going to be a father when the only thing you care about is the continued worship of you?"

"That's not true. Is it so wrong to want a little validation?"

No. It was something she'd secretly yearned for her entire life. "Okay, for what it's worth, you are easily the most heartbreakingly handsome cowboy stud I've ever seen. If you hadn't been, I never would've slept with you."

"Thank you." He winked. "It's about time you admitted it."

"Beast!" she cried, giving that gorgeous chest of his a swat. "Are you ever going to feed me? Or are you just going to stand there admiring yourself?"

"THIS IS THE one place in town I've never been." When Cash had agreed to take Wren to the library, he hadn't planned on going inside, but now that he had, he found it wasn't half-bad. Bond money had newly remodeled the space to be light and airy with skylights and plenty of picture windows overlooking the town duck pond. Potted plants filled every corner and the children's area with its thick blue carpet, yellow furniture and green-eggs-and-ham wall mural looked straight from the pages of Dr. Seuss.

"You're kidding?" Wren said, heading straight for a spinning rack loaded with more of her pirate books.

"Nope. In fact, I've made it a mission to stay away. Many women have tried coercing me in here, but all until you have failed."

Hands on what was left of her hips, she cocked her head, spilling her cute ponytail over her right shoulder. Her gray eyes were bright, her complexion glowing—

he'd have been hard-pressed to find a more attractive woman. Not that he'd ever tell her. The house wasn't big enough to hold both their egos should she realize her own level of attractiveness. "You are so making that up."

"You got me." He cracked a smile. "But if you hurry, we'll have time for the lunch special at Ron's."

"What's that?"

"Best hamburger in the state. It's out by the toll road, but well worth the drive."

Glancing at the cover of a book and then the back, she said, "I'm still full from breakfast."

"Then as a favor to me for coming here, you can at least sit while I eat."

Sighing, she agreed.

"What do you see in these?" He grabbed one showing a guy wearing jeans and chaps and a woman spilling half out of her prairie dress.

She dived for another book. "Adventure, a smidge of history and loads of romance."

Making a face, he noted, "Couldn't you have all of that with a real-live man instead of just reading about it?"

"I don't have time for a real man."

He gave her a dirty look.

"Except, of course, for you."

"That's better."

"Seriously, though…" Her latest pick featured a castle. "Until I have a spare moment for real-life romance, books carry me through. You might give them a try."

"Me?" He laughed. "I could have a date in the next hour."

"True, but with someone you wholly want to be with? A woman who feeds your mind and spirit? Do you plan on spending the rest of your life in pursuit of the eternal party?"

Hell, yes. Since when had fun been declared a bad thing? "What's it matter to you?" he said. "You'll soon be gone. Besides, you don't even know me."

"What little I do know, I discovered on a one-night stand."

"And seems to me you weren't opposed to our night."

"I never said I was." Blushing furiously, she looked away. "All I meant was that sooner or later, that kind of outing will eventually lose its thrill."

He coughed. "Speak for yourself."

Though he'd been teasing, Wren didn't look amused. "You know what I mean."

He did, but since he had no intention of marrying, he failed to see how in his case a lofty ideal such as finding a woman to feed his mind and soul applied.

Clearing his throat, he asked, "We about done here?"

"SURE YOU'RE UP for this?" Sunday afternoon on their way into Cash's mother's home, he took her hand for a brief squeeze. Though there hadn't been tension between them, there also hadn't been a whole lot of meaningful conversation since their library trek. The hour drive to Tulsa to visit Cash's neighbor, Delores, had been even worse.

"Yeah, I'm good." Forcing a deep breath, Wren tried believing her words. Truth was, her stomach was in knots, her ankles were swollen and more than anything she'd have liked to be lounging by the pool with her latest read. While Doc Haven hadn't placed her on total bed rest, the worse she felt, the more she feared losing her last bit of independence.

"You don't look it."

"Thanks." Just what she needed was Mr. Handsome to confirm her suspicion that she looked like crap. Though she'd been with Cash nearly two weeks, she hadn't encountered his mother again. The thought of the older woman once again urging her to marry, to enter into a lifelong relationship with a man she hardly knew, was too much to comprehend. Wren understood that in sharing a child, she and Cash would be irrevocably linked, but that was vastly different from being legally linked.

"Hey…" He drew her into a hug. "You're beautiful. Really, truly pretty. I just meant that I can tell you're having a rough day."

She tried pushing him away, but he held firm. "You're not going anywhere until you slow down your breathing. Are you really this upset over sharing a meal with my family?"

"Yes—no," she said against his chest. "I don't understand why I'm reacting like this. My heart's beating a mile a minute and…" She held on to him for dear life.

"It's okay. Everything's going to be fine."

"I don't know why, but your mom's opinion means something to me. It makes no sense. I've never had parents, so why would I care what your mother thinks?"

His fingers gentle beneath her chin, he raised her gaze to meet his. "Mom told me that—"

"You and your mother talked about me?" Horrified didn't begin to cover the emotions surging through her.

"Relax. She understands how important our baby is to you—that you'll finally have a family. Do you think seeing me close to my family has stirred up feelings for you?"

"I don't know… Maybe. I just want to feel normal

again, but the more pregnant I get, the more messed up I seem to be."

"You do a good job of hiding it." He kissed her forehead. "Most days you only seem mildly crazy—nowhere near certifiable."

Growling, she tried pushing away again, but he wasn't letting go. And, oddly enough, though she'd never verbally admit it, she didn't want him to.

"So here Cash was," Cash's oldest brother, Dallas, said to their middle brother, Wyatt, "drunk off what had to have been half a keg when he…"

Georgina leaned toward Wren. "How about we leave my boys to their tall tales while we go for a garden stroll?"

"Uh, okay." After enduring a family meal including Dallas's rambunctious five-year-old twin girls and their nanny, the last thing Wren needed was more awkward conversation.

Trailing after the Buckhorn matriarch, Wren focused on slowing her pulse. As long as she held firm to her convictions, nothing Georgina said could hurt her. She was a grown woman with every right to live her life as she wanted.

Exiting the home through French doors transported Wren to a world that felt more like a European wonderland than Oklahoma. Everywhere she looked were roses and ivy-covered trellises and gurgling fountains. The sweet scent of snapdragons mingled with freshly cut grass so lush it could've been living velvet.

"Aside from my kids and grandbabies," Georgina said, "this is my passion. It gets so dry here in the summer that sometimes I water three times a day. Dallas says if there's ever another Oklahoma dust bowl my garden will be to blame."

"It's amazing," Wren said, fighting a childlike urge to kick off her shoes and run barefoot down winding stone paths. "Outside coffee-table books, I've never seen anything like it."

Pausing at a covered seating area featuring wicker rockers with sunny yellow cushions, Georgina gestured for Wren to have a seat.

After a few moments of awkward silence, Georgina said, "Cash informed me I owe you an apology."

"Oh?" Fussing with her fingers, Wren wasn't sure what else to say.

"It seems I overstepped my boundaries when I cornered you about marrying my son. The bribery also wasn't one of my prouder moments." For the longest time she stared off into space. When next she spoke, her voice was raspy, as if she held back tears. "But you have to understand that this baby you're carrying represents a part of my husband. A man I loved to a degree I'd never dreamed possible. The thought of you bringing this precious child into the world, and me never getting to see him or her, well…" Cash's mother no longer bothered trying to hide her pain. "I—I know you and my son hardly know each other, but if you could just find it in your heart to let Cash in, I'm sure…"

Wren stood. "I'm sorry, Mrs. Buckhorn, but I can't do this. Cash and I have already told you we have no intention of marrying, and for you to press the issue is upsetting."

"The idea of you taking off halfway across the country with my grandchild is abhorrent."

"Again, I'm sorry. It's not my intention to keep this

baby from you. You're welcome to visit any time you like."

"It's not the same as if you and the baby lived with Cash. If you won't marry, would you consider staying in Weed Gulch?"

Hands over her womb, Wren struggled for words.

How did she begin explaining to her child's grandmother why she needed to keep her distance? Yes, back in Baltimore she had her residency, but technically, she could complete that in almost any large city. As much as she craved family, a part of Wren feared it—not having her own baby, but the notion that if she were to one day marry, her husband's folks might not find her worthy of their son. If that happened, what if he abandoned her just as her parents had? Her heart couldn't bear finally finding people with whom she could find a home, only to lose them. It would be unfathomably cruel. Which was why Wren had long ago decided never to entertain the thought.

Chapter Six

"Daddy says you've got a baby in there."

Wren had made slow progress on the short walk back to Cash's house, only to encounter the look-alike girls she'd first met that afternoon in the Buckhorn dining room.

"I think it's a girl baby." Betsy, the one wearing a purple My Little Pony shirt, performed a pirouette on the driveway.

"It could be a boy baby," Bonnie said. Wren recognized her because of the pink Hello Kitty T-shirt she wore.

"What if it's an alien in there?" Betsy giggled.

The ridiculous question coaxed Wren's smile out of hiding. "I've thought of that," she teased. "If I did have an alien, I'd want it to have polka-dotted skin."

Both girls took a minute to let this sink in.

"Cool!" Betsy said.

"Yeah!" Bonnie skipped in a circle.

"You two always have this much energy?" Wren asked, continuing her journey.

"Uh-huh." In unison, they now skipped and hopped.

Just think, in five short years she'd have one of these little walking atoms of her very own.

"Wait up!"

Wren looked behind her to find Cash jogging up the tree-lined driveway. As usual, he favored his right knee. Out of respect for his privacy, she'd stopped questioning him about it, but still wondered about the full extent of what was wrong. And if that was the reason he hadn't been in a rodeo—or even a sponsored media event— since she'd lived in his home.

"Uncle Cash!" The energy balls ran to meet him.

Bonnie said, "Your girlfriend told us she's gonna have an alien baby with polka dots and green-and-purple blood."

"That so?" Cash scooped up both girls, charging with them squealing all the way to where Wren stood smiling.

"For the record," she noted, giving both girls noogies, "I never said that about the blood."

"With these two—" Cash set them down "—I've gotten used to there being more fiction than fact."

"Give us another ride," Betsy demanded.

"No way. Uncle Cash is broken. Ask your dad to saddle up your ponies."

"Okay!" As suddenly as they'd arrived, the duo was now dashing off for a new adventure.

"Those two are a mess." Cash fell into step with Wren.

"I didn't want to ask at dinner, but where's their mom?"

"Family graveyard. Died in labor."

"Wow." Heat rushed through her. From what she'd read, giving birth was like landing a plane. A delicate process that usually went well, but sometimes horribly wrong. "Wish I hadn't asked."

"Was a freak thing. She started bleeding and didn't stop. Dallas was destroyed. He and Bobbie Jo were together for as long as I can remember. Literally since, like, the sixth grade."

"I can't imagine surviving such a loss." Which proved Wren's point that giving your heart was more likely to cause harm than good.

"You scared about the baby's grand entry?" On the tail end of his question, Cash caught her gaze.

A part of her wanted to be truthful that, yes, she was terrified of not only the birthing process, but everything that came after. Having had no mother of her own, would she instinctively know how to care for their child? Another part of her thought it best that she follow her long-standing rule of keeping her most private thoughts inside. That way, when she and Cash went their separate ways, he wouldn't keep part of her with him.

"I'm taking your silence as an affirmative." Casually resting his arm across her shoulders, he gave her a squeeze. "Sorry I told you about Bobbie Jo. Should've kept it to myself."

"That's okay. It's not like I haven't learned people die."

"True." When he released her, for a split second she was lonely. Then she regained her senses.

They walked for a few minutes in companionable silence, listening to wind whisper through tall grasses. Oklahoma had a grandeur she hadn't been prepared for. Rolling, cattle-dotted hills that stretched all the way to the horizon. The sun was setting, making the September air nippy while at the same time washing the sky in a hundred shades of orange, lavender and gold.

Had she and Cash been a couple, now would've been the perfect time to snuggle against him, sharing his warmth.

"I'm almost afraid to ask," Cash said once they were

almost to the house. "But what did my mother have to say out in her garden? I wanted to warn you that nothing good ever comes from conversations held out there, but Dallas and Wyatt wouldn't let me get a word in edgewise."

"They're a couple of characters."

He chuckled. "That's putting it mildly. But back to Mom…"

"Same CD, different track. If I can't bring myself to marry you, she wants me to at least move to Weed Gulch."

"How are you supposed to finish your residency here?" He mounted the wide slate steps leading to the front door.

"My point exactly. My mentor, Dr. West, has said she'll help me return to the program, but if I'm not in her hospital, I doubt knowing her will pull much weight."

"You'll work it out. I have faith in you."

His words warmed her heart. Wren stood staring at Cash until he held open the door, gesturing for her to enter first.

It felt good to be back. The house had become her haven, with its soaring ceilings and walls of glass. Scents of lemon oil and the lingering fragrance of whatever Mrs. Cahwood had cooked for dinner. The housekeeper was typically in and out before Wren had even showered. Ever since moving in with Cash, her usually frenetic pace had become downright decadent. She now read exclusively for pleasure, snacked and lounged. At first her new routine had felt like a hard-won vacation, but lately she'd grown a little bored and frustrated. She struggled to squelch the constant feeling that she should be doing something more productive than resting.

"It's chilly," Cash said. "Want me to build a fire and you pick a movie?"

"Sounds nice." A wonderful departure from worrying about their baby's delivery or Cash's scowling mother. "I haven't seen a movie in probably a year."

"Really?" At the hearth he meticulously laid a kindling base, setting larger sticks atop that and finally adding a couple of logs. "Dallas's kid duo conned me into a Disney marathon a few weeks back." After striking a match, he eased it under the smallest twigs, soon immersing the room in a dancing glow.

His every movement mesmerized her. He was so capable and sure. Granted, he'd only built a fire, but with all her book smarts, it wasn't something she could do.

Staring into the flames, he said, "Don't tell anyone, but *Pocahontas* and *Beauty and the Beast* were pretty damned good."

Wren laughed. "Afraid you might tarnish your manly-man image?"

"Never." His cocky grin convinced her all was well when it came to his ego. "I just want to ensure those little monsters don't make a habit of crashing at Uncle Cash's. Took me a couple days to fish all the Gummi Bears out of my furniture."

"Betsy and Bonnie are adorable. What're you talking about?"

"Don't let those sweet facades fool you." He parked himself on the opposite end of the sofa to her. "Well?"

"What?" When he smiled, she lost track of time. The man was so handsome, it hurt.

"I did my part for the evening's entertainment. Where's our movie?"

Yawning, she admitted, "I forgot. You pick."

"Woman…" He rolled his eyes. "I suppose you want me to make that popcorn for you, too?"

Beaming up at him, she said, "Now that you mention it, that would be—oh."

"What's wrong?"

"Nothing." Hands over her belly, she said, "The baby's feeling his oats. I think he just took out one of my ribs."

"Mind if I…" He cautiously approached, holding out his right hand as if he wanted to feel the phenomenon for himself, but was afraid to ask.

Snagging Cash's wrist, Wren drew him close, placing his large hand on her stomach. Within a few seconds their baby kicked again.

"Holy crap…" Eyes wide, he shook his head. "Does that hurt?"

She shook her head. "Usually just feels funny—like an inside tickle."

Sitting on the sofa beside her, he now had both hands over her belly. When the baby kicked again and again, Cash grinned and said, "Screw the movie. Our kid is way more entertaining."

Funny, she was just thinking the same thing about him.

"You're glowing," he said, holding her gaze the way he had in Vegas. With just a look, he stripped her bare. Made her long for an indefinable something she knew she shouldn't crave. "Crazy beautiful is what you are and I'm going to kiss you."

She should have stopped him, but when he slipped his left hand under her hair with his right still hugging their baby, denial was an impossibility. He kissed her softly and then hard and then every way in between. He stroked her tongue and then lifted her on top of him, urging her legs apart to straddle his waist. With her knees pressing into the soft sofa cushions, an infinitely more sensitive area sat atop throbbing proof of his still-thriving attraction for her.

When she moaned, he eased his hands under her shirt, smoothing her back while bucking in a slow and easy rhythm old as time.

Voice raspy, Cash asked, "What'd the doc say about us makin' whoopee?"

"I—I never thought to ask."

"Yeah, well, you should...." He kissed her a few more times. "But until you find out, you're going to have to excuse me before all the gentleman in me runs out."

"Ouch. Looks like you got up on the wrong side of the bed."

The next morning, tired and cranky after an exhausting night spent wide awake and lusting, the last person Wren wanted to see was Georgina, but there she stood in all of her towering, Buckhorn glory at the open front door.

"Good thing I brought fiber muffins. They'll perk you right up." Bustling past Wren, the older woman strode to the kitchen, setting a cloth-covered basket on the granite counter. Over her shoulder she'd slung a large bag, the contents of which she'd yet to reveal. "I don't know about you, but every time I got pregnant, my body played a new trick. With Cash, my lower tummy refused to play nice. My mother—bless her soul—made me this recipe and it always did the trick."

"Um, thank you." Was she truly standing in the kitchen talking about an insanely personal issue with a woman she hardly knew?

"My pleasure," Cash's mom said. "Now, let's get

you back on the sofa, where I'm going to teach you to needlepoint."

"That's an awfully nice offer," Wren said, already tired from the short walk, "but I'm clueless when it comes to crafts."

"Needlepoint isn't a craft," she said, shooing Wren back to her blanketed sofa nest, "but a womanly art. Next time you're over for dinner, I want you to get a good look at the dining-room chairs. My ancestors stitched every one of the cushions."

"Seriously?" Wren had heard of such things—families holding on to those kind of priceless antiques—but she'd never seen them.

"Of course I'm serious. And trust me, you'd be better off starting on your first project before the baby comes. Once your little bundle of energy arrives, your life will never be the same."

"Haven't seen much of you lately." Dallas did a head count of the cattle in the northeast pasture. Usually Wyatt would step in to help their oldest brother, but he'd taken a sick calf into town to the vet.

"Been busy." Cash tipped his hat brim in an attempt to keep cold rain from his eyes. It was a miserable morning to be a working cowboy. Especially after the three long, miserable nights he'd spent horny for the woman sleeping in the room across the hall. Damn, but his baby's mama was a sexy little thing.

Since feeling their baby kick, Cash had made a conscious effort to keep her smiling. They'd made another library run and a trip to the grocery store to stock up on the purple grapes and Doritos she'd been craving. He'd even put wildflowers in a vase on her nightstand. Truth was, the mother of his child was growing on him—figuratively and literally!

From the first time she'd placed his hand on her belly, it was as if he'd been possessed with thoughts of not only her, but their child. Were they having a boy or a girl? Would he or she be healthy? Would Wren's blood pressure remain normal?

As Dallas logged the count with wax pencil on a laminated chart, Cash wondered how he kept his head from exploding with all his efficiency. Their father had never relied on charts or graphs. He'd stored everything upstairs.

Reining his mount toward the northwest pasture, Dallas asked, "What have you been doing? Wyatt says you've been slacking on your rehabilitation. You told us you'd be back on tour in a couple weeks. I realize Wren's been a distraction, but Wyatt figures you've missed at least three stops and enough sponsor events to get yourself fired."

"Wyatt needs to mind his own business."

"Sorry to break it to you, but you are our business. Mom's pushing me over the edge with nagging." He snorted. "Not only is she worried about your knee, but she thinks I can shame you into giving Wren and your baby your name."

"Stop. When you called at an ungodly hour asking for help today, I didn't think your ulterior motive was to ambush me."

"More like talk sense into you. The clock's ticking and before you know it, this baby will be here and gone. That what you really want?"

Approaching a steep slope, forcing his attention to directing his horse, Cash wasn't sure what he wanted other than for Dallas to shut his piehole. "Look, Wren's my business. As is *my* kid."

"That's where you're wrong. This child is a Buckhorn, and don't you forget it." Dallas's horse turned skittish at his harsh tone. "First and foremost, you are to remember your family name. When Dad died, he left me in charge, and I refuse to allow you to bring scandal upon his legacy."

"For God's sake," Cash shouted back at his big brother, "would you please step out of the Old West and into the new millennium? Obviously I have no business being a husband or father. Yes, I'll be sad when Wren takes the baby with her, but what if I'm also relieved? Did you ever think of that?"

"If I weren't mounted, I'd slug you right in the jaw." As the rain fell harder, Dallas worked his fists. "Can you even imagine what my girls have been through not having their mother? All the time, they're asking me girl stuff for which I don't have answers. What is your son or daughter going to do when they have questions? What's the reason Wren's going to give them for why their daddy stays away? No, he's not in heaven, just too caught up in his own good time to give a damn about his offspring."

"THIS IS DELICIOUS, Mrs. Cahwood. Thank you." While the housekeeper hovered, Wren pressed a napkin to her lips. Back in Baltimore, breakfast consisted of an energy bar. If she were really lucky, she might also have time for yogurt or a banana. "You're spoiling me."

The perpetually cheerful older woman shrugged. With her hair in a messy French twist and usual white blouse always paired with pearls, she'd have been a dead ringer for June Cleaver if she hadn't also habitually worn blue jeans. "I like spoiling you. Plus, it'll be nice having a little one around the house."

Wren's stomach sank. Was it a middle-America thing that had everyone in her current circle assuming that just because she carried Cash's baby they'd be together forever?

She finished her latest strip of turkey bacon. "I guess Cash hasn't told you, but after I have the baby, I'll be moving back to Baltimore. I need to finish my residency."

"But isn't that very time-consuming?" The woman quickened her pace on wiping the counters. "Who will watch your child? I have four, and trust me, that first one sucks the life right out of you."

"The hospital where I'll be working has an excellent day care. Plus, my mentor, Dr. West, has more contacts than anyone I've ever known. She's already offered to help."

"I understand that sort of thing if you have no other option, but when you have a built-in support system right here in Weed Gulch, why would you want to leave?"

She made it sound so simple. As if giving up on a goal she'd worked her entire life to achieve was no big deal. "Please don't take this the wrong way, but did you ever want more from life? Something other than caring for your own or someone else's home?"

"Sure. Believe it or not," she said with a pat to her ample behind, "I dreamed of becoming a Rockette. I did it, too."

"Really?" Wren was so surprised she dropped her toast.

"You don't have to look so shocked."

"Sorry. I just never would've suspected it."

Brandishing still long and lean legs, Mrs. Cahwood said, "I danced in a reunion show just last year. A lot of my old friends got caught up in reminiscing, wishing they could be back in the limelight. But you know what I remember most about that time?"

Leaning forward, Wren asked, "Adoring fans? Gorgeous costumes?"

"Nope. I could never stop thinking about home. How much I missed my mom and dad and kid sister. I'd obtained something I'd worked for since my first dance class when I was only three years old, but without anyone there to share it with me, my victory felt hollow. Once my contract was up, I got a bank loan and set up my own little dance studio here in Weed Gulch. Turns out I loved teaching dance just as much as performing. Sure, it wasn't anywhere near as flashy, but as I got older, my values changed. I discovered true happiness wasn't in achieving an end goal, but in the journey." Slipping the bacon pan into the sink, she added, "You might think about that next time you're daydreaming about returning to the big city."

Chapter Seven

Thursday afternoon Cash had finished his chores and found Wren reading by the pool. It was a gorgeous afternoon. Bright and sunny with temperatures in the mid-eighties. Perfect for drowning out Dallas's condemning speech with fun. "Wanna join me for a swim?"

"Love to," she said, "but I don't have a maternity suit."

"How's that a problem?" He grinned. "Especially when God made you a perfectly fine birthday suit."

She rolled her eyes. "I thought until the doctor clears me for, um, *action*, we weren't going to do any more of that kind of activity?"

"Lord, woman, I didn't say I was makin' love to you in the pool. I'd just be getting an eyeful. Hell, if you want, I'll let you look at me right now." And to prove it, he unbuttoned his trunks.

"Stop!" she screeched with her book over her eyes.

"Okay, but if you ever want a peek, all you have to do is ask." When he winked, her face turned red as a beet. "Until then, come on, let's get you something pretty. There's a specialty shop over in Fouke. I'll bet they have something big enough to fit."

"Beast!" She threw her book at him. "First you want to see me naked, now you're calling me fat?"

"Never." Leaning low to kiss her, he said, "Sorry if it came out wrong. I realize my big baby boy is making your stomach huge."

"Like that sounds any better?"

"Whatever. I'm sorry if I offended you. Bottom line, it's a freakishly gorgeous day and I don't want to swim alone. Now, will you go shopping with me? Or is your refusal a subtle way of telling me you'd rather skinny-dip?"

IMPOSSIBLE DIDN'T BEGIN to describe Cash.

An hour had passed since his raunchy suggestion and Wren now stood in the dressing room of Fouke's Baby Barn. Surveying her image in the mirror, she wasn't sure if the pink floral suit made her look more like a cartoon hippo or a funky lounge chair. Either way, she wasn't wearing the getup in public any time soon.

"Does it fit?" Cash asked. He'd insisted on occupying the chair right outside her room.

"Technically, yes. But that—"

The dressing-room door creaked open. "Damn, woman…" Cash's smiling image appeared in the mirror alongside hers. "You look hot."

"Get out!" she snapped, grabbing for the white T-shirt she'd worn to at least partially cover herself.

"Have you seen the size of your—" At least having the decency to redden, he cleared his throat. "Suffice to say, our baby will be well fed."

To heck with modesty. She straightened her shoulders, giving him a real eyeful of her newly enlarged *assets*. "It's a shame you'll miss the party."

"Woman," he said with a growl, "I *am* the party." His agility meant he'd easily drawn her in for another kiss. "Shoot, if you weren't already having my baby, I might hire you for the job."

"Stop!" she begged in a stage whisper. "You're making a scene."

"So are you with your baby-enhanced boobs." After a quick check over his shoulder to make sure no one was looking, he ducked into the already cramped room.

"What are you doing?"

Easing his hands around her, smoothing them in a lazy up-and-down motion that did wild things to her pulse, he said, "What's it feel like I'm doing?"

"Wreaking havoc?"

"I should hope so." He focused on her neck, nuzzling and kissing and flooding Wren's body with aching, forbidden want.

"Really," she said, pushing him back the whole four inches the space allowed, "you have to stop."

"Why? It's not like we haven't already done all of this and more."

"I know, but..." It felt so good being back in his arms. Oddly right. What would it hurt indulging in this little bit of pleasure?

What would it hurt?

Try everything!

Not only didn't they have Doc Haven's safety clearance, but she had way too much at stake to risk losing it all on a casual affair. Getting pregnant had been bad enough. As much as she now wanted her baby, she was that much afraid of how she'd manage being a good mother and a doctor. No way could she toss being a good *girlfriend* for Cash into the mix.

Cash sidled right back beside her. "Just one kiss," he whispered, his breath warm and moist in her ear.

A knock sounded on the dressing-room door. "Is anyone in here?"

Heart pounding, Wren answered, "Um, yes! A-almost done."

"Just one," he urged, lips hot against the base of her throat. "Promise, if it's that awful, you can pretend you've never met me."

"Need any other sizes?" the sales clerk persisted.

"N-no, thank you."

"You know you want me." His raspy whisper caused hot and cold shivers. Of course she wanted him. *Want* wasn't the point. Sanity dictated she keep her distance. A repeat of their Vegas adventure would only make it tougher for her to eventually say goodbye. "C'mon…"

Glancing into his green eyes was her undoing. Everything about him invited her in. He represented the world of forbidden pleasure she'd spent her lifetime working to resist. Chocolate and staying up too late and dating rather than becoming one with her anatomy tomes.

"I—I want to," she said, licking her lips, "but…"

Kisses on her forehead, her cheek, the palm of her hand gave her only a sampling of what he ultimately offered.

"Ma'am?" The sales clerk rapped again. "If you're finished, we have a line waiting for the room."

"All right," Wren answered.

Cash made a face toward the door.

Abandoning her logical side, Wren slipped her hands behind Cash's head and pressed her lips to his. It took everything in her not to groan, and when he eased his hands under the top of her tankini-style suit, skimming them along her sides, teasing the sensitive skin near her breasts, she feared her legs would crumple from pleasure.

"Need help getting out of that sexy thing?" Cash teased.

Thank heavens they were in a public setting or she might've taken him up on his latest offer.

"Ma'am?" The clerk's tone had turned sharp. "Is someone in there with you?"

When Cash launched into a fresh set of mocking faces, Wren couldn't hold back a giggle, which quickly turned into a laugh.

Snatching the tag from her suit, Cash opened the door. "We'll take it," he said, handing the clerk what she'd need to ring up Wren's purchase.

Wren cringed in horror, tugging the door closed before dragging her shirt and maternity jeans on over the ugly suit.

Leaving the room with her bra shoved into her purse, Wren strove for a devil-may-care attitude on her walk of shame past the gaping crowd of moms and grandmothers. A scowling grandfatherly type clamped his hands over a squirming toddler's eyes. Wren opted for the long route to the front of the store, zigzagging through clothing racks and a towering infant car seat display to eventually stand alongside Cash.

"Will the swimwear be all?" The clerk glared at them over the top of her reading glasses.

"Sweetheart," Cash said to Wren, kissing the crown of her head, "need anything else? Thongs? Bras? Guess there's no need for condoms."

"Sir," the clerk admonished, handing Cash his change, "this is a family establishment."

"And clearly," Cash said with a pat to Wren's tummy along with his trademark grin, "we're in a family way."

"YOU'RE AWFUL," WREN noted an hour later while lounging on a hot-pink air mattress in the center of the pool.

"I'm also the one who made your current comfort level possible."

"That may well be, but as long as I live, I'll never get that clerk's horrified features from my mind."

He dived under the heated water, popping up alongside her. "Admit it, that was the most fun you've had in a while, if not ever."

In the glare, all she could focus on was the white of his smile and water beads gathering on his muscular, sun-kissed skin. Mouth dry, she managed, "I will admit nothing."

"Because you're ashamed of craving more of the same?" He formed a cup with his hands, scooping water into them and trailing it over her overheated chest. "It's okay to admit. Promise, I won't turn you down."

Lips pursed, she sighed. "What's wrong with you? In a single day you've transformed from all-around good guy to raving horndog."

"It's your fault," he complained, "parading around with your *goodies* on display."

"My *goodies* were safely tucked away in a dressing room!" Rolling off her pool toy with as much grace as she could muster considering she carried her own built-in floatie, Wren sloshed toward the shallow-end stairs.

Unfortunately, Cash followed. "I'm sorry, okay?"

Out of the pool, she took her towel from a lounger, wrapping it sarong-style—only, it didn't cover her bulging belly. Great.

Hands over her shoulders, causing unwitting havoc with the simplest of touches, he said, "Guess I've gotten used to having you around. I don't know if it's the unseasonably warm weather or what, but it felt good not worrying about anything and just having fun. I should be working my knee. I need to make amends with my mom, and now Dallas."

"What's wrong with him?"

Cash released her, slicking the water from his hair. "What's that expression you used? Same CD, different track?"

"That's the one." Taking another towel from the pile Mrs. Cahwood had thoughtfully set outside, Wren put it around her still-tingling shoulders.

Perching on a low rock wall, he said, "I get where they're coming from—the whole give-our-baby-the-Buckhorn-name thing. But it's not like you don't see Hollywood types not marrying."

"Considering where you live and your family's standing within the community, I wouldn't expect that argument to hold water."

"That's such BS." Now pacing, he said, "My big brother is well on his way to following in our dad's footsteps, as is Wyatt, but I've always been a disappointment."

"I don't believe that for a second." Wren's heart went out to him. All her life she'd wished for a family, but never once had she considered the pressure of living up to their expectations. "You're a rodeo star. Every ranch needs one of those."

"Mom and Dad dreamed of me becoming a veterinarian. What I do is a far cry from that."

Not thinking, just following her gut feelings, Wren went to him, wrapping her arms around him for a hug. "What you do is entertain everyone who sees you. You give them an escape from their everyday drudgery. If your mom and brothers don't see the importance in making people smile, then that's their problem."

"Who knew I had a little scrapper living with me?" He kissed the tip of her nose.

"First off, there's nothing *little* about me. Second, I'm not sure what I expected to find just dropping in on you like I did, but in light of the circumstances, you've been as welcoming as anyone could be."

"Thanks. Coming from you, that means a lot."

"Why from me?"

Releasing her to pace again, he said, "You're a family virgin."

"A what?"

"You know, since you haven't had a real, blood-related family, you don't know what a pain in the ass they can be. Which is one more reason why for us, marrying would be stupid."

But we're not blood related. The only thing linking them was smoking-hot chemistry.

A fact she'd be better off forgetting.

Chapter Eight

"Am I cleared?" Cash winced while hopping off the exam table in the National Bull Riding Team's Dallas facility.

His longtime friend and team doctor, Mack Duggan, consulted MRI images on a computer screen. "'Fraid not."

"Why? I've rested for six weeks."

"Right, and I told you after that time we'd take another MRI and reassess. Bottom line, just as I'd suspected, you have a nasty anterior cruciate ligament tear and I'm not clearing you to rejoin the tour until you've had corrective surgery. Even then—" he patted Cash's back "—there are no guarantees."

Though in his heart Cash had feared the news had been coming, that didn't make it easier to stomach. Slamming the nearest wall with the heel of his right hand, he said, "Dammit, I don't need this right now. Can't I just man up and deal with the pain?"

Making notes on Cash's chart, Mack said, "If you want me to lose my job. C'mon, work with me. Have the surgery. We're talking six months recovery max, and then we'll reassess."

With a sarcastic snort, Cash added, "Yeah, with pissed-off sponsors and no income."

"Look," his friend said, "you've already earned more at rodeo than a lot of people do in a lifetime. You're a young man. This isn't a death sentence. Worst-case scenario, a possible change in your life's course."

Cash's drive home was long.

He was used to a lot of time on the road. What he wasn't accustomed to was having his mind run faster than his truck's engine.

News that he'd have to go under the knife wasn't what most bothered him. It was the fact that on the off chance the surgery didn't go well, he might never ride again, at least not at a professional level. Screw the money—time on the road was his lifeblood. It was the only place he got validation that he was okay. He sure as hell didn't hear that news from Dallas or his mother. Yes, he was a screwup with women, but he'd always been a phenomenal bull rider. No matter what, he'd always had that to fall back on for all of his financial and emotional needs.

Without it, where did that leave him?

Worse yet, he had the added worry of sweet, funny, very pregnant Wren. Was she faring all right on her own? If he went under the knife ASAP, who would care for her then?

True, Mrs. Cahwood handled the household feeding and cleaning, but Wren needed rides to the library and plenty of chocolate-dipped cones at Queenie's. Who would make sure Wren didn't capsize in the pool or always had fresh wildflowers on her nightstand?

By the time he'd turned onto the road leading to his home, it was well past midnight. He'd expected the house to be dark, but lamplight shone through the windows, and on the couch he saw Wren curled up with one of her books. The sight of her warmed him. Made him feel oddly whole. As if even though his professional life was quite possibly shot to hell, everything would turn out all right.

Out of the truck, knee throbbing, Cash tried shaking out the stiffness. As usual, it didn't work. But for once, mounting the porch steps, the pain was okay. For better or worse, it was part of him. Just like the woman waiting up for him inside.

"Did you win?" Wren asked, sleepy eyed and hair tousled. She rested her book atop her baby bulge.

"Nah." He'd told her he'd spent the day competing. He hadn't needed her questions or pity. Now he almost wished he'd taken her with him. She'd have been able to not only explain the medical implications of surgery, but alleviate his no doubt irrational fears of possibly never riding bulls again. "Didn't even place."

"I'm sorry." Rising, she slipped her arms around him for a hug. "Mrs. Cahwood made blackberry cobbler. Want me to warm you a piece?"

"Sounds delicious," he said, nuzzling her sweet-smelling dark waves. "Do we have ice cream?"

She laughed. "That's like asking if I'm ever up all night, peeing."

Trailing her into the kitchen, he settled in at the table, appreciating her curves while she bustled to prepare his snack. "I should be waiting on you."

"Give me a break," she said with a pretty grin in his direction. "I've been sitting all day. It feels good to be productive."

While the cobbler was being nuked, she smoothed the hair back from his forehead, rubbing his temples and then aching shoulders. "You're one big knot."

"Tell me about it."

Still kneading, she asked, "What can I get you to drink?"

"Shot of Jim Beam."

She leaned over to view his expression. "Seriously?"

"Better make it two."

"All right…" Ignoring the beeping microwave, Wren pulled out a chair and tried straddling it, but her belly got in the way. "Rats." Once she turned the seat back around and plopped down in the usual way, she said, "Pardon that brief interruption. Now, what happened that's got you turning to drink? Did you get hurt physically, or is this an ego thing?"

Should he tell her the truth?

"Cash?" Her eyes begged him to let her in, but was he strong enough? If she knew all of his secrets and fears, what else stood between them to keep their attraction at bay?

Leaning into her, he rested his head atop their baby. "I'm sorry. I lied about where I've been."

The color drained from her face. "Were you with another woman?"

"What?" Raising his head, he took her hands. "Trust me, it's nothing like that. Why would that even cross your mind?"

"I don't know." She lowered her gaze. "It's stupid— and none of my business. If you want to be with somebody, then…"

He kissed her. Nothing fancy or calculated to make her want more, but brimming with emotion straight from his heart. "You've been on my mind all day."

Hands to her lips, she said, "You shouldn't have done that."

"I know. But how else could I get my point across that there's no other woman?"

"That's *my* point." Taking his cobbler from the microwave, she said, "We don't have that kind of relationship. Because of the baby, we'll always share that connection, but nothing more."

"Why do I get the feeling you're working overtime to convince yourself that's what you want?"

Ice cream in hand, she slammed the freezer door. "I don't know what you're talking about."

"Can we call a truce?" Standing behind her, he pinned her at the counter, fighting his every instinct to nuzzle her neck.

"Fine." After topping his dessert, she pushed him aside to return the frozen treat to the freezer.

"Does that mean you'll share this with me?" Knowing full well she'd never met a sweet she didn't like, he wagged the bowl.

"Thanks, but I'm ready for bed."

So much for telling her why he'd lied. She hadn't even cared. Chalk this up as just one more reason why Cash didn't need a woman in his life.

Wren closed her bedroom door and leaned against it.

"Baby," she whispered, feeling like a fool for talking to her belly, "your father is infuriating. Worse yet, his kisses are dreamier than lemon meringue pie. I've got our whole lives carefully mapped out for us, and nowhere on that map is a sign leading us straight into the arms of a too-handsome-for-his-own-good cowboy."

Her baby kicked.

"Thank you for agreeing."

As Wren readied for bed, the trained doctor in her knew late-night indigestion was what had her baby more active than usual. But she ignored that reasoning in favor of the idea that she and the baby were already emotionally connected.

Worse yet, Cash had admitted to lying about where he'd spent his day, but she'd been so wrapped up in the thought of him being with another woman that she hadn't even asked where he'd been. Not a good thing, considering the multitude of places a man like Cash could find trouble.

"You ever talking to me again?" In Doc Haven's waiting room Monday morning, Cash slapped down a copy of *People* magazine and glared at Wren.

"Maybe." She didn't bother looking up from her *US Weekly*.

"Let me get this straight," he said in a hushed tone. "You're miffed because I kissed you and you liked it."

"Did not." She tried acting offended, but the underlying flush to her complexion told him he'd pushed the right button.

Doc Haven's nurse opened the exam area's door. "Wren Barnes."

Cash stood along with the mother of his child.

"Oh, no," she whispered. "Don't think for a second you're going back there with me."

"It's my baby and I have every right to hear how *he's* coming along."

"*She's* doing great." The strap to her purse got hung around the chair arm. Cash cheerfully unhooked it for her.

Instead of thanking him, Wren glared harder.

"Good morning," the nurse chirped when they approached. "How's the momma today?"

"Miserable," Wren said with a pained look in Cash's direction.

"Isn't she cute?" Once they'd passed through the door, Cash put his arm around her.

In the exam room, when Cash tried helping Wren onto the bench table, she snapped, "I can do it myself."

"Go for it." He released her, only to quickly see she hadn't a prayer of safely making it without major assistance.

Though she didn't look happy about it, Wren grabbed hold of him, clutching him for support. "Thank you."

"Any time."

The nurse made a note on her chart.

"Miss Barnes, if you'll lend me your arm, I'll go ahead and take your blood pressure."

Wren removed the sweater she'd squeezed into to counteract the October chill. Indian summer was gone, replaced by blustery wind and a cold drizzle. Thrusting out her arm, Wren said, "Do your worst."

"I'll try to be gentle." A few minutes later the woman removed her stethoscope's earpieces and frowned. "One fifty-six over ninety-four."

"That good?" Cash asked.

"No." Wren put her hands to her forehead.

"Is she okay? Do we need to run her to a Tulsa hospital?"

"Not just yet," the nurse assured him. "Let Doc Haven take a look, and I'm sure Mommy and baby will be fine."

After another reassuring smile, the smiley blonde left them on their own.

"Tell it to me straight," Cash said to Wren. "How serious is this?"

She shook her head. "It's probably nothing. Stress related."

"What are you stressed about?"

She crossed her arms, and her scowl hit him like a well-aimed slug.

"Do you even have to ask?"

"Me? You're upset over me?" He laughed. "That's the stupidest thing I've ever heard."

"Maybe to you, but obviously my blood pressure doesn't lie."

Doc Haven bustled into the room. "Sally tells me my favorite patient's vitals aren't ideal?"

"True," Wren said.

"You've been taking it easy? Eating right?"

"Yes and yes," Cash answered.

Extending his hand for Cash to shake, the doctor said, "Nice to see you taking an interest in your future child's health."

What was he supposed to say? *Sure, Doc. Up until now I just didn't give a damn?* Cash had always cared— he just hadn't realized how much.

"Wren, before we snoop on your little guy's or gal's heart rate, in general, how have you been feeling? Swelling in your extremities?"

"No." Easing her back on the exam table, the doctor extended it to make room for her dangling feet, and then raised her shirt, exposing Wren's belly. "Nothing out of the ordinary."

She sucked in her breath when he squeezed clear gel from a bottle.

"Cold?"

She nodded.

"Sorry. They make gizmos to heat this gunk, but I haven't gotten around to ordering one." He waved a wand over Wren's belly until all of a sudden a rapid-fire thumping sounded from what looked to Cash like one of the twins' old baby monitors. "Whoa. Sounds like you have a track star growing in there. Nice and strong."

Wren released the breath she'd been holding.

"The next few days," the doctor said, wiping her stomach and then tugging down her shirt, "I'd like you to do better at keeping off your feet as much as possible. Cash, that means whatever this little gal needs, you're to deliver. Ice cream, pickles, late-night fried chicken— within reason, whatever she wants."

"Yes, sir."

"Also—" the doctor took a tissue from a box on the counter, using it to clean his glasses "—I want you back here Friday. If we don't see an improvement, I'm checking you in to Saint Francis in Tulsa for observation."

Chapter Nine

"Now you simply have to marry her." In the kitchen with her son, Georgina Buckhorn spoke as if Wren wasn't even in the house.

Wren had set up camp on the living-room sofa.

Outside, cold rain had set in and the wind howled, making Wren grateful for the crackling fire Cash had made.

Snuggling deeper into the fuzzy pink blanket he'd brought her, she closed her eyes, inhaling deeply through her nose and exhaling through her mouth.

"God forbid, what if something happens? What if that poor little baby is stillborn without ever having had a proper name?"

"Mom," Cash said, clanking around in the kitchen, "Wren isn't supposed to be upset. If you won't let this go, you'll have to leave."

Georgina lowered her voice to the point Wren could no longer hear.

Eyes wide open, she fought to achieve the comfort level she'd found before Cash's mother had stopped by for a supposedly friendly chat.

Cash appeared, carrying a plateful of the turkey-and-Swiss sandwiches Mrs. Cahwood had left for lunch. His smile was forced.

His mother marched behind him with sliced apples and bananas as if Wren were a toddler incapable of chewing whole food. "Here you go," she said, setting her load on the coffee table. "All nice and healthy for you. Lots of fiber, too." She winked.

"Thanks."

The older woman had brought an extra plate and now assembled snack-sized portions she handed to Wren. "When I carried Wyatt, I was perpetually hungry. His sister, not so much." Fleetingly enough as to make Wren wonder if she might've imagined it, a wistful look saddened Mrs. Buckhorn's features. "First losing your father, then Daisy... When you get to be my age, multiple losses seem to exponentially increase heartache."

"You talk as if she's dead, Mom." Cash grabbed a sandwich. "My gut tells me Daisy's great—just for her own reasons choosing to live on her own."

Hands to her temples, Wren said, "If you all don't mind, I think I'll go to my room and have a nap."

"I've upset you, haven't I?" Fussing with Wren's still-full plate, Cash's mother dabbed her napkin at a few crumbs on the table. "It's just that with my daughter Lord-only-knows where, and now my future grandchild about to meet the same fate..." Hand to her chest, she dragged in a breath and shuddered. "It's oftentimes more than I can bear."

"Quit being melodramatic." Cash slammed his plate on the table and was on his feet, pacing before the windows. "You hate losing control."

"I didn't raise you to be cruel."

Turning to her, he asked, "What did you raise me for?"

Wren cleared her throat. "I—I'm going to give you two some privacy."

"No." When she rose, Cash urged her back down. "Whether we're legally wed or not, you're carrying my child. That makes you family." To his mother, he said, "All my life you and Dad told me what to do. Quit riding bulls. You'll only get hurt. Go to college. Do something valuable with your life. Marry a nice girl. Settle down. Never once in all of those demands did either of you just wish me happiness. Why is that, Mom?"

"What's wrong with you?" With her napkin, Georgina blotted tears from her eyes. "Why are you acting this way?"

Wren resisted the urge to pull the blanket over her head and hide. How long had she dreamed of belonging to a real family? If this was what it was like, then she truly was better off on her own.

"I'm hurt, okay? My riding career might be done. That make you happy? Finally hearing me admit you and Dad were right?"

"Of course not. Your father may have wished you'd chosen a more academic path for your life, but that doesn't mean he wasn't proud of you." His mother tried embracing him, but he nudged her away.

"The team doctor says I have to have surgery. Even then, I might not be cleared to ever rejoin the tour."

"Oh, honey…" She again reached out to hug him, only this time he fell into her arms.

Wren remained frozen on the couch.

Why hadn't Cash shared this with her? Lack of trust? But then, why should he trust her? Aside from sharing great sex, they were practically strangers. Was seeing a specialist what he'd gone to Dallas for?

"If I can't ride again," he asked, "what am I going to do?"

Stepping back, Georgina braced her son's shoulders.

"You're going to be the man your father knew you to be. First we'll get you a second—even third—opinion. If all of those doctors are in agreement, you'll face that reality when and if it comes. Until then—" she turned to Wren "—we have much to be thankful for. Together we'll ride out any storm."

"You're quiet," Cash said to Wren an hour after his mom had left. Rain still fell, and the KOTV weatherman said by night it could change over to an early snow.

"I'm reading." She didn't look up from her book.

"Must be a good page, seeing how you haven't turned it the whole time I've been sitting here."

Resting the book on the sofa back, she said, "Truthfully, though I understand why you wouldn't confide in me about your knee, I'm hurt. I wouldn't have expected details, but why couldn't you have at least told the truth about your Dallas trip?"

Fear? Embarrassment? Hell if he knew.

"I thought we'd grown close. At least become friends. Now…" She smoothed her hands over their baby. "I have to wonder if I mean anything to you at all. And that seriously messes with my head, considering I've been adamant against us sharing anything beyond the most basic of platonic relationships once our child is born."

Cash added a log to the fire. "Of course we're close. I tried telling you about my Dallas trip, but then we kissed and everything got messed up in my mind. I had this image of me being the perfect guy for you. Making boatloads of money and buying you and our child everything you'd ever need. But if I'm off the tour, all that changes. I'm back to earning a living the old-fashioned way, which is something I've never done."

"Please face me." When he did, she said, "Beyond

helping people, a large part of why I wanted to become a doctor was to be self-sufficient. No matter what, as a healer, my services will always be in demand. So as far as money goes, I couldn't care less what you earn or if I ever see a dime of child support. In the short term, I'm dead broke. And because I've been blessed enough to have scholarships that negated the need for student loans, once my residency's over I'll make more than enough to support myself and our baby. The last thing you should worry about is taking care of me."

What if I find myself in the unexpected position of wanting to care for you and our kiddo? Cash wasn't sure how, but Wren had become a lifeline. She was the only thing keeping him sane in his otherwise upside-down world.

"Cash?"

He looked up.

"Talk to me. What's going through that handsome head of yours?"

"Finally admitting it, huh?" With a pinched smile nowhere near as potent as usual, he took one of the sandwiches left to wilt on the coffee table. "I'm the best-looking man you've ever seen?"

"That's a given. What I need you to be is the most communicative."

"Girl," Delores Hawke said Friday afternoon at her home's front door, "you've grown big as a house. Get in here before we both catch our death of cold."

Passing Cash's elderly neighbor, Wren barely got around her new aluminum walker. The woman's hip surgery had been a success and after weeks in a convalescent home, she'd been released to care for herself.

Cash had taken Wren to visit several times and they'd become fast friends.

At her doctor's appointment that morning, Wren's blood pressure had been back to normal, meaning when she'd heard from Doc Haven that Delores had been sprung, it was the perfect way to celebrate Wren's own good health.

Collapsing onto her new power chair, Delores said, "Be a dear and fetch us some cookies before we settle in for a nice visit. All I have are store bought until I'm back to one hundred percent."

Laughing all the way to the kitchen, Wren hoped she had as much spunk when she was eighty.

Armed with two tumblers filled with milk and two saucers of coconut macaroons, Wren returned to the living room and sat on a loud floral sofa featuring crocheted doilies on the arms and across the back. Cool weather had helped considerably to tame the scent of mothballs and Bengay.

"Where's that man of yours?" Delores asked after downing two cookies and half her milk.

"First, Cash is hardly mine, and second, Dallas sent him to the feed store with a long list. He's picking me up on his way home."

"No wedding bells, then?"

"Not you, too," Wren said with a sigh. "What is it with this town? Everyone's obsessed with marriage."

"Oh, don't go getting your panties twisted." She popped another cookie into her mouth and chewed. "Isolated as we are, Weed Gulch has old-fashioned values. Back when I was your age, an unwed mother would make front-page news. I know, to your generation it sounds crazy, but that's how it was. We had no such thing as divorce statistics, because folks didn't get divorced. More often than not, you grew to love each other. Good or bad, you stayed together until death do you part."

Grinning, Wren had to ask, "So then everyone understood if you ended up killing each other?"

"HAVE A NICE VISIT?" Cash had gone inside to chat with Delores for a short while, but once he'd got wind that the topic centered on marriage, he'd ushered Wren to the door.

"Fine," she said, accepting his help climbing into the truck.

With her safely buckled in, he got behind the wheel, starting the engine for the short ride home.

"How was the feed store?"

"Good. I bought you a present."

"More popcorn?" Since her first batch, she'd taken to having some every afternoon, munching while reading. She usually dropped a bunch, making a hellacious mess wherever she'd happened to park herself.

"Since that's a given—it doesn't count. Guess again."

"I don't know, it's the feed store. A new hoe or rake?"

"Hmm… No and no." He couldn't ever remember being so excited to give someone a gift—not even when he'd made his mother a Popsicle-stick log cabin in 4-H.

"You do know it's not nice to tease pregnant people? We're prone to snap."

He flashed a smile. "I'll take my chances."

The drive time couldn't have been over fifteen minutes, but it felt like an eternity. What would she think? Was his gift too personal? Would she even like it? How could she not? He probably shouldn't have left it in the truck bed, but the woman who'd sold it to him said it would be all right for the short trip.

He stopped in front of the house. "You stay put. And close your eyes. I don't want any peeking."

"Yes, sir," she said with a saucy salute.

"You all right?" Cash asked, scooping the cutie out of her blanket-filled box. The hamster-sized puppy—supposedly a Yorkie-Chihuahua mix—licked his nose.

"Hurry!" Wren shouted. "I have to pee!"

"Your mother's very demanding," Cash whispered, cradling the furball to his chest.

"*Really* bad!"

"How about holding it long enough to meet the newest member of our household." Cupping the puppy in his palms, he presented it to Wren. "Okay, open your eyes."

She did, only her reaction wasn't quite what he'd intended. Instantly tearing, she looked at the puppy for the longest time, then cried, "Cash, how c-could you?"

Now in full-blown sobs, Wren gave the trembling pup one last look before running into the house, slamming the door behind her.

Chapter Ten

Having locked herself in the bathroom for at least twenty minutes, Wren wasn't surprised when Cash pounded on the door.

"Come on, she's just a puppy. How scary can she be?"

"I—I'm not scared," Wren wailed, "but sad."

He persisted. "Same question, different word. She's adorable, not sad."

Wren cried harder.

"Hope you're decent," Cash called, "because like it or not, I'm coming in." The doorknob jiggled and true to his word—albeit with his eyes closed—he barged in. He'd brought the puppy with him, a fact that did little to help Wren's emotional train wreck.

Seated on the tile tub surround, she covered her face with her hands.

Cash knelt in front of her. "Honey, what's wrong?"

"Nothing!" she wailed. *Everything!*

"Okay, breathe…" He set the puppy on Wren's baby belly. Lowering her hands, she looked down at the squirming, shivering mess of a tiny dog. It whimpered and looked up at her, melting her into hundreds of shattering pieces. Scooping it up, she cradled it between her breasts, nuzzling the puffy fur between the dog's ears. "Better?"

She nodded. "Sorry. This baby has my emotions all over the map. You couldn't have known."

"That I'm living with a psycho?" He laughed.

Wren didn't.

With Cash stroking her hair and the dog licking her nose with the sweetest puppy breath, had Wren been a cat, she'd have purred.

"I'm kidding," he said, "but when you get a second, I'd love you to let me in on what it was about this goofy-looking dog that sent you over the edge."

"It's stupid. *I'm* stupid for letting something that happened a hundred years ago affect me today."

"You don't look that old." He tugged a lock of her hair.

"I feel it." Yawning, the hamster-sized dog still held close, she asked, "Wanna take this conversation to my bed?"

"Thought you'd never ask."

Cash had never seen a prettier sight than Wren sleeping with his gift snuggled into the crook of her neck. She'd broken his heart with the story of how she'd found a puppy hiding in the bushes at her orphanage. For weeks she'd secretly fed it and cared for it, visiting every chance she'd gotten. Then she'd been caught sneaking it lunch scraps. By that afternoon, the pound had loaded it into the back of a truck and she'd never seen it again.

Since then, she'd avoided anything with fur like the plague. Fur equaled pain. Though she hadn't said it, he assumed she felt the same way about forging emotional connections.

So that was her reasoning. What was his excuse?

Wren was a great woman. Any man would be thrilled she was having his baby. Any other man would have also long since proposed, but not Cash. No matter how perfect Wren might be, he wasn't the marrying kind.

Didn't have it in him.

"What are you doing?" Wren asked, catching him standing over her.

"Thinking."

"About what?" She yawned, in the process waking the fur ball—who also yawned.

"You two look alike." Both of his girls had crazy bed hair and sleepy eyes.

"I'll take that as a compliment." She gave the dog a rub.

"Got a name for her?"

She took a minute to answer. "I named my first dog Waldo, after the books. I loved them."

"Waldo?" Cash made a face. "Not a very pretty name for such a gorgeous little girl." Snatching the dog for himself, he held her out in front of him, surveying her mutton-chop sideburns.

"How about Wenda?" Wren suggested. "That's his girlfriend's name."

"I thought his girlfriend was Wanda?"

Laughing, she asked, "Got your iPhone? Let's look it up." Ten minutes later they'd discovered Wenda and Wanda were twins. Waldo had officially dated both.

"Kinda kinky if you ask me," Cash said, "which is always a good thing, but that still doesn't help with a name."

"True." Sitting up in the bed, Wren turned thoughtful. "I had a friend at the orphanage named Priscilla. She had the prettiest blond curls and was adopted just before her sixth birthday. Losing her was as tough as losing my dog."

"Do you have any childhood stories that aren't tear-jerkers?"

"Not so much," she admitted, "but anyway, what if we call our puppy Prissy? She's not blonde, but she does have an angelic, beauty-queen look to her that leads me to believe she'll have a great career in breaking doggy hearts."

"We talking about the same mutt?"

In a surprisingly agile move considering her size, she took the dog from him. "Come here, Precious. Don't listen to a thing he says."

"Thought you wanted to name her Prissy?"

"It's a woman's prerogative to change her mind."

Heading for the kitchen to warm the dinner Mrs. Cahwood had left them, he asked, "You're not going to pull that name-change stunt on our boy, are you?"

"Nope," she said, trailing after him with the dog riding her belly. "Especially since we're having a girl."

"You DO REALIZE we have a human baby due in four weeks and should be shopping for her?" In the south Tulsa Pet Warehouse, Wren peeked into her purse to find Prissy napping on the miniquilt Delores had made. "Not to mention Christmas is also barreling toward us. Have you thought about gifts?"

"Four weeks is plenty of time to get human baby gear and presents for the family." Cash grabbed a cart. "This dog baby, however, is here now and needs toys and clothes and that special food I saw advertised on TV."

"Cash, you're spoiling—ooh, look at that rhinestone collar." She made a beeline for a specialty Princess Pup endcap. Who knew there were so many adorable pooch clothes? Dresses and T-shirts and even hats and match-ing booties packaged in sets of four.

"Let me get this straight—if I want to buy Prissy special food, that's spoiling, but you can pick out fancy clothes when God already gave her a fur coat and that's perfectly fine?"

Wren stuck out her tongue and selected a blinged-out T-shirt that said I'm a Princess...You Scoop It!

Thirty minutes later the cart was so full with a bed and food and a plush carrying case that Wren had to ask Cash to push it to the checkout stand.

In the truck with Prissy on her lap, Wren dressed her and put on her new collar and bow.

"Know what we forgot?" Cash asked, veering the truck onto Highway 169.

"Looks like we've got everything to me." Holding up Prissy, Wren couldn't remember a time in recent his-tory she'd ever been more content. "She's gorgeous."

"She also doesn't have a name tag. We should've at least gotten one with a phone number on it in case she gets lost or runs away."

"What number would we put? Right after the baby's born, all three of us will return to Baltimore."

Fury didn't begin to describe the sudden change in Cash's expression. Blaring the horn, he passed the car in front of them that was going five under the speed limit.

"Cash?" Wren tightened her hold on Prissy. "I've never seen you like this. What's wrong?"

"What do you think?" Cash passed another car and another.

"You know that just as soon as I'm able, the baby and I and now my puppy will all need to go home. To Bal-timore. I have my residency waiting and I've even re-served a spot in the hospital's on-site day-care program.

It's award winning. Our baby will receive groundbreaking infant care."

Turning on the radio, Cash flipped through stations, ultimately settling on pounding rock.

"Avoiding the issue's not going to make it go away."

"Excuse me for caring." Turning off the music, he focused on the road. "Sometimes I wish we'd never even met."

It didn't matter that he'd spoken the words out of anger—they still hurt Wren to her core. "Don't even bother going to your house. Take me straight to Tulsa International."

"Don't be ridiculous." Though they passed an exit, he didn't even slow.

Shifting on the seat, she said, "You're the one acting like a child about my leaving."

"You running away is grown-up?"

Lips pressed tight, she vowed to remain silent the rest of the way to their ranch home. Only, the place she'd once viewed as a temporary haven no longer existed. Cash had ruined it.

"Dammit, Wren, answer me. Tell me why you're still leaving. Couldn't you do your residency in Tulsa or Oklahoma City? Think about it. During the week, I can be with the baby. Isn't that better than him spending fifteen to twenty hours each day being raised by strangers?"

The last thing Wren wanted was to dignify his question with an answer, but he'd left her no choice. "Of course being with you would be better, but you're missing the point. I'm not a team player. Never have been, and I have no intention of starting now. Any time I've ever grown attached to someone or made a friend, they leave me. You'll do the same. Only instead of just me being hurt, our child will be, too. As a good mother, isn't it my job to protect my baby from pain? Especially when it inevitably stems from being abandoned by her own father?"

Shooting her a disgusted glare, he asked, "You honestly think that little of me?"

Cuddling Prissy, she snapped, "I try not to think of you at all."

"Liar."

Yes, she was. But to let him know how much his friendship had come to mean would be foolhardy. She hadn't gotten where she was today by letting people in, but by shutting them out. Remembering that was key to escaping Cash with her heart intact.

"YOU NEED TO EAT," Cash said over the chick flick he'd popped into the DVD in hopes of making Wren smile. As she no longer fit in the kitchen-table chairs, they'd taken to dining in the living room. Only, tonight she wasn't watching the movie or vacuuming her food.

"Why do you care? Remember how you wish we'd never met?" Feigning great interest in the movie, she nibbled a green bean.

"You know damn well I didn't mean that."

"Then why say it?"

"I don't know." *Probably had something to do with hurting you the way you hurt me.*

Outside, cold wind howled. Hard to believe it was already December. Where had autumn gone?

Putting her plate on the table with considerable effort, she rolled onto her side, away from the TV and him.

"Just because you can't see me doesn't mean I'm not here."

"Did I say it did?" Her voice was muffled due to her having drawn her blanket over her head.

He turned off the movie. The sudden silence was jarring, but not as much as this constant bickering.

"I was watching that" came a halfhearted complaint from somewhere under the sofa mound. Prissy peeked out from under the covers, eyeing Wren's thick-cut pork chop.

"How long do you think we have left together? Assuming the baby's on time, four weeks, and then what's a standard maternity leave? Six weeks more?"

"I've already taken too much time off. I'd like to be back in Baltimore by the first of February. As it is, I'll be lucky if the dean lets me rejoin the program midyear."

"No."

She tossed back the covers hard enough to damn near knock off the dog. "What do you mean, *no*? Last I heard you don't have a whole lot of say in the matter."

Prissy used the boost to leap onto the coffee table, helping herself to Wren's meal. Lightning fast, uncaring she'd dredged her brand-new pink shirt through ketchup, Prissy tugged the chop and herself to the table's edge, vanishing under the couch.

"Did you see that?" Cash couldn't help but laugh. "If our kid's anywhere near as sly as our dog, we've got trouble."

"No kidding." Wren also sported a slight smile.

Until their eyes met and hers filled with tears. She held out her arms and he went to her, holding her tight, praying she understood he didn't want to marry her, but he certainly didn't want her to go.

"We're going to be all right," she promised. "But this

fighting has to stop. It's not good for any of us—especially my puppy, who will probably throw up all night."

Cash grinned past the knot in his throat.

Somehow, some way, bull riding was no longer his top priority. His biggest problem now? Learning to breathe without Wren and his baby and a seriously cute mutt dog.

Chapter Eleven

"How's Mommy?"

Wren cringed upon opening the door Monday morning to find Georgina carrying more fiber muffins and slung over her shoulder a bag that no doubt carried a new form of torture. "Good morning. I'm doing great. How are you?"

"Honestly," she said on her way to the kitchen, "I had my annual physical this morning, and my blood pressure is up, too. Curiously enough, when I told Doc Haven that my diet is quite healthy and I exercise every day, he suggested all of the unknowns surrounding my third grandchild might be causing me stress."

"Oh?" Ignoring Cash's mother's not-so-subtle dig, Wren helped herself to a muffin. "Thanks for bringing these. They are super-duper effective."

"You're, ah, welcome."

Catching Cash's mother off guard had become a hobby of sorts. After all, it wouldn't hurt her to at least call before her visits.

"Since needlepoint wasn't your thing, I brought you a new hobby in which I know you'll excel." When Wren returned to the sofa, head filled with remembrances of the knotted catastrophe that had occurred the last time she'd tried being crafty, Georgina pulled out a cellophane-wrapped box, brandishing the cover like a *Price Is Right* model. "Taa-daa! You're going to make a latch-hook rug to hang in the baby's room. Aren't the blue booties adorable?"

"Yes," Wren said, "but I'm pretty sure I'm having a girl."

"Nonsense." Opening the box, she drew out a large chart and a tool she pronounced to be the latch-hook instrument. "Everyone knows that if a woman craves boiled eggs during her pregnancy, she'll only give birth to boys. Mrs. Cahwood told me you've been eating dozens of her deviled eggs, which are made from boiled eggs, so there you go."

WEDNESDAY MORNING WREN found herself back in Tulsa, only this time for an ultrasound.

Constant arguing between herself and Cash had morphed into a bittersweet understanding that their remaining time together was already brief. Why poison it with petty bickering when they'd be better served preparing mentally and physically for the new life to come?

"This your first?" the ultrasound tech asked.

"Yep," Cash answered from his chair alongside Wren's padded table.

"Nervous?" the tech asked.

"Is that snow outside cold?" Again Cash acted if he was the one hauling around his thirty-pound baby!

The pretty, petite blonde laughed.

Wren suppressed the urge to smack him. Wasn't there a rule about guys who were expecting a child not flirting?

The pressure of the tech and her wand was making Wren have to pee.

"I've got a great shot of your baby's sex. Want me to print a copy for you?"

"No!" Wren snapped.

"Yes!" Cash leaned over her, trying to get a view.

"Oops." The screen had already gone blank. "Once *Mommy* told me she didn't want to see, I exited."

"Damn," Cash mumbled, shoulders slumped.

"What does it even matter?" Wren asked.

"Oh—it matters." He helped wiped the gunk off her belly, tickling in the process.

"Stop," she said with a giggle. "You know I can't stand it when you touch there."

Which only made him do it more.

"You two make a darling couple," the tech noted. "Good luck with your new family."

Wren started to correct her, but didn't.

AFTER SCRAPING SNOW from the truck's windows, Cash hopped into the warm cab alongside Wren. "While we're in the big city, does Prissy need anything? I noticed she's running low on Tiny T Bonz. She prefers the filet flavor over the porterhouse."

"It frightens me how you know that." She directed a heater vent toward him.

"What can I say? I take my parenting duties seriously."

"After the pet store, we really should make a stop at Baby Depot. What if she surprises us by coming early and we don't even have a crib?"

"You're right," he said, turning on the wipers and lights. "Wanna stop for lunch first? I'm seriously craving a nice, thick steak." He winked. "I'm sure our boy is, too."

After watching the mother of his child wolf down

more food than he'd thought humanly possible, Cash bundled her back into the truck and headed for the baby store.

A good six inches of snow had already fallen, with no signs of a letup. Traffic was nuts, with far too many rotten drivers out on the roads.

Finally in the store's lot, Cash put the truck in Park, leaving the heater blasting. "Think I should call Mom and have her check on Prissy?"

"Probably. I would hope Mrs. Cahwood is home in front of a nice fire by now."

He dialed his mom's cell, only to five minutes later wish he hadn't. "I swear that woman's sole purpose in life is to make me miserable."

"I highly doubt that." Wren tugged on her mittens. "What'd she say?"

"Just that we need to quit playing house, pretending a puppy is our child when what we should be doing is stepping up to the real-life obligation of planning a custody visitation schedule before her blood pressure gets any higher."

"Ouch." Nibbling her lower lip, Wren asked, "Does that mean she's not checking on the puppy?"

"She'll do it, but I wouldn't be surprised if the price we pay for her services is having to hear more of her wishes and wisdom."

Once Cash had Wren safely in the store, overwhelmed didn't begin describing his avalanche of emotions. Grabbing a few things for Prissy had been fun. Selecting everything from toys to safety equipment to rectal thermometers for his child was a task he wasn't equipped to handle.

"I think I need to sit." Judging by her wide eyes, Wren wasn't faring much better.

"Want to come back when the weather's nice?"

"That's a great idea," she said, going limp from what he guessed was relief. "In the meantime, we can make a list. I'll go to some baby websites and figure out which basics we'll most need."

"Good thinking." He hustled her toward the door.

"Excuse me?" A kindly, middle-aged clerk wearing a pink-and-blue-striped Baby Depot T-shirt approached. "I couldn't help but overhear your conversation, and since I'm in charge of gift registry and have five little ones of my own, I'm fully qualified to help."

Wren was back to nibbling her lower lip.

Cash's stomach hurt.

"I, um, think we need more time." Wren hedged closer to the exit.

"Judging by the size of your baby bump," the clerk noted with a big grin, "your time is almost up."

"COULD YOU BELIEVE that woman?" The first thing Wren did when they got home was scoop up Prissy, showering her with love. Next, she took off her heavy coat, hat and gloves before kicking off her rubber snow boots. "One would think baby-store employees would be trained to lay off the high-pressure sales tactics."

"No kidding," Cash said right behind her, scratching behind the puppy's ears.

On her way to the kitchen, Wren said, "I'm starving. Want me to make you a plate of whatever Mrs. Cahwood left?"

"Absolutely."

"On second thought…" She veered toward the bathroom. "Nature's calling."

"I knew you'd wriggle out of cooking."

"You have to admire my skill!" she shouted on her mad dash down the hall.

After washing her hands, she wound her way toward her closet to change into more comfy clothes. On such a cold night, her green fleece sweats would be extra warm.

Humming the jazzed-up version of "Rock-a-Bye Baby" that had been playing during their failed shopping mission, Wren quickly changed and then headed for the kitchen, where she hoped Cash had found something good.

Rounding the living-room corner, she found Georgina and wished she'd stayed in her room.

"Hello," Cash's mother said, rising from the sofa to give her a hug. "You look ready to pop."

"Um, thanks?"

"Have a seat," she urged, patting the sofa. "Cash tells me you two had an ultrasound this afternoon."

"Y-yes, ma'am..." Was it wrong for Wren to be terrified of what the Buckhorn matriarch might say next?

"He also said you chose to not learn the sex. I don't blame you for wanting to be surprised."

"Thank you," Wren said, relieved by Georgina's seemingly mild-mannered turn. Lowering her gaze, she laced her fingers atop the baby. "As long as he or she is healthy, I'll be happy with whatever we get."

"As long as it's a boy." Cash lit the fire and then turned to face her. Wren had always been a sucker for his smile, but something about this night's version made him extra attractive. It'd been a good day. Riding snugly alongside him in the truck while gumball-sized snow cocooned them in their own special world.

"I don't mean to be an interfering mother," Georgina said, "but Cash also told me about your failed mission to the baby store. When you two do finally get around to making a temporary nest, keep in mind that you'll want to get two of everything. One set for here, and one for Wren to take with her to Baltimore."

Though Wren was thankful the woman had finally digested the fact that she and the baby wouldn't permanently reside in Weed Gulch, something about her tone was off-putting. "Mrs. Buckhorn," Wren couldn't keep from asking, "what is it about me you don't like?"

"Excuse me?" She pressed her hand to her chest. It was a work- and weather-roughened hand with nails not painted and fancy, but filed short. "How did you draw that conclusion? I hardly even know you."

"From the day we met, I've gotten the sense that you disapprove of everything about me, from my career goals to my nonexistent craft skills to my refusal to marry your son. But one fact you need to understand is that the last thing Cash wants is to be tied down with not only a wife, but a child. Do you really want to railroad your son into a lifetime of misery out of your antiquated sense of honor?"

"Anyone up for hot chocolate?" Cash clapped his hands, smoothing them together. "Yeah, I'm thinking that's just what we need."

"Son? Is what Wren said true?" Though her eyes teared, Georgina still looked as tall and unyielding as ever.

Cash turned his back on his mother and hustled toward the kitchen. "I think Mrs. Cahwood bought me some mini-marshmallows. I'll check."

"If it is true," Georgina said, hot on his heels, "I'm sorry." The older woman's hands fluttered about her long hair, and her lips quivered.

Wren should've minded her own business, but if

Cash was going to endure another attack, she felt honor bound to stand by him.

"Knowing you like I do," his mother continued, "I never thought you'd be the sort to engage in a one-night stand unless you felt an extra spark for a woman. All this time I assumed you and Wren were just playing hard to get, but would eventually realize you've fallen in love with not only each other, but your baby." Looking out the window at the still-falling snow, she added, "Again, I apologize for being a foolish old woman with ideals better suited for the last century."

At the back door Georgina took her long leather duster from a hook. After slipping it on, she removed gloves and a hat from the pockets.

"Mom…" Cash abandoned his marshmallow mission. "Don't leave like this."

"It's all right," she said. "You're an adult. Do let me know when you're having your surgery, though."

When she walked out, he chased after her. "At least let me put boots on and drive you home. You shouldn't be walking in this."

"Your father and I delivered calves out in the pasture in worse storms than this."

"Mom, please…"

Already halfway across the drive, she waved. "You two have a nice night."

Inside, with the door shut on wind and blowing snow, Cash took off his wet socks and flung them against the stone hearth.

Again Wren followed, wishing there was something she could do to if not comfort him, at least help him calm down.

"Damn her," Cash said.

Going to Cash, she slipped her arms around his

waist, wishing the baby wasn't blocking her from fully pressing against him. "I'm sorry. I don't know what got into me, confronting your mom that way. I guess that's one more thing to blame on hormones."

"Don't sweat it." He returned her hug, shielding her from whatever hurt in her world. Cash was big and strong and capable. The opposite of how she currently felt. "God's honest truth… What just happened is a huge part of why I want nothing to do with setting up my own family. I loved my dad, but as you can see, even with him gone, I still don't measure up. As great as he was, he set what, for me anyway, were unobtainable expectations."

"Did he say that? Or was it your conscience always wanting to please him?" Wren ached for Cash.

Never had she considered herself lucky for growing up not knowing her parents, but maybe there was a certain satisfaction that stemmed from having to please only herself.

Mouth dry, holding him for dear life, she said, "Did it ever occur to you that you could make a conscious decision to not be like your father? Create your own rules. Keep the parts of your upbringing you cherished, while at the same time raising our son or daughter with the qualities you wished your father had had."

"Great plan," he said with a sad laugh. "Only one problem."

"What?" Pulse racing, she prayed that problem had nothing to do with her. She'd grown to enjoy Cash's company and never wanted to hurt him.

"Practically as soon as our kid is born, you'll be taking him or her away. It's hard to implement all of these brilliant ideas when I won't even have the damned dog to practice on." He turned away from her, striding to the corner wet bar to pour a shot of Jim Beam. Downing it in one gulp, he poured another.

"That's not fair." Taking the glass from him, she dumped the amber liquid down the drain. "And getting rip-roaring drunk won't do a thing to help your emotional clarity."

Rolling his eyes, he noted, "This from our resident basket case who cries during every sappy commercial?"

"I really dislike you," she snapped.

"Ditto."

Tears started and wouldn't stop.

"Oh, come on," he said. "It's been a long day. Let's rest, and hopefully we'll wake sane in the morning."

"That's it?" He was shredding her heart, and rather than discuss it, he wanted to sleep? She longed to rail at him, but then remembered her heart had nothing to do with their situation. Per her request, they were casual friends. Yes, they'd soon share a child. Yes, Cash would forever be in her life. No, they would never share anything more.

Hand to his forehead, he sighed. "What do you want?"

"Nothing." Fighting a fresh onslaught of tears, she woke Prissy from where she'd fallen asleep on a sofa cushion. With the dog in her arms, Wren retreated to her room.

Unfortunately, Cash followed. "Obviously you expect more of me, or you wouldn't have asked the question."

"All right…" Arms crossed, she said, "I've always heard it's not wise for a couple to go to bed angry. But since we're not a couple, in our case, that rule doesn't apply."

A muscle ticked in his jaw. "Let me get this straight—

after weeks of you declaring your independence, you now all of a sudden want there to be a *you and me*?"

"No." *Yes!* But she didn't understand why. With every fiber of her being she no longer wanted to leave him. Trouble was, no matter how badly she might want to, she absolutely couldn't stay.

Chapter Twelve

"Cash?"

He woke from a deep sleep to find Wren standing alongside his bed, clutching her belly. Bolting upright, he asked, "What's wrong? Something with the baby?"

"I think so," she said, fear lacing her voice. "I woke with a horrible headache, ringing in my ears and I'm dizzy."

"Could you be getting a cold or flu?"

"I suppose, but all of those are signs of high blood pressure." Wringing her hands, she looked lost. "I've been meaning to get a home pressure monitor, but they're expensive and I felt funny asking you for money when the last time we were at the drugstore I felt fine."

"Are you kidding me?" Out of bed, he rummaged through his dresser for a clean T-shirt and socks. Finding yesterday's jeans where he'd left them over the end of his footboard, he pulled them on over his boxers. "What's wrong with you? You didn't mind me spending a small fortune on new clothes for your dog, but when it came to watching your own health, pride got in the way?"

"It wasn't like that," she said.

He snorted. "You already call Doc Haven?"

"Uh-huh. He said with the weather, it'd be fastest for

you to drive me into Tulsa. He's called ahead to Saint Francis hospital, so they'll be expecting us."

"What're they going to do?" he asked as he headed for her room, where he found her a giant sweatshirt to slip on over her flannel nightgown.

Miraculously, she didn't fight him about his choice, instead lifting her arms for him to help put it on. "I would imagine order a twenty-four-hour urine test for protein. Put me on a fetal monitor to test the baby's heart rate and to see if he or she is feeling any stress."

"Less chitchat, more action." Nudging her toward the front door, he asked, "Need anything else?"

"What about Prissy? She's too tiny to stay here alone." Wren was so unsteady on her feet that Cash had to reach out a couple of times to steady her.

"Your mutt will be fine," he assured her. "In the morning I'll call Mrs. Cahwood and ask her to take the dog home with her until we get back."

"Thank you," she said, standing on her tiptoes to kiss his cheek. "This is scary enough together. I can't fathom going it alone."

He wished for an elegant turn of phrase to comfort her, but he was fresh out of poetry. "Wait here," he said after pulling on her coat, hat and mittens. "I'll be right back with the truck. And while you wait," he called halfway out the door as an afterthought, "sit."

Thirty minutes later Cash barreled down the Turner Turnpike as fast as crappy road conditions allowed. One lane had been plowed, but no way was he able to go his usual seventy-five.

Wren intermittently dozed, and if it hadn't been for her seat belt holding her upright, he was fairly certain she'd have long since slumped onto his lap.

What had her sweet kiss been about? Why did he

care? It bugged him that in such a short time she'd become his everything. Before her arrival he'd fixated on nothing but his knee. Calculating over and over the time until he rejoined the tour. Now he had fleeting moments when he wasn't so sure he even wanted to go back out on the road. As much fun as he had playing with Wren's pup, he couldn't fathom what holding his son for the first time would do to his heart.

Piggyback rides and sledding and building snowmen and forts in the winter. In the summer he'd sign him up for Little League and 4-H—all the things his father had done with him. All four Buckhorn men and Daisy would fish and hike and sit around campfires soaking in stories of how their great-grandfather and Duke had pieced their land together like a patchwork quilt. Buying parcels here and there until he'd made it into the powerhouse it was today.

Dallas and Wyatt oversaw the farming and running cattle. Breeding top-notch quarter horses and even pumping oil. It was a huge undertaking keeping all their father's endeavors in good order. His mom worked too hard. As did his brothers. None of them seemed to resent his spending nearly every weekend on the road, but secretly, did they?

Wren stirred. "Where are we?"

"Just east of Sapulpa. Won't be long now." The snow had stopped and this part of the state hadn't been hit nearly as hard as the ranch. "While you're up, I've been meaning to ask what kind of trouble high blood pressure can cause. I mean, you hear about it with older folks, but I never thought of it as being a problem for pregnant women."

She yawned and rubbed her eyes. "As a formal diagnosis, it's called preeclampsia. The main concern is in causing narrowing of blood vessels, including the ones in the placenta and umbilical cord. This leads to the baby not getting enough oxygen or nutrients." Drawing a snowflake on the fogged window, she added, "If left untreated, it can lead to placental abruption, seizures, premature birth, coma."

"Swell." Instinctively he reached for her hand, easing his fingers between hers. "But that's not going to happen to us, right? Because we're treating you and the baby in time?"

"Right." Taken at face value, her answer was positive enough, but knowing her as he did, he knew she couldn't hide her lingering fear. He recognized it in the dampness of her palm. The way her expression had glazed—as if she hadn't shared the full extent of her worries.

How long until she trusted him completely? Would the time ever come? Considering how standoffish he'd been in regard to their one day being a couple, did he deserve having her rely on him? Not only for her and their child's financial support, but emotionally?

"You gave me quite a scare," Doc Haven said to Wren in her hospital room the next morning. She and the baby were hooked up to so many monitors she felt more like a robot than soon-to-be mom. "Thought you'd been taking it easy so this wouldn't happen?"

"I was, but Cash and I got into a tiff and I guess things went downhill from there."

"Your vitals look good for the moment. Blood pressure's higher than I'd like, but I've seen worse and still delivered plenty of healthy babies. Once I've got your urine results, we'll reassess."

Nodding, she said, "Thanks. This is the first time

I've seen a hospital from this perspective, and it's scary. I much prefer being the doctor to the patient." The newly remodeled maternity wing featured wood laminate flooring and soothing floral wallpaper. There was an oak rocker, built-in sofa and even a recliner. Botanical prints and striped curtains finished what designers had hoped to be a warm, friendly birthing environment. A thoughtful nurse or aide had even hung red and silver garlands for the holidays. If it weren't for the monitors, Wren could almost have imagined herself in a hotel.

Chuckling, the white-haired man made a few notations on her chart, then promised to release her as soon as he felt it was safe for her and the baby.

WREN HAD FINALLY managed to drift off to sleep when Cash bumped open the door and entered the room.

"Everything okay?" Carrying three bags of chips, a microwave burrito and two Cokes, Cash said, "I ran into Doc Haven in the hall."

"Our baby's fine. Me, too," Wren assured him. With the exception of the butterflies winging through her stomach every time she saw her baby's father, she thought. He'd been so good to her. The whole night, never leaving her side. His jawline sported dusky brown stubble and his longish curls looked as if they'd developed a halo. Wren knew the effect was caused by perpetual hat head, but she'd grown to like it all the same. Then there were his eyes. Darker this morning—like the perfect Christmas tree she'd wanted to hike through the woods to find.

"Did the doc say when you're getting sprung?" Upon settling into the recliner, he carefully arranged his snacks on Wren's nightstand.

"Probably tomorrow. And FYI, the smell of that burrito is *no bueno*."

Poised with the offensive thing at his mouth, he asked, "Want me to eat it out in the waiting area?"

"No. I could probably still smell it from there."

He downed it in three bites. "Did I do anything in particular to tick you off—besides eating?"

"Sorry. I'm antsy." Hands folded on top of her belly, Wren sighed. "Throughout my pregnancy I guess I've played this game in my head that it wasn't really happening. Sounds nuts, but it was a way to cope. I'm afraid of everything. How I'm going to do justice to both being a parent and completing my residency." Covering her face with her hands, she was even afraid of crying again.

"Time out." Cash abandoned his food to draw down her hands, easing his fingers between hers. "For the moment, how about we tackle one problem at a time, which is getting you out of here and back home."

She nodded, holding on to him for dear life.

"After that, you and I are going to sit down and come up with a list of kid gear. If we managed to get a puppy through her first weeks at home, being two reasonably intelligent adults, we can do the same for our child."

"You think?" At the moment she didn't feel capable of walking to the bathroom on her own. Weak and trembling and bigger than three houses, Wren was shocked by how rapidly her hard-won independence had faded. Had she ever truly been in control of her life, or had that control been an illusion?

"Honey, I remember when my sister-in-law was close to delivering Betsy and Bonnie and trust me, she was nutty as a Christmas fruitcake. Crying constantly, and when she wasn't sporting tears, she'd snap like a pit bull. It wasn't a good time. I can't imagine what you're going through, but you have to get it through that thick head of yours that no matter what, I'm here for you."

"But you shouldn't be," she argued, crying anew. "You need surgery right away so you can rejoin your tour."

"What I need..." He released one of her hands to tuck flyaway strands of her hair behind her ears. "Is for you to understand my bull riding is on the back burner. Even if my knee were a hundred percent, I wouldn't leave you or our baby in this condition. Now, take some deep breaths and focus on nothing but getting our baby safely into our arms."

"SURPRISE!"

Hands to her chest, Wren felt her legs nearly go out from under her in the doorway of Cash's home as she saw every person she knew in Weed Gulch smiling and clapping in welcome. Delores and Doc Haven. Sally, Doc's nurse. Georgina and Stella. Dallas and the twins and Cash's brother, Wyatt. Mrs. Cahwood—even Henry, the ranch foreman, whom Wren had met only twice. After two days in her quiet hospital room, the noisy show of affection brought on instant tears.

Someone flipped a switch, immersing the room in an incredible holiday glow. Tiny white lights had been strung in a fragrant pine. Glittering ornaments had been hung from each bough. Beneath the tree were presents. Dozens—maybe even a hundred. Every inch of the house had been decked out in Christmas cheer, from the three stockings hanging from the mantel to fresh pine garlands strung over each door. The scents of evergreen and cinnamon and freshly baked gingerbread completed the holiday wonderland.

Georgina stepped forward, crushing Wren in an un-expected hug. "You gave us a scare. I'm so glad you're feeling better. We all are."

"Thank you. It's good to be home."

When Cash entered, his brothers and friends drew him aside for plenty of laughter and backslapping.

Georgina drew Wren a short way down the hall. "Before your baby shower really gets under way, I owe you another apology. I'm sorry we got off on the wrong foot. *Really.* Chalk it up to an old woman's insecurities. I hate that it took you being in the hospital to force me to my senses, but that's the truth. I thought by sheer stubborn will I could make you and my son fall in love, but if it's not meant to be, then so be it. I can't live with this animosity between us. Whether you're here or in Baltimore, I'd very much like to be part of my grandchild's life."

"Of course," Wren said. "A baby can never have too much love. I'm sorry, too." And Wren truly was. There had been times she could've taken the higher ground and backed away from their confrontations, but hadn't.

Taking Wren by the arm, Cash's mother helped her off with her outer garments before guiding her to a comfortable armchair. The twins pushed an ottoman beneath Wren's swollen feet.

Delores leaned in, giving Wren's shoulder a squeeze. "A little birdie told us you and Cash are behind on baby shopping."

"That's an understatement." Wren shared a smile with her friend, realizing that in the short time she'd lived in Weed Gulch, she'd met people she never wanted to let go. For the first time in her life, she felt part of something bigger than herself. As if she was a better person for knowing everyone in the room.

With Prissy squirming in her arms, Bonnie asked, "Do we have to wait for *all* of those presents to open before we get cake?"

Everyone laughed.

Dallas ruffled his daughter's hair. "This is Wren and your uncle Cash's party. You'll have to ask them."

Cash deferred to Wren, pouring on his ample charm with a lopsided grin that left her feeling drunk on happiness. "Ma'am?"

"Tell you what," she said, tweaking Bonnie's nose and then the puppy's, "if you promise to bring me a big piece, then I say you should have all the cake you want."

With their guests retreating to the kitchen, Cash sat on the arm of her chair. "Having fun?"

Unable to speak past the knot in her throat, she nodded.

"Me, too."

"I—I'm assuming you planned all of this?"

He shrugged. "I had a lot of help from the ladies in my life. While Betsy and Bonnie took their dad to the bakery for the perfect cake, Mom, Stella and Delores went on a baby gear roundup." After kissing her forehead, he leaned back, allowing their gazes to lock. Their connection was dizzying. The equivalent of six glasses of champagne.

"What's happening?" she whispered.

"I'm no expert," he said, close enough to her lips for his warm breath to tickle, "but if I'm lucky, I'm getting the strangest suspicion Mommy may be falling for Daddy."

Chapter Thirteen

"If those people were truly our friends," Cash said the next day from the floor of Wren's bedroom with Prissy looking on, "they would've stuck around to help put this stuff together."

Wren didn't look up from the crib assembly manual she was reading.

"Are you even listening?" he complained.

"What?" She looked up, in the process releasing a cascade of her long dark hair over her shoulder. He'd always considered her a beauty, but the way she sat in a pool of bright winter sun made her skin glow. If they had a baby girl, would she be as pretty as her mom?

"Last night," Cash said, pulse racing faster than it had conquering his toughest bull, "I said something that I no doubt shouldn't have, but…" He cleared his throat. "I—I need to know if what I was feeling was just an issue of circumstance—you know, both of us wrapped up in the festive mood—or more?"

"I can't do this," she said, sharply looking away.

"Can't do what? Answer my question? Take a chance on me? *Us*?"

Sighing, she tried standing, but ended up looking like an upside-down ladybug.

Prissy barked, thinking it was time to play.

"Need help?" Crouching behind her, he hefted her onto her feet. The motion hurt his knee, but that didn't bother him nearly as much as Wren's refusal to talk about issues that mattered.

"I'm tired. Would you mind if we finish later?"

"Take your mutt and nap in my bed," he suggested. "Unless you want our baby sleeping in a dresser drawer, this needs to get done."

"Please don't be angry. I heard you—I just don't know what to say. Truth? I felt the same. Like in that moment everything we'd ever dared dream of might be coming true. But they're called dreams for a reason, Cash. Because for the vast majority of people, they only occur deep in people's minds in the black of night. They aren't real."

Slamming down his screwdriver, Cash used every ounce of control not to punch the wall. "On the flip side," he pointed out, "my parents were very happily married for thirty-eight years. Dallas and Bobbie Jo are another classic case of love conquering all."

Making her escape, she called over her shoulder, "Sure, Cash, let's talk about how great those relationships turned out for both your mom and brother. Your dad and Bobbie Jo are dead. Dead, Cash."

He followed her out into the hall. "Despite that, I know for a fact that had Mom and Dallas known in advance their spouses would die too young they would've married anyway."

Spinning to face him, she said, "You're not even making sense. You've told me a half dozen times you want nothing to do with marriage."

"I know, but what was it you told me not too long ago about having the prerogative to change your mind?"

She opened her mouth, only to cover it with her

hands. Turning from him, she walked straight to the freezer and grabbed for her Chunky Monkey ice cream.

Prissy sat at her feet, begging.

After getting a spoon, Wren scooped a small portion into the dog's crystal bowl, then ate her own straight from the container.

Cash pushed himself up to sit on the granite counter. "All the ice cream in the world isn't going to change things between us. Your advice on me remembering my father and upbringing but raising our kid with my own style—it made sense. Seeing you in the hospital, realizing how much having you in my life means…" Hopping off the counter, he took the ice cream and spoon from her, setting them on the table before cupping her face with his hands. "Marry me, Wren, not because my mother and the entire town think it's the right thing to do, but because you'll die without having a cowboy stud like me permanently entrenched in your life."

"But we hardly know each other. There's my residency and…"

Tracing the delicate arch of her eyebrows, all the while never dropping her stare, he dared her to deny him. "I was really touched by my family and friends coming together for us last night. It made me see that maybe beyond my fear of not being a good father or husband was an extra-large helping of Buckhorn pride. For as long as I can remember I've done the opposite of what people expected or wanted me to do, sometimes for no good reason other than being ornery. In our case, I now realize that in letting you and our baby go, I'd only be spiting myself."

"How?" she fairly squeaked. "How do you know? Is it a feeling deep inside or a voice? I'm so afraid if I allow myself to fall for you, I'll never be independent again. I'll never complete my residency or earn my medical license. I'll become a lonely drifter like most of the kids I grew up with. Can't you understand?"

He traced her lips. Full, lovely, kissable lips he was finished even trying to resist.

Pressing his mouth to hers earned him the sweetest mew. She leaned fully into him, clinging to his shirt with the kind of openmouthed hunger he'd craved ever since their wild Vegas night.

"Marry me," he demanded rather than asked.

"Okay," she said, kissing him again as if he were her air. "But if we go bad, don't say I didn't warn you."

"OVER THE TOP?" Stella asked three days later.

Not wishing to hurt the woman's feelings, Wren wasn't sure how to reply. They sat in the duck-themed living room of Marva Wells, who was apparently the master baker for all of Tohwalla county. With the wedding scheduled for Saturday, Georgina was back home with the florist, making hasty plans for every inch of the main house to be decked out in Christmas finery.

Sandwiched between Stella and Cash, Wren perched on the sofa with Marva's portfolio balanced on her knees. The current page showed a six-tiered wedding cake complete with a fountain and glittering swan topper that was magnificent, but more fitting for royalty than a sweet ceremony intended for family and a few close friends.

"Um." Wren struggled to form a thought past how amazing Cash's leathery aftershave smelled. Never would she have predicted her life would turn out this way, but now that it had, she abandoned herself to the giddy, girlie pleasure of planning their special day.

"Maybe something smaller would be more appropriate."

"I disagree," Cash said, all too pleasantly pressing against her as he reached for one of the sample cake pieces Marva had placed on her coffee table. Ignoring the plastic fork, he dredged his finger through the frosting. "Mmm...good." Repeating the motion, he offered the same sugary treat to Wren.

Momentarily forgetting the other two people in the room, she licked and sucked his finger clean. When their eyes met, there was no denying the heat she'd long suppressed.

Stella gave Cash a swat. "I'm glad your mama's not here, or she'd tan your hide for such a public display."

Wren's cheeks flamed from the remembrance of every bare inch of Cash's splendid *hide*. Was it wrong for her to now be as happy as she'd once been confused?

"It's quite all right," Marva assured her. "Just last week I worked with a drunken groom who requested beer-flavored frosting."

Stella blanched.

Cash grinned. "Damn. Why didn't I think of that?"

Wren rolled her eyes. "Consider yourself booted from the cake committee."

Talking to Wren's belly, he complained, "Can you believe the way your mother treats me? We're not even married and already she's bossing me around."

"Ignore him," Stella urged. "We have to make this decision ASAP, as we still have a dress to find."

"Give me that book," Cash said, and flipped rapid-fire through the pages. After twenty or so, he pointed to a dreamy quadruple-tiered confection. Since the tiers were small, it had the feel of a classical wedding cake without being overdone. The bottom layer was square with diamond-patterned piping. The next layer was round with wide fondant stripes, followed by another square layer with lacy piping. At the top was a tiny round cake dotted with sugar pearls and a white bouquet of sugar roses. Each layer was ringed with more sugar pearls and roses. "This work for you?"

Tossing her arms around his neck, she answered with a kiss.

Clearing her throat, Stella said, "Marva, it seems we've made a decision."

The cake lady laughed. "That was the easy part. Now you have to select the flavors and fillings."

"I DON'T KNOW about this, man." If Dallas scowled any harder, Cash was pretty sure his face would forever freeze that way. "Mom's gonna eat you alive for not picking a more conservative suit."

Surveying himself in the dressing-room mirror of the Woodland Hills Mall Dillard's, Cash couldn't help but grin at his own reflection. "Damn, I'm good-looking."

Arms folded, Dallas tapped the toe of his boot. "Time's ticking, bro."

"And? I'm done."

"This is a mistake," Dallas said. "Weddings should be solemn occasions. As such, you should dress the part."

"Tell you what." Cash took off his jacket. "If I ever marry you, I'll be sure to keep that in mind."

Twenty minutes later they stopped off at the food court before the long ride home.

Dallas had salad with low-fat dressing.

Cash had Frito chili pie.

Joining Dallas at a table in the seating area, Cash dug in.

"How did all of this come about?" Dallas asked, still fussing with his napkin on his lap.

"What? The wedding?"

Big brother nodded. "Last I heard you and Wren were dead set against marital bliss."

"We were. To a certain extent we still are. But the whole hospital thing gave us a hellacious scare. For me, anyway, it got me thinking about my priorities. It pains me to admit it, but you were right. No matter what, family comes first. Before Wren, my next bull ride was my world. Now..." Choked up, he looked away and smiled.

"I'm happy for you." Holding his hand across the table, Dallas grasped Cash's hand. "Welcome to adulthood. It's been a long time coming."

"Happy?" Georgina asked Wren during a lull in the rehearsal dinner conversation. The Buckhorn main house had been transformed into a Christmas wedding wonderland—white and purple poinsettias, pine garlands and plenty of sparkling lights, candles and silver ornament accents.

"Aside from constant heartburn, a tiny elbow between my ribs and swollen feet, I'm floating on clouds."

Cash's mother laughed. "Ah, I remember those days well. At least it's almost over."

"True."

The meal had been a decadent blend of steak and lobster tails, twice-baked potatoes and pencil-thin asparagus dripping in butter and Parmesan cheese. Cheesecake, coffee and herbal tea had provided the perfect end to an enchanted evening.

The guys were engrossed in talk of football playoffs, and Stella had taken the twins off to bed. Delores had gone home early, leaving Wren and her soon-to-be mother-in-law on their own.

Georgina said, "You had me convinced that this wedding wasn't in your cards."

Grimacing, Wren admitted, "I didn't think it was. Even though Cash and I connected the second we met, I refused to believe it possible to merge a husband and baby with my medical career."

"Will you be completing your residency in Tulsa?"

"Most likely." Taking a roll from a basket, she daubed on butter. "I've started the transfer process with my dean, but there's a lot of paperwork involved. This late in the year, I might have to start over in July, but we'll see. Winning my Baltimore residency was quite a coup. Only ten out of two thousand applicants were accepted."

"Wow…"

Wren forced a breath. Caught up in the wedding excitement, she'd forgotten what an honor she'd been given.

"Please don't take this the wrong way," her future mother-in-law said, "but I had no idea you were so accomplished. I can only imagine what a shock your pregnancy must've been."

No kidding.

Mouth dry, Wren struggled with a moment of panic over her recent hasty moves. Then she looked to Cash. He met her gaze and they shared a smile. Calm flooded through her. In marrying him, she was making the right decision. For her baby and for herself.

"I found out I was carrying Dallas at a point when his father was constantly on the road working for an oil exploration company. The thought of raising him without Duke was almost more than I could bear, but the time flew by and I actually missed some aspects of being solely in charge."

"How did you reconcile your professional needs with those of your family?"

Turning introspective, Georgina folded her cloth napkin. "When Duke and I were married, women didn't really have careers. Sure, there were nurses and secretaries and schoolteachers, but I'd never even met a female doctor or dentist until I was in my fifties."

Which was yet another facet of why continuing her career meant so much to Wren. She'd always had an innate need to prove herself. Being married wouldn't make that go away.

"Did you know Mrs. Cahwood was a Rockette?"

"Did I know? I begged my parents to let me go with her. She was the exception to the Weed Gulch rule that women belonged in the home. When Yvette danced, you just knew she was destined for more. I was heartbroken when she gave up New York City to return home, but she's told me on numerous occasions that she never regretted her decision."

"Did you?" Wren was almost afraid to ask, but she was enjoying getting to know Cash's mom as a woman rather than his parent, and she genuinely wanted to know.

"You mean did I resent giving up any dreams I might've had to support Duke in achieving his?" Again her expression seemed far-off. As if she'd become so comfortable in her current role as matriarch that it required a trip back in time to touch base with the woman she'd once been. "In retrospect, no. I've led an amazingly blessed life. But I'd be lying if I told you Duke and I didn't suffer our share of growing pains. Once the boys and their sister were all in school, I wanted to take a floral-design class in the hopes of being hired by the florist in the next town over. Well, once Duke heard the class met during the day and that I would need his help with laundry and the meals and such, he flat-out refused. Said he'd rather spend the money on buying me new dresses. For months I resented him."

"What happened?" Leaning forward, Wren asked, "Did you ever take the class?"

"Years later, on my fortieth birthday, Duke surprised me with fully paid tuition. As well as an apology for taking such a hard-line stance the first time around."

"Did you ever land a job in floral design?"

"I did." Laughing, she said, "It was right around Easter and turns out I was deathly allergic to lilies. I lasted all of a week until I was missing volunteering at the kids' school and my weekly bridge games and church meetings. Still, it meant the world to me that Duke finally came around to encouraging me to try following my own dreams. One thing about Cash is that I believe he'll wholeheartedly support you in whatever course you decide is right for you."

Placing her hand over Georgina's, Wren confessed, "If I didn't believe that, we wouldn't be having a wedding tomorrow night."

Chapter Fourteen

"In all of the excitement," Cash said on the short walk home, "I forgot to mention how amazing you look in that blue sweater."

"Thanks." Wren snuggled against him to ward off the crisp December chill. Though the brick-paved road had long since been cleared, snow still covered much of the rolling prairie. Reflected moonlight illuminated their every step. "For the record, it's aquamarine. You're looking quite dapper in pomegranate."

"Do you have any idea how hard my rodeo buddies would laugh at me for having the words *aquamarine* or *pomegranate* in my vocabulary?"

"From what I've heard," she teased, "*real* men aren't afraid of color."

Cash used her dig as his invitation to tickle.

He loved Wren's laugh. Her shrieking giggles were the stuff dreams were made of. She all too soon begged him to stop or she'd wet her pants. Knowing how much she'd peed of late, he knew she wasn't kidding. He also knew how much he wanted to kiss her.

Hugging her to him, he pressed his lips to her forehead, her nose, her lips. Her soft, pliable delicious lips that no matter how many times he sampled, he never tired of tasting.

"Mmm…" She clung to him, moaning for more, which he was only too happy to give. Pressed against him as she was, Cash had a tough time remembering to be a gentleman. He hadn't dreamed it possible, but her breasts had grown even larger and felt incredibly hot in his palms.

Their kiss deepened to the point his head was swimming from the rush of blood servicing his erection. "I want you so bad."

"I know," she said, panting breaths clouding the frigid night air. "We were so busy arguing at my last doctor appointment, we forgot to ask permission."

"Doesn't matter," he said, his forehead against hers. "At this stage, I probably shouldn't be fooling around down there."

Giggling, kissing, she asked, "*Down there*? What are you, twelve?"

"Judging by my current frustration level, that's about how old I feel. At least I got some boob action."

"You're incorrigible," she playfully scolded.

"And damned good-looking."

"Goes without saying."

"And for the record," he added, "back to your anti-quated definition of *real* men, honey, I'm as real as it gets and I am afraid of my very pregnant almost-wife catching a chill. Want me to carry you the rest of the way?"

"Does my waddle embarrass you?"

"Not a bit. But your chattering teeth I find most alarming." Almost to the house, he asked, "You and Mom seemed to be engrossed in something. She wasn't complaining about me, was she?"

"To the contrary, much of the conversation centered

around her life, but she did add what a great man you've become."

"Really?" Eyebrows raised, Cash had a tough time believing his mom didn't view him as a total screwup. Especially now that his knee was so wrecked he might never ride again.

"You seem surprised."

"I am. As the youngest of our clan, I've spent my life in everyone else's shadow. Wyatt has a fancy business degree he uses to help Dallas with the ranch. Dallas's degree is in animal husbandry—like, what does that even mean? My sister's raking in big bucks with her law degree. Then there's you. You'll have a string of credentials after your name, half of which I won't even understand."

"If you want a PhD, sweetheart, then go to school. It's not that big of a deal."

Inside, Cash helped her off with her winter gear.

While she changed into her pj's and slippers, he started a fire. He was getting married the next day to a woman he couldn't get enough of, so why was he all of a sudden feeling blue?

Staring into the flames, he lost himself in fears.

What happened if his surgery didn't work and he was kicked off the tour? Yes, he had more cash than he knew what to do with in savings, but that wasn't going to last forever. Would Wren eventually think him less of a man for not sharing her education level?

"What's wrong?" she asked, in her fleece looking like a fluffy bunny he wanted to hold on his lap and stroke.

"Nothing." Forcing a smile, he motioned her to join him on the hearth.

"No one has a pout quite like you, Cash Buckhorn.

Out with it." She tried sitting beside him, but didn't fit. "Guess it's the sofa for me."

"At dinner, my brothers spouted statistics about how marriages where one spouse has a degree and the other doesn't typically end in divorce. I don't want us to end up as a statistic."

Shaking her head, she sighed. "You, dear, have too much time on your hands. Mark my words, once the baby's here and you're back into your training you'll feel more like your own self."

"Promise?"

"Wish I could," she said with genuine concern. "But that would be like you reassuring me my residency transfer will magically go through. In marrying, we're both assuming a certain amount of risks."

Though he hated asking, he couldn't stop. "For you, are those risks worth it? Playing devil's advocate, if your transfer doesn't get approved, will you resent me?"

Her flicker of indecision told him more than he'd ever cared to know.

"YOU'RE A BEAUTIFUL BRIDE," Mrs. Cahwood gushed while easing rhinestone pins into Wren's hair. To accommodate her lacy veil, the front was swept away from her face, while the back was a cascade of curls.

"Thank you." Wren hadn't thought it possible to find a maternity wedding gown that made her feel like a princess, but she should've known better than to underestimate the power Georgina had in moving mountains to get her way. After selecting her dream satin gown in a Tulsa bridal shop, it had then been rush altered to fit. With a full, tulle-lined skirt, sweetheart neckline, miles of white satin and enough seed pearls and crystals for her to blind airline pilots were she to stand in the sun, Wren hoped her groom found her as beautiful as she felt.

Prissy, snoozing on the bed, wore a specially made rhinestoned doggy dress for the occasion.

"Nervous?" her friend asked, standing back to appraise her work.

"Funny, but no. It's almost as if my entire life has led me to this moment." She did, however, have a slight stomachache. Almost like period cramps, but considering her current state, that was unlikely.

"Good." The housekeeper squeezed her in a hug. "There are, however, a few items we're missing. For something old, I thought you might do me the honor of wearing these…." Eyes shining, she took a Tiffany box from her purse, opening it to reveal spellbinding diamond cascade earrings.

Wren gasped.

"Impressive, huh?" Helping Wren put them on, she said, "They were an opening-night gift from a Wall Street tycoon named Geoffrey Bartholomew Wentworth IV. He wanted me to marry him in the worst way, but I just kept telling him I couldn't be bothered with wifely duties." She winked. "I'd been born to dance. I've kept them all these years as not only a keepsake, but a nest egg. Now I want you to have them."

"I couldn't," Wren insisted. "They're too valuable."

Mrs. Cahwood waved off Wren's objections. "Making you smile is far more valuable. Please, I want to know that even after I'm gone, they'll still be treasured."

Hugging her friend, Wren said, "I love you." And she meant it.

A knock sounded at the guest room's door. In popped two matching girls, followed by their grandmother and nanny.

"Lovely," Georgina said, catching her first glimpse of the bride. "Cash is going to be blown away."

"I hope so," Wren admitted.

"Yvette," Stella said, "those earrings of yours are even prettier than I remember. Why didn't you bring them out at my wedding?"

"You never asked," the former dancer teased.

"Since I see you're already wearing your something old," Cash's mom said, "we still need borrowed, blue and new." Nudging her granddaughters, she said, "Ladies, do you have something for your new aunt?"

Bonnie held out an exquisite pearl-and-diamond bracelet. Her expression very serious for a five-year-old, she said, "If you don't like this, I'll wear it."

"Thank you," Wren said, touched beyond words by not only the bracelet's beauty, but the love that had gone into selecting such a perfect piece. "I can't begin to describe how much all of this means."

"You don't have to," Stella said, brushing tears from Wren's flawless makeup. "It's written all over your face." Stepping back, she put her index finger to her lips. "You're looking pretty darned good, but there are still a couple of things missing. Betsy, hon, it's your turn."

With much pomp and ceremony in her fancy long satin dress, Betsy held up a lacy handkerchief that had been meticulously embroidered with bluebonnets and ivy. Scrunching her face as if trying to remember a speech, Betsy said, "This is really, super-duper old and I forget who used it, but there aren't any boogers."

Georgina gasped. "Betsy Buckhorn, after practicing all morning, that was the best you could do?"

"Sorry, Grandma, but I'm awfully hungry and hafta make a pee-pee."

Laughing, Wren said, "You did perfect, and I'm sure your grandmother can fill me in on the details."

"'Kay." Crossing her legs and doing the potty dance, Betsy asked, "Can I go now?"

While her twin scampered off without permission, Bonnie shook her head. "She's so childish."

"For the record," Georgina said, "that handkerchief was made by my Irish great-great-great-grandmother Kate and has been carried in every wedding in my family line since."

Tears stung the back of Wren's eyes and her throat felt in danger of forever knotting. Her stomachache was now working overtime. Regardless, she was determined to enjoy this magical afternoon and night. "You all are the best. Thank you doesn't seem adequate."

"It's perfect," Stella said while fussing with more makeup repair. "So where does that leave us?"

"Borrowed," Georgina said, stepping forward with Wren's final gift. "On the surface, this may seem ridiculous, but Cash's father won this for me on our first official date at the Tulsa State Fair. Now, to an Oklahoman, it's still a big event, but all those years ago it might as well have been Christmas, Easter and Thanksgiving all rolled into one."

"Amen," Stella said with a firm nod.

Mrs. Cahwood yawned. "Frankly, I always found the whole thing overrated."

The comment earned her swats from both of her contemporaries.

"As I was saying," Cash's mother continued, with her object still hidden, "Duke won this for me and I believe it's brought me luck ever since." Opening her hand, she revealed the ugliest, ragtag Kewpie doll ever on God's green earth. It wasn't much over two inches tall, but the hair was orange, body naked and eyes a little spooky with glowing red stones. "Isn't he the cutest thing ever? I'll tuck him in your bouquet and no one will ever see him."

"Grandma," Bonnie said, hiding behind Wren's train, "that thing's scary. Put it away."

Though she'd never let on to her future mother-in-law, Wren couldn't have agreed more.

WATCHING HIS BRIDE descend the staircase he'd sledded down as a little boy, Cash felt ready to bust with pride. The closer Wren came, the more he wanted the ceremony over and the honeymoon to begin—not that they were headed anywhere. Doc Haven had ordered her straight to bed after all the excitement. Still, Cash couldn't wait to finally, officially have her all to himself.

His mother had hired a local band to play for the ceremony and reception. "Here Comes the Bride" had never sounded sweeter than with acoustic guitars and a few fiddles.

Bonnie and Betsy made adorable flower girls. Granted, some of the red rose petals hit the walls and guests like projectiles, but at least the girls looked good while acting like the hellions they usually were.

Wren was next down the temporary aisle. Stella and his mother had found a good fifty woven willow chairs, softened by Santa-themed cushions. Candles and holly and the rich scent of pine had transformed his family home into a Christmas wedding wonderland.

Despite all of his mom and Stella's work, the most exquisite part of the ceremony was his bride. "You take my breath away," he said when she reached him.

"You're not looking too shabby yourself." Her hands lightly trembled, but the light in her smiling eyes told him all he needed to know. "I'm loving your derriere in those blue jeans."

He tipped his black cowboy hat. "Dallas thought you wouldn't, but I knew damn well you would."

The preacher performing the service cleared his throat. "Whenever you two are ready, we'll begin."

Most weddings Cash had attended were dignified and brimming with deep meaning. His was a seriously good time with both the groom and the bride making plenty of mix-ups and flirty double entendres until at long last reaching the most important part.

Reverend Winthrop seemed grateful to wrap things up. "I now—thank heavens—pronounce you husband and wife. Cash Buckhorn, you may kiss your bride."

Whoops and hollers from all in attendance prefaced a kiss that rocketed through Cash with enough force to make him weak in his knees.

"Mrs. Buckhorn," he whispered in his wife's ear on their walk down the aisle, "what are you getting me for Christmas now that I have everything I've ever wanted?"

Wren grimaced in pain then stopped to clutch her belly. "W-will a son or daughter work?"

Chapter Fifteen

On their own for the brief time it took their guests to rise from their seats, Cash asked Wren, "Do I need to get you to a hospital?"

"No," Wren said, wincing through a smile. "I want to enjoy our reception. I've had a few contractions today, but I'm pretty sure they're just Braxton Hicks."

"In English for the nondoctors in the crowd."

"Practice contractions. Unless they become regular, we have nothing to worry about."

"Are you sure?" Cupping her cheek, he searched her eyes. Did he think she'd lie about something like this?

"Sweetie, of course I'm sure. I may be a disaster when it comes to shopping for baby gear, but on the medical side, I've got it—" ouch "—under control."

The rest of the night passed in a pleasantly painful blur. The Braxton Hicks continued, but Wren was having too much fun to worry about the timing.

The band was amazing, mixing romantic slow songs with plenty of rowdy country tunes. Though she didn't know the vast majority of guests, the longtime family friends and neighbors proved to be great partiers.

Taking a breather in the kitchen, she found Georgina directing a caterer on adding more sherbet to the punch.

"I can't thank you enough," Wren said, pulling her

aside. "This night will forever top my favorite memories."

"I'm glad you enjoyed it." Turning her head to swipe tears, Georgina excused herself to find a tissue.

"What's wrong?" Wren asked her mother-in-law.

"Has Cash told you much about his sister, Daisy?"

"No." Silently bearing another contraction, Wren took a second to catch her breath. "Just that she lives in San Francisco and you don't see her as much as you'd like."

"I understand she's busy, and we're all proud of her for earning her law degree, but for the life of me I can't fathom what could keep her away from something as important as her baby brother's wedding."

"I'm sorry." Wren took her hand. "I'm sure whatever Daisy's doing, you're on her mind."

Hugging Wren, Georgina said, "I'm so happy to have you as my daughter. Even better, as my friend—although that may be on a probationary status if I don't get a decent craft out of you."

"Sure you're all right?" Helping himself to thirds of the cake he'd selected, Cash worried his bride had overdone it. Her color was *off,* and her smile no longer reached her eyes.

"Please, Cash, just let me enjoy—" Her face wrenched in pain, and he had to grab hold of her to even keep her upright.

"That's it…" Abandoning his cake plate on the table, he guided his wife to the nearest willow chair. "Don't move an inch. I'm finding Doc Haven."

Wren hadn't wanted to believe she could be in early labor, but with each new contraction she feared that might be the case. Two weeks before her due date, her baby would be smaller than ideal, but still healthy.

"This better be good." All smiles, Doc Haven was clearly winded. "That's the most fun I've had dancing in at least thirty years. Delores does a mean two-step."

"I'm sorry Cash interrupted you. I'm sure these are—*ooh*…" Pain had her gripping the sides of her chair so hard that her nails dug into the soft wood.

"Wedding *and* a baby all in one day." Slapping Cash's back, the doctor said, "Good work, son." To Wren, he asked, "Can you make it to the nearest bedroom?"

"I—I think so…." She was all at once hot and cold. But on the inside. The pain was escalating. Almost more than she could bear.

"Wyatt!" Cash called to his brother. "Help me carry Wren to the guest room."

"Too much cake?" Wyatt asked. Unaware of the seriousness of the situation, he kept on with his shtick. "Maybe your stomach's too big from swallowing a watermelon? Or wait—brother Cash, did you have the honeymoon before the wedding and your bride's preggers?"

"Lay off," Cash ground out from between clenched teeth. "She's having our baby."

"Here? Now?" Wyatt paled. "I'm not so hot at this sort of thing."

"Would you shut up and grab the arm of her chair?" In case his daft brother still didn't grasp the plan, Cash pointed where Wyatt's hands should be.

A few minutes later Wren had been hefted onto the comfy canopy bed she'd napped on only hours earlier. "Doc Haven, why is this happening?"

"Who knows why anything happens when it does, dear." Easing extra pillows beneath her head, he said to Cash, "Fetch my bag from the back of my van. After that, have your mama boil water so I can sterilize my equipment. After that, come right back here. Your wife's going to need you. Oh—and I also need towels. Dozens, if you can find them."

"It hurts," Wren complained.

"I know," the doctor soothed. "Not sure how we're going to get you out of this dress, but let's try."

"I—I want Georgina. She'll know what to do."

When Cash returned with everything the doctor had requested, he was sent back out to put someone else on boiling-water duty.

"Honey," Georgina said, finally by her side, "Cash told me you asked for me? What can I do?"

"Please help me off with my dress. I want it pretty for m-my—" she rode out another contraction "—my own daughter."

"Good idea." As Wren had known Georgina would, she got straight to work unfastening rows of satin buttons on her back and sleeves.

Crying and laughing while shimmying out of the gargantuan gown, Wren managed, "Next time we're wedding-dress shopping, remind me to opt for cocktail length and Velcro."

"You got it," the older woman promised. "Only, let's hope that'll just be your vow renewal to my son."

A knock sounded on the door, and in walked Stella and Delores carrying a fancy, silver-wrapped box. "Pardon the interruption, Wren, but we thought this might be useful, if not exactly what it was originally intended for."

"C-could you please open it for me?"

Inside was a peach chiffon nightgown and matching robe far too pretty to give birth in.

"I can't wear that," she complained.

"Of course you can." Delores assured her. "It's your wedding night, and even if you're not feeling your best, you should always look it."

"Ladies…" Doc Haven cleared his throat. "If you don't mind, it'd be helpful for me to get within at least a couple feet of my patient."

After much grumbling, Wren's two friends set off to make sandwiches for the guests, who'd all sobered enough to start a betting pool on the baby's sex and exact time of birth.

"All right." Tossing back the covers, the doctor said, "Now that we've got you dressed in something a little more appropriate, let's see how far along you really are."

Having already tucked towels beneath her and alongside her, Doc Haven performed his exam. "For a future doctor, you're not very in tune with your own body."

"Wh-what's that mean?" Indescribable pain rolled through Wren, making her want to pummel her gorgeous new husband for putting this baby inside her.

"Honey," Doc Haven noted, "you're fully dilated. It's time to push."

"B-but my water never broke."

"You should know as well as I do that sometimes that's the way it goes. Mother Nature doesn't want us knowing all the answers. This is going to be on your final exam, so listen up. What you're experiencing is a dry birth. Pretty rare, but I've seen it a few times. We'll get you through."

The pain had grown so intense Wren didn't know whether to scream or cry or both.

Georgina held her left hand and Cash her right. "Come on, honey, you can do it. Not much longer now. You were pretty lucky to have a wedding distract you from all of the long boring parts of giving birth."

"Arrgh." With all her might Wren pushed until she feared she'd black out.

"Good girl," Doc cheered. "A few more like that and we'll be in the baby business."

"D-did we remember to b-buy diapers?" Wren asked anyone who'd listen.

"Relax," Cash said. "Delores and some of her beauty-parlor friends bought us six months of cloth-diaper home delivery service."

"That was so *sweeeet.*"

"Uh-huh." Cash wiped her sweat-drenched forehead with a cold washcloth. "Breathe, sweetheart. Save your energy for pushing."

"I'm afraid we forgot a lot of stuff."

"Of course we did. That's why God invented grand-mas. Right, Mom?"

"Absolutely."

"Less chitchat, more push." Doc Haven turned to Georgina. "She's crowning. Did anyone sterilize my surgical scissors?"

"They're on the towel on the dresser."

"Great." To Wren the doctor asked, "How about an-other push?"

"I don't think I can…." Thrashing her head, she fisted the sheets. "It hurts…it hurts."

"I love you," Cash said. "Hang in there, sweetheart. It'll be worth it. Just think of how good it's going to feel to hold our son in your arms."

"I hate you and we're having a *daughter*!" She used the vehemence behind what would hopefully be the end of this argument to be the fuel for her most pow-erful push.

"Almost there…"

Gritting her teeth, Wren fought to bring her baby into the world—and succeeded.

"Congratulations, newlyweds! You have a gorgeous baby girl."

"How's that possible?" Cash asked.

Georgina laughed, "Because God in all of His wisdom knows this family is desperate for females. I'm happy for you," she said to Wren. "She is lovely."

The doctor wrapped the baby in a blanket, resting her on Wren's chest. Transfixed, Wren couldn't stop staring. "Cash, look at her tiny fingers and toes."

"She's off-the-charts beautiful—like her mom...." He kissed Wren. "But I'm telling you now, no boy is ever getting near her."

"Slow down," the doctor said. "Let's tackle getting this charmer and her mama comfortable before you go pulling out the shotguns."

"THOUGHT YOU WANTED a boy?" Wren crept up behind her husband, who stood at their daughter's crib, drinking her in. Two days had passed since her birth, yet Wren still couldn't believe she was really here.

"Hush it and revert back to our earlier conversation on changing one's mind. She's perfect. Everything I ever wanted. She does, however, need a name." He stroked his daughter's perfectly pink cheek. "I was thinking Cashita. Cashalinda? Cashley?"

"Would you be serious," Wren scolded. "We've got to get her birth certificate and social security card." Wren's head spun just thinking about the amount of government paperwork.

Grinning over his shoulder, Cash reminded her, "Let's not forget to put her on waiting lists for all the best Weed Gulch preschools."

"You're awful." Taking his hand, she led him from the room. On the sofa, she resumed wrapping Christmas gifts—most of which had been ordered weeks earlier from the internet. "So? Names?"

He added another log to the fire. "Actually, you'll be happy to know I've put a lot of thought into this subject."

"Oh?" She cut a square piece of elf-themed paper.

"It makes me sad that our baby girl has no history on your side of the family. What she does have, however, is an awesome mom."

Eyes stinging, Wren said, "Thanks, but no need to butter me up. We're already married."

"Hear me out. My mom, and her mom, and even her mother's mom all share the same first initial and middle name—Marie. What if you did the same thing with our baby, only with bird names?"

"You're crazy." She put the singing-bass plaque Cash had selected for Dallas on the paper.

"A while ago—I think we were in the pool—you told me the women at your orphanage called you Wren because you were plain and sweet and never caused trouble. They made your middle name Katharine because one of them was a huge Katharine Hepburn fan and wanted you to eventually find that kind of brassiness for yourself. So what if we call our baby Robin Katharine Buckhorn. Thus combining pretty with sass and a last name that's become Oklahoma legend?"

"Robin..." Wren was beyond touched that Cash not only cared about their daughter's name having meaning, but that she knew from her first breath she was loved. "I like it. But what if the boys at school call her Robin the Robber? Or Batman and Robin?"

Cash punched his hand with his fist. "Dare one of them to try."

"It's official, then? We'll call her Robin Katharine Buckhorn?"

He held out his hand for her to shake, but then used her grip to pull her off the sofa and into his arms. "Didn't think you were getting off that easy, did you?"

"I hope not." When he pressed his lips to hers, no words described the champagne bubbles that seemed to have taken up permanent residence in her heart.

Without the baby between them, all mystery was gone when it came to how ready Cash was to finally pick up where they'd left off in Vegas. As soon as she got Doc Haven's okay, she planned to reacquaint herself with every one of Cash's gifts.

The more he kissed her, the more a sweet, aching hunger cried for more of him. Because he was now officially hers, she took the liberty of sliding her hands under his shirt and up his chest. His pecs were masterpieces in muscle, and before too long she removed the cloth barring her way from kissing every inch of him.

He groaned, easing his fingers into her hair. "You've got to stop."

"Why?" she teased, feigning innocence. "All I'm doing is this…." Kissing the line where his jeans hung low against his groin, she unfastened the top button, fully intent on giving her new husband a much-deserved *happy* ending.

An hour's worth of fun later, Wren woke to find herself having fallen asleep beside Cash on the sofa. "Hi."

"Yes, I am," he said with his grin. Playing with a strand of her hair, he asked, "When you first arrived at the ranch, did you ever dream we'd end up this happy?"

"No, but before you get too content with the status quo, we both have major hills to climb." Yawning, she managed to push herself onto her feet. Leaving him, she put a bow on Dallas's gift and set it under the twinkling tree.

"Like what? From where I'm sitting it all looks downhill from here. I'll get my knee fixed and go back out on the road. You get all those fancy initials added on to your name, then we pack up the munchkin—hell, we might have two or three more by then—and we'll all go on the road together. I'll buy us one of those tricked-out RVs. You'll love it. A lot of rodeo wives have them and swear they're like living in rolling mansions."

Freezing in front of the Christmas tree, Wren asked, "Did you think about a word you just said? Newsflash, but I never planned on spending ten years of my life to become a doctor, only to spend my life preggers and cheering from the sidelines while alternately praying I'm not watching the inevitable ride where you fall off a bull and never get up."

Chapter Sixteen

"I didn't mean it, okay?" Cash said later that night. Though he and Wren shared his king-size bed, as far as he was concerned he might as well have been sleeping with the ice chunk that'd taken over the front pasture pond. "Of course you'll do your doctor thing. When you can't, Mom can stay with Robin. Shoot, we could even pay Stella to take on our kiddo, too. Bottom line, we've got months and months till any of this comes to pass. Why are we fighting about it now?"

"Why?" Wren rolled to face him, in the process inadvertently knocking Prissy from her appointed pillow. The dog shot Cash a look nearly as offended as his wife's. "When we married, it was with the understanding that you not only knew how demanding my career is, but that you were fine with it. Now all of a sudden you're spinning cowboy fantasies of the *little woman* standing by her man."

"Ouch." Cash clutched his chest. "At least you'd be standing alongside a damned good-looking man—rich, too, once I get my sorry ass back on a bull."

Growling, she flopped back over. "You're impossible. Dense as that disgusting concoction you make for oatmeal whenever Mrs. Cahwood takes her days off."

Scooting over to her side of the bed, he spooned her,

loving that her tummy now fit in his hand rather than the barn wheelbarrow. "Add bad cooking to my list of sins, but I'm still freakishly gorgeous, right?"

She hit him over the head with her pillow.

A WEEK AFTER Robin's birth, smack-dab in the center of the Woodland Hills Mall, Cash helplessly watched while the kid screamed bloody murder. He'd just bought her that year's special-edition Eskimo Joe's holiday T-shirt and tugged it over her little head. Hell, when he'd been a kid, he'd lived for this annual tradition. "What's wrong?"

"How should I know?" Wren jiggled the baby and rubbed her head, but nothing calmed her.

"You're supposed to be a doctor," Cash reminded her. "What good is your fancy degree if you don't know something as basic as why our baby's turning red?"

"Oh, dear..." A blue-haired onlooker shook her head.

Cash glared at the nosy old biddy.

Wren glared at him.

"What?" he asked, barely able to hear himself think.

"You should be nice to old people." Rocking and jiggling and cooing only infuriated Robin all the more.

"Seriously," Cash said to his new wife, growing more uncomfortable by the second as every passerby stared. "Do something."

"What would you suggest? I nursed her an hour ago. She already had her postlunch burp and poo. Want me to whip out a tranquilizer dart?"

Cash didn't appreciate Wren's sarcasm. "Aren't wives and new moms supposed to be pleasant?"

"If we weren't in the center of a crowded mall," she ground out from between clenched teeth, "I'd beat you silly."

"Nice, Wren." Hands on his forehead, Cash wished himself anywhere but his current location. "Our kid is dying and all you care about is smacking the crap out of me?"

"Robin's not dying," she growled, her pinched expression not as confident as her words.

With their wailing baby in the crook of one arm, she managed to steer the Mack truck of a stroller his mother had given them alongside a wooden bench. Unfortunately where Robin was concerned, adding sitting to her jiggling, rocking repertoire did little good.

"That crying is really getting to me," he confessed. "Mind if I go ahead and get back to shopping?"

"Y-you're kidding, right?" His clenched stomach told him Wren's narrowed eyes weren't a good thing.

Meanwhile, now even the kids in line for Santa pics had started to stare.

"Excuse me." A fellow mom with two sticky-faced toddlers rolled to a stop in front of Wren. "I see your baby has one of this year's Eskimo Joe's shirts. Did you check the inside of the tag? Last year my Lucy got one with a staple that poked her. Luckily she was old enough to tell me what was wrong."

Tugging the back of Robin's shirt, sure enough, Cash found the price tag had been stapled in place. It was positioned just right to stab his baby girl. In under ten seconds he had it removed and his daughter's screams faded to indignant "what took you so long" sniffles.

"Thank you," Wren said to the stranger. "I feel so stupid. She's only a week old, and we're just starting to figure out her noises."

"Glad to help," the woman said, already on her way. "You'll get the hang of it."

Cash perched alongside Wren. "Looks like we flunked that parenting test."

"I feel awful." Nuzzling the side of Robin's head, Wren inspected the angry red scratch on her back. The staple hadn't broken the skin, but the way his baby girl had screamed, he'd have expected barbed wire sticking out of her tag.

Furious, Cash stood. "Wait here."

"Where are you going?" she asked while Robin sucked on her chubby fist.

"To give that store a piece of my mind. They can't just go around hurting children. Aren't there laws for this sort of thing?"

"Yeah." Smoothing her hand up and down the baby's back, Wren said, "There are also laws against bad parenting. We should've known to check the tag. In some of my prebaby reading, an article said the best way to prevent skin irritation is to remove tags."

Arms crossed, he asked, "Then why didn't you do it?"

"You seriously didn't just ask that." After easing their sleeping baby into her stroller, Wren was on her feet, weaving through the hellish holiday crowd.

Hands shoved in his jean pockets, Cash doggedly followed. "It's an honest question."

"Where?" she sassed over her shoulder. "In Cowboy Land? Surgical price-tag removal isn't taught. It's learned through firsthand parenting experience. Something neither of us have, but most especially you. Aside from changing a few diapers, what have you even done?"

"Plenty," he said as she entered a kitchenware store, maneuvering the stroller to a quiet side aisle. "I've changed diapers *and* made a late-night diaper run when we ran out of the cloth ones."

She put her hands on her hips, and mean flashed from her eyes. "Congratulations. I suppose that qualifies you for father of the year?"

"I'm trying, all right? And anyway, it's not like I can feed her. As for the whole bath thing…" He shook his head. "Nope. Not for me. She's tiny and slippery and if I accidentally hurt her, I don't know what I'd do."

Jaw hard, staring at the ceiling, Wren looked so far removed from the woman he felt he'd grown to know and married that had he been a sci-fi fan, he would've wondered if she'd undergone an alien switch.

"I'm sorry, okay?" His hands on her hips, finally able to ease in as close to her as he wanted, he brushed the pad of his thumb over her full lower lip. "I'm not sure what I'm apologizing for, but I obviously said bad, bad things. I deserve to be punished." She still wouldn't meet his gaze. "Seriously, spank me. Cuff me. Whatever you feel fits the crime." He winked and grinned, but it was tough working his charm without an audience. "If you'd look at me, my rugged sexiness would go a long way toward helping you select a proper punishment for my crimes."

Oh, she looked at him, all right, but not with lust—more like disgust.

Cash's stomach sank.

Had marrying Wren been the worst decision he'd ever made?

It was Christmas Eve. The first ever Wren had experienced not with friends who took pity on her for being alone, but with a family truly her own—Robin. Her baby girl. Flawless in every way. Cash—her husband. The man she'd believed to be her best friend. If it hadn't been for the chill that'd settled between them ever since their disastrous shopping trip, she might have been happy. As it was, she felt trapped in limbo between a potential fairy tale and a nightmare.

In the kitchen late that afternoon, while Robin napped, Wren prepared a veggie tray to share that night with Cash's family.

Prissy lounged near her feet, eyes wide in hope of snagging a falling snack.

As she chopped cauliflower, Wren's memory regretfully wandered back to their mall outing. To their baby's crying. To the way once they'd discovered the problem, Cash had seemed furious with her for not having known what to do. His unrealistic expectations had been not only ridiculous, but cruel. As if because she'd been to medical school she should be a better parent than she currently was.

"Need help?" Fresh from the shower, Cash strolled into the kitchen with rumpled damp hair, wearing nothing but half-zipped jeans. Had she cared, she thought his six-pack abs would have qualified for the eighth world wonder. He stopped behind her, close enough for his radiant heat to muddle her thoughts. Wren pretended he'd never even entered the room.

"No, thank you."

He stole a baby carrot. "Wyatt's going to love this. When we were little, every holiday whenever we had a platter—cheese, meats, cookies, whatever—he used to sneak them from the table and run off to his room so he didn't have to share."

"Should I make two so he can have his own?"

Laughing, he said, "He does better with the whole sharing thing now than he used to."

She wanted to come up with some witty reply, but had nothing left in her to say. During their outing he'd really hurt her.

"We all right?" Cash nuzzled her neck, pressing warm, wet kisses in places he knew damned well turned her on. Maybe that was the problem with their whole stupid upside-down relationship. From the first night they'd met, he'd learned her every intimate secret. Now there was nowhere left for them to go.

"Honestly," she mumbled, resting her cheek against his chest, "I don't know. Your reaction at the mall was crushing. I wanted you to be jazzed that though we'd done it in an unorthodox way, together we figured out what was hurting our daughter and fixed it. Instead, I got the impression you blamed me from the start. That crack about me not learning about prickly tags in med school was not only uncalled for, it was insulting."

"I'm sorry." Judging by the darkening in his eyes, the lack of sexual innuendos, this time around he was sincere. "The munchkin's crying flipped me out. I wasn't prepared for that level of panic."

His raw confession touched her. She'd felt the same, but didn't think dads even cared about babies' crying. Oh, of course they cared, but not in the soul-deep way moms did.

"As for me not helping you out more on the late-night shifts, what do you want me to do?" He launched a heavenly shoulder massage. One that made her purr with contentment. Not that she wasn't still upset with him, but considering how much her back had been hurting, she put her fury on hiatus.

"All I want from you, Cash, is to know you're there. Half the time I'm sleepwalking, yet you don't seem fazed by Robin's attack on our schedule."

"Oh…" He pressed the heels of his hands to his eyes. "Trust me, I'm fazed, but again, I need guidance. When you're breastfeeding, I'm not even sure if I'm welcome in the room."

"Of course you are. Why wouldn't you be?"

"That's just it…" His back to her, he thumped the heel of his fist against the stainless steel fridge, and Prissy scampered to the living room. Cash continued, "When it was just me and you and occasionally my mom or Mrs. Cahwood around the house, I knew where I stood. I knew when you needed refills on herbal tea or when the flowers on your nightstand needed changing. Now, as much as I love Robin, I'm scared of her. She can't tell us what's wrong or what she needs." Taking over with the chopping of bite-size broccoli chunks, he added, "She reminds me of a Chinese exchange student Dallas brought home. We tried bending over backward to make the guy feel comfortable, but because of the language barrier, nothing worked. The week he was here felt like a start-to-finish disaster. Kind of like I feel as a father."

"First, comparing our daughter to a Chinese exchange student is crazy. Second, the more you're around Robin, the more instinct kicks in. By this time next week we'll both recognize the meaning behind her every burp and coo." Wren took mayo, buttermilk and sour cream from the fridge, intent on making homemade ranch dip for the center of her tray.

"How do you know?"

Artfully arranging black olives alongside celery, she noted, "Believe it or not, that's one area we did cover in med school."

Tackling the few dishes in the sink, he said, "I didn't mean to tick you off again."

"You didn't."

"Then why are you still refusing to look at me?"

Good question. One she suspected that were she to dwell on it for the next two weeks, she still wouldn't have an answer for. "Please," she implored, pushing stray hairs from her flushed cheeks, "can't we get through tonight and tomorrow without further deep discussion?"

Drying the cutting board he'd scrubbed, he turned to her, cracking a smile. "That mean you'd rather spend our time on more productive matters? Like making out?"

After the deep admissions they'd both shared, his reverting back to his usual carefree ways irked her to no end. Was the man ever serious? If not, was she willing to spend the rest of her life trying to tame him?

Chapter Seventeen

Christmas Eve, after their meal of turkey, ham and tur-ducken with all the trimmings had been eaten, Cash sat with Wyatt and Dallas in his mom and brother's living room, watching a John Wayne movie marathon. Instead of a white Christmas, their part of the state had been slammed by pouring rain that showed no signs of letting up.

Robin, wearing a fuzzy green elf suit, had crashed on his chest. He loved how her eyelashes were already long enough to sweep her cheeks and every so often her little lips suckled.

"Been getting much sleep?" Dallas asked during a commercial for trash bags.

"Sure. Lucky for me, Wren's breastfeeding, so I usually get plenty of *zzzs*."

"Bad idea, man," Wyatt counseled. Prissy had long since crashed on his chest. "Friend of mine slept through every night feeding and found himself kicked to the curb after the kid's first birthday."

"Like you'd know," Cash argued. "You don't have a wife or kid."

"May well be…" Dallas sipped from his beer. "But this is one case in which I agree with Wyatt. You're playing a dangerous game in not sharing every part of the pleasure and pain of raising that baby girl."

"I change diapers."

Cash's oldest brother grunted. "Not nearly enough."

Tired of being nagged by the two guys he thought most likely to have his back, Cash picked up Robin and headed into the kitchen. Hopefully he'd fare better with leftovers and woman talk.

"Georgina," Cash overheard Wren saying, "he means the world to me, but how do I make him understand that so does earning my medical license and then joining—possibly even starting—my own practice?"

"Give it time. You two are just starting out. Adjusting to the baby and married life doesn't happen overnight."

Tiptoeing from the door he'd been hiding behind, Cash whispered to Robin, "Looks like Daddy needs to ramp up Mommy's Christmas surprise."

He took the back stairs two at a time. When he reached the twins' closed door, he slowly turned the knob and then crept the door open, inching his way inside.

"Who's there?" Bonnie asked, blinding him with the Barbie flashlight that had been in her stocking. Dallas being a softy where his girls were concerned, he'd allowed them to open one gift each and their stockings after dinner. "I've got an Old West sheriff rifle and I'll put on my badge and take you down!"

"Yeah," Betsy said, completing his twin torture by nailing him with her laser pointer. "I've got a hamster and I'll get him to go ninja on you!"

Robin started to cry.

"Ladies," Cash said, entering the room and closing the door before turning on the lights, "who taught you to be so violent?"

"Uncle Cash!" Bounding out of their beds, the girls danced around him as if it'd been a year since their last visit.

"I wanna hold the baby," Bonnie demanded.

"No, me!" Betsy tugged Robin's foot.

Robin's scream was loud enough to wake the entire population of Weed Gulch.

"Knock it off," Cash said to the little monsters his brother was raising. "And keep your grubby paws off the baby."

"We're not grubby." Betsy was back to shining that damned laser thing in his eyes.

"Give me that." When he took it from her, she started to cry.

Bonnie kicked his shin.

Wincing in pain, but thankful she hadn't messed with his bum knee, he said, "You little bugger. Get back to bed pronto, or I'm calling Stella."

They feared their nanny far more than Dallas, who was the world's biggest pushover, so they scampered into their beds. After jiggling and patting Robin, Cash finally got her quiet, too.

"Now that everyone's settled down—" Cash perched on the foot of Betsy's bed "—I need a favor."

"I don't like you anymore," Bonnie announced.

"That's fine. Just give me your doctor kit."

"I *love* my doctor kit." Bonnie bolted back out of bed and sat on her toy box. "You can't have it."

"Please?" He wriggled Robin's arms to look as if she was begging, too. "I'll buy you a new one just as soon as I can get into town."

"What're you doing with it?" Betsy asked, plopping alongside her sister. "'Cause if you need to fix a broken gut or something, it doesn't *really* work."

Tired of sass, Cash placed Robin on Betsy's bed, surrounding her with pillows and animals so she wouldn't roll off. Next he hefted a twin under each arm and set them on Bonnie's bed. "Stay."

While the twins pouted, Cash rummaged through naked Barbies with chopped-off hair, missing limbs and eyeballs. Sparkle dresses and shoes and enough Lego to build a life-size house. Finally he found Bonnie's kit. It had been attacked with markers and crayons, but was basically still intact.

"Come on, munchkin." He scooped up Robin, glared at his nieces and said, "Wish Santa had known how ornery you two were before he bought your gift."

In unison, Betsy and Bonnie stuck out their tongues.

"WHEW." AFTER FEEDING Robin and tucking her into her crib, Wren collapsed on the sofa beside Cash. "Mothering is exhausting."

Prissy usually occupied the spot next to Wren, wherever that might be. But at the moment she was too busy with a chew bone to notice Cash horning in on her territory.

Lightly massaging Wren's neck, he asked, "Any thoughts on how you'll handle nursing once you're back at work?"

The question brought on an instant headache, as well as a hot rush of panic. Yes, she'd given the topic a lot of thought and with always the same result—how would she realistically have it all? Marriage? Motherhood? The career as a doctor she'd worked years to achieve? It felt just within her reach, if only she were smart enough, energetic enough, stubborn enough to juggle it all.

"Well…" She forced her breathing to slow. "Since the day care is on-site, I'll pop in to feed Robin whenever possible. If that doesn't work, I can always pump milk or supplement with formula."

"And us?" He shifted on the sofa, his proximity making it impossible for her to look anywhere but at him. At those gorgeous green eyes that had first drawn her in. Since having Robin, Wren had harbored horrible thoughts of wondering where she'd be now if she'd never met him. Midway through her first year of residency would she be happier? More fulfilled? Or was it the exhaustion of new motherhood forcing her thoughts to gloomy places?

"Cash…" How did she begin sharing her thoughts with him? No man wanted to hear his wife of barely two weeks already confessing doubts about their future. "I'm tired. We have Christmas with your family in the morning. Do we have to have this conversation now?"

"No. Sorry." He smiled, but even having known him as briefly as she had, Wren knew by his lack of dimples that his heart wasn't behind the expression.

"Ready for bed?"

"Actually—" he nodded toward the Christmas tree "—while you were with the baby, Santa left you an early gift." He presented the simply wrapped box with a flourish. "He advised me to give it to you now, before the family crush. Besides, after the past few rocky days, I wanted to…" Voice cracking, he looked away. "Look, I've been an ass. Said things I regret, and I'm sorry. Considering where we are in our relationship, this gift is backward, but…" He nodded toward the box. "Go ahead. Open it."

In the months Wren had lived with Cash, she couldn't remember him being more humble. Cupping her hand to his dear cheek, more than anything she wished she could've met him five years down the road. By then she would've been established. Ready for more than the one hot night they'd intended to be all they'd ever share. Now, even though she wasn't sure, she felt caged by circumstance. She needed to file for her residency transfer, but couldn't get Dr. West's voice from her head. *I've lost a lot of promising candidates due to so-called love, and I refuse to lose you, Wren Barnes.*

Not that Wren hadn't known full well what she'd been doing when she married Cash, but she felt as though she now had the stomachache of a child who'd eaten too much candy when her entire life before meeting him had been sugar free. Was what she shared with Cash the real deal or her mentor's *so-called* love?

And then Cash melted her heart as if it had been made of chocolate. Inside the box was an obviously well-loved child's doctor kit just like the one she'd had at the orphanage. Only, the stethoscope on this model included a spellbinding square-cut diamond ring.

On his knees in front of her, Cash said, "You should've had this before our wedding, but I hope you'll forgive me enough to not only wear my engagement ring, but honor me by becoming the first full-fledged doctor in the Buckhorn clan." After slipping it onto her trembling left ring finger, he kissed it. He then rose to kiss her lips.

"Th-thank you," she said, voice husky, eyes shining. "It's beautiful, but Cash, it's also unnecessary. I don't need a ring to seal me to you."

Rising, he threw his hands in the air. "Dammit, I'm not trying to *buy* you, but show you I care. I'm going to be a better father to Robin. A better husband to you. I'm sick of bickering and—"

Wren crushed him in a hug. "I've been so afraid that since we're married, you expect me to give up my career to raise Robin on my own. Don't get me wrong, I love everything about being a mother, but..."

"I get it," he explained, raining kisses over her cheeks and brows and finally, deliciously, her lips. "I'm going ahead with my surgery. You're going ahead with your residency. Together, we'll be unstoppable."

She wanted to believe him. Oh, how she wanted to trust in Cash's every word, but more than anyone, Wren knew dreams rarely—if ever—came true.

"THANK YOU, UNCLE CASH and Aunt Wren!" Upon unwrapping their kid-sized, battery-powered Hummer, Dallas's twins wriggled and screamed to such a degree Cash was afraid they'd wake Robin, who was finally asleep in the portable crib his mother had set up in a relatively quiet corner of the main house's living room.

Prissy wriggled along with them, but then found a candy cane and snuck off with it under the couch.

"You're welcome," Cash said, hugging them both, "but please, keep the celebrating quiet."

"Okay!" The girls' exaggerated whisper was hardly an improvement.

"Can we drive it now?" Bonnie asked.

"Let's go to the mall," Betsy said.

"And get ice cream." Bonnie ripped at the supersized box.

"Slow down," their father said. "The end of the driveway is as far as you two will be traveling."

With both girls pouting, Georgina said, "Wren, I wasn't sure about your size, so if your blouse doesn't fit, I have the receipt. It's from the cutest Utica Square boutique. If you need to take it back, we'll do lunch."

"Sounds fun," Wren said, fingering the white silk

blouse Cash's mom had given her, "but it's so beautiful, I'm hoping it looks great."

"Ladies never need an excuse to do lunch," Georgina noted, gathering the crumpled wrapping at her feet.

Wren laughed, helping with the cleanup. "Thank you, everyone, for such a fun morning. I've never had a family Christmas, and…" Seeing his wife choked up formed a knot in Cash's throat. Waving her hands in front of her suddenly red face, she managed to say, "You all are amazing. I'm lucky to have found you."

"Feeling's mutual," Georgina said, practically pushing Cash to give his wife a hug. "I'm so glad you've decided to stay with us. I realize even with your residency in Tulsa you'll still be busy, but at least we'll see you every once in a while."

Cash witnessed Wren's smile fade to a frown. What was she thinking? Was she sad about her change in plans? Would she grow to resent him for it? Or worse yet, did she already? On the surface, everything between them had never been better. They shared meals and jokes and he'd been doing more diaper changes on Robin. What more did Wren want from him?

Dallas patted Cash's shoulder. "Love the new fly-fishing gear."

"Good." Cash wanted to say more, but at the moment didn't have it in him.

"Wanna give me a hand?" Wyatt nodded toward both of them to help get the Hummer from the box.

With the twins dancing around their gift, his mother and Wren cleaning and Stella with her own family in Stillwater, the old place felt almost as it had back when his father had still been alive. What would Duke say about Cash's predicament? Would he think his son was overreacting? Was now the time for Cash to man up and tell Wren how things between them were going to be? Her transferring her residency would be best for not only him, but Robin. Surely she knew that, so why was she apparently still riding the proverbial fence?

"IT'S DONE." HAVING set his knee surgery appointment for a few days after New Year's, Cash hung up the phone.

"How do you feel?" Wren asked from the living-room sofa, where she nursed Robin.

Prissy protectively sat beside them.

"With all this rain, my knee hurts like hell."

Making a face, she said, "That's not what I meant. Are you satisfied you've made the right decision?"

"What other decision is there? Either I have surgery or I'm off the tour."

She switched Robin to her other breast. "I'm hardly an orthopedic surgeon, but once you heal, you should be good as new."

Grunting, he stared out the window at the puddles forming on the drive. "Never thought I'd say this, but lately I've been wondering if that's what I want. You know, to be good as new? Before I had a family of my own, I used to feel invincible. Now I worry if something happens to me, where does that leave you and our baby girl?"

"Good question. Not gonna lie, but I worry about you getting hurt again—only next time, worse." Robin had fallen asleep at her breast. Wren repositioned the baby, tugging up the flap of her nursing bra and pulling down her T-shirt. "I'm a big girl. I'd survive without you."

"Gee, thanks." He looked away from her in disgust.

Securing Robin on the sofa with a wall of pillows, Prissy on the opposite end lightly snoring, Wren slipped her arms around him, resting her cheek on his chest. "That's not what I meant and you know it. What I was trying unsuccessfully to convey is that I know how much riding means to you. I would never ask you to give it up in order to give me a false sense of security. Let's pretend you quit riding and worked the ranch full-time. Who's to say you couldn't be just as badly injured falling off a horse or being maimed in some—" she tossed up her hands "—I don't know, some rattlesnake attack?"

"Did I truly marry that much of a city girl?" He kissed the bridge of her nose.

"It could happen. Snakes attack, don't they?"

"Sure, but typically not unprovoked. Certainly not en masse."

"Yet it *could* happen?" She played with the ribbing around the collar of his T-shirt, unwittingly turning him on with the soft backs of her nimble fingers. Cash could've strangled the physician who had invented the "no sex for at least six weeks after having babies" rule.

"Honey," he said with a low growl, "for you, I would do my damnedest to move the stars, but I would hope you wouldn't want me to coordinate a snake attack for the sole reason of proving you right."

"No, thank you." Smiling sweetly up at him, she said, "Although I suppose if you get tired of riding bulls, you could always try your hand at a carnival sideshow featuring various fanged creatures."

"The only freaky sideshow I want to star in," he said along with his most charming grin, "would feature you and our bed—without your attached-at-the-hip dog."

"Three, two, one...Happy New Year!"

On her tiptoes, Wren kissed her husband, tuning out the crowd around them. Georgina loved a party, and in true Buckhorn style, half the town had shown up to ring in the New Year.

Streamers and champagne flowed. Balloons and confetti and noisemakers accompanied the same country band that had played at Wren and Cash's wedding. "Auld Lang Syne" performed with fiddles took on a slow, reminiscent quality that quieted the once-boisterous crowd.

"A year ago," Cash said, hands on her hips, swaying her in time to the music, "would you have ever believed we'd be married with a dog and a baby?"

"Would've been tough, considering I didn't even know you a year ago."

"So true." He returned her kiss. "Guess that's why you're the brains of this organization."

"Don't you forget it." Standing in his arms, Wren would have been hard-pressed to remember her life before meeting him. He made her feel safe and adored. Yes, they'd had their issues, but lately, the more he helped with Robin and the more affectionate they'd become, the more she found herself wanting to be with him night and day.

"What's your resolution?" he asked.

Up until now she hadn't given it much thought. "I suppose I should be more productive. Since moving in with you, I've turned into quite the slug."

"At least you're an attractive one." As Cash gripped her tighter, Wren reveled in his all-male form against her. Unlike her, the man didn't have an ounce of fat on him. His every inch had been honed to perfection, partially in his home gym, but mostly from plenty of hard outdoors work.

"Mmm…" She snuggled closer. "Right back atcha."

After a few moments more dancing, she asked, "How about you? Any special goals for the coming year?"

"I want to be a really great dad. My own father had some amazing qualities, but I always felt pretty far down on his to-do list. Robin needs to know that she and her mother come first."

Cash's words warmed Wren through and through.

They also worried her. Though she and the great Duke Buckhorn had never met, she suspected they shared the same level of determination. Now that she'd held Robin in her arms and assumed her daily care, Wren realized just how difficult raising her child and completing her residency would be. She knew quite a few guys in her program who had kids, but they also had wives to care for them. Come to think of it, she couldn't name a single other woman in her particular residency program with kids. Not even Dr. Abigail West, the world-renowned heart surgeon. Her lack of family was the price she'd chosen to pay for success. But was Wren willing to go that far? She hadn't even summoned the courage to complete her transfer forms.

"Tired?" Cash asked when Wren turned quiet.

She nodded.

Robin had long ago conked out in the twins' room in her portable crib.

"It's been a wonderful night," Wren said. "Special in every way." Aside from nagging worries about her residency that refused to release her.

"Not *every* way," he whispered in her ear, his warm voice making her shiver. The thought of being with him again brought on a hot and dizzy rush. His raw sex appeal had been what had landed her in this mess in the first place. But then, looking back at the past nine months, was Robin a mess? Of course not.

And your marriage?

Caressing the base of her throat, Cash kissed her deeply enough for Wren to feel it in her toes. Her whole body hummed with awareness. His merest touch made her feel electrified. As if every inch of her body had been massaged to a hypersensitive glow.

Was this love? Having never before experienced it, how did she know?

Chapter Eighteen

"Sure you have enough food?" January 3 in the black before dawn, Georgina stood alongside Cash's truck wringing her hands as if he were going off to war.

"Mom," he said, "I'm having a simple outpatient surgery done by one of the best knee guys in the whole damned country. Hell, if his work fails, I've got my own doc right here." Reaching behind the already snoozing munchkin in her car seat, Cash gave Wren's shoulder a squeeze.

"I know," his mother said, "but I still feel like I should be with you."

"You're welcome to ride along, but with all of Robin's gear, you'd have to sit in the back." Grinning, he nodded toward the truck's bed.

Judging by her crossed arms and pressed lips, his mother didn't find him amusing. "You know I've always hated your bull riding. Your cocky nothing-can-hurt-me attitude is just one more reason why."

"On that note..." Cash started the engine.

"Wren," his mother called past him, "you call with regular updates."

"I will," his wife promised.

Five hours later they'd reached the office of the orthopedic surgeon his team doctor had recommended.

Next came an hour's worth of paperwork and changing into a blue-striped dress that would show off his ass to any and all who cared to look.

His surgeon stopped in for a visit, explaining in a little too much detail exactly what he planned to do. By this time, Cash wanted the damned thing over and done with. It was long since time to get back to work.

Through all of this, Wren struck him as strangely silent. Not so much nervous, but melancholy. As if she'd lost her favorite pirate book. Was worry about him what had put the furrow between her eyebrows?

"Baby, I'm going to be fine," he assured her, taking her hand in his.

"I know." She jiggled Robin, who was wide-eyed and drooling at the bright lights of her new surroundings.

"Then why can't you smile for me?"

She forced it, but even a dumbo bull rider like himself knew she was faking. "Sweetie, seriously, before you know it, I'll be sprung from here, taking you out to a fancy early supper."

"Uh-huh." Rising, she managed to hold Robin with one arm while still fussing with his blankets. "I appreciate the thought, but I'm taking you straight home. You're going to hate me once we start your range-of-motion exercises."

"I could never hate you." Gazing upon his wife and child did funny things to his chest. He felt a squeezing pressure, but not in a bad way. More as if he didn't know where he left off and they began. As if without them, he might survive, but never again thrive. "Come here."

Wren perched on the edge of his gurney-style bed. "You should rest."

Slipping his hand beneath her hair, he pulled her in for a kiss. "You should stop being bossy long enough for me to tell you I love you." It was the first time he'd told her since she'd been in labor. That time, she'd declared hatred for him, which, considering her pain, he hadn't blamed her for, but this time he wanted more.

"I—I think I love you, too." Laughing, maybe even crying a little, she added, "Sorry, that came out wrong. Honestly, you're the first man I've ever said those words to."

"Kiss me," he demanded. Fortunately for him, she for once did as she was told and did a properly hot job of sending him off for medicinal torture.

"Whoa..." Cash's nurse bounded into his curtained cubicle, only to shield her eyes with his chart. "Should I come back later?"

"We're good," he assured her, wishing he'd had a few more minutes alone with Wren, but eager to get on with the next phase of his life.

"Great," the tall blonde said with enough exuberance to make him wonder if she'd been a college cheerleader. "Let's go fix your knee."

PACING WHILE ROBIN napped in her carrier, Wren could scarcely contain her emotions. Back and forth she traveled across fawn-colored carpet so thick her footfalls made no sound. Upholstered red leather chairs held two other people. Calmly reading magazines, they didn't look half as nervous as she felt.

Before she'd seen Cash wheeled away, surgical procedures had seemed to her like high-tech video games. Patients hadn't been real, but more like characters presenting problems for her to study.

The practical side of her knew Cash would be in recovery in just over ninety minutes. She knew after that he'd face painful rehabilitation, but a probable full recovery. He'd return to his bull riding and she...

What would she do?

Did Tulsa hold the same opportunities as Baltimore? What about Weed Gulch? After all, staying with Cash meant living with him on the ranch. He'd never leave it, and she'd never have the gall to ask him.

Warding off a sudden chill, Wren hugged herself. Cash's unexpected declaration of love hadn't lightened her heavy heart. Having had a family as well as countless lovers, Cash had the advantage of at least knowing the word's definition.

Despite that fact, it took only a glance at her sleeping child to remind Wren that she was on the fast track to achieving her every familial dream.

Minutes ticked into an hour and then more. Finally Cash's surgeon sauntered into the waiting area. When he smiled, relief shimmered through her.

"Cowboy Cash did great. I want him in recovery at least a couple of hours, and then you can take him home."

"Thank you," she said, almost afraid to stand for fear of her shaky knees giving out. "Any special aftercare?"

"My nurse will give you an instruction packet. I want his brace on with an ice pack for the first five days. He'll need to be up on crutches ASAP, contracting his thigh muscles, rotating his feet—it's all in the packet." The surgeon held out his hand for her to shake. "Also, I'll give you the number of my favorite physical therapist up in your neck of the woods."

Mouth dry, mind overwhelmed, Wren nodded.

What was wrong with her?

"Have a safe trip home." Just as abruptly as he'd arrived, the man was gone. Wren had worked herself into such an emotional state, she couldn't even remember the surgeon's name.

Before having Robin, before meeting Cash, orthopedics had been one of the residency rotations she'd most looked forward to. Now she just wanted to see her husband.

The notion was all at once thrilling and terrifying.

Her entire life she'd leaned on no one but herself, and had been successful. She'd lived by the principle that being on her own was streamlined efficiency at its best.

Upon returning to her residency, she'd have neither time nor energy for Robin, let alone Cash. The presumption wasn't some pie-in-the-sky ideal, but fact. How did she meld the two halves of her new life? Was it even possible?

After she called Georgina and Mrs. Cahwood to share the news that Cash's surgery had gone well, adrenaline turned to exhaustion, forcing Wren back into her chair. Movie magazine in hand, she thumbed through starlets' dresses and managed to read a piece on the latest Hollywood scandal before her eyes drifted shut.

"Mrs. Buckhorn?" Two hours later a nurse jolted Wren from a light sleep. "Your husband's awake and asking for you."

It took Wren a minute to gather Robin's things and her purse. After that, she followed the nurse down a short maze of brightly lit halls, finally entering the quiet area reserved for patients returning to consciousness from general anesthesia.

"Hey, gorgeous," Cash said with just enough potency behind his handsome grin to make her eyes sting with relief. "Hope you brought mashed potatoes."

"Sorry," she said, holding Robin close while leaning

over to kiss his forehead, "my purse happens to be fresh out, but I'll call Mrs. Cahwood to put in your request."

With a sleepy, smiley nod, he drifted back to sleep.

"Wake up," she coaxed with a gentle nudge. "I want you out of here."

"Did our bags make it all right?"

"What?" Wren laughed at Cash's latest drug-induced question.

"Can't start our Vegas honeymoon without my wife having her suitcase." Eyes already closed, he added, "It's a secret, so don't tell her you know."

Two days later Cash woke to his knee still feeling as if he'd wrestled with a hundred hornets and lost.

"Wren!" he hollered from their room.

She bustled in with Robin.

Prissy followed, looking none too happy about the baby taking her usual spot in Wren's arms.

Wren said, "Breakfast is almost done."

He winced. "I need something for pain."

"I want you to take it with something to eat, so you'll need to wait about five minutes."

Trying to shift positions and only causing more burning agony, he growled.

"How did you cope with pain while riding?"

"That was different. A man can't show he's a wuss in front of thousands of people."

"Uh-huh…" Wren plopped the baby next to him on the comforter before making a nuisance of herself by fluffing his pillows.

Robin fussed.

Cash tried reaching to comfort her, but couldn't quite pull it off.

"Let me," Wren said, snatching her up. "You rest."

"I'm tired of resting."

"Want me to turn on the TV?" Wyatt had needed a part for one of the oil rigs, which had called for a trip to Tulsa. Since he'd been only a few miles from an electronics store, Cash had coerced him into picking up the new flat screen now parked atop the dresser.

"No, thanks."

"Other than a pain pill and breakfast, what do you want?"

He sighed. "To feel normal again. Do you have any idea how long it's been since I've put in a full day's training? Or even helped Dallas with the ranch?" Judging by her hasty look away from him and out the wall of bedroom windows, she knew exactly how long it'd been since either of them had worked at anything besides caring for her, then newborn Robin and now him. Were their lives forever destined to stagnate in this holding pattern?

"I'm as frustrated as you, but it won't be too long until you're on a busy rehabilitation schedule." Her back to him, with Robin calmed and resettled on the bed, she began putting up the clean clothes overflowing the laundry basket. "Plus, I'm not exactly thrilled with this situation, either."

"Way to make a man feel loved." Was he imagining things, or for a fraction of a second after his quip, did she freeze? As if she hadn't viewed his joke as all that amusing. *Did* she love him? She'd sure shown him in a hundred ways. By nursing him around the clock. Doting on their daughter and dog. Those kinds of things were enough to prove love, right? He was hardly insecure enough to need something as lame as a verbal confirmation.

"I've been thinking…" Continuing with her task, she

said, "Though you may not believe it now, by the end of the week you'll be off your crutches and busy with strengthening exercises."

Why did his stomach now hurt more than his knee? "What are you saying?"

"We'd planned for me to resume my residency in February."

"Yeah, but in Tulsa, right?"

Either she hadn't heard him or was deliberately ignoring him. Knowing her as he did, he voted for the latter.

"What's going through that pretty head of yours?"

She tucked her bras into his sock drawer—his tip-off that something was going on.

"Talk to me, Wren."

"I'm fed up, okay?" She spun to face him. "Your whole life you've been programmed to care for dozens of people. Your mom and dad. Brothers and sister. Neighbors and friends. I'm a loner, and all of this domestic bliss is getting on my nerves."

Liar. In his esteemed opinion, she was scared. But that was okay. He had enough love in him to see all three of them through. He might've been out of it after his surgery, but he also remembered her shining eyes. The way she'd sweetly kissed him—as if he'd been a dream she was afraid would fade away.

Trying to lighten the mood, he asked, "I don't suppose I could trouble you for breakfast and a pain pill before you go?"

"I'm sorry." Face reddening, she crushed him in a hug. "I don't know what got into me."

"It's all right," he assured her. "Between your pregnancy and my knee, we've both been at this bed-rest thing for too long."

"Speaking of which..." Reclining on her side of the king-size mattress, Wren tickled Robin's chubby tummy. "Not sure if you remember or not, but when you were waking from surgery, you spilled the beans on a Vegas trip. Was that for real or drug-induced rambling?"

Stomach hurting again, only for a much different reason, he asked, "Am I going to be in trouble if I confess to ignorance?"

She shook her head.

"I'd like to take you. Have to admit it sounds fun. We could book the same room." He winked. "Reenact our first night together."

"On that note—" she sat up "—I'm off to get your breakfast. Need me to take the baby?"

"Leave her. She's a good distraction."

His wife flashed a pinched smile before closing the bedroom door. Hard to believe a few minutes earlier, his throbbing knee had been his only problem. Now he was also left to dwell on not only what Wren wasn't telling him, but how he was going to find out.

IN CASH'S STUDY with the door closed, well away from the prying eyes and ears of not only her husband, but Mrs. Cahwood, Wren's hand's trembled to such a degree she had difficulty punching Abigail's private cell number into the phone.

Wren had hoped her talk with Cash would've gone better, but then, how could it when she feared he wasn't going to like what she had to say?

"Happy baby, Miss Barnes!" her friend uncharacteristically gushed after two rings, no doubt recognizing the Oklahoma number on her caller ID. "When am I going to see you? Sometimes I feel like you were the only competent candidate on our team."

"Actually, that's why I called." Though flattered, Wren knew Abigail's complaint was pure fiction, considering the *team* consisted of ten of the brightest young medical minds in the country. "I spoke with the dean about a possible transfer to University of Oklahoma's Tulsa residency program. He sent the papers a while back, but I have yet to sign them."

"I thought that was a joke." In her mind's eye Wren saw the always perfectly dressed, unflappable surgeon seated behind her French provincial desk, no doubt multitasking as she talked. "I'm sure Oklahoma produces fine physicians, but Wren, you and I both know you're special. Destined for greatness that can only be fostered by greatness. That sort of training can only be found in a handful of programs. Ours happens to be one of them. There's a reason you haven't filled out those transfer forms. Deep down, you know I'm right."

Twirling a pencil between her fingers, Wren searched for a legitimate argument, but came up lacking.

"Now, the committee agrees that due to your pregnancy, you've missed too much of your first year to make up. No worries, though, as I've already found you a plum research position. Really top-notch, which you'll be able to start right away. Meaning, you've been hiding out on the prairie long enough. I want you and baby back here pronto. You're even welcome to stay with me, which I wish I'd suggested in the first place before you took off for the wilds. I should've hired a private medical jet to safely carry you home." Barely pausing for breath, she added, "What's done is done. All that matters now is making up for lost time. Tell me your address and I'll send you and baby your itinerary and flight information. Do babies fly free?" Laughing, she said, "I have no idea, but my secretary should know."

"Dr. West—Abigail…" Wren's mouth was so dry, her tongue could barely move. Her mentor held the key to her every dream. Even her housing problem had been magically whisked away. Abigail had taken on the role of her fairy godmother and as such, seemed determined to knock down any obstacle. Little did she know Wren's only roadblock happened to be a husband.

"Sorry to cut this short. I didn't realize the time, and I'm due in surgery in ten. Let me transfer you to Eloise and she'll get your address."

After a brief conversation with the secretary that basically consisted of turning traitor on her new family, Wren hung up the phone.

Chapter Nineteen

On crutches, six days after his surgery, Cash hobbled from the front door to the barn, trying not to squash Prissy in the process. The mutt danced around him, growling at the metal frames as if they were dragons. His knee still throbbed, but it felt great to be out of bed and into bright sun. Though the temperature was barely fifty, his efforts already had him working up a sweat.

"You're doing great, sweetheart." Wren, with a bundled-up Robin in her arms, walked alongside him. "Don't be afraid to admit you need to rest."

"No way," he said through gritted teeth. "I'm going for it." His body said otherwise. Refusing to give in to the pain, he split the difference by leaning back on his crutches.

Out on the dirt road a dust cloud rose, caused by a speeding FedEx truck.

"There's something you don't see every day," he noted. When the vehicle turned onto their drive, he asked, "You order something?"

Her face paled. "No."

"Maybe he's headed for the main house and took a wrong turn?"

The driver parked and hopped out. "Morning. Either of you Wren Barnes?"

"She's Wren Buckhorn." Grinning, still resting on his crutches, Cash hooked his thumb in his wife's direction. "Guess someone didn't get the memo about our wedding."

Not looking amused, the driver held out a computerized clipboard for Wren to sign.

She did.

The driver in turn handed over a ten-by-thirteen envelope. "Have a great day."

"Who's it from?" Cash asked, peeking over her shoulder. Unfortunately, Robin blocked his view.

"It's no doubt paperwork on my residency transfer."

"Open it," he urged, more than ready for her stay in Oklahoma to become officially permanent.

"Later. Now you have work to do." Smacking his butt with her package, she said, "Come on, get moving to the barn."

Midway there, Robin began to fuss.

"What's wrong?" Cash asked their daughter in a coochie-coo tone.

Wrinkling her nose, Wren said, "Surprise! Your baby left a smelly package for you."

"Not me." Hustling toward his goal, he said, "Remember? I've got more work to do."

"Will you be okay on your own?" Her furrowed brow didn't show much faith in his hobbling skills.

"I'm fine," he promised. "Go ahead and get her changed. I smell her from here."

IN THE HOUSE, Wren quickly changed Robin's diaper before placing her in her living-room playpen. After a hand wash, Wren sat on the sofa with her envelope. Abigail's return address already had her dreading the contents.

She'd just torn the zip closure when Cash fumbled through the door, Prissy leading the way.

"How's that for record timing?" he asked with the same broad smile that had first drawn her to him so many months ago.

"I'm impressed." She was also finding it hard to breathe now that his growing efficiency with his crutches had him already across the room, collapsing onto the sofa beside her. "Good job."

"Thanks." He seemed expectant. As if he wanted something.

"Thirsty?" she asked, already rising. "Need me to take off your shoes?"

"What's in the envelope, Wren?"

If her heart raced any faster, she'd keel over. "I—I already told you I don't know."

Sighing, he raked his fingers through his hair. "In all the time we've been together, I don't think you've ever just out-and-out lied to me. Why start now?"

She wanted to continue the lie indefinitely, but couldn't. It wasn't fair to him or his family, who had been nothing but welcoming to her from practically her first day on the ranch. Yes, she and Georgina had gotten off to a rocky start, but now that Wren was a mother, she understood why her mother-in-law had been so preoccupied with the interests of Cash and her future grandchild.

"Talk to me." He took her hand, tracing the outline of her fingers. "What could be so bad?"

"I—I have to go." Tears streamed down her cheeks, hot and messy and strangely quiet. As if the pain stemmed from so deep inside her that the secret place had never before been exposed.

"Go where, honey?"

"Back to Baltimore. I never even applied for a transfer. I started to—many times—but couldn't. The chance to one day work with Dr. West is just too rare."

"And you and me and Robin? What we have isn't rare?"

"Cash, please..." Still crying, she struggled with a way to make him understand just how much she hated doing this to not only him, but herself. "My leaving is for the best. I've been fooling myself in ever thinking the two of us could last anywhere near forever. Since the day we first met, I've told you I'm a loner. I just wasn't made for a shared life."

He didn't look at her. Didn't move a muscle other than an errant nerve ticking in his jaw.

"When you were in surgery," she said, "it destroyed me. And that was a relatively minor thing. I would die should something more serious ever happen—like I permanently lose you."

After a sharp laugh, he said, "So instead of letting fate take its course, like most sane married couples do, you're grabbing the bull by the horns and just leaving me?"

"It's not that simple," she tried to explain. "My whole career is at stake. Everything I've worked so hard for."

This time when he pushed himself up, he stayed on his feet while reaching for his crutches.

"You should rest," Wren advised. "After such a long walk, you have to be exhausted."

"Don't," he ground out. "Don't you dare pretend to care."

"I do. You mean the world to me. I—" *I love you.* Trouble was, she wasn't even sure what the words meant. Life experience had taught her love equals pain. Growing attached to someone or something equaled eventual loss. It was as simple as that. Why couldn't Cash understand?

"How long have you been planning this escape?"

Raising her chin, she admitted, "From the day I set foot on your property."

"Why'd you even bother marrying me? Other than making me out to be a fool?"

"I don't know." Covering her face with her hands, she now knew that to be true. At the time she'd been caught up in the romance of it all. The cake and gorgeous white dress. The fairy-tale hope that maybe just this once, dreams really would come true. But then she'd talked to Abigail and realized her actual dreams resided back in Baltimore. With the goals she'd held dear ever since playing doctor on her little dog Waldo all those years ago.

"I suppose you're taking the baby?" he asked.

"Of course. I'm still breastfeeding."

"All right, then." Hobbling toward the back door, he said, "Let me know when you need a ride to the airport. I'll make sure there's someone around to drive you."

His cold demeanor was more than she could bear.

"Please, Cash..." She went to him, put her arms around him, expecting his usual strong embrace. The one that made her feel safe and secure and capable of meeting any goal she'd ever dreamed of achieving. But instead of wrapping his arms around her, he stood ramrod still, hands curved tight around his crutch handles. "Talk to me," she begged. "Tell me you still want to spend time with Robin and me during your touring breaks."

"Right now," he cruelly noted, "I'd gladly see my daughter every day. As for you, I'd probably get along just fine never setting eyes on you again."

AT FIVE THE next morning, the lights from Henry's pickup shone through the front windows.

Having been up most of the night tossing and turning in the guest bed, Wren stood in the living room waiting. Robin slept in the carrier portion of her car seat that Cash had informed her he'd already switched to the foreman's truck. Prissy also slept, only in her designer pooch purse.

Her actions braver than her emotions, Wren mechanically walked toward the door, telling herself she'd made the right decision for her daughter and her. The opportunities for Robin in Baltimore would be limitless. Here in Weed Gulch she'd be lucky to win a spelling bee, let alone a prestigious debate title or science scholarship.

"Sure you want to do this?" Henry asked when Wren opened the door.

Not sure at all, she went through the motions, assuring him in a falsely bright tone that if she wanted to be a doctor, returning to Baltimore was her only option.

Wren had hoped Cash would at least step out of the room they used to share long enough to say goodbye, but he didn't.

And so she left, leaving behind no traces she'd ever been there save for Robin's crib and changing table and the light floral scent of her own perfume in the air.

The ride to the airport was uneventful.

Henry wasn't the talkative sort, and Wren was thankful for the fact. Pulling up to the curb nearest her airline, he unloaded everything, slipped the porter a twenty and then with the slightest tip of his hat, climbed back behind the wheel and drove off.

Standing in the surprisingly long security line, Wren reflected on how many people she'd hurt by not at least saying goodbye. Georgina and Stella. Delores, Mrs.

Cahwood and Doc Haven. Even Dallas and Wyatt and the twins. Surely she'd see all of them again. After all, they were family.

Then why are you leaving?

The question hit from nowhere with the force of an Oklahoma twister to her gut. Had it not been for the knowledge that Abigail was expecting her in Baltimore, Wren might've called Cash, begging him to forgive her for putting a stupid job before their marriage. But then she came to her senses. Becoming a doctor was a goal she'd worked hard for. It wasn't stupid, but noble. Once licensed, she knew she'd be able to do good for so many people, rather than merely a few.

Having convinced herself that her deep affection for Cash, his family and their friends had been a fleeting thing, she edged forward in the suddenly moving line. And when she thought she saw her husband out of the corner of her eye near a coffee stand, she chalked it up to exhaustion. Instead of admitting that in reality, her seeing him everywhere, in every face, was the desperate act of a woman praying her very own cowboy would ride in on his white horse and bring her to her senses.

Only problem with that scenario was that Cash not only didn't own a white horse, but no matter how much she craved her own wildly romantic ending, she was grounded enough in reality to know her leaving was the right decision.

JUST TO THE LEFT of Tulsa International's Starbucks, Cash tugged his best straw hat over his eyes. Had he not seen Wren taking his baby and his dog for himself, he might not have believed they were really leaving.

He wasn't supposed to be driving and he sure as hell wasn't supposed to be fawning over a woman who obviously loved her damned job more than him, but he couldn't help it. Wren had gotten under his skin, and until he discovered a way to exorcise her from his system, he'd have to throw himself into his work. He'd have to push himself harder. Ride as if there was no tomorrow. Because without Wren and Robin and even little Prissy in his life, there might as well not even be a tomorrow.

Solely so she could be a big-city doctor, Wren had broken his heart. And from where he stood, he doubted all the fancy degreed doctors in the world would be able to fix it.

"WHAT DO YOU MEAN Wren's gone?" Georgina stood with her hands on her hips in Cash's home gym, staring at him as if he'd sprouted horns and a tail. "Like, on a shopping trip to Tulsa?"

"No, Mom. Like in she moved back to Baltimore." It'd been forty-eight hours since his bride had vacated the premises and as far as he was concerned, Cash preferred to never speak of her again.

"Why'd you let her go? She didn't take Robin, did she? What about the dog? Even a runt dog like Prissy needs fresh air and plenty of country to roam around in."

"Look…" He stopped his workout and grabbed a nearby water bottle. "Long story short, she felt her work was more important than me—or the rest of her family and friends. End of story."

"Well, what are you doing here?" his mom demanded. "Go after her. Drag her back caveman-style if you have to, but get her back."

He rolled his eyes.

"You think I'm kidding? Any fool could see the girl's

crazy about you. And no grandchild of mine needs to be growing up without her daddy."

Easing up from his weight bench, Cash tossed a towel around his neck and limped to his gym's door.

"Don't ignore me, son. I've been on this earth a lot longer than you and recognize true love when I see it."

Cash snorted. "You must need a new eyeglasses prescription, because where me and Wren are concerned, there never was much between us but lust."

ONE MONTH LATER Wren sat alone, save for Prissy, at a mahogany dining-room table large enough to seat twenty. Exhausting work hours had forced her to wean Robin so that the nanny Abigail had found could bottle-feed her.

It was ten at night, and she'd been home only fifteen minutes. Just long enough to peek in on her baby, grab a quick shower and scoop up her dog.

The housekeeper had informed her that Abigail and her significant other were at a fundraiser and not expected home until late. Mrs. Rodriguez had then warmed Wren a pasta-and-chicken dish that was too heavy on olive oil and garlic to suit her taste. What she could use was a big slice of Mrs. Cahwood's meat loaf with sides of green beans and buttery mashed potatoes.

Wren offered Prissy, who occupied her lap, a pea-sized bite of chicken, but the dog took one whiff of the pretentious food and went back to sleep.

Picking out the tomatoes and nibbling on somewhat edible garlic toast, Wren wondered for the umpteenth time what she was doing with her life. She hadn't wanted to be in research, but to heal people. Granted, because of her pregnancy she'd been forced out of her current year of residency, but might she have been better off staying at the ranch until July?

Living with Abigail, she'd managed to save enough money for her own place, but her friend had insisted she and the baby stay. After all, it wasn't as if their paths crossed that often in the rambling estate.

She'd sent apology letters to Georgina and her friends. She'd also packed her mother-in-law's Kewpie doll in a tissue-lined box, returning it with a note of thanks. So far she'd received only short, sharp notes from Mrs. Cahwood and Delores, imploring her to return home.

But had the ranch ever truly been her home? Had she ever in her life had a genuine home outside the fantasy image she carried in her mind?

The one where she wouldn't have met Cash until she'd been well finished with her residency. The one where she certainly wouldn't have had a child until she could afford to take off enough time to be with her.

As it was, what had Wren accomplished besides being lonely and bored with every aspect of her life, with nothing but memories of happier times?

"YOU EVER GOING to go get her?" Dallas asked Cash one early-spring afternoon when it seemed as if every blooming thing in the world was coming alive save for him. They'd been riding fences, and had yet to find one in need of repair. Cash figured his brother just wanted an excuse to not only get him out of the house, but nag his little brother.

"If by *her,* you're referring to my wife," Cash said, "then nope."

"Mom told me what a screwed-up childhood Wren

had. Think she might need lessons on the meaning of love?"

Frowning, Cash asked, "Isn't it a little early in the day for you to be hitting the bottle?"

"I'm serious. If I could have Bobbie Jo back for just a minute, I sure as hell wouldn't waste it fighting. Your woman and child and even your dog are just a few states east. All you have to do is fly over there and get 'em."

"Yup." Cash spotted a loose place in the fence and reined in his mount to climb off and set about fixing it.

"Then why don't you?" Already down from his horse, Dallas reached into his saddlebag for a hammer and nails.

"What don't you get about the fact that she left me? My knee's getting better by the day and I'm already in talks to head back out on the road. I'm a hot commodity and I'll be damned if I let some woman determine my self-worth."

"Been watching much of those daytime talk shows?" his brother asked with a chuckle. "You're starting to sound like that Oprah."

"Oh, yeah? Well, you sound like a pain in my ass."

"I'm sorry," Wren's supervisor said over the phone Thursday morning, "but with patient trials starting, I can't spare you today."

"My infant daughter has a 103-degree fever," she explained. "I don't feel comfortable leaving her with a nanny."

Nathaniel cleared his throat. "I don't mean to be rude, but isn't that the whole point of hiring a nanny? So that parents don't have to be inconvenienced by these things?"

"These *things*?" Wren tried slow breathing to keep

from blowing her cool, but failed miserably. "We're talking about my baby girl. As a doctor, didn't you take an oath that warmth, sympathy and understanding may outweigh the surgeon's knife or the chemist's drug?"

"Pollyanna," her boss said in a snide tone, "when you get a chance to fly back to reality, give me a call. Until then, consider yourself on probation."

"Never mind," Wren said. "I quit." Pressing the off button on her cell, Wren should've been upset. But all she really felt was an enormous sense of relief.

Maybe she'd return to Baltimore to restart her residency in July or maybe not. One thing she was sure of was that when she did finally earn her license, she wouldn't do it at the expense of her daughter.

Taking Robin from her crib, she dismissed the nanny for the day and then sat in a rocker in front of the nursery's bay window. Singing a soft lullaby, stroking her daughter's downy hair, it occurred to Wren that this was the first time since leaving the ranch that the two of them had spent quality time together.

The fact not only shamed her, but empowered her.

For Wren's entire life she'd searched for family. For a career that made her feel needed and whole. She couldn't believe that once she'd finally found it all, she'd thrown it away. How many times had she sworn that when she had a child, she'd be different from her own parents? She'd never abandon him or her to be raised by strangers. But look what she'd gone and done. For all her certainty that returning to Baltimore was right for her, she'd never considered how incredibly wrong it was for Robin. In Weed Gulch her daughter had a father and doting grandmother and cousins and uncles. Living in this mausoleum, she had a full-time nanny and all the priceless objets d'art anyone could ever want. But when it came right down to it, this place wasn't a real home any more than Wren's orphanage.

Home had nothing to do with a roof, but the people residing under that roof. People who loved you and comforted you and made you feel whole. People like Cash—her *husband*. The man she loved with every breath in her body.

Wren might be highly educated, but when it came to common sense, she was sadly lacking.

Key word—*was*.

From here on out, no more putting work above family. Not only was she no longer afraid of giving her heart to others, but she'd found a new mission. One designed to win back the hearts of those whom she'd no doubt badly hurt.

Chapter Twenty

"As I live and breathe..." Delores held open her front door. "Get in here before all three of you catch your death of cold."

"Thanks." Teeth chattering, Robin and Prissy in her arms, Wren said, "I'd forgotten how Oklahoma wind can turn what would otherwise be a perfectly nice afternoon into a walk-in freezer."

"You've got that right." To the baby she said, "Look how she's grown. When she sees her, Georgina's going to bust with pride."

Though it'd been only a little more than five weeks since Wren had been gone, it felt like a lifetime. Had she been as brave as she'd felt back in Baltimore, demanding Abigail sign her transfer forms, she would have gone to the ranch before stopping anywhere else. As it was, Wren needed to test the waters. Hear from a trusted source whether or not she was even still welcome at the place she used to call home.

After ten agonizingly long minutes of small talk, Delores finally got around to the important stuff. "Much as it flatters me to think you missed me bad enough that I'm the first one in Weed Gulch you'd want to visit, I suspect the real reason you haven't yet been out to the ranch is you're wanting the inside scoop on how Cash and the rest of your kin took your leaving."

"H-how do you know I haven't been to the ranch?"

"Girl, you forget, nobody comes down this road without me knowing." Laughing and patting her thighs, she said, "How about you hand over that baby and then I'll tell you everything you want to know."

THIRTY MINUTES LATER Wren turned her powerful SUV, the first car she'd ever owned, down her home's drive. It was funny how she loved the freedom of finally having her own vehicle but no longer cared for sleeping alone.

Since quitting, then telling Abigail that just because she believed Wren was well suited for being the next cardiac superstar didn't mean that was the path she wanted to take, this was the first time she'd been without Robin or Prissy. Besides learning just how angry Cash was with her, Wren had also been in desperate need of Delores's services as a sitter. Should Cash decide not to give her a second chance, she didn't want their daughter witnessing the ugly scene.

As she approached the achingly familiar house, a knot formed in her throat she feared wouldn't soon go away.

After parking and exiting the car, she added a light tremble and upset stomach to her body's list of complaints.

She rang the doorbell, only to have no one answer.

A glance at her watch told her that by three in the afternoon, Mrs. Cahwood was long gone.

Worrying her lower lip, Wren looked to the barn, only to now lose all of her air. Exiting the corral was

Cash in all his cowboy glory. Walking tall with no sign of a limp, he wore his favorite cowboy hat, a dust-covered white T-shirt, faded jeans and those damned chaps that had first landed her in trouble all the way back in Vegas.

Never had she seen a more handsome man—or one whose expression looked more thunderous.

Pulse racing to a degree she'd never dreamed possible, her mouth summer-drought dry, Wren raised her chin and continued walking toward her husband. She wanted to run. Toss her arms around him and never let go. But in leaving, she'd given up that right and didn't blame him for his icy reception.

"Where's my baby?" he asked, his jaw hard and his normally welcoming green eyes icy-cold.

"Safe and happy with Delores. Prissy's there, too. If you don't mind, I'd like a few minutes on our own, not being parents, but a couple."

Gazing across rolling prairie, he said, "I've been thinking a lot about filing for divorce. If that's why you're here, I'd be the last person to stop you from making the death of our marriage official."

It crushed her to know the man she'd finally realized she loved thought so poorly of her. But in the same respect, learning he hadn't already taken it upon himself to draw up a legal separation was great news. That meant the door for reconciliation might not be wide open, but it also wasn't padlocked shut.

Forcing a breath, she managed to whisper, "I'm not here to divorce you, Cash, but confess how much I love you."

He tensed. "So help me, if this is some big-city game designed to trick me into signing over my legal rights to Robin, I'll—"

Desperate to derail his negative train of thought, Wren used the only *trick* she knew. The one stemming from the sexual chemistry neither had ever been able to control.

Arms around his neck, she kissed him as if there was no tomorrow, because from where she stood, there might not be. She kissed him hard and softly and every way in between, not only hungry for his taste, but desperate for his understanding.

"I'm so sorry," she murmured between kisses. "My leaving was the most harebrained thing I've ever done. I had to, though, to prove to myself what we shared was real. A thousand times more important than some residency at a prestigious hospital. I no longer even want prestigious, but meaningful. I want what Doc Haven has—not just patients, but friends. I've already made calls, and my former dean promised to put in a good recommendation for me with OU. If all goes well, I'll start in Tulsa in July. It'll still be rough, being apart from you for even days, but the end prize will mean I could set up a practice right here in Weed Gulch. I even bought an SUV for just that reason. So that even in bad weather I'll be able to get to anyone who needs me."

"Woman," Cash noted, "you first showed up on my property talking a mile a minute and telling me how things were going to be. Well, hate to burst your bubble, but you wearing the pants in this relationship no longer works for me."

Terrified he was on the verge of telling her to climb back into her car and drive on out of his life, her fingertips turned numb.

"At the airport, watching you go, I knew you were making a huge mistake, but—"

"You were there?" Hand over her mouth, eyes tearing, she said, "I knew I saw you, but I thought my imagination was playing tricks on me."

"Oh…" He laughed. "I was there, all right, telling myself over and over about that old saying. You know the one? How if you love something, you have to set it free?"

Nodding and not bothering to hide her tears, she said, "If you'll have me, Cash, I'm back, and wanting nothing more than to be your wife."

"You just refuse to let me have the last word, don't you?"

He tried looking stern, but his scowl transformed into the grin that had never failed to turn her tummy upside down. "Robin will always be welcome, but if I'm going to let you and your silly little dog back into my bed, there are going to be changes."

"Whatever you'd like." Dizzy with relief even though she still had Georgina's wrath to face, Wren was more than willing to make a few concessions.

"First," he said, holding her tight while kissing the crown of her head, "well, second after I get my hands on our gorgeous baby for a nice long hug, we're going on a proper honeymoon. You teased me back in Vegas and then here, prancing around in your pregnant glory…"

Now she was laughing. "I would hardly call my blimp-like shape glorious."

"Trust me, it was. And I've been horny for you for months. Third, you ever so much as think about leaving me again, I want it in writing that I have permission to lasso you to the bed."

"Done," she said, warm and shivery at the thought of him once again having his cowboy way with her.

"Finally—and this one's a biggie—you will have to tell me on a daily basis that I'm the most handsome man you've ever seen, ever hope to see and will *ever* see. Think that's something you can manage?"

Laughing and crying at the same time, Wren wholeheartedly agreed.

* * * * *

We hope you enjoyed reading

HER COWBOY'S CHRISTMAS WISH

by *New York Times* bestselling author

CATHY McDAVID

and

THE BULL RIDER'S CHRISTMAS BABY

by LAURA MARIE ALTOM

If you liked these stories, then you will love **Harlequin® American Romance®** books.

You love small towns and cowboys! **Harlequin American Romance** stories are heartwarming contemporary tales of everyday women finding love, becoming part of a family or community—or maybe starting families of their own.

 HARLEQUIN®

American Romance®

Romance the all-American way!

Enjoy four *new* stories from **Harlequin American Romance** every month!

Available wherever books and ebooks are sold.

www.Harlequin.com

*Looking for more all-American romances like the one
you just read? Read on for an excerpt from
Cathy Gillen Thacker's LONE STAR CHRISTMAS
from her McCABE MULTIPLES miniseries!*

Nash Echols dropped a fresh-cut Christmas tree onto the bed of a flatbed truck. He watched as a luxuriously outfitted red SUV tore through the late November gloom and came to an abrupt stop on the old logging trail.

"Well, here comes trouble," he murmured, when the driver door opened and two equally fancy peacock-blue boots hit the running board.

His glance moved upward, taking in every elegant inch of the cowgirl marching toward him. He guessed the sassy spitfire to be in her early thirties, like him. She glared while she moved, her hands clapped over her ears to shut out the concurrent whine of a dozen power saws.

Nash lifted a leather-gloved hand.

One by one his crew stopped, until the Texas mountainside was eerily quiet, and only the smell of fresh-cut pine hung in the air. And still the determined woman advanced, chin-length dark brown curls framing her even lovelier face.

He eased off his hard hat and ear protectors.

Indignant color highlighting her delicately sculpted cheeks, she stopped just short of him and propped her hands on her slender denim-clad hips. "You're killing me, using all those chain saws at once!" Her aqua-blue eyes narrowed. "You know that, don't you?"

Actually, Nash hadn't.

Her chin lifted another notch. *"You have to stop!"*

At that, he couldn't help but laugh. It was one thing for this little lady to pay him an unannounced visit, another for her to try to shut him down. "Says who?" he challenged right back.

She angled her thumb at her sternum, unwittingly drawing his glance to her full, luscious breasts beneath the fitted red velvet Western shirt, visible beneath her open wool coat. "Says me!"

"And you are?"

"Callie McCabe-Grimes."

Of course she was from one of the most famous and powerful clans in the Lone Star State. He should have figured that out from the moment she'd barged onto his property.

Nash indicated the stacks of freshly cut Christmas trees around them, aware the last thing he needed in his life was another person not into celebrating the holidays. "Sure that's not Grinch?"

Look for LONE STAR CHRISTMAS
by Cathy Gillen Thacker from the
McCABE MULTIPLES *miniseries from*
Harlequin American Romance.

Available December 2014
wherever books and ebooks are sold.

www.Harlequin.com

American Romance®

He's out to get her back

In the fifteen years she's been gone, Bella Biondi forgot
how sexy Travis Granger could be. And she can't afford to
remember. She's back in Briggs to seal a real estate deal,
that's all. No more tears or heartache, no reminiscing,
definitely no kissing. However, Travis has other ideas.
He's sure he can crack the wall Bella's built around
herself. She's the girl who loves Christmas in ranch
country even more than he does.

Look for
Christmas with the Rancher
by MARY LEO

Available December 2014
wherever books and ebooks are sold.

HAR75546

ⒽHARLEQUIN®

American Romance®

A love song that goes on forever

His heroic rescue of a stranger caught in a flash flood just changed Liam Murphy's life—big-time. With Whitney Marlowe's help, the laid-back saloon owner and aspiring country-and-western singer could be a star. Only now, with the dynamic L.A. talent scout temporarily stranded in his Texas town, Liam has another dream: to turn their perfect harmony into a permanent duet!

Look for
Christmas Cowboy Duet
by MARIE FERRARELLA

From the
Forever, Texas miniseries
from Harlequin® American Romance.

Available December 2014
wherever books and ebooks are sold.

HARLEQUIN®

A *Romance* FOR EVERY MOOD™

Stay up-to-date on all your
romance-reading news with the
Harlequin Shopping Guide,
featuring bestselling authors, exciting new
miniseries, books to watch and more!

The newest issue will be delivered right to you
with our compliments! There are 4 each year.

Signing up is easy.

EMAIL

ShoppingGuide@Harlequin.ca

WRITE TO US

HARLEQUIN BOOKS
Attention: Customer Service Department
P.O. Box 9057, Buffalo, NY 14269-9057

OR PHONE

1-800-873-8635 in the United States
1-888-343-9777 in Canada

Please allow 4-6 weeks for delivery of the first issue by mail.

HARLEQUIN®

A *Romance* FOR EVERY MOOD™

JUST CAN'T GET ENOUGH?

Join our social communities
and talk to us online.

You will have access to the latest
news on upcoming titles and special
promotions, but most importantly,
you can talk to other fans about your
favorite Harlequin reads.

Harlequin.com/Community

Facebook.com/HarlequinBooks

Twitter.com/HarlequinBooks

Pinterest.com/HarlequinBooks

HSOCIAL